BOOK ONE OF THE *LIVES LESS ORDINARY* SERIES

A PLACE OF OUR OWN

BOOK ONE OF THE *LIVES LESS ORDINARY* SERIES

A PLACE OF OUR OWN

Dr Dmis

Contents

CHAPTER 1

The Raid

The black metal catch lifts and the stained wooden pantry door slowly opens with a creaking from the dry metal hinges. A small candle set in a brass cup is thrust forward and lights the way into the kitchen, where two Great Danes in the corner of the room raise their heads to view the intruders. With passing curiosity, they watch as the figures move round the large wooden chopping block, between the crockery racks and then cross in front of them, moving to the far side of the room.

Stepping up onto the raised tile plinth by the large stone sink, the visitors peer out of the window into the walled garden, looking for anyone who may be walking past as they must be careful not to be seen. It takes a while for their eyes to adjust to the low light and they wait patiently until confident the coast is clear.

Now bored of watching and with a muffled yawn as they reposition themselves, the dogs lower their heads back into their thick, red tartan blankets and return to getting comfortable. To Apollo and Zeus, this is just another night like many others, with no rewards on offer. It's not worth them getting up and greeting these frequent visitors, so for now they are ignored in preference of sleep.

The two figures move down off the step and head to the back door, where both catches are quietly raised and released. The candle, for now unrequired, is snuffed out and put on the window ledge ready to be used later. From now on it will be the moonlight and oil-lit wall lamps that will guide their way through the extensive gardens.

They step out onto the white marble doorstep and down onto the short path leading onto the gravel walkway. Each step is taken with great care, ensuring they plant their feet squarely on the ground to minimise any noise as they head up past the vegetable patch, through the raised rose beds until they come to the garden's most prized feature: the long-walled greenhouse. Each day, it is opened to the first rays of the sun's light and warmth, remaining in its grasp for most of its rotation during the day. The heat generated inside, combined with the ducting and low trenched gullies, ensures the glass and timber building is always several degrees warmer than outside. This makes it one of the few places that exotic fruits like pineapples, figs, oranges, lemons and grapes can be grown in abundance in the colder English climate.

To our intrepid duo it's just another obstacle to pass by. Following along the path beside the greenhouse, they reach the fruit trees. These prime examples are not like normal fruit trees; they are trained to run along wires and trellis against the wall, with heat from the sun in front and residual heat held in the wall behind keeping them warmer than standalone trees. With several expert gardeners ensuring they are well-watered, fed, manicured and handled with the utmost care, they produce an abundance of early-season fruit that is the envy of all who are fortunate to attend the many banquets thrown at this estate house.

The two ghostly figures stop, pull out large brown cloth sacks from under their coats and approach the bounty in front of them. 'Make sure you pick the fruit well-spaced apart so they don't know we've taken some.' It's the only time someone speaks as they get to work along the row, collecting several apples and pears from each tree. They slip the part-filled sacks over their shoulders, step onto the grass that now runs beside the path and hastily head to the gate at the corner of the wall. The long door bolts are retracted, and the door is quietly opened.

A head leans out of the doorway and views up and down an unlit alleyway, listening for footsteps and any other sounds. With the coast clear, they step out into the darkness. Looping a small piece of string round the catch on the back of the door, they attach the other end to a rusty nail poking out of the frame. To a person looking at the gate from a distance, the door looks like it is locked shut, as it can only be bolted closed from inside the garden. With the addition of the string, it is now held closed but can still be opened from the outside.

After one more check to ensure the coast is still clear, they make their way up the dingy track, moving from shadow to shadow, ensuring no one sees them. Just a few yards from where this path meets the main village street, they tuck up behind an old wooden cart and wait.

'Looks like we're the first ones here again,' a quiet voice whispers.

'If that's the case, why have we been waiting here so long?' comes a reply from the other side of the wagon. They both lean out and look round the side of the cart. Three more silhouettes can be seen, crouched tight to the side of the vehicle.

'Is that you, Megan?'

'No, it's Maddi.'

Shuffling round, they all group together at the back end of the cart. 'We will give the others five more minutes and then we must move, for time is against us.'

They stay crouched for another few minutes, waiting patiently, then from behind them, way down the bottom of the alleyway, steps can be heard approaching. As they quietly watch, more figures prance from shadow to shadow. The ghostly figures move swiftly along the path, taking only a few minutes to join the others behind the stationary cart.

'Watching them was like watching mice run from a cat,' says Oliver.

'Sorry we're late. Susan's parents did not retire to bed until later than usual.'

'That's fine, Topper, we've not been here long,' replies Edward as he looks around at all present. 'Let's go,' he whispers as they move round the cart and up to the entrance where the alley meets the village road. It is always the most difficult part to cross but is the most direct route with enough light to see where they are going. The recent rain showers have made the cobblestones shine and reflect a yellow glow from the oil streetlamps, as well as making it very slippery underfoot.

Looking round to the left and right, the group see two thief-takers (constables, in a modern-day comparison) replacing the candles in a wall light at the far end of the street. A couple bursts through The Hare and Hound tavern doors, laughing and joking. They start kissing and playing around, the older man whispers something in her ear, and the young woman laughs. 'You'll have to give me a lot more than that if you want me tonight. I don't come cheap, you know.' The couple sees the two men and instantly they release each other from their embrace and move off down the road. The two constables watch the couple's mannerisms. They have stirred their interest and they stop what they are doing, turn and slowly follow them at a distance, watching.

Once the couple and their followers are out of view, the group prepare to make their move. They shuffle up and crouch at the edge of the road in preparation for their dash across the gap. Just as they are about to slip across the road and down an alleyway on the other side, they hear a horse trotting down the cobbles. 'Back, quickly. Back down into the alley,' Edward says. They scurry back behind the cart and watch as a dark horse pulling a wagon trots into view with a driver and passenger up front.

As it passes, they can see about a dozen large coal sacks heaped in a pile on the backboard. The driver raises a bottle to his lips and as he swigs he pulls the reins to one side. The horse responds, moves to the left and the wheel clips the high kerbstones. With a massive jolt, the driver is bounced sidewards, and the bottle falls from his grasp and shatters in the footwell. The back metal-rimmed wheels slide out of control on the wet road and several of the coal sacks spill off onto the cobbled floor with a hollow thud.

The driver instinctively pulls back on the reins and with his left hand clutching the wooden wheel brake, he pulls back, applying pressure to the left wheel. 'Woah!' he shouts as he slows the cart to a stop.

'You clumsy fool, look what you have done. Now get off and reload them sacks on the back,' shouts the passenger. 'Be quickly about it, damn your eyes.' The passenger rotates slightly and, as the driver turns to dismount, he reaches out with his leg and boots him off the side. The driver loses his balance and falls into a heap on the floor. He takes a second to realise his position, collects his thoughts and stands up, brushing himself down. He looks up at the passenger, his fists clenched.

There's a look in his eyes like he's about to commit to something without holding anything back. But as he goes to move forward, there is something in his subconscious mind that tells him he will come off second best – if not now, later. The passenger, unaware of the driver's intentions, is busy kicking the broken glass off the footboard. He mutters to himself about the evils of too much drink and the weakness it brings to those who indulge to excess.

Half hearing this, the driver lets go with a few choice words of his own. 'Yeah, well, try doing what I have to do without a wee dram inside. It's not right, what we are doing. Not right at all.' He pauses for a second, then continues. 'In fact, get off your high and mighty and give me a hand. Some of these sacks are heavy.'

Still mumbling to himself, the passenger stares at the driver then dismounts and helps retrieve the fallen sacks.

All of what unfolded has been fully viewed by the small party at the end of the alleyway behind the cart. They watch intently as the sacks are collected and deposited on the back of the wagon.

'Whatever is in them sacks, it is not coal,' Topper whispers.

'How do you know that?' Edward asks.

'Look at the one he's carrying now – it's only half full. And the shape's all wrong as well. It's sticking out all over the place. Coal in a coal sack is fairly even in size and all the sacks look and weigh the same, filled to the top. My father took me to his coal yard just last week and I watched them count, weigh and load the sacks onto the wagons destined for the factory's furnaces. Also, they do not work in the coal yard at night and would not be delivering coal to the factory at night either. So, the question on my mind is, what ARE they transporting in them coal sacks? And why is it being done at night?'

The men swing the last large sack onto the cart and mount up. Collecting the reins and unlocking the brake, the driver clicks at the horse and flicks the reins to get the wagon and its unusual load of sacks moving. The group watch from the safety of the dark alleyway as the wagon disappears around the corner. Soon all they can hear is the faint rhythmic tapping of iron horseshoes on cobblestones fading off into the distance.

'Let's not waste any more time,' Maddi says as they move up to the edge of the road again. After checking the coast is clear, they swiftly slip across and head down the alley on the other side. They follow the narrow paths round the back of the houses, ducking under lit windows and around glowing streetlamps, avoiding all contact with anyone they come across. The last few road crossings are uneventful until Susan steps into a pile of fresh horse apples. 'Er, that's disgusting.' She squeaks and wipes her shoe on the grass verge. It is not long before the group is at the outskirts of the village and they can they see their objective: an old, abandoned house on the side of a large rock face.

'Come on – we've wasted enough time and we've so much to do,' Edward says as he tries to pick up the pace a little. With a quick check up the road and back down towards the village, he leads the group as they scamper across the last twenty or so yards of scrub. Some press their backs up against the building's wooden walls, while others scurry round into the darkness of the open barn attached to its side. Edward reaches for the door handle, twists it open and pushes it back. He stealthily sneaks inside and a few moments later the others hear the words they are waiting for. 'All clear, come on in.'

Inside the dilapidated building, they rally in the living room. 'This place is so disgusting. It's dirty and damp and smells of wet dog,' Susan says as the others snigger.

'You say the same thing every time we arrive here. Why don't you think of the others and not yourself for once?' replies Maddi.

'Let's go while we still have time on our side.' Edward leads them up the worn rickety wooden stairs to the room above.

These are no ordinary village children; their hand-stitched, polished boots and shoes in bright colours show they are from families with money. Susan's vibrant red shoes in particular (even with the piece of horse apple still clinging to the heel) are a fine piece of workmanship that only the affluent could possibly afford.

Upstairs, they head over to the far wall and each lift off a set of filthy old clothes from a peg. There is a hive of activity as they change into these old garments. One by one, the eight pegs fill with pristine, fine clothes. Below each set, a pair of fine footwear is placed.

'Is everybody ready?' Edward asks. All in the room either nod or murmur their agreement. 'Right, we have not got much time left, so Susan, Maddi and Dicky head to the bakery and see what you can get. The bakery always leaves the old bread on the racks, while they start the dough for the next day. Who knows, they still might have a few other items lying around as well. Topper, Harriet and Megan head off to the orchards and see what fruits are left on the trees. They've been picking plums this week, but I'm sure they would have missed some, along with the greengages and damsons. Check out what's available and take what you can, as quick as you can. Oliver and I will go around the houses and see what clothing and tools we can lay our hands on. Don't forget to take your sacks with you and we'll meet at the fireplace at midnight, no later.'

'How will we know the time?' asks Megan.

'Listen for the new park clock Lord Fitzgerald has installed. It rings on the quarter hour and chimes on the hour, and it is loud enough to be heard for miles and miles. Now be careful and watch for each other. Above all, don't get caught. If you feel you're being followed, don't rush back here. Head towards the brook or the factory. Dump anything you have and double back home through the back alleys. We know these tracks better than anyone else by now, so use them to your advantage and keep out of sight.'

The group quietly head back down the stairs and across the living room. They stop only at the fireplace. One by one, they rub their hands in the sooty residue and wipe their faces and necks.

'I hate this part the most,' Susan says in disgust.

'Stop being a glamour queen. You can wash it off later. Besides, I think it makes you look better.' Maddi chuckles as she wipes the soot onto her cheeks.

Susan scowls. 'Oh, ha ha.' She tries to put as little of the black dust on her skin as she can, while following the others into the kitchen. The group pause at the front doorway while Edward opens the door and takes a quick view outside, then turns to look at the others. 'It's all clear. Good luck and stay safe. Just remember we have a lot of friends relying on us to come through for them.'

The two parties of three are first out the door, disappearing into the darkness and heading in different directions.

Edward looks at Oliver, who is now putting on his black pirate bandana with the skull and crossbones on the front. He shakes his head and smiles. 'You always want to be a pirate, don't you?'

Oliver grins at his brother and lets out a quiet, 'Yo ho ho and away we go.' The two of them step out and move off in yet another different direction.

The route the boys take has them moving through some willow scrub and round the back of the building. They have to climb along some of the protruding rock face, but it gives them good cover and an easy way into the village along a little-used track well-hidden with brambles and hedgerows. They follow this path to the edge of the village and along the walls of the first few houses. As they turn into the first dark alleyway, Oliver takes the lead and starts up the muddy track, reaching a recessed gate at the back of the printer's house. He stoops down to re-tie his shoelace. Edward watches his brother from about ten feet down the path, behind a large holly bush.

Without warning, the gate beside Oliver swings open and three men come rushing through the gap. Oliver is still crouched down and the first man trips over him, hurtles over the top and straight into a muddy puddle. The second fares no better and follows his associate into the dirt. The third man almost manages to stop but is too unbalanced to hold his stance and ends up landing on the others. Oliver stands up and looks at the men in shock as they get back to their feet and start brushing themselves down.

'What the hell is going on here? Who the fuck are you? And what are you doing here?' bellows one of the men. The other two are scowling and cursing as they try to clean off some of the mud.

One of them grabs Oliver by the shoulder. 'He's seen our faces. What shall we do with him?' he hollers.

'We need to go. Bring him along. I will deal with him away from here,' another replies.

Edward steps out from behind the bush. 'Leave him alone. He did not mean anything.' The startled men turn around and look at him, then at each other.

Staring into their faces, Edward instantly recognises two of them as part of Lord Fitzgerald's group of henchmen: Brannigan and Sykes. Fortunately for Edward and Oliver, with soot on their faces and rags for clothes, Brannigan and Sykes do not recognise them.

'Christ, how many of them are there?' says Brannigan, looking around for any more people who may appear from the bushes.

By now the noise and commotion has started to draw the attention of people in nearby houses. Rooms are lighting up as people head for the windows with lit lamps. 'We need to get the hell out of here, and fast,' says Sykes.

'What about these kids? We cannot leave them – they have seen our faces.' One of the men reaches for a knife attached to his belt.

Edward steps forward to be closer to his brother.

'We have no time to deal with this now. We have to go,' Sykes replies before looking back at the children. 'Count yourself lucky today, you… you…' He looks at Oliver's bandana. 'Little pirate! But if you ever mention seeing us today, or I see you again, it will be a different story.' Sykes growls and pretends to snap something in front of the boys before turning away. 'Come on, let's get out of here before someone recognises us.'

As they run away, the men mutter to each other about whether they should have dealt with the children in another way, and about how they shouldn't leave loose ends.

Edward grabs Oliver by the hand and leads him towards the village. 'That was a close-run thing, Oliver.' He nudges his brother, trying to make light of the situation. Deep down, Edward is not so sure this is over. If it were not for the people turning on their lamps, this might have been a very different and dire situation.

In another part of the village, Susan leads her team towards their objective. Slipping from shadow to shadow, they make good time. They are dodging around the back of the houses, nipping in and out of gardens and alleyways when suddenly a window swings open above them. With cat-like reflexes, Susan steps back and hugs the wall tightly as an old woman leans out the window, letting fly with the contents of a chamber pot; the children are left looking at the bush opposite, which is still shaking from the impact.

Although they cannot see it, they can hear the liquid dripping through the bouncing leaves to the ground below. With a cough and a splutter, the old woman tucks back into the house and closes the window. The children remain stuck to the wall for a minute, looking up at the window. Sniffing the air, Maddi gets an invasion on her senses and chokes. 'Oh my God, that is disgusting.' She turns to look at Dicky. 'I think that woman must be dead and just doesn't know it yet?'

He lets out a small chuckle and smiles, but it is short lived as soon the smell hits him. He gags as the pungent, acrid odour fills his nostrils and turns his stomach. But before he starts to retch, Susan leads them down the path, giving the bush plenty of room.

They round the corner of a large, whitewashed timber building and at the end of the lane, they crouch down on both sides of the path, tight to the hedges, to view their quarry.

The bakery is opposite them, between a cobbler's shop and the village general store. Through the large display window, they can see the wooden racks holding the remains of the day's bread. It will be sold tomorrow at a cheaper price, then anything left over will be ground into breadcrumbs and used to bulk up pie fillings and pastries. A light coming from the back room means they are preparing the dough for tomorrow's bread.

'There's a lot of bread still on the racks tonight,' Susan says.

In the darkness, Dicky grins. 'All the better for us.'

'We will have to be quick. Get what we need and run for it,' Susan adds. They can see down the road to a group of people viewing the display in the tailor's shop window. In the other direction, two of the local thief-takers are walking towards them, one swinging his baton on its cord.

'I don't like the look of this,' Maddi whispers. 'Let's wait here a minute and see where they go!' They move back down the alleyway a few feet and disappear into the shadows, watching intently.

The door of the bakery opens, and two men step into view. One flicks his coat collar into position and turns to the other man. 'I reckon we can get more bread out if we bulk up with a bit more sawdust and make more money in the process.'

(A common trick used in past times by unscrupulous bakers.)

'It's an idea, but if we bulk up any more and people find out, we'll be strung up by our bootstraps. So no, let's stick with what we've got now and not get too greedy. Anyway, to more important things. I think we can get at least two hours in before the bread rises enough to bake, especially as the nights are becoming a lot colder.'

(The colder the night, the longer it takes for the yeast to work and the bread to prove.)

'Time for a few tankards of ale. Maybe even enough time to see that new wench Cora and claim a bit of that one-on-one attention I so deserve.'

The other man smiles. 'Only after I've had my turn first.' They both laugh and head off in the direction of the local inn. Not twenty yards down the road, they meet up with the local constabulary, greeting them as friends. After a few words they all start laughing and move towards the tavern, talking amongst themselves as they go.

'Dicky, here's our chance. Go see if they have left the door open.' Susan prods Dicky. With a quick check to ensure the group is still window shopping at the far end of the street, he slips across the road and up to the bakery door. He turns the handle, the catch clicks, and the door gives way.

'Quickly.' He beckons the girls. 'Let's take advantage while we can.' The girls hotfoot it across the road and Dicky swiftly closes the door behind them. Within moments, brown sacks are pulled out from under their clothing and bread is swiftly stuffed inside them. Barely a minute has gone by, and the entire selection is cleared from the shelves, along with two pies – contents unknown – and several other pastries. The children huddle back at the door with sacks full to bursting and, with a quick check to ensure the way is free from prying eyes, they make good their escape.

Dicky and Maddi are first out the door. They cross the road and tuck back into the shadows, awaiting their companion. But as Susan runs out the door, her sack catches on the handle. The door slams shut with a *crash*, shattering two of the small glass panes and pulling her backwards and onto the floor. The sack is ripped from her grasp and some of the contents spill out onto the ground. Instinctively she stands up, grabs the sack and pulls to free it from the door. A sliver of glass cuts deep into her hand and she lets out a scream. Pulling herself together, she collects some of the fallen items and runs across the road, dragging the sack behind her.

In the background, she can hear people calling after her. 'Run,' she shouts as she passes the others and heads off down the pathway at full speed. They run down the back alleyways at a rate of knots, hearing whistles being blown behind them and people shouting loudly. They turn right as they follow the track past a row of workers' cottages, through a gateway in a hedge and into the church grounds. They weave in and out of the headstones, climb over the small stone wall and head off down a footpath to the brook.

Now slowing, the three of them try to catch their breath a little. Maddi and Susan constantly look back to see if anyone is following them. More and more lamps light up the sky as shutters are opened by curious residents looking out.

'That was close,' Maddi says, looking at Susan and still trying to catch her breath. 'I thought you were a goner.'

Susan looks at her but says nothing, her face expressionless as she begins to tremble. Seeing tears in her eyes, Maddi realises something is not right. Looking around her body she notices Susan's clenched, bloodstained hand.

'You're bleeding,' she yells, reaching out to inspect the wound.

'Ah, please be gentle. It hurts.'

Maddi can now see the blood has smeared over a large proportion of Susan's hand and has been running down her clothes as they ran.

'I cut it on some broken glass from the door.'

Maddi gently lifts up Susan's hand to make the best of what little light is coming from the moon. 'There's still a bit of glass in the wound.' She pauses for a second as she looks closely at it. 'It's going to hurt a bit, but we need to pull it out.'

There's a moment of silence as Susan prepares herself for what must be done next. She takes one last deep breath and gives a small nod to show she's ready and Maddi gets to work. Holding the shard of glass between thumb and forefinger, she teases the object around before pulling it free from the wound and throwing it away. Closing her eyes and gritting her teeth, Susan lets out a quiet whimper and starts to cry as the blood begins to flow more freely.

'There, it is out. Now close your hand to stop the bleeding and we'll clean it up in the brook.' Susan closes her hand and hugs Maddi for comfort while Dicky picks up her sack as well as his own.

'Let's go. We'll be safer the further we are away from here,' Dicky whispers as he takes the lead and heads towards the small brook. He is closely followed by the two girls, who are now arm in arm, with Maddi dragging her sack behind her.

* * *

In the orchards on the far side of town, the commotion has not gone unnoticed by the three intrepid fruit gatherers. Topper looks up from his viewpoint at the top of a damson tree. Various buildings light up as shutters are opened and lanterns illuminate the sky. He turns to look back at the others and yells out, 'That's it, someone's been rumbled. Time to take what we've got and meet back at the house.' A leg drops down from the next tree along, followed by a second as Harriet leaps from the lower branches to the ground.

'Come on, Megan, time to go,' she calls as Topper steps down from the tree and swiftly starts collecting the picked fruit off the floor. With a quick double-check for any missed offerings left on the grassy ground, they pick up the part-filled sacks and make their way through the trees to the far side of the field.

'I wonder what has happened?' Megan asks.

'We'll find out soon enough,' replies Topper as they now follow the footpath along the hedgerow towards the brook and then on to where it joins the river.

The orchard run is one of the safest raids for the group, as it's away from the main village and not many people walk that way at night. It's not that it's dangerous to be out at night – far from it, for a small village it has one of the largest forces of thief-takers (men who solved petty crime for a fee) or – as most of the new people who moved down from London called them – 'runners' or 'constables' after the famous Bow Street Runners of London town.

These thief-takers are entrusted to keep order in this now wealthy and affluent region of the county, handpicked from society for their toughness and ruthlessness against the criminal element of society. They are paid direct from the magistrate's office in the middle of the village, a building owned by Lord Darius Fitzgerald – the main landowner for the district and the person who just so happens to donate most of the money to fund this operation. His cousin Wolfgang Bergman is chief magistrate, and between the two of them, they have a more than healthy influence on all that happens in the village and surrounding areas.

Some in the past questioned this relationship and what seems to be their own private army, but after failing to get support from the rest of the original residents, they simply fell into line or moved to another county away from the reach of Lord Fitzgerald and his associates.

All in the village acknowledge the improvements and investment Lord Fitzgerald has made for the community, including the huge new factory, better roads, drainage system, large community park with fountains, rebuilt shops, pumped fresh water and new housing. All this has created an expansion of new jobs and wealth for a growing workforce. For the first time, prospects for the local people look good. Although the cost of such improvements is yet to be fully determined, some visual side effects are obvious:

With the local workforce having such a limited skill base and education, almost all the higher paid and prominent positions are taken by people moving in from the cities.

Shop owners are paying more rent to the landlord, who just happens to be Lord Fitzgerald as he has now bought almost all the buildings from the previous landowners. Once they fall behind on rent, he removes them and rebuilds the shops, thus removing people who have run the businesses for many years, in some cases generations. Without breaking any laws.

Large portions of the old village have been levelled to make way for modern housing and amenities desired by these new wealthier residents.

The cost of living has gone up, so fewer of the original residents can afford to remain in Pippinsford Village unless they get a better paid position in the new factory, and not many of them become available to local people.

For most of the residents, long hours of backbreaking work in the fruit fields are their only option if they want to remain in the village area.

No locals can afford to buy a new house in the village, so all the younger generation either move away or become servants and maids to the wealthy outsiders who can afford to purchase these newly built country estate buildings and own houses.

Lord Fitzgerald also tried to lay claim to building the new school, and for the expansion in fruit production, along with the trading of fruit and fruit products like jam, fruit drinks and honey directly with the capital city of London for better prices for the growers. But most in the know would comment that Steven Todd built the school and brokered the trade routes and deals on pricing with the city brokers – so the farmers' children could have a place to get better educated and the landowners could afford a better standard of life for themselves and their tenant farmers.

By far the biggest impacts on the village so far have been the loss of community spirit and close-knit family ties, and the huge divide between the poorer original village folk and the newly arriving wealthy – and in many cases arrogant, rude and obnoxious – city migrants. Some would say this is progress, a vision of the future coming through to fruition. While others take a different view, one thing is for certain for this village community: things will never be the same again.

For the children who move here from the large towns and cities, this is all one great adventure. There are huge green fields, woods, clean rivers and unpolluted water, with lots of open space to explore and investigate. Compared to what they were used to, the freedom, total safety and fresh air is beyond anything they could have wished for. The problem is, with so much freedom, sometimes they see things they should not. With children being what they are, they will always investigate the odd and unusual. And in a village like Pippinsford where growth and development are in conflict with tradition, this can be a costly mistake.

As Topper and the girls make their way quietly along the path towards the brook, they hear the faint pounding of footsteps coming towards them. As they get louder, panic starts to set in. 'What shall we do?' Megan asks Topper.

'Shh. Quiet,' is the instant response. After a quick view of the surrounding area, Topper points to a gap in the hedgerow about ten yards ahead. 'Quickly, move over there into the gap in the bushes.' They swiftly cover the ground and one by one crouch down and sink back into the small dark recesses of the hedge. Quietly, they watch the crossroad ahead, where the track from the field meets one from the village and a path to the footbridge over the small brook.

Within minutes, shadows begin to appear in the distance and hastily move towards the hidden children. Moments later, three people appear in the moonlight as they move down the track from the village. As they reach the crossroads, they stop. Puffing and panting, they drop their sacks on the ground. One of them speaks.

'We're nearly at the brook. We can rest there for a moment.'

Megan makes out her best friend's voice instantly. 'Maddi? Is that you?' she whispers.

Maddi steps about two feet backwards and all three of the newcomers crouch down low to the ground, looking at each other, terrified that somebody has spoken out to them. It remains eerily silent for a while before Maddi plucks up the courage to speak. 'Who's out there?' she whispers, her heart pounding as if about to burst out of her chest.

'It's me, Megan.' For a few seconds there's a deathly silence, then Maddi speaks out.

'How do I know it's you?'

'Who else would be calling your name in the middle of nowhere, from the depths of a smelly hedge?' Maddi and her group slowly pick themselves up, still staring at the hedge, where the other children are now revealing themselves.

'You scared the devil out of me,' Maddi says, walking towards Megan. As she reaches her, their arms spread out and a big hug ensues. Never has Maddi been so glad to see her friends.

'What happened in the village?' asks Harriet.

'We could see the village lighting up, and hear whistles,' Topper adds.

'We were running out of the baker's shop and my sack caught the handle on the door,' says Susan. 'It slammed shut and shattered the glass with an almighty noise that alerted the village.'

'Show them your hand,' butts in Maddi. 'She cut her hand on a shard of glass. She's terribly brave.' The children view the wound. 'We were heading to the brook to get it cleaned up, then off to the house with our sacks.'

'Then let's waste no more time. We're due back at the house soon anyway and we must clean Susan's wound and see how bad it really is. Besides, it would be safer down the tunnel while the village people are looking for us, rather than out here in the streets,' says Topper.

Dicky is the first to pick up his and Susan's sacks and he leads the way, closely followed by the rest of the group. They reach the brook, where Susan sits down and – with the help of her best friend – starts gently washing her hand to remove the clotted and dried blood. But as she opens her hand, it begins to bleed profusely, and she quickly closes her hand tightly again. The two girls look at each other. A physician is needed to attend to this injury as soon as possible.

'I need to get you home quickly,' says Maddi. 'The others can take our sacks back to the house while we work out a way to explain this without incriminating you at the bakers.' She fumbles in her pocket and pulls out the only clean item she possesses: a small white handkerchief with a red letter M stitched in the corner. She wraps it around the wound and ties a small knot to bind the makeshift dressing together.

'That will hold for now.' Turning to the others, Maddi explains, 'I've got to get Susan home. You lot will have to add the contents of our sacks into yours and go down the tunnel without us.'

'But you still need to get back to the building to get her clothes,' says Topper. 'Otherwise, Susan's parents will know something is up!'

Maddi rethinks her strategy. 'Actually, a better idea is for me to go with you to the house and collect Susan's clothes and my own, bring them back here, wash and get cleaned up at the brook and then head back home. I will also need someone else to take our rags back and hang them on the pegs ready for the next time.' She looks around. 'Harriet, you'll have to do that for us.' Harriet gives a nod of approval. 'Then it's settled. Harriet, you stay with Susan while I bring all our clothes back in one of the empty sacks. The rest of you, along with Edward and Oliver, will have to finish off what needs to be done.' She turns back to look at Harriet. 'Once we've changed, you will have to take our clothes back to the house before returning home.'

With the plan decided, the reduced group head off back to the empty building, leaving Susan behind under the care of Harriet. They stop just short of the main road out of the village, taking refuge in a bramble thicket. From this viewpoint, they can see people are still roaming the side streets and gardens with lanterns, shouting to each other as they check every inch of the village. The group crouch down low as a pair of horses trot up the road from the direction of the factory. As they pass, the children can see it is two mounted constables, who pull to a stop around ten yards along from the group.

The children crouch even lower, in some cases even hold their breath in the hope it will prevent them being spotted. With one last check of the scrub area, the riders kick their spurs into the horses and trot off towards the people searching in the village some way off in the distance.

After giving the riders a few minutes to disappear from sight, the small party makes its way across the road and into the derelict building, with the last one in sliding the wooden bar through the wall to seal the door shut.

There, in the darkness, looking out of the window is Edward, with Oliver sitting on a small wooden stool beside him. He turns to the group. 'We had to cut short our raid due to some sort of commotion. But we did manage to get some clothing off the washing lines, and Oliver grabbed a few pairs of shoes from the doorway of the cobblers, as well as the fruit from our garden.'

Maddi explains to Edward about the accident that befell Susan at the bakers. Edward gasps and his eyes widen. 'Don't worry, she will be alright,' Maddi says. 'I'll get our clothes and make my way back to them immediately.' After giving Edward a reassuring hug, she moves off up the stairs and, within minutes, returns wearing her original attire and clutching a sack full of their friend's clothes. With a nod to the others, she heads for the door then pauses and turns to Oliver. 'One of you will have to lock the door behind me and wait here for Harriet to get back with their old clothes.' Oliver smiles as he opens the door, allows Maddi to leave and then slides the bar back across. From the window, he watches as Maddi darts in and out of the shadows until she disappears into the darkness. Then he turns and looks at his brother.

'Aye, I know,' Oliver says. 'I'm the smallest, so it's up to me to wait here.' He picks up the stool and parks it by the door. 'I'll wait just here then, right by the door.' He sits down, folds his arms and leans back against the door. The others chuckle as the little pirate, still with his bandana on, sits resolute on his stool guarding the door.

'See you soon, little brother,' says Edward as he picks up one of the sacks. He walks over to the fireplace and kicks the brass fitting. With a clunk, the back wall jars open, showing an open slit down the corner where the walls join. Dicky leans forward and pushes on the wall and it rotates open, showing a secret tunnel behind. Just large enough for them to slip through with their sacks. Megan is the last to enter the void, and as she disappears into the darkness, the wall slowly grinds back into position, leaving no sign of any hidden passage.

* * *

Oliver's been sitting on his stool for about half an hour.

'I'm bored,' he mumbles to himself as he rocks backwards and forwards. A large bent nail catches his eye, and he edges his right foot towards it. Being just out of reach, he shuffles to the edge of his stool and stretches his leg out further. Still unable to reach, he leans out his whole body and stretches some more, but is still not able to reach it. He thinks for a moment, then rocks the stool onto one of its legs and reaches out a little further.

It was inevitable he would overreach, and sure enough a few moments later there's a loud *crack* as the stool gives way, sending him crashing to the ground.

'Owwww,' he yelps, swiftly picking himself back up and brushing himself down. He heads to the window. Looking left and right, and then left again, he's relieved to see his escapade has drawn no attention. Letting out a sigh of relief, and with nothing stirring outside, he returns to the bent nail. Picking it up, he realises it's quite a chunky piece of metal and begins flicking it up and down in his hand as if trying to guess its weight. He pauses for a second before slowly walking towards the fireplace. He steps under the lip of the flume and, reaching up, he scratches a short line on the soot-covered wall. Impressed with how well it shows up, he writes his favourite phrase on the wall. With his tongue partially sticking out, he carves out the words 'Yo ho ho', speaking the letters as he writes them. He steps back and smiles at his handiwork. In a moment of inspiration, he realises there are eight children in their group, and he carves 'pieces of eight' on the wall below his first words.

An idea forms in his head. He looks around the floor, walls and broken furniture until, at the bottom of the stairs, he finds the object he wants. Grabbing the broken bit of timber hanging off the step, he snaps it off, then – using the bent nail – he taps out the knot in the centre. 'Perfect,' he mutters, taking it back to the fireplace. Standing on an old black pot, he offers up the piece of wood to the back wall above his writings and starts to scratch out a circle. He does this eight times, leaving eight creamy white disc shapes against the black sooty background.

Thud. Something hits the outer wall of the building. Oliver freezes, his heart instantly pounding. *Thud.* Another item hits the outer wall. It's all he can do to turn his head in the direction of the noise. Something is moving along the outer wall.

Through the small cracks along the wall, he can see a shadow slowly moving. As it reaches the boarded-up window, it stops, lowers and moves along under the window towards the door. Oliver tries to move, but fear has made him unable. The shadow reaches the door and stops. Oliver's heart is now pounding so hard he is sure the 'shadow thing' can hear it beating.

The door handle slowly turns to the left and then to the right.

Click. It drops forward onto the wooden bar. Oliver is now physically shaking.

'Oliver,' a voice whispers. 'Let me in.'

It knows my name, he thinks, frozen to the spot with fear.

A little wet patch forms in his trousers as tears start to fall. He is barely able to draw breath as he trembles in terror of what lurks outside. At this moment in time, he is truly petrified.

'Oliver! Let me in,' the whispery voice says again. His whole body is now shaking profusely. Unable to draw breath, he is running out of air in his lungs. 'Oliver, open this door at once. It's Harriet,' she says in a slightly angry and louder voice.

Oliver takes in a huge gulp of air and tries to compose himself. He wipes the tears from his eyes and looks down at the wet patch on the front of his trousers. Although he can feel it, it's very hard to notice in the dark and gloomy room with the rags he is wearing. He slowly moves over to the door and slides the bar across. Harriet forces her way in, turns, slides the bar back across the door and grabs Oliver by the hand, pulling him towards the next room.

'About time! People are coming up the road with lanterns.'

She has no idea of the state Oliver was in and drags him towards the gap under the stairs. Throwing the sack of clothes across the room, they tuck themselves tightly against the back wall and kneel down in the darkness, making themselves as small as possible.

They hear voices, quietly at first but growing louder, and soon the glow from the lanterns is throwing moving beads of light through the holes in the walls and half-boarded windows.

'This place should have been pulled down years ago,' yells one of the men.

'If he owned it, he would have, but it still belongs to the widow Greaves,' replies another.

'My God! She still alive?' the man answers back.

'Alive and kicking. And her hatred for the boss still burns deep. She lives in the city with her fancy magistrate son. They know how important this bit of land is to his plans. Refusing to sell it to him, and having people in high places to protect them, is her way of getting revenge for what he did to her husband in the tunnel collapse a few years back.'

'I've heard about that accident. Terrible shame, all them residents killed at the opening of the tunnel road. I hear the village has never really recovered from the loss of so many.'

'Accident! You call it that if you choose to believe it was an accident. But if you do, you're a fool!'

'Oh, and I suppose you know better, do you?'

'Still got the pick, shovel and half a keg of black powder at home! How do you think he got access to so much land and housing so quickly? Not to mention the loss of so many people who were all opposed to his development plans? My advice to you as a new person here is to do what the boss asks and take the money. Leave the questions to some other fool, Crossy.'

The door handle rattles. As with Harriet, the door clicks and drops onto the wooden bar. The man gives the door a violent shove, but it holds firm. Stepping back, he lowers his right shoulder and gives the door a solid ramming. The door, doorframe and whole front wall shudder. A grating sound makes the men look up and they catch sight of half a dozen slates slipping off the roof.

'Look out!' shouts Cribbs. All four men dive for cover, each going in a different direction.

'Aah, God damn it,' echoes through the air as a roofing slate strikes one of the men down the side of his face, cutting into his cheek and severing part of his ear.

'Crossy? Are you OK?' yells Fletcher as the men rush to his assistance.

Cribbs raises a lantern. 'That's a nasty cut.'

Fletcher and Brannigan try to stem the blood running down the side of Crossy's face and neck with a scarf.

'This place is a bloody death trap,' sputters Crossy as blood spurts out from the cheek wound.

'Come on, let's pick him up and get him to the physician. Cribbs, go ahead to The Hare and Hound and drag Doc Pilkins from the bar. I only hope he's still sober enough to stitch this back up!' says Brannigan.

'What about checking the house?' Fletcher asks.

'Be dammed with the house,' shouts Brannigan. 'No bugger in their right mind's going to be in that death trap.' Slowly the group heads back towards the village, cursing the bad luck and misfortune that has befallen one of their own.

Throughout this commotion, Oliver and Harriet have been pinned to the back wall of the stairs, quiet as mice and still as statues. They have heard everything and now wait for the voices to fully fade away to nothing before getting up and moving to the window. In the distance, they can see the men being greeted in the village by a crowd of people. One of them points to a building ahead and a few of them head off in that direction while supporting Crossy as he staggers along, holding his head. Others continue to wander the streets, presumably looking for the people who broke into the bakery.

'That was close.' Harriet looks at little Oliver and gives him a hug. Oliver is far from over his experience. What has happened in the past hour has rocked him to his very core. He is still in a shocked state, unable to speak without stuttering or trembling.

For a few minutes they watch out the window, looking towards the village for any sign of more people coming back to check the house. Eventually, Harriet turns to Oliver. 'I think we will be alright now,' she says. 'Most of the people seem to have gone, and the lights in the houses are starting to go out.'

They hear a click from the fireplace, then a grating noise as the secret passage slowly opens as the four children emerge. Leading the way, as always, is Edward. Barely have they got out of the fireplace before Harriet and Oliver are explaining what has happened over the past hour.

Edward and the others listen intently, while Dicky closes up the tunnel entrance. Once the debriefing is over, the children head upstairs to get changed into their own clothes. Topper is carrying Harriet's sack of old clothes with him, and they will be put back on the pegs ready for the next excursion. Harriet, already changed, remains downstairs and keeps watch out of the window.

Dicky wipes his face with a handkerchief that he has dipped in a bucket of water as Edward looks at the others. 'This has been an eventful night. I think it's better we wait a few days before we venture out again, especially with one of them being injured and the whole town on the lookout.'

'But our friends! You've seen the state of them down there. How can we leave them for a few days? We need to do more!' says Topper with a frown.

'I know. It's tough, Topper. More so for you with two cousins there, but if we are caught, all of us will be with them and nobody will come to help. We have to be careful. But I promise you now, we will not abandon them. We will try and get them out as soon as we can.' Every member of the group nods and, after a short debate on where to meet up before school the following day, they are ready to leave.

Unlatching the door, they first view the surrounding area for any people still out and about, then slip out and quietly disappear into the darkness.

Walking home, Edward puts his arm round Oliver's shoulders and gives him a squeeze. He knows his little brother has been through an experience that most children his age would have nightmares over. Oliver looks up and stares at his older brother. The hug makes him feel a bit better, but Edward can see in his eyes that he is still traumatised and will take a while to recover. 'You have done so much to help me with these people,' says Edward. 'But I think you should stay at home for a little while, just until you get your confidence back.'

Oliver knows his brother is right, but there is this drive in him that wants to do more, even if it means he must put himself through nights like tonight. 'I was a little bit scared, but I can do it. I did get the shoes, and I can do more. I know I can. I won't let you down again, I promise.'

Edward lets out a big sigh. 'You have never let me down. In fact, you are the bravest pirate I have ever known. But even pirates need to lie low for a while and recover.'

Oliver eventually concedes to his brother's wishes and agrees to take a break for a while, but only if he can keep watch from the kitchen window for his return each time he goes out.

They reach the back gate to the gardens shortly before three in the morning. Edward closes it behind them and releases the piece of string that holds the lock open. A few minutes later they are at the marble step and slipping into the kitchen. This time, the dogs are up and alert, sniffing Oliver and Edward as they enter the room. Both animals are whimpering and baying for a bit of affection from the boys, knowing this is the time they will be receiving a treat. Edward lights the candle and heads to the pantry. He always gives them a titbit when he gets back to keep them content and quiet. It also gets them used to him sneaking around late at night.

Tonight's treat is some slices of leftover beef from yesterday's dinner. It's enough to keep the dogs quiet, but not so much that the cook will miss it from the pantry. Edward makes the dogs sit, before flinging the chunks of meat towards them. Every piece is snatched out of the air. The boys give the animals one last pat on the tops of their heads before heading off up the stairs. By quarter past three, the two of them are tucked up in bed, whispering about the events that have unfolded that night. The two exhausted children do not speak for long, and soon succumb to their eyes closing.

CHAPTER 2

Defending the Youngerns

Edward and Oliver are woken by their sister Edith. As with every morning on a school day, she bounds into the room, pulls back the curtains, opens the windows and squawks about how wonderful the day is.

'Come on, you're both late as usual. You're not even washed, and breakfast will be ready soon. And as it's Friday, it's your favourite, smoked haddock with poached egg, so hurry up as Cook won't be happy if it gets cold.'

Oliver is first to raise his head above the sheets. The icy blast that blows through the window sends a shudder down his spine and he shrinks back down under his sheets. 'It's freezing,' he says, burying his head back into his pillows. Edward doesn't move at all. He just slowly opens his eyes, rumbles out some sort of grunting sound and closes them again.

'Father wants to speak to us all before he goes to work, so up and get washed now!'

Edward opens his eyes again. This time he sniffs the air. Sure enough, he can smell the sweet scent of smoked fish. Summoning what little drive he has to get up on a cold, school-day morning after very little sleep, he swings his legs out of the bed and shuffles his feet into his leather slippers.

'Time to get up,' he says to Oliver. 'We don't want to make Father angry.'

Oliver sits up and rubs his eyes. He's just about to speak when a bellowing voice comes from downstairs.

'Boys, hurry up and get down here. We're waiting on you!'

'It's Father. Quick! Get washed and dressed! We don't want to keep him waiting.'

Edith chuckles to herself. All her effort to get her brothers up in the morning has very little effect, but a couple of words from Father and they are zipping about like moths around a flame. Within minutes, the two boys are tearing down the stairs while still putting on their waistcoats. Edith follows behind, picking up a pirate bandana that Oliver dropped from his pocket on his way out of the bedroom. Truth be known, she absolutely adores her brothers. Despite not being able to get up in the morning, they will do anything to help 'big sis'. Her only regret is that soon she is to marry, and the boys will no longer be as large a part of her life. Still, until then she will have all the fun she can with them.

Near sprinting along the hallway, Oliver and Edward race to take the lead. From the doorway to the left, a young servant walks out carrying an armful of sheets. Splitting left and right, the boys avoid slowing down while almost knocking the maid over as they race into the dining room, where Father is seated at the head of the table.

Mother – Mary by name but called Mother by all – is seated at the other end of the table. Sisters Victoria and Rebecca are always on the far side of the table and the boys take their places on the near side with one empty chair between them. However, this is soon filled up as Edith arrives. The boys eagerly look at Father, waiting for him to say something. The expression on their faces and in their eyes is of pure excitement, but inside, Edward is praying he does not know about their escapades last night.

'Now, children,' Father begins. 'I would like you to be careful when out and about in the village. And for the next few days, I want you all to go to school in a group with Springer escorting you. When school finishes, he will be waiting outside to return you all home safely.'

The children all look at each other, then Victoria asks, 'Pray, Father, why all this caution in a quiet village like this? Has something happened?'

Father leans forward on the table, rubbing his two thumbs together. 'It would seem that last night a group of thieves and murderers went on a rampage in the village. Shops were pillaged, people's houses were burgled and plundered. Worst of all, Mr Jenkins, the producer of the local paper – if that is what you can call it! – was found murdered in his bed with his newly wed wife, Edwina.'

There are a lot of gasps around the table, for all knew of the man and his passion for the village of Pippinsford, even if Father did not approve of him and his six-page-a-fortnight paper due to his criticisms of Lord Fitzgerald.

'It just so happens that Mr Jenkins had recently produced an article on the front page debating the core values of the village community. It went on to question the influx of the new wealthy arrivals and their effect on the rural economy. The most scathing criticism was against Lord Fitzgerald himself, stating he is creating his own empire at the expense of the local people who can no longer afford to live in their own homes. The article outlined how the low-paid farmers and labourers have had their wages cut by forty percent as a direct result of Lord Fitzgerald purchasing all the farms in and around the village and dropping the wages to deliberately remove tenants and labourers from the land. The report finished off with a comment that Mr Jenkins had been unable to contact any of the locals who had been forced out of their village homes by rising living costs. Even those who had sold up – after receiving more than generous payments from Lord Fitzgerald – were unable to be traced.' Father pauses and looks around the table. 'Mr Jenkins' only interest was apparently to see how moving to another district had changed their lives. To find out whether they felt they had made the right decision to move rather than work for Lord Fitzgerald in his new factories or as servants, maids and gardeners to the wealthy families that have moved to the village. Unfortunately, in all his time of searching, he was never able to find anyone who has left Pippinsford in the past few years.'

Edward and Oliver looked at each other. Surely people were not implying they had done murder!

'Now I don't want you to be alarmed, but after speaking to Mother this morning, we felt it best to talk about this as a family rather than have you hear all the rumours that will be circulating when you go to school. I do not believe for one second that you are in any danger, but – being new to the area and me being in a position of importance working for Lord Fitzgerald – I am not prepared to take any risks involving my children. So, from now until the end of next week, you will go to school, return from school and play in the grounds of our house under the supervision of Mother and Edith. At the weekend you will stay in the grounds unless we go out as a group, or I agree that you can go to a specific destination.'

Father looks at Edith. 'Edith, you may be collected by Chester as long as you both stay in the company of others when out of this house. All staff will be on full alert when on duty as the gardeners have noticed footprints in the grounds near the fruit trees. I will also have someone staying in the lower lodge at night, patrolling the grounds while we are asleep.'

The children look at Father and then to Mother, hoping she will say something to ease the restrictions Father has set. But in Victorian times, the husband sets the rules of the house. What he says goes without question. It is the wife's duty to support her husband and organise the children, servants and household in his absence to the requirements he sets. And Mother was going to do just that.

Edward plucks up the courage to ask, 'How long is this going to last, Father?'

'I think the matter will be closed in a few days. The magistrate has recalled all his men to investigate the issue. Heading up the enquiry is none other than Mr Cribbs himself. Now that Cribbs has retired from prize fighting, Lord Fitzgerald has promoted him to Chief Constable, a fine reward for a man who hasn't lost a fight in the past five years. I fear for any man who crosses him.' Father chuckles to himself. 'I've seen that man in action many a time, and what a sight it was to behold! Broken jaws, smashed bones, blood everywhere. I even have a tooth fro—' Mother coughs politely, and he takes the hint. 'Now enough of this and let's get on with breakfast. Mother, will you do the honours?'

She looks up at the housekeeper and gives the nod. The housekeeper then nods at a maid, and service begins. Mother and Father are served first, followed by the children. A fine spread of food is placed before them as toast and preserves, bacon and sausages are put in the centre of the table. The fish, still steaming and each with a perfect poached egg on top, is served on a plate which itself is on a silver tray. 'What a wonderful smell,' says Oliver, sniffing the air above his fish.

'I know.' Edith smiles. 'What a treat smoked haddock is for breakfast.'

'Shall we begin?' says Father. 'And I don't expect to see any empty plates at the table today.'

Not that that was ever going to happen. The children are always expected to eat whatever is presented in front of them, but in the case of Edward and Oliver, the fish was lucky if it touched the sides going down, such was their love for it.

Near the end of the fish course, the maid wheels a small silver trolley over to the side of Mother. On the top of it stand two large tortoiseshell boxes with gold inlay, and a large silver pot. Mother turns from the table, reaches up to the locket round her neck and opens the clasp. A small key falls into her palm and, reaching forward, she opens the two boxes. Inside the protective silver lining is one of the rarest commodities of the Victorian era: tea. Mother has two blends of tea that she mixes to make Father's favourite tipple. She opens the lid of the silver teapot, takes the deep-bowled silver spoon and adds two spoons of tea from each box into the teapot. On the fourth spoonful she looks at Father and waits.

He thinks for a bit and nods his head to the left. Mother smiles and adds another spoonful from the left box and looks up again. This time he thinks for a bit longer, rubs his chin and double nods his head to the right. The children giggle as Mother, still smiling, puts half a spoon more from the right-hand box.

Father tries to act serious, but in this case he relents and lets out a small smile as he shakes his head. Closing the boxes, Mother puts the key back in the locket, rolls the lid back over on the teapot and covers it with a thick blue cosy decorated with lions and unicorns sewn in golden thread. She then signals to the maid to move the tea to one side to be infused for a few minutes. On its return, it is poured through a strainer into cups and served to the family sitting around the table.

Breakfast over, the children prepare themselves for school. The mood in the group is quiet, as Father's words are still on everybody's minds. Only three of the children are of an age to go to school. With Victoria and Edith being older, they have other duties in the family home, most of which entail socialising, organising afternoon teas, shopping and assisting Mother with whatever she is doing.

Father's personal butler, Springer, arrives at the front door to escort the children to school. To all who look at him, he is an ordinary man, just a little taller in stature and wider across the shoulders than most. He is well-dressed in his butler's attire today, but usually he is dressed more casually for working and organising the farmhands while running the yard for his master.

Few of the locals know he is an up-and-coming prize fighter – ready for a big fight in the not-so-distant future – under the guidance of Cribbs. He has been put in the position of a personal butler and yard foreman by Lord Fitzgerald and Henry (Father) to hide his arrival from the local bare-knuckle-fight scene until the best and most rewarding bouts come along. The intent being to make a large amount of money by putting his skills to the test against the very best in the business before the odds reduce on this talented young fighter.

Springer caught Henry's attention a few months earlier when on a trip to Northumberland. While drinking in the tavern where he was staying the night, Henry overheard a conversation about a local man who had earlier that week single-handedly taken on and defeated three would-be opportunists who were attempting to steal lead from a warehouse roof. One of the men pulled a knife on Springer and, as a consequence, will never walk again. The others did not fare much better, but the brutality of the beatings they received had not gone unnoticed by the county magistrate.

This had left Springer in prison without means, and a magistrate with a problem.

On the one side, this man had done the job he was paid to do. He'd protected the warehouse and defended himself when in danger. The owners of the warehouse wanted their employee back on duty as it would now put fear in the hearts of any other would-be thieves. On the other side, these three local men had been brutally beaten to within an inch of their lives. Despite them being thieves and criminals, their families and friends were starting to create unrest in the deprived sectors of the town. Meaning more time and constables were required to quell disputes than in any other part of the district. This left the wealthier parts of town short on security at a time when crime levels were on the rise. The rich were being targeted more and more by pickpockets, housebreakers and suchlike as they were the ones with better loot for the taking. For if a thief is to put his life on the line, the reward needs to be worth the risk involved.

Henry had made enquiries and on finding out the local magistrate had a few gambling debts, he decided to take over the marker, pay the debt and go after the man himself for payment. After a short meeting with the magistrate, a wiping clean of the marker and a small sweetener being paid, Springer was released into Henry's charge on the condition that he was never to return to Northumberland. The magistrate spread the rumour that Springer had been dispensed with aboard a ship bound for the Far East under the service of the crown. This resolved all issues, cleared his debt and made him a small profit.

Springer now had a new employer and owed a debt of gratitude to a man he had never met before. This new employer then spoke to *his* employer, Lord Fitzgerald, who was heavily into the fight scene. Now Springer has two new masters eager to exploit his talents and make money at the expense of his fists. In a way, they all got what they wanted: Lord Fitzgerald has a new fighter; Henry looks good in his boss's eyes and gets a boost up the ladder; and Springer gets out of prison with some money in his pocket and a place to live while he works for Henry on his estate.

'Right, youngerns, let's be going. We don't want to be late to learning, do we?' A fighter Springer may be, but his use of the Queen's English? Not so good. He rounds up the small group of children and heads off out the door, leading them down the long gravel driveway.

Springer has a soft spot for children, for – being kinder and with no underlying objectives – they treat him better than most adults. He also finds them easier to understand and get on with.

In many ways, he is far smarter than people give him credit for. Sharp in the mind and agile on his feet, he can read people and their character very well. Speaking slow and in simple English makes many around him think he is stupid, but the truth is far from that. It just takes time for people to understand his ways.

As for Springer, he is fully aware of his new master's objectives, but for the moment this situation is comfortable and suits him. Not to mention he has a soft spot for Miss Victoria, who he considers the finest woman he has ever seen. Any time spent in her company is treasured, and in his eyes and mind, that is well worth the odd punch up or broken nose.

The small group led by Springer head off along the lane to the village. The school is situated on the other side of the park, about twenty minutes' walking distance from the estate. The building itself has recently undergone a large extension, ready to cater for the additional children now moving to the village. An extended and higher level of learning – with new, highly skilled teachers able to set a better standard of education for the children of richer families – has also been put in place by Lord Fitzgerald as a sweetener to attract the people he wants in his growing empire.

Edward turns to Oliver and whispers, 'I don't think we will be able to meet up with the others before school. We'll just have to find a way to meet up in our lunch break or something.' Oliver looks back at Edward and gives a nod.

Springer ushers them through the black metal gates that lead into the school grounds. 'Now be remembering, all of thee are to wait for me here after schoolin' be ended. Be not forgetting now, youngerns, and cheery bye until then.'

The children soon blend into the crowd of bodies shuffling across the playground towards the main entrance, where the school's junior teacher swings a large brass bell. Being such a small person in stature, it takes both his hands to swing the heavy bell with its foot-long wooden handle. And even then, it's in the most ungainly technique, like a man trying to swat a fly with a sledgehammer.

As the children enter through the main doors, they split up into relevant age groups and head towards their respective classrooms. Rebecca moves to the far side of the school, where the oldest children are in their last year of schooling. Edward gives Oliver a flick across the head as he passes. Turning on his heels, Oliver spots Edward and tries to return the favour. But being much shorter, he is unable to reach, swishes his hand through the air and misses his faster brother by some distance while nearly falling over with the effort. They both laugh before Oliver turns and runs off.

As Edward enters his classroom, he feels a sharp pinch to his ribs. Looking round, he stares right into the face of Susan.

'And where were you? I waited for nearly half an hour for you to turn up.'

Edward sighs. 'I know, I'm sorry. But Father had his butler escort us into school. Apparently some people were murdered in the village last night and they are blaming it on the thieves that were seen stealing from the houses and shops. Father thinks we are in danger, so we are to be escorted to and from school until the constables have finished their investigations.'

Susan pauses for a minute to think. 'That's us! They think it was us who murdered people in the village.' The whole classroom looks round at the two of them.

'Keep your voice down, Susan,' Edward says quietly. 'Yes, we were out last night, and no, we did not kill anyone. It just so happens we were not the only people out with an agenda to fulfil. It looks like someone is taking advantage of the fact that you were spotted at the bakers. Don't forget Oliver and I had a run in with Brannigan, Sykes and some other man outside the home of the family who were murdered.'

Edward looks round. All the other children in the class are still staring at them and whispering to each other. 'We'll talk later,' he says.

They walk to their desks. Susan is seated beside Edward but on the other side of the walkway. From the moment she takes her seat and while she lifts the lid up on her desk and collects her books from inside, she stays in constant eye contact with Edward. Mouthing words he cannot quite understand, she only turns away as the teacher walks into the classroom and passes between the two of them to the front of the class.

'Good heavens to be,' she lets out. 'I hope you children are all alright and the events of last night have not disturbed you too much.'

By now most of the children have heard about what happened in the village.

'Be assured that the school is very safe, and the magistrate has stationed one of their constables here every day to ensure our safety until the culprits are apprehended.'

This seems ironic to Edward. With all that is going on in the village, from families going missing, several people passing away under strange circumstances and unusual goings-on all over the region, only the events of last night are being highlighted to such a level, causing panic throughout the village. Why would the magistrate be so concerned about the children that they would put someone in the school to protect them? Or is there an ulterior motive behind all of this? Edward starts to recall his encounter with Brannigan and Sykes. It seems to him now that it was no coincidence they were near the printer man's house that night. Perhaps they had something to do with the demise of the couple who lived there. If they did, it would put his brother and him in a very difficult position. They saw the killers first-hand, just after they had done the evil deed.

The teacher reassures everyone again, then after a brief discussion about not walking home alone and the dangers of strangers and what to do if someone approaches them, the lessons continue in their usual way. All Edward can think about is lunch break, when he can see his friends and talk to them about last night and all the goings-on that had occurred since, but the morning seems to drag on for so long. Each time Edward looks around, Susan waves her bandaged hand under the table and opens her eyes wide with concern. A constable is walking round the school grounds, constantly looking in the classroom windows as if searching for someone. It's not a moment too soon when the teacher says, 'Children, you are dismissed for lunch.'

Edward's out of his chair like a bullet from a gun, fast-walking past the teacher, through the door and down the hallway, weaving in and out of other children as he goes. Susan struggles to keep up, and as they head across the yard, she runs after him. 'Edward, wait up!' she calls and grabs his arm. 'Ouch,' she yells and lets him go. Only with the pain does she realise she grabbed him with her bandaged hand.

Edward stops, turns around and looks at her, only then realising how fast he's been moving. He looks down at her bandaged hand. 'Are you OK?' he asks. 'How's the hand?' Reaching forward, he holds her hand and turns it to view the palm. Small beads of red start to stain through the white bandage and expand. The cut was disturbed when she grabbed Edward's arm. His eyes move from her hand to her face, and he watches as tears run down her cheeks. He holds her waist and embraces her. It's all the encouragement Susan needs, and she wraps her arms around him and holds him tight for nearly a full minute.

Edward has no intention of letting her go until she is ready to release him. Inside, he is feeling guilty and sad that she is in pain.

Finally, she whispers into his ear, 'My hand needed to be sewn up with several stitches, and it hurts and throbs so very much. I have to see the matron soon to have the bandage removed. She'll put iodine put on the wound and wrap it up again. Now it's bleeding, I know it will sting even more when she does it.'

'You poor thing,' Edward replies. He thinks for a moment. 'In fact, let's go now. I'll escort you there.'

Susan's eyes light up. 'Will you?' She releases him, wipes her eyes and goes to turn away, then stops, turns back to Edward and gives him a kiss on the cheek.

Edward starts to blush. He's a little shocked, but in a good way. A small smile appears on his face as he realises what Susan already knows: that he has very strong feelings for her. 'How did you explain the cut to your parents?' he asks as they walk towards matron's office.

'Oh, that was Maddi's idea. Once I had sneaked back into the house, I smashed the glass lantern on the floor, opened my hand and allowed some blood to drip around the area. Then I let out a scream! When Mother and the servants came, I explained I could hear noises from the village and how I'd tried to light the lamp. Father, having some knowledge of cuts from his days in the army, started work on my hand while waiting for the physician to arrive.'

Edward smiles. 'That Maddi could find an excuse for anything. And if it was a sport, she would win every time.'

Leaving Susan as she enters the matron's office, Edward heads back out into the schoolyard. He looks around at the groups of children, trying to find the rest of his friends. He needs to find out more about what happened last night. And try to fathom out the events that have been unfolding at school.

He shudders, as if someone has just walked over his grave. An eerie sense befalls the whole of his body, and he has a strange feeling as if being watched by someone. His pace slows dramatically, slower and slower, until he stops and pauses momentarily. Slowly he looks around at all angles of the playground. He can see no one looking directly at him, nor anyone looking in his general direction. *That's odd*, he thinks as he wriggles and shuffles his body in an attempt to shake the eerie feeling. He takes a few steps forward, but the feeling persists. Goosebumps appear on his arms, and the hairs are standing up on the back of his neck.

Stopping again, he thinks for a second then quickly kneels and pretends to tie his shoelace. His thinking is that in a crowded playground, kneeling down will mask his position and flush out the person watching him. He waits to see who will approach, looking in all directions from his low viewpoint. It doesn't take long before the legs of two adults head in his direction. Curiosity now has the better of him. Keeping a low, crouched position, he scurries along the floor, ensuring he stays on the far side of a group of children. Being able to hide his movement from the two arriving adults for a few moments helps him gain an advantage and, passing a line of children playing hopscotch, he makes for the corner of a school outbuilding. He finally stands up, quickly pressing his back up against the wall, then turns to look at the people who were observing him.

'Oh no.' Edward groans. 'It's Sykes.' Why would the magistrate send one of Lord Fitzgerald's enforcers to watch over the children at a school? Surely it would be considered a menial task for one such as him! Sykes is accompanied by one of the new teachers who started at the school this term, Elroy Snape – a strange, tall, thin and balding man, quick with punishment and slow with praise, wearing a long black fishtailed cloak. Edward is not in his classes but is aware of his reputation. His nickname with the children is The Stick – not just for his build, but also for his use of a bendy willow cane that he regularly flicks over a child's shoulder so the thin end whips down and stings the back of its victim's hand, leaving a red mark that lasts for hours. Edward has been told it's a painful experience.

As the adults arrive at the spot where Edward had been, they look around. Edward strains his ears, trying to hear what they are saying.

'I'm sure I saw the boy in question standing here,' says the teacher. 'He cannot have gone far.'

'Don't worry yourself, Snape. I only want to have a word with him and see if he saw or heard anything of what happened last night. Anyway, with my experience, I will know if he has any information just by looking into his eyes. They have a way of talking to me, you see… Even if the owner does not speak.' Sykes turns and, with one more look around the yard, speaks again. 'It's of no importance. I can catch up with him later in the classroom and talk to him then. It's not as if he's going anywhere!'

Edward thinks on his options. He realises Sykes is going to find him at some stage, so he may as well get it over with now and find out what he wants. His first thought is that Sykes wants to know if it was him they bumped into last night. And if so, whether Edward recognises him. He decides that no matter what happens, he will play ignorant and pretend to know nothing. With that fixed in his mind, he takes one last deep breath and steps forward. Pretending to join in with the other children, he deliberately puts himself in view of the adults while letting out a large laugh.

Instantly, Sykes spots him and yells, 'You, boy,' while pointing at Edward. The children in close proximity go quiet and all look in the direction of Sykes' outstretched arm.

'Who, me, sir?' Edward replies, touching his chest.

'Yes, you. Come here at once, boy.'

Moving slowly towards the constable, Edward puts on his blank 'I know nothing' expression. He stops in front of Sykes and slowly raises his head until he is looking straight into the eyes of this evil man. 'Yes, sir?' he says in a quiet voice.

Sykes slowly looks the boy up and down from top to bottom, twice over, watching for any tell-tale signs that he recognises him from the previous night. Then he asks, 'What do you know about the incidents in the village last night?'

'Last night, sir? I know only what my father told me this morning at breakfast and what the teacher said in the classroom earlier.'

Sykes eyes him up and down again. 'Well, see you let me know if you hear of anything that might be of use to help us apprehending these awful villains. Who knows, you might even see them swing from the gallows. If they don't send them to Australia.'

Edward takes a deep, sharp intake of breath. Sykes sees the expression on Edward's face and decides to play on him a bit more.

'Course, if you 'ave never seen a man dangle by his neck, all blue in the face and soiling himself as he flaps like a puppet on a string, it can be a disturbing sight,' he says. Then he deepens his voice and slowly growls, 'It's even worse if they don't get the drop right. Too shallow and the neck does not snap. The choking and gurgling can last for five or ten minutes. Ghastly they say, just ghastly. Or if the drop is too long, the head pops off like the cork out a bottle. The body drops to the ground, jumps up and runs around like a chicken.' Sykes laughs a horrible grating cackle. Edward starts to feel sick.

'That's enough!' the teacher yells. 'Edward, take no notice and be on your way. And you,' Snape says, pointing to the constable, 'you should know better than to fill the heads of children with such horrible thoughts. You could give them nightmares.' Sykes chuckles to himself as he sees the fear he has set in the child's eyes, for it will now give him the upper hand when he speaks to him again.

Edward hastily turns to run away and bumps into another child, knocking himself and the other person to the ground. He staggers to his feet and offers his hand to the unfortunate victim. 'I'm so sorry,' he says as the smaller child turns around and looks at him.

Edward is faced with a huge smile and the words, 'That's alright, brother. I've been knocked over by you harder than that playing bulldog in the garden.'

Edward smiles as he grabs his brother's outreached hands and pulls him to his feet. 'Where did you come from?' he asks.

'I've been looking for you, to let you know that Syk—'

Oliver stops in mid-sentence, for he has just seen, over his brother's shoulder, the large and looming form of Sykes. His eyes widen and he grips tight to his brother's hands as fear takes him over.

'Yes! You do recognise me, don't you, boy? For I remember you,' Sykes mutters in a slow, calculated voice. It is all Oliver can do to shake his head at the accusation.

Edward realises Oliver is in a compromising position and is swift to try and defuse the situation. He spins his brother around and pushes him away from Sykes' prying eyes. 'Come on, let's go or we will be late for class.' The two of them turn, swiftly weave around the groups of children and head towards the entrance to the school.

They can hear Sykes bellowing in the background. 'We'll talk later then, shall we?' But the boys ignore him. As they reach the safety of the school building, Edward looks round to check where Sykes is. As he expected, Sykes has not moved from the spot. He just watches them with a keen interest.

Edward knows this is not the end of the issue, but the start of a problem he does not yet know how to fix. With one last look back at Sykes, he turns and heads off into the classroom to ponder the problem.

All through the afternoon, Edward wracks his brain to come up with a solution. He needs to keep his younger brother away from the horrible Sykes. Periodically, he looks out of the window. And each time he sees the horrible figure of a man standing by the school gate glaring right back at him through the window. He knows Sykes is going to ask his little brother some questions. Or worse, put him and his brother in front of their father and start questioning them. They will both deny being out last night, and Father will believe it and support them by stating his boys were in bed.

But he knows now that Sykes will not leave it at that. He will want to be thorough, and Oliver may not be up to the questioning. Somehow he must be convinced that Oliver and Edward were not the children he bumped into at the printer's house. For otherwise, Edward is sure there is no limit to how far Sykes will go to ensure no witness to his crimes is left alive. He is aware Oliver will panic and break down if Sykes starts to question him in the school, but if Edward can get him home in his own environment and prepare him a little, make it some sort of challenge or a game, Oliver might be able to pull it off.

But how can they get back home before Sykes gets hold of them? He wonders for a while. The only person who could help him is Father's butler. He is big enough and strong enough to defend himself against Sykes, but how far would he go to protect his master's children?

Edward has no idea of Springer's talents as a bare-knuckle fighter. The only concern in his mind is how he can avoid Sykes and get his brother home safe and sound. A few minutes before the end of school, the crowd of parents arriving to walk their children home grows, much larger than usual. But given the circumstances and reports on the goings-on last night, it is of no surprise that more escorts than usual are arriving.

Edward can see the big figure of Springer through the mass of people, at the back of the adults. Beside Springer he can make out the bonnet of his sister Victoria. To an extent, Edward is relieved there are two of them as it may help to protect his little brother from the intimidation Sykes will throw at him.

As the teacher releases the children, Edward quickly nips to the front of the room and is first out of the door. He makes his way to the coat rack and waits for his brother and sister. Oliver is the first to arrive, but before Oliver says a word, Edward starts to speak.

'Now listen to me carefully, Oliver. Sykes is still outside; he will want to talk to you about last night. You must be strong and not be intimidated by him. Just tell him you were in bed by eight and you heard nothing. Do not show any fear in your eyes and definitely do not let on that you recognise him from last night. It's important that you do this for me.'

Oliver looks into his brother's eyes. At first, Edward sees just a worried little boy, but as the young lad gets his mind around what his brother has just said, he can see a bit of calmness and resolve returning to his features.

'I understand, and I will show you I can be brave. I won't let him know we are the ones who saw him last night.'

Edward smiles. 'That's my little pirate.'

'Aarrrr,' comes the response from little Oliver.

'Oh, and one more thing, do not let Rebecca know anything about what is going on, as she will go straight to Mother, and we will get in trouble and be grounded.' Oliver gives a small nod and taps his nose with his finger.

Rebecca arrives, pushing past the both of them to collect her coat and scarf. 'Well, I hope your day has been better than mine. All I seem to have done today is answer questions about you two with that creepy teacher, The Stick. He is not a very nice man.'

Edward looks at her and asks, 'Why was he teaching you? He's not your normal teacher.'

'He was filling in for Miss Millen, who was called away during the first period for something.'

'What kind of questions was he asking?'

Rebecca huffs at all the questions from her younger sibling. 'Oh, silly ones like does Oliver often go out late at night? Who are your closest friends? Where do you go to play with your friends?' She sighed. 'I mean, you go to bed one hour before me, so you are never out late at night, and we all play together in the same places with the same group of friends. I just think he's a sad, old creepy man.'

Edward thinks for a bit. 'Perhaps you're right. I just don't trust him or his motives, that's all. Anyway, Victoria is by the gate with Springer. If you head out to them, we'll catch you up once we've put our coats on.'

'What? Vicky's outside! Oh, that's grand. Why didn't you tell me sooner? We have so much to talk about with Edith's wedding coming up and I will have her all to myself for all the time it takes for us to get home.' Rebecca hurries off to join Victoria without so much as a by your leave.

Edward peers out of the main entrance, crouching low and ensuring he is shielded from view by all the children leaving. As expected, Sykes is just outside the doors, waiting for them to appear. Quietly, Edward retraces his steps and turns to Oliver. 'Now she's gone we need to move fast. If we follow the south wing corridor, we can slip out the side door, follow the path to the maypole gate and go along the outside of the school boundary wall. This should hide us from Sykes until we meet up with the others.'

The pair of them scurry off down the corridor, head out the side door and, within minutes, are running along the school wall towards Victoria and the others. Just before the boys get to Rebecca and Victoria, Springer looks up and spots the lads running towards him from an unexpected direction.

'That there be a different way to be getting to us,' he says. But before they can answer he continues, 'Still, mind thee not. You be here now. Hope you youngerns had a good day's learning.' Springer pauses before addressing the group. 'Well, let's be getting thee back. Your mother be waiting with a bobbin puller to measure Victoria and Rebecca for their new dresses, and you two youngerns for the suits ye be needin' to wear.'

The two sisters giggle with excitement and walk off arm in arm, chatting while Springer walks beside Victoria, keeping pace. Behind them, the boys follow in close order. Every now and then, Edward looks back over his shoulder to see if Sykes is behind them. Each time the coast is clear, and he feels a little more at ease.

They take the shortcut across the meadow, around part of the lake and re-join the path just before a crossway lined with hedges. As they turn to the right to follow the track home, Edward gets that strange feeling again and looks round. To his horror, right behind them is Brannigan and another man in a long dark trench coat. This man Edward has never seen before.

"Ello, boys. Nice day for a walk, isn't it?' says the strange man. Edward turns his head back. Fear grips him, but he manages to hold his nerve. *Is this strange man the third person from last night?* he wonders.

The whole group feels uncomfortable with the men behind them, and the girls stop talking and concentrate on walking a little faster.

The strange man calls out to Edward and Oliver. 'What do you boys know about last night, then?'

The boys ignore him and continue walking on.

'Boy, I'm talking to you,' bellows the strange man. He grabs Oliver by the shoulder and pulls him back. Oliver lets out a yelp and buckles down to his knees with the force of the grip.

Springer spins round and grabs the man by the wrist, squeezing tightly. 'Let the youngern go or it will end badly for thee,' he says, looking hard into the man's eyes. The pain exerted by Springer's grip is clear in the man's face and from the whitening of the skin around the area he has grasped. The stranger swiftly releases Oliver's shoulder and steps back as Springer also lets go.

'Now leave this place afore I throw you a beating,' Springer says as he stares both men down, clenching his fists.

The man pauses for a second before letting out a roar and lunging forward, swinging wildly at Springer's head. The move is way too slow and also expected. Springer tucks under the blow and brings up his right hand to hit the man in the stomach. He winces and buckles up and Springer unleashes a second, left-handed punch, impacting the back of his head. The force knocks the man forward and he collapses, spread out, face down in a muddy puddle.

Brannigan lets out a yell and swings at Springer with a flurry of right- and left-handed punches that Springer blocks with his forearms and shoulders before countering with a straight right onto Brannigan's chin. Brannigan staggers back about three feet before stepping forward and delivering a sharp left to the side of Springer's head, followed by a right to the other side. The follow-through of the right-handed punch spins Springer round almost one hundred and eighty degrees. And as he retracts back, he bends his arm and sticks out his elbow, driving it with maximum force onto the bridge of Brannigan's nose. The subsequent crack is heard by all but felt by only one. The children wince and grit their teeth at the hollow sound of broken bone. Brannigan falls backwards and hits the ground like a sack of potatoes. He lies there motionless with blood pouring from his nose and an open wound running across his eyebrow.

All goes quiet for a while, then the group slowly moves towards the downed men. They spread apart so all can get a good view of the damage inflicted on Brannigan and the stranger.

'Wow,' says Oliver. 'Look at his nose. It's everywhere. I mean, it's all over his face! And look at the blood he's cov—'

'Now you youngerns had best not be seeing this. But them there men should not have touched young Oliver that way, and they had fair warning afore I gave reckonin',' says Springer as he stretches out his fingers and rubs his hands together to take out the sting.

All the children and Victoria are staring at the bloodstained faces of Brannigan and the other man, who just manages to crawl out of the puddle a little before collapsing on the floor again. First to snap out of it is Victoria, who turns and looks at their saviour.

'Oh Springer! Are you alright?' She grabs his arm and holds it tightly.

'Now don't ye fret, little Miss Victoria. I be fine and all be safe. Now let's not be hangin' about 'ere and get to going. We need tell your father what be going on, find out who be these men and send for a sawbones to fix them up.'

Victoria instantly backs Springer up. 'Now come on, away with you boys. There's nothing to see here for the likes of you.' She grabs both the boys' heads and turns them away, ushering them towards home, before re-clasping Springer's arm.

Rebecca has taken Oliver's hand and is walking alongside Edward. They all slowly reposition themselves and head towards the house, stepping around Brannigan and the man who had grabbed Oliver's shoulder. He's quietly moaning. Oliver looks back at him. He cannot help himself and he turns around and kicks him in the ribs with all his might. 'That's for touching me!' he cries as the man gasps at the impact of Oliver's boot.

'I think that there brother of yours is recovering well. Packs a good wallop when he be of a mind to do so,' Springer says to the smiling Victoria.

They make their way down the path and back to the house. All of them have different thoughts running through their heads.

Victoria looks up at Springer. 'Thank you for protecting my brothers,' she says. 'That was a very brave thing to do, standing up against two men like that. I'm not saying I agree with what you did, but I am glad we are all safe. And that is all down to you.' She smiles at him, then after another few minutes of holding on to his arm, she finally lets go, turns to Rebecca and comforts her for the rest of the journey home.

Springer, on the other hand, does not remember much about the altercation. The fight was just an instinctive reaction, adrenalin running through his veins and great skill against undisciplined opposition. What he remembers is spending precious time with Miss Victoria, the feel of her holding his arm for a while, her smile, the blue of her eyes, her smell and the way she softly spoke to him. It's been a long time since he last felt content as a man and for a brief period of time today, he'd had the honest affections of a fine upstanding woman. And in this act alone he felt like a human being again, not a bruiser baying to the crowds for pay.

It takes them another ten minutes to reach the grounds of the estate. Once there, Springer knows the first thing he must do is see the master of the house and explain what has happened. While he heads off to see Henry, Victoria and the children walk round to the rose garden teahouse, where they join Mother and Edith for afternoon refreshments.

Victoria is still thinking about what happened earlier, and also about Springer. She recalls that since moving to this area, she has always felt uncomfortable and a little afraid. The only time she feels truly safe is when Springer is around. Not only does she feel more secure, but also more at ease and able to be herself with confidence. Now that he is on her mind, she tries to work out which of his qualities makes him stand out from all others.

She puts together a mental list of all the good things he stands for: his gentleness; the fact he is always there for her and any others who approach him, willing to listen and answer with an honest opinion; the kindness he shows for such a powerful man and the way he softly speaks to people no matter what the issue. He has never let her down or crossed a bad word in her presence. Even the manner in which he speaks his words in that slow, old-fashioned simple country style makes her smile. It soon becomes clear to her that despite the huge difference between their lifestyles, wealth and family backgrounds, with Springer around her and close to hand, she is a far happier person and in a far better place.

So deep is Victoria in her thoughts, she becomes oblivious to her surroundings and walks blindly into one of the many garden ornaments – in this case a huge marble seashell about six feet high displaying a variety of flowers in various shades of blue. Giving a high-pitched squeal, she bounces back off the stone shell and into a heap on the floor.

Springer, who has just reached the doorway, hears her distressed call and looks back just as Victoria crumples to the ground. 'Oh Lordy,' he mutters to himself as he rushes to her assistance. He offers her his hand and eases her up, his other hand on the small of her back.

'Miss Victoria, is thee alright?' he asks. She looks back at him with those clear, bright blue eyes and an embarrassed smirk on her face. But before any words are spoken, Mother and all with her arrive and take over. Shuffling Victoria along to the teahouse, they sit her down on one of the now vacant seats, offering her a drink of some description to calm her down.

During all this commotion and moving of Victoria, Springer has barely moved. He is still looking only at Victoria, and Victoria – at every un-obvious opportunity – looks back at Springer. He ponders for a minute, with thoughts above his position in society, then shakes his head and returns to his original business with the master of the house. This time the journey is uneventful, and on arrival at the side door, he wipes his feet and enters the building.

Unfortunately, the same cannot be said for the children with Mother. All they can talk about (and display again and again by swinging their fists) is what Springer just did to the two men who attacked them.

'Mother, you should have seen him! He was so fast! And the blood…' says Oliver.

'Yes, yes!' replies Edward, swinging his fists through the air.

'Enough!' responds Mother in a stern voice. 'Now go and play.'

Edward is about to comment when Mother raises her eyebrow. He realises that whatever he says will not help the situation, so he grabs his brother and the two of them head off into the garden, still throwing punches and pretending to be Springer beating up on the two bad men.

Victoria also has other things on her mind. She stands up and leaves the attentions of her mother and the others behind as she heads back to the house. She has an impulse to speak with Springer. She still does not know what she wants to say, but approach him she must. She watched him enter the house and close the door behind him, but knowing the man, she is aware of where he will be going and why. She moves off in a brisk walk to catch him up before he reaches her father – as once there, he will no doubt be tasked with other duties, and she may not get the chance to speak to him for a while.

CHAPTER 3

The Announcement

Springer walks through the hall of the large house, unaware of Victoria rushing to catch him up. Turning right at the two Chesterfield wall bureaus adorned with porcelain figures and other decorative fineries, he continues on at pace until reaching the large wood and brass study door, stopping only to brush himself down and ensure he is tucked in fully while putting on his white butler's gloves. He takes one final look at himself in a hanging hall mirror then raps three times on the door.

'Enter,' a voice calls from inside the room.

Springer briskly enters the room and swiftly closes the door – which bounces on the catch but does not fully shut, leaving it slightly ajar.

Victoria was about to call out to Springer but was just too late. She reaches for the door handle and pauses when she realises the door is not fully closed. She waits, listening through the gap for the right time to announce her presence and enter the room.

Inside, Springer finds Henry standing by a shallow table with Lord Fitzgerald, admiring a full suit of oriental samurai armour. The helmet and mask combine to display the head of a fearsome dragon, while the body armour is made from what looks like reed, leather and silk in the colours of black and red. Engraved on the front is a large body of a golden dragon that spirals all the way round and down the entire suit, finishing on the shin protector plates.

To the left of the suit is a small stand upon which lie three swords horizontally in size order. The top one is approximately three and a half foot long, below it is a two-and-a-half-foot example, and below that the last one is a foot or so long. All three are black, with gold and red braided handles and a dragon's head at the end of the hilt. 'They were made by the famous Japanese swordsmith Muramasa from the sixteenth century,' Henry says, taking a sip of brandy.

'It is truly exquisite. I cannot believe you got this all for under two hundred guineas! Where on earth did it come from? And how do you know so much about it?' asks Lord Fitzgerald.

'The captain of the ship said it was from a noble family in Japan. It was being transported to France as a wedding gift with their daughter, who was to marry a diplomat in Paris. The name of the swordsmith is hidden inside the handle on the hilt and the blade is decorated with a dragon image stained into the metal itself. I can assure you its provenance is without question, and the story of how it got here is quite true. I was just fortunate to be in the right place at the right time, Lord Fitzgerald.'

'Yes, but how did it fall into your hands, Henry? For this is no ordinary suit of armour. It was a gift for a wedding – how is it now in your possession?'

'Unfortunately, the bride died on the voyage over, with what the doctors think was consumption. I acquired it from the captain to pay for the funeral and travel expenses to send the body back to Japan. Though what she will look like by the time she gets back is anyone's guess. The one thing I do know is she left the docks in a vat of the finest brandy I could lay my hands on.'

'You know, I must have it for my collection. I simply must. I will give you three hundred guineas for it. How's that for a fine offer?'

'It's a very attractive offer indeed, my lord. But I do not intend to sell it. I plan to display it on the far side of this study once a better frame and mount has been made.'

Lord Fitzgerald thinks for a moment – it is almost possible to feel his mind working things out and scheming to his own advantage.

'I'm not so sure,' he says. 'I do not believe it would fit in with this modern house. I'll reappraise the offer. I'm prepared to go up to—' He pauses before looking into Henry's eyes and continuing in a sterner voice. 'Let's say four hundred guineas and we will remain good friends over the matter.'

Henry knows he has no choice but to sell his prize find, or risk angering Lord Fitzgerald. 'Well, my lord, I had not intended to part with it. But you put such a generous offer on the table I guess I just cannot refuse.'

'Oh, capital! I will send my benefactor round this very afternoon to procure my merchandise. All I need do now is find the right place in my armoury to display it. What a talking piece it will make when my guests walk around my estate.'

Springer waits for the two gentlemen to finish their conversation. Henry looks up and beckons him closer. 'Yes, Springer? What can I do for you?' he asks.

'Sorry to disturb you, me'lord, but I thought thee be best aware of a reckonin' that happened on the way back from collecting them there youngerns from schoolin'. Up yonder at the crossroads, we be approached by two men, one—'

'Youngerns? Up yonder?' says Lord Fitzgerald. 'My God, man, you really need to work on your English. Anyway, I sent two of my men to intercept your journey.' He turns to Henry. 'You see, I heard a disturbing rumour that your boys were out last night and might have seen something they should not have.'

Henry looks at Lord Fitzgerald in amazement while shaking his head. 'You said nothing to me about this!'

'Oh, that was forgetful of me. Then again, that was the reason I came around in the first place. Unfortunately, I was side-tracked by this wonderful set of oriental armour. Well, I hope they did not frighten you, or cause you fret. They are quite big men,' he says, chuckling to himself.

Springer thinks for a second, then responds, 'Well, more fool them for not introducing themselves proper like, me'lord. And cos they ort not to have laid hands on young Oliver like they did, them being strangers an all to the likes of us.'

Lord Fitzgerald stops chuckling. 'What do you mean? What has happened to them?'

'They grabbed the master's youngern from behind and I had to defend him, and a right thumping they got from me too.'

'What? Show me your hands! Are they damaged in any way?' Lord Fitzgerald grabs Springer's hands and, after pulling off his white gloves, inspects his knuckles, squeezing down on all the bruised areas to ensure no deeper damage is present.

'I be fine, sir. It's them there others that need attention. I left them snapping at the grass with their teeth, and I feel a sawbones be needed to help them.'

'Be damned about them,' Lord Fitzgerald yells before turning towards Henry and speaking again. 'Be a good fellow and send a wagon to pick them up at once and deliver them to my gatehouse cottage. Have the driver pick up the village physician on his way through and tell him to keep them at the gatehouse until I arrive and be sure they tell no one of this affray. I cannot afford for anyone to know about this man's talents before Saturday's fight. I have too much riding on the outcome and don't need loose tongues wagging beforehand.' Lord Fitzgerald looks at Springer. 'As for you, go soak those hands in salted water while I have a word with Henry.'

Springer looks at Henry and, with a nod of approval from his employer, he turns, tilts his head at Lord Fitzgerald and leaves the room by the side door.

Victoria is still listening at the main entrance to the study. She is just about to leave when Lord Fitzgerald speaks up again. 'I did not expect this, but if he can take out Brannigan and Fletcher, two of my best men, you might be right about his abilities as a prize fighter and money maker. Well, at least for as long as he is in good health and able to keep winning, that is. Now, back to the business at hand. As you know, I have invited important investors down today to view the factory and its works. One of them has invented a new type of steam engine that could power four to six of our cotton looms on its own. I mean, think of the savings on wages and labour. Why, I could save a fortune! Not to mention the fact these contraptions could run indefinitely, day and night. No sleep required with them, what! They don't need to be trained or replaced when they have an accident or become sick, just one skilled man to keep the lines running and one to keep the steam engine fuelled and water topped up. Just think, a constant flow of evenly machined fabric, yard after yard without even the risk of a bloodstain to taint the colour of the product.'

Lord Fitzgerald smiles and taps his cane on the floor. 'Things just keep getting better and better. We must think of the future, you know. Progress is the way forward – yes, life is capital, that's what I say. I will also have a guest from France with us, called Pierre. He represents the interest of Madam Kelly – a lady friend of mine going back many years who has expressed an interest in expanding her business into our capital city. She'd like to invest in our expansion plans here so she can have a place of her own in the country as city life would not be for her. She is a powerful and very influential person with many contacts who could open a lot of doors for us. So whatever Pierre wants, ensure he is fully provided for.'

Henry nods in acknowledgement.

'They will be staying at Aubrey Manor with me tonight and reviewing the new housing designs on Saturday in the factory planning room. With any luck I can tempt some of them to invest in this steam engine project as well, and perhaps sell a house or two at the same time. I may even offset his machines against our expansion plans and offer a deal of a free house just to get them on board with me.'

'A good plan, my lord. But giving away one of your new buildings for free is not like you at all.'

'Ha, you know me too well, Henry. What I give with one hand, I certainly intend to take back with the other. In the afternoon, we will be attending your special entertainment in the park. I expect to have a good, uninterrupted view of the proceedings for myself and our honoured guests – as most of them will be putting heavy wagers on McAndrew's champion prize bull, Gripper "The Bear" Jones. Especially when I give them an introduction to the man himself and after that offer very favourable odds. You see, I intend to take a lot of coin on this fight, especially from our guests. Greedy men are easily baited, and I intend to have many of them beholden to me and in my pocket by the end of the fight.

'That is why I will keep those two unfortunates that met Springer away from everyone until after the fight – unless they can convince me they will keep a low profile and not cause any disruptions. You, my good man, will also need to have a word with your children. Nothing must be said in public until after we have concluded our business on Saturday. Is that clear?'

Henry nods. 'Well, of course, that goes without saying as I also have personal interests in this man. I intend to be collecting on my investment as well, my lord.'

Lord Fitzgerald looks at him sternly. 'Yes, well, I cannot disagree with that. Just remember not to get too carried away. If you bet too high, people will smell a rat. I am looking to gain well over a few fights with this venture of ours, especially with my connections and associates. Then, once this man Springer has won a few and becomes the champion favourite, we will have him throw a fight against a nobody and take the money betting against him. After that, we will dispose of your fighter in the usual way before people can trace him back to us.'

Henry is a bit shocked at Lord Fitzgerald's callousness, but still nods.

Lord Fitzgerald turns and slowly makes his way towards the door. Victoria hears the footsteps heading towards her and swiftly retreats down the hallway and slips out through the dining area to join her mother in the garden. She cannot believe what she has just heard, and her opinion of Lord Fitzgerald has been greatly challenged, along with that of her father.

As Lord Fitzgerald reaches the door, Henry nips past him and swings it open, allowing him to continue without stopping. 'Don't forget to send a wagon or something for my men,' says Lord Fitzgerald. 'I would collect them myself, but I find the thought of having such dirty and distasteful men in my new carriage so unappealing. Oh, and do remember to have a word with your boys. If they were out last night, ensure they did not see anything. I would hate to send out more people to assess the situation and tie up any loose ends. If you get my meaning.'

'I can assure you my boys were in bed by eight p.m. I walked up the stairs with them myself, as I do every night when at home.'

Lord Fitzgerald gives a small nod as if accepting Henry's comment. 'Well, time waits for no man. I must be on my way. I've people to see and a factory that will not run itself.'

As he reaches the front door, a young housemaid arrives with his top hat and cloak. He stops, views the young girl from top to bottom and stares quite obviously at her assets. 'Why thank you, my child,' he comments as he collects the items from her, his eyes never leaving her amply proportioned breasts.

With the front door being opened for him, he moves out onto the marble steps, crosses the gravel path and climbs up into his waiting carriage. With one final look back at the maid through the carriage window, he hits the inner roof of the carriage with the top of his cane and yells to the driver, 'On with it, my good man, and don't spare the horses.'

The driver flicks the reins and the pair of bay horses set off. Within a few paces they are at a swift trot and maintain that pace down the long driveway and onto the park road, still being watched by Henry, who is standing at the front door watching his employer leave his estate.

Henry breathes a big sigh of relief. 'I'm glad that's over with,' he comments to himself as he turns and walks down the hallway. A small smile appears on his face as he notices Springer, who has just resurfaced from the cloakroom wearing a more workman-like set of clothes, ready to oversee the running of the estate.

'Ah, Springer. Just a quick word – I would like to thank you for protecting my family. It's something I will not forget in a hurry.'

Springer gives a small tilt of his head. 'Think nothing of it. They were both deserving of a bit of learning.'

'Do you know where my children are now? In particular the two boys?'

'I believe they be still out in the garden with your good lady, reviewing the events of the journey home.'

'I will speak to my family and explain what I can of the situation to keep them from talking to anyone else about what happened today. It would seem Lord Fitzgerald wishes to keep the event under wraps until after the fight.' Henry thinks for a moment, then speaks again. 'I require you to get the stable boys to hitch up the hay wagon and collect the physician from the village, then collect Lord Fitzgerald's men from the crossroads and deliver them to his gatehouse. Don't go yourself – I want you around my family for now. You're one of the few people I trust with my children's safety.'

Springer acknowledges the compliment with one of his typical tilts of the head. 'Well, I be on my way to do your asking then.' He again tilts his head before he leaves to do his employer's bidding.

Henry watches as Springer walks away then turns and views his finely decorated hallway. He moves over to a brass statue of a horse on the greeting table. Reaching out, he rubs his hand over its head and body while thinking to himself. *Is all this worth the aggravation my new employer is putting me and my family through?* He ponders this thought for a few minutes, then decides it is a small price to pay to be in such a fine house in a wonderful country location in comparison with the filth, squalor and sewerage smells of old London Town.

He taps the horse's head three times for luck and walks off – a superstitious thing that Henry has always done before leaving the house. As he approaches the front door, the young housemaid arrives from a side room with his coat, scarf and gloves. 'Thank you, Nancy, that will be all for now.' The young maid opens the door and sees the master of the house out.

Henry walks round the side of the building and into the beautifully manicured rear garden. There he can see Mother talking to Edith and Victoria on the patio, while the three children are sitting round the summer table enjoying light refreshments. As he approaches them, he puts his hand in front of his mouth and lets out a low rumbling cough, as if to announce his arrival.

Mother, Edith and Victoria look round and politely acknowledge his appearance. As for his younger children, they have already spotted Henry and are running towards him, calling out as they go.

'Father, Father, you won't believe what happened on the way home from school!' shouts Oliver as he runs up to his dad.

'Oliver, please contain yourself. That is not the way to approach your father,' comments Mother from afar. But it's way too late. The three of them are already with Father and all talking at once like a gaggle of geese.

'Wow, slow down, children,' he says. 'Let's take this from the beginning with you all talking one at a time, starting with you, Rebecca.' Henry listens to their stories as if he has never heard them before, expressing amazement at the ability of his butler to defend them in such a violent manner, and praising his bravery.

Knowing the children's fondness for Springer, Father outlines his opinion on the situation. 'Now listen to me carefully, children. Springer has done the right thing in defending you, but in the eyes of the law, he has beaten two men quite badly – if what you say is correct. If it was to be presented to the magistrate, he would be sentenced to prison for some time.'

The children are mortified at the thought of losing Father's butler and, more importantly, their friend – especially after protecting them like that.

'Now I am sure I can make amends with the men involved, but you have to promise not to bring up what has happened with anyone else. Nobody outside this family must be told about the incident if we are to keep our friend Springer out of prison.'

Instantly the children promise not to tell another living soul. Father explains – again – the importance of being careful and sticking together in these difficult and dangerous times. He also reminds them that if any strange men approach, they are to yell and scream for help and run to the nearest group of people.

'Now, Rebecca, go over to your mother while I speak to the boys for a moment.' Rebecca holds out her arms for a hug and Father obliges without hesitation, stooping forward and lifting her off the ground and spinning her round as he does so.

'Go, my little angel. See to your mother while me and the boys have a private conversation.' Rebecca skips off in the direction of her mother and sisters, leaving Father to address his sons.

'Edward and Oliver, come join me for a walk down the garden.' The boys move swiftly to catch up with him as he walks towards his hot house on the far side of the estate. 'It's been brought to my attention that you two may have been out in the village last night. And that, furthermore, you might have run into some men while you were out – possibly including the two gentlemen Springer dispatched earlier.'

Edward answers swiftly, but behind his back he has both fingers crossed. 'What us, Father? No, Father, we were tucked up in bed last night, just where you left us.' He thinks for a second. Maybe Father heard them going up or down the stairs in the night. 'The only time I got up was to raid the pantry of a couple of slices of that beef left over from dinner, but it was only a tiny amount, and it was so very tasty.'

'You're growing boys. A few slices of beef do not bother me in the least. In fact, you should copy what my old friend John Montagu the fourth Earl of Sandwich did – and I still do when playing cards. Put the slices of meat between two pieces of bread. That way, the juice goes into the bread and not down your arm. Anyway, that's not what concerns me – your safety does. And at the moment I want you to be extra conscious. Lord Fitzgerald's men are a bit full-on, and for my peace of mind as well as your safety, I want you to stay away from them at all costs.'

The boys look at each other and then back at Father. 'Yes, Father,' they say at the same time.

'Now, into the study. I'm sure you must have some homework to do.' Edward and Oliver both groan with disappointment. Their misery at the thought of doing homework while it is still daylight outside is written all over their faces.

Overhearing the end of the conversation, Rebecca excuses herself from Mother and calls out, 'Come on, boys. I'll join you in the study and assist. Who knows, I might even be able to help you with your sums.' She pauses for a short while. 'That is if they are easy.'

As Oliver passes the summerhouse table, he swipes a big red ripe plum off the top of the fruit bowl and pops it into his pocket. Thinking he has got away with it, he walks past Mother and Victoria with a smile on his face.

Quick as a flash, Victoria spins round and slaps Oliver's thigh, squashing the fruit flat in his pocket, leaving the juice running down the inside of his leg. 'I'll get you for that!' calls out Oliver, peeling the squashed flesh of the plum from his now out-turned pocket and flicking his leg out in a vain attempt to stop the sweet sticky juice running down his leg.

Victoria wears a wicked smirk on her face as she turns back to Mother to continue their conversation.

Mother pretends not to notice the incident, but Victoria sees the rare smile she is trying to hide behind a solemn look and gives her a devilishly cheeky grin, forcing Mother to comment. 'Well I never. Is that the behaviour expected from a young lady of your standing, Victoria?' They both stare at each other for a minute with poker-like expressions before bursting into laughter. 'Come, let us plan what we are to wear for tomorrow's occasion.' They link arms and walk towards Father.

Henry looks at his wife and gives a small but noticeable nod. She responds with a subtler, but still understood, flick of her hand.

'I think I will have a walk round the garden and see what needs to be addressed,' Henry says. 'There is always something that needs my attention. I will leave you ladies to attend to whatever it is you get up to.' Henry moves away towards the vegetable plot, leaving the two ladies to continue their discussion.

Although she smiles with Mother, Victoria is still thinking about what she overheard. It does not sit well with her, and she feels the need to find out more about Father's associate. 'Mother, what do you know about Lord Fitzgerald? Is he a good man?'

Mother stops walking and pauses for a moment, then looks up solemnly into Victoria's eyes. 'Lord Fitzgerald is your father's employer; he is an important man in these parts and very influential when it comes to commerce with the local businesses. Father owes him a great deal for our house in this village and for his position within the foundation that he has set up here.'

'That I understand, Mother. But did not Father also invest a great deal of money into the development of this venture? I thought he was a partner, not just a man working for him?'

Mother looks back at Victoria, a bit taken aback that her daughter is aware of so much and has a better understanding of what is going on than she should. 'Now, my dear, this is a complex arrangement, and these things are best left to your father to deal with, for he is the head of the house. It's not for the likes of us to be involved in such dealings.' Mother smiles. 'Besides, we have far more important things to deal with. In fact, now seems a perfect time to discuss one of them.'

Victoria looks at Mother with an expression of curiosity. 'Well, Mother, you have my undivided attention. What kind of assistance do you require? A partner for bridge? Help to organise a crochet evening or afternoon tea with the vicar?' she says, giving one of her smiles and lowering her eyelashes.

'No, nothing like that. This is more on a personal basis. You are a grown woman now, and your father and I have been approached by several suitors who wish to be introduced to you.'

Victoria stops in her tracks, aghast at the idea she has been spoken about in this way, without knowing. Perplexed, she tries to think of the words to say, but so many of them fill her head that none come out. After attempting to compose herself for what seems an age, her mind begins to collect itself and she speaks. 'Mother, I am only twenty-two years old. Surely it will be down to me to decide when and with whom I would like to spend the rest of my life with.' She takes a deep breath. 'I cannot believe I have been discussed like a piece of meat on a butcher's slab, without being consulted first!'

Mother gives her a stern look. 'Now, my dear, that is quite enough. Your father and I have talked about this at great length, and it is our responsibility as your parents to guide you in the right direction for your future. Anyway, it has only been in the last few days we have decided upon a suitor worthy of consideration. From good stock and financially well-positioned, he will be allowed to come calling on you with our blessing. Tomorrow's celebrations will be the first day you will be seen together. This is why we must ensure the day is such a success. You will be seen together by all the influential people from society, and first impressions are important. We must show we belong in this community, and that we are associated with people of high importance in the region. You see, image and social standing are important, and you need to be seen with the appropriate people.'

Victoria's heart sinks. 'Do I dare presume from this discussion that the people who want to fit in with high society are you and Father? And that the bargaining for this would be myself handed over to the person with the greatest influence? I always thought I would follow my heart and find my true love, regardless of where in society they were positioned, just as Father always told me.'

A shiver suddenly runs down Victoria's spine. A cold feeling of dread wells up inside her. *Surely not*, she thinks, *they couldn't, they wouldn't. Could they possibly be considering him?* 'And who would this fine, upstanding person from society be? Who is to come calling on me and escort me to the celebrations tomorrow, may I ask?' She braces herself for an unwelcome answer. Inside, she is praying she does not hear his name, hoping at least her father would save her from that awful man, even if Mother would put their positioning in society above that of her daughter's integrity.

'Why, it's Lord Fitzgerald, my dear. He has asked about you on many occasions, and we feel the time is now right for you to be properly introduced into society as a couple.'

Victoria's world collapses. She looks down at the green grass at her feet. Time seems to stand still for a moment as the whole of life drains from her body. She cannot even bring herself to speak. The words are not there to describe the utter sadness that she feels inside, the total devastation of all that she holds dear. *How can they do this to me! It's like they do not even consider my feelings on the matter at all.* She remembers what she overheard at the door, recalling how Lord Fitzgerald forced Father into selling something he highly prized. The way he speaks to people, chastises and belittles all who are in his way. How he looks at and treats women he wants, then casts them away once he has had his fill. She does not want to be just another notch on his stick, to be at his beck and call when needed and fobbed off when something else catches his eye. This is not what she envisaged as her lot.

After a few minutes, she looks back up at Mother. Before she can utter a word, Mother speaks. 'I knew you would approve of our decision, my dear. We only have your best interests at heart. I am so excited that you approve – it will be the talking point of the whole community. I simply cannot wait to tell everybody the good news, including your father. He will be so happy that you are in agreement of our choice for you.'

She turns away from Victoria and heads off towards the house at a brisk walk.

Victoria is still numb. She hasn't moved. No words have been uttered from her mouth. She looks around and spots a chair on its own by the side of the summerhouse. Her shoulders slumped, she slowly stumbles forward, shaking her head and full of disbelief as she takes a seat. Her head is spinning with thoughts, but none of them are making the moment better. Leaning back, she lets out a small sigh and stares at the grass forlornly. Her eyes fill up with tears until they burst and start to run down her cheeks, then quietly she sobs in her own company.

Over in the coach house, Springer is speaking to the stable boy who is on the front of the wagon about to collect the two men who were left beaten. 'Now you be knowen where to find them and pick up that there sawbones on the way, for he be sorely needed by them I gave a good seeing to. So be on your way, young James.'

The young man nods and smiles at Springer. 'I would have given a week's wage to see you give them men a walloping, for the other week that Brannigan set about my brother for no more than bumping into him in the tavern and spilling his tankard of ale. He is not a nice man, and my brother still carries a limp and black eye a week later from the kicking he got.'

'Aye, he be a wrongun alright, but he won't be so full of himself now, that's for sure.' Springer slaps the horse on the rump to start it on its way and watches for a minute or so as the cart trundles down the track, bouncing on every bump and hollow. With the boy now sent on his way, and all other duties completed for the moment, Springer heads to the kitchen to see if he can charm something to eat from Cook.

Entering through the kitchen door, he wipes his feet on the grating so he leaves no visible tracks on the floor. He wants to avoid the wrath of Cook as he announces his presence and desire for a good feed. 'Afternoon, Cookie. How be thee on this fine day?'

'Don't give me that old hat. Have you wiped your feet?' comes the response bellowing from the main kitchen in the next room.

'That I have, my dear. That I have.'

'Well, sit yourself down at the butchers block. I will be with you shortly.'

Two minutes later, Cook appears from round the corner. She slides a plate in front of Stringer with some boiled potatoes, slices of beef, a few carrots and a wedge of bread and places a tankard of cider down beside the plate.

'Get that down you while it's still warm. The master told me to feed you when you came in today, and for the next two weeks.'

Springer doesn't need telling twice. He tucks into the food, and the cider doesn't even touch the sides on the way down.

'I heard what happened earlier with the children. I'm grateful you protected them, but those men will not take it lightly that you have showed them up. They will be looking for retribution, and they will ensure the odds will be in their favour next time.'

Springer pauses for a bit then looks up at Cook. 'Aye, I gave 'em a thumpin' this time. The next time may not be so good, that's true, but it will take better men than them afore I be put to ground.' He eats for a moment, then speaks again. 'I be takin' a chance here, but I be trustin' you, Cook. Your old man be Dan the poacher, an' he can get round a bit without makin' a fuss true?'

Cook sighs before answering. 'I don't like him being called that, but yes, my Dan, he knows a few people.'

Springer puts his hand in his pocket and pulls out a small worn leather pouch and drops it on the table. 'That there is all I own in this world: a pocket watch, Ma an' Pa's wedding rings, some jewels, trinkets and five gold pieces. Not much for a lifetime, but all is mine. If you would be so kind as to ask Dan to trade all into coin, add to the gold pieces and wager on me to win come the day of the fight, I would be much obliged.' Springer leans forward and gently holds Cook's hand, turns it over and places the small bag in her palm.

Cook looks into his eyes, then at the pouch resting in her hand. She can see the worn wedding bands and a dented watch through the opening. Looking back at Springer, she can also see what this means for him to ask this. Without saying a word, she closes her hand over the bag and slowly nods her head.

'I would see him paid fair for time he spends a sortin' this out, I promise thee,' Springer mutters.

Cook moves back into the main area of the kitchen, still carrying the pouch in her hand. When she returns to top up his tankard of cider, Springer is gone. The plate is empty and the chair neatly tucked back in its place. Her thoughts go back to a story her husband told her a few months earlier.

Dan had been poaching on Lord Fitzgerald's beat on the river and the salmon were running well. He was staggering up from the riverbank under the weight of a sack full of fine specimens he had tickled from the rapids below the weir pool. Fitzgerald's men were combing the sides of the river on a tip-off from one of their many snitches that Dan was working Lord Fitzgerald's land. Dan was known well for his ability to poach game of all varieties as it came into season, and sometimes even when it was not, depending on demand. The locals welcomed it, as it was fresh meat and fish at a cheap price or in some cases just trade. Also, for the people it was one in the eye for Lord Fitzgerald – a man who so many had every right to hold a grudge against, going on past experiences with him and his associates.

Unfortunately for Dan, on this occasion someone else in the village had the attention of Sykes and Brannigan, and to save any more of a beating, they had hinted Dan was at work that day. Oh, how Sykes and Brannigan would love to catch Dan in the act and impress their boss Lord Fitzgerald at the same time. It would be a feather in their caps, along with a good reward for their troubles.

Dan was heading towards the village to distribute his catch between the many customers who would take kindly to his delivery of fresh fish. The path he chose to walk was just off the main track and about two hundred yards from the riverbank – as the cover was good and the ground was firm underfoot. Being a poacher, Dan was always quiet and alert to his surroundings. So when a few deer broke cover in front of him and split to his left and right at the last moment with no thought of his presence, he knew they had been spooked. Instantly, he crouched down and within a minute he could hear people pushing through the bushes in the distance. A line of people, spread out evenly, could be seen making their way along the valley towards his position, thrashing the undergrowth as they went.

He was in no doubt they were there looking for him. And if they found him, it would be his last day of poaching, if not his last day of freedom and probably his life. Dan's options were very limited. He could not make it to the river and dump his catch as he would be seen on the open ground. Nor could he go forward as there was a line of people heading towards him. To the left and up the valley was a bit of cover, then open ground and a sheer rock face some eighty feet high, so he would be seen again. If he dumped the fish now and they found it, they would know they were on to him and have the evidence to find him guilty and that would be his end.

For now, his only option was to head back along the path beside the road in the opposite direction, but the sack was heavy, and Dan is a light frame of a man. He struggled on along the path for around another four hundred yards before he needed to stop and take a breather. In front of him, the vegetation was sparse, and cover thinned out as the road started to turn left round a large sweeping bend. As he rested to recover and assess his situation, he could hear the noises of the men closing in on his position getting louder and louder.

He had to move on, as his life depended on it. Swinging the heavy sack back over his shoulder and groaning under the weight and effort, he moved off again, walking as fast as he could. The men were getting ever closer. Looking over his shoulder, he made the decision to go onto the track and walk part of the bend on the more level ground for better time. As he reached the drystone wall on the other side of the road, his plan was to hop over and loop back into good cover and hope to lose them in the denser undergrowth.

Suddenly, he heard approaching hooves hitting the stone-covered road at pace. In complete panic, he started over the wall with the sack of fish still hanging over his shoulder. There was a lot of weight on his back and Dan mustered all his might to get him and the sack over the top of the wall. As he climbed up, he lost his balance and tried to swing the sack up as he attempted to leap off the wall to the ground on the other side. But the sack had other ideas and it became wedged between two rocks. With the momentum of Dan going forward and the sack holding fast on the top of the wall, combined with his refusal to let go, there was only one outcome, and he was catapulted backwards off the top and down onto the track. His head hit the ground with an echoing thud, leaving him motionless for a moment. To Dan, it was like a blinding white light, then nothing as he had all his senses knocked out of him.

The front hooves of two horses pulled up just in front of the crumpled body and a man climbed down from the front of the wagon. The frame of the wagon creaked and rocked under the movement of the person's weight distribution. 'What do we 'ave 'ere then, for I be sure this be no common man,' said the driver.

When all was going wrong for Dan, he finally caught a break on this bad day. For standing over him was Springer. The new yard foreman and personal butler to the owner of one of the local estates. He was bringing back a cart full of straw for bedding in the stable yard, and a few sacks of grain. He looked over the fallen man and, by his description, recognised Dan as Cook's husband.

The sack full of salmon, which was now back on the track with some of its contents strewn on the floor, was a sure sign of his trade.

With what Springer had just been through back up the road, he knew all there was to know about the situation, along with Dan's predicament. He pushed back some of the straw in the wagon, then picked up the fallen man and placed him in the open cavity, followed by the sack and most of its contents. He then covered them over with the straw. 'Best thee be quiet for a while,' he said, moving more of the straw over him for good measure. Springer then mounted up and with a flick of the wrists, he got the horses moving down towards the village.

He got no more than a few hundred yards down the track before a man appeared out of the bushes and grabbed the reins connected to the head of the nearside horse.

'Easy, girl,' the man muttered as he put his other hand on the horse's nose to comfort the beast. Behind him, another two men stepped out into view, armed with loaded pistols. 'What have we got here, then?' one of them asked.

Springer did not recognise the men as he had only been working in the area a few weeks. 'Straw for the master's horses,' he responded. 'I've been up yonder to collect additional beddin'' from a storage barn, as we be expecting some foals from a couple of brood mares to drop this week.'

Brannigan nodded his head and casually wandered around to the back of the loaded cart, viewing the pile of bright, fresh-from-the-barn yellow straw. He pulled down one of the three pitchforks that were lined up against the cart's buckboard. Staring at Springer, he rolled the pitchfork in his hands. 'Well, let's see what else we have in here then, eh?'

He watched for any reaction from Springer, but Springer just casually looked away, showing no emotion. Brannigan pulled back on the pitchfork and prepared to ram it deep into an area of the straw when a voice cracked the quiet tension. 'Have you found him yet?' Everyone looked up to see Lord Fitzgerald cantering down the track with three other riders in tow. 'I say again, have you found the scoundrel yet?' he bellowed out loudly.

'Well, no, not yet, sir. I'm just about to see if he is hiding in this straw,' replied Brannigan.

'My God, man, do you not think we checked this load at the crossing bridge? We've been through every bit of it not ten minutes ago. He is not hiding in the back of this cart. However, do you see that bend in the road back there?' He pointed back up the track with his leather, brass-tipped riding crop. The horse flinched and spun around as the movement of the crop past its eyeline spooked him.

'Stand still, damn you,' Lord Fitzgerald shouted at the horse, yanking on the reins to regain control of the scared animal. He re-pointed his whip back in the direction of the bend. 'On that bend, by the side of the wall, on the floor is a salmon. My salmon. My salmon from my river. That thieving bastard is up there, not here, but up there. Now go up there and find him. I don't care if you call out the hounds – I want him found now!'

'Yes, sir, right away, sir,' responded Brannigan in a growl before turning to Springer and swinging his arm to wave him on his way.

Springer obliged by flicking the reins and calling, 'Get thee up there,' at the two horses. They responded immediately and slowly moved off down the track.

'Five guineas to the man who catches him,' Lord Fitzgerald shouted out as he turned his horse and charged back up to the bend in the road. The three horses led off, with near a dozen men now following them on foot at pace, all eager to claim the reward.

Brannigan realised he still had the pitchfork in his hand. 'You in the wagon,' he called out. Springer was slow to react, but as he turned round, the pitchfork came hurtling through the air and impacted the pile of straw. Brannigan had thrown it a good thirty yards and it had imbedded in the straw just above where Dan had been hidden. Springer raised his hand in the air as recognition to Brannigan. He did not bother to look up at him. Inside, he was just relieved that the pitchfork had landed away from his hidden guest and not in him.

Half an hour later, Springer arrived at the yard. He pulled round to the side of the barn to hide the cart from the main view of the house, dismounted the rig and placed a short wooden log either side of the front wheels to stop it rolling forward.

Moving to the back of the load to see the condition of his passenger, he pushed the straw apart. It soon became apparent that the guest was recovered and had absconded. In his place were two plump salmon, covered in a small piece of cloth to protect the straw. Chuckling to himself and shaking his head, Springer picked up the fish by the gills and headed over to the kitchen door. He tapped on the window and entered, walked over to the empty sink and deposited his catch in the bottom of the bowl.

Cook, with her steely-eyed glare, had watched him since he entered the room and unloaded the fish. 'And where are they from, then?' she asked, folding her arms.

Springer had moved to the water pump and worked the lever to wash his hands. He looked up at her with a smile on his face. 'Well, Cook, I think I've just had the pleasure of meetin' with that there husband of yours, at work down yonder on Lord Fitzgerald's beat. It seems they be biting well at present, and he be a busy man ensuring his fill. If I were thee, I would use those right quick as they be a little warm to the touch, if you know what I mean.'

Her face started to glow red as she looked down at the floor and then back up at Springer. 'I think I will be having a word with that perishing bleeder when I next see him. He be making me look bad being caught. I thought he was better than that.'

Springer nodded and chuckled in agreement. 'He be close to being caught this time. It was just luck it be me and not them there holding a grudge that found him.' He wiped his hands on the cloth by the sink, then headed back out the door and down towards the stable yard.

Cook returns from her thoughts. She clears up the last few items from the table and places them in the pantry, undoes her apron and folds it neatly over the back of the chair then looks at Springer's small leather pouch. 'You're a good man, young Springer, with a heart better than most I know,' she mutters to herself. Picking up the pouch, she places it in her pocket, grabs her shawl and jacket from the peg on the wall and heads out the door.

CHAPTER 4

The Fair Arrives

Edward slowly stirs from his sleep. The distant, muffled sounds of voices and a range of unusual thuds and crashes travelling on the wind have woken him rather earlier than usual. To start with, he just lies there rubbing his eyes and trying to make sense of the noises, but a slow drawn-out yawn is caught short as he suddenly realises what is going on. His eyes fly wide open with excitement. It is the day of the fair.

He flings the sheets off his body and jumps up. Taking a sharp breath, he sits back down again – the floor is colder than expected. He shimmies along the bed and stretches out his feet, sliding them into his leather slippers, then swings his dressing gown around his shoulders.

Looking over the wall surrounding the house and way off into the distance, Edward can see the top of the big canvas marquee. This is no surprise, as the wooden frame has been going up for the last couple of days. But now there are loads of smaller tents, and a whole hive of activity setting up the stalls. To the right of the marquee, he spots the four large square posts he's been waiting for.

'The prize ring,' he says. On his way out of the room, he stops to shake Oliver awake. 'Get up! Get up!' he yells, pushing down on his brother, making him bounce. 'The prize ring is going up!'

'What's going on?' Oliver asks, blearily rolling onto his side and snuggling back into his pillow. But by the time his words have been uttered, Edward is long gone. All Oliver can hear is his brother tearing down the stairs, and his calls of 'Father, Father!'

At this moment in time, young Oliver is really not that bothered with all the ongoing commotion. His warm bed has a far greater appeal, and he is not ready to leave its comfort just yet. Maybe in an hour or so he will stir, but for now there is not a chance of him getting out of bed.

Edward rushes along the corridor, peering in all the rooms in search of his father. He steps into the dining room without looking and nearly collides with Maria – the new Spanish scullery maid – who is carrying all the linen and place mats to set up the grand table for breakfast. Only with a swift twist to her body and by raising her arms at the last moment does she avoid impact. Rotating a near full three hundred and sixty degrees, she ends up facing the shocked young Edward. With several tuts, a shake of the head and a few words in Spanish, she continues preparing the table for breakfast.

Lowering his head, Edward shuffles across to the right. The next stop in his quest is the kitchen – but this time he looks round in the doorway before entering.

Cook is fussing over the stove, with pans of thick-cut bacon and sausages sizzling on the flat top. Edward lifts his nose and takes in the fine aromas being given off. Cook moves left and right, shaking the pans on the oven top as she goes, then uses the long, narrow shovel to scoop coal from the scuttle in the corner, adding it to the firebox. With a quick shuffle of the embers, she closes the hatch and drops the shovel back in the scuttle.

Her attention now turns to a second hatch on the right side of the oven. Picking up a cloth, she opens the door and extracts two large black metal tins – both topped with the unmistakeable golden domes of loaves of bread. Quickly turning, she slides the tins onto the table behind her, releasing the cloth at the very last moment and shaking her hands as if to cool them.

Without even looking round as she closes the door, she speaks. 'Not today, Edward. I'm too busy for any of your tomfoolery. Now be on your way until breakfast is ready, that's a good lad.'

Edward is a little taken aback. He didn't know Cook had even seen him.

'I'm sorry, Cook,' he replies. 'I was just looking for my father.'

'Your father was here earlier to talk about the food required for tonight's dinner guests but left some time ago to see Arthur and the other gardeners. I'd wager it would be to do with Springer's fisticuffs later today.'

Edward lowers his head. He knows he's not dressed enough to go outside. 'Thanks, Cook,' he mutters as he slowly turns around and heads back the way he came. Cook pauses for a moment, then reaches into a stone jar and slides a couple of biscuits towards the corner of the table.

'Edward,' she whispers while tapping the table with a spoon.

Edward's eyes light up. 'Thank you!' he says, snatching the golden biscuits and grinning at his bounty.

Cook smiles as he disappears into the dining room, then her attention swiftly moves back to the tins of bread. Grabbing the first one back in the cloth, she slams the tin down on the table and turns it upside down to release the loaf. The same is done with the second tin and both loaves are placed on an adjacent cooling rack. The tins are put straight back on the shelf, ready for tomorrow's bread. Black iron moulds are never washed – this would take off the black coating that has built up over years of use, making the bread stick and the rise uneven. They will be wiped and warmed in the oven just before the dough goes in them tomorrow.

Nobody, but nobody, dares touch Cook's tins, along with many other items in the kitchen. Her wrath would have no bounds if outsiders meddled in her domain. Even Henry knows better and dares not involve himself in how Cook runs the kitchen.

Outside, Henry has long since left Arthur and the gardeners and is now overseeing the assembly of the prize fighting ring – ensuring everyone is aware of how tight he wants the ropes around the edge, and how much gap there should be between the ring and the raised staging area looking over it. He moves up to the viewing point and takes a seat at the front. He wants to be sure the positioning is exactly right for Lord Fitzgerald and his honoured guests. The staging is high enough to see over the two levels of rope and close enough to see all the action but not so near that the duellers could fall through the ropes and land on them. *Yes*, he thinks. *This is how I envisioned it.*

Looking at one of the carpenters, he says, 'This is exactly the right distance. Now clamp it in place to ensure it does not move, and we are done here.' The man nods and tilts his cap at Henry before locking the platform to the stage with some additional planking.

Henry stands up and casts his eye over the whole area. From this vantage point, he can see most of the fair and its stalls and stands. To the left, a high slide is near completion. Beside this, the Punch and Judy kiosk is having the curtains fitted and chairs are being placed in the viewing area. An array of swings and small entertainment stalls are being fitted out and various tents are being assembled and guide ropes hammered down. To the right, a big firepit lined with stone is being prepared for the spit-roasting of a large wild boar. Tables are filling up with all kinds of preserves and edible treats, and through the second-largest marquee, he can see various jugglers and tricksters practising their talents.

Far to the back of the fields, the rifle and pistol ranges are being paced out and marked up, wooden cut-outs of animals are being staked into the ground at various distances, and weapons are being cleaned and checked and loaded.

The largest marquee – the beverage tent – is about thirty yards from the prize ring. It's full of tables and chairs which spill out into the open air, and Henry expects it will sell a lot of ale and wine. He will also have some champagne available upon request, but he's not expecting to sell much of that to the local farmers and villagers – just to the new bloods, for they will expect the better things and will want to show off their wealth.

As Henry looks around, he feels a surge of pride in his chest. Everything is coming together. He rolls back on his heels and takes his watch from his waistcoat pocket. 'Five and twenty past eight,' he mutters to himself, closing the lid and swinging the full hunter around on its chain before sliding it down into his pocket. Rolling on his heels one last time, he stretches his back and arms as he yawns then makes his way back down the steps.

On his way past the prize ring, he grabs the top rope and gives it a hard tug, then pushes it away and back towards himself again. With a point of a finger and a flick of the head, he summons the carpenter. 'My good man, I would like that top rope to be just a little tighter. I think at present there is just a little too much play in it.'

The carpenter grabs the rope and gives it a push and a pull. 'Yes, sir, I will adjust it immediately.' With his apprentice, he tightens the rope then gives Henry a nod.

'That's more like it,' Henry says after tugging on the rope. 'Thank you, my good man. That is much better.' The carpenter again tilts his cap at Henry, then secures the brass ring on the back of the post.

Walking back towards the house, Henry quickens his pace – he's already late and wishes to minimise the deficit. The house has a stone-pillared, metal-arched entrance. A lion and a unicorn sit on each post, and the house name, 'Hope's Folly', is written into the ironmongery arch in gold paint, against a background of black, twisting metal vines and leaves.

Many a time Henry has paused here to look at the house, as it reminds him of how far he has come since his humble beginnings. But not today. He is late and walks briskly along the grey gravel driveway to the house. Looking down, he can still see the carriage tracks have heavily grooved through the gravel and left several ridges. It might be a small matter, but it does annoy Henry that all is not perfect for today's guests.

The front door opens wide as he approaches. 'Good morning, sir,' Nancy says as he walks past her. At the side bureau he grabs the cord attached to the bell for the housekeeper and tugs it twice. The bell pings into action here in the hallway and simultaneously in other areas of the house via a complex line of wires.

'If only everyone was as efficient as you, Nancy,' Henry says.

She smiles and dips slightly before returning to her duties – which at the moment involve brushing the master's jackets and shoes in the closet.

Within a minute, Miss Lewellen arrives. Her dress uniform is black from top to toe – including a black bonnet and black shoes – with never a crease out of place. Small in stature she may be, but she is big on impact. On the outside she is a stern woman, her face emotionless as if cut from granite and a smile is unheard of. A stickler for discipline and correctness, everyone seems to up their game when she is around. The staff fear her wrath as she inspects everything and misses nothing. In truth, she is the perfect person for a head housekeeping position. And although many have wondered if she is different away from her duties, none dare to ask her. Such is the staff's fear, and also their respect for her.

She approaches Henry. 'Yes, sir, what can I do for you?'

Henry was, less than a minute ago, incensed. But now in the presence of Miss Lewellen, he pauses and chooses his words carefully.

'Ah yes, Miss Lewellen. I could not help but notice that the drivewa—'

'Was rutted, sir. Yes, it is already in hand. The gardeners needed additional time to finish putting down the markers you requested for today's activities on the estate grounds. I gave them until eight forty-five sharp before they must start to rake, then go over it with the heavy roller.' She leans around Henry to view out of the window. 'As you see, sir, they are raking the area now.'

To Henry's surprise, two of the gardeners are frantically raking over the gravel as they speak, while another is pushing a heavy stone roller behind them.

'Will that be all, sir? Or is there something else you wish to discuss?'

Henry looks at her expressionless face, then back through the window in disbelief. How the hell did this woman do it?

'Umm, no. That is quite all, thank you.' He pauses for a moment before speaking again. 'I think I will now join my family for breakfast.'

'You will find them all in the dining room awaiting your arrival, sir, as it is gone the hour.'

He goes to reply, but then stops as nothing constructive comes to mind – for he is late, and she has just dropped a subtle hint that he should be more punctual. With one more look out of the window, he moves off towards the dining room wondering how she is always one step ahead of him.

Miss Lewellen watches Henry until he is gone from sight, then turns her attention to Nancy. 'Once you have finished the master's coat and shoes, start polishing the best silver for the dinner tonight. The master will be expecting everything to be immaculate for his guests.'

Nancy doesn't even turn around, for she was fully expecting Miss Lewellen to approach her and inspect her work closely. 'Yes, Miss Lewellen,' she replies, still beavering away at the last of the master's jackets.

As Henry enters the dining room, Mother nods to one of the servants. The swirl of conversation between the children stops and everybody stands up at the table. 'Please, sit down and continue. I'm sorry to be late. I've been checking on the layout of the stands and entertainment. There just seems so much to do and so little time left to do it.'

He looks around the table at his children – all of whom are wide-eyed with excitement – and it's clear from the fidgeting that several of them are bursting to say something to him. But nobody does, until Mother finally speaks. 'Hello, dear. I asked the children to be quiet and just to allow you to eat something first, as I know this is going to be a busy day for you.'

Before he can respond, breakfast arrives: hot toast, bacon, sausages, mushrooms, eggs and many more items.

Henry looks at the feast spread out before him. 'Well, let's tuck in while it's hot, my children. Then, as Mother says, we can talk about the day's events.'

Everyone selects items for their plates, while Henry looks lovingly at his wife with all the pride a man could have. It's only now he notices the place beside Edith is empty.

'Where's Victoria?' he asks, looking around the table.

'I saw her heading to the fair just after you left this morning,' says Rebecca. 'I believe she was looking for you, Father. Something to do with a conversation that took place yesterday.'

Mother and Father look at each other before Henry speaks. 'Oh, I see. Well, I'm sure she will be back shortly. I will have a word with her on arrival.'

This is one conversation he always knew he was going to have to face up to. In his mind, he tries to convince himself it is a wise and good marriage union for Victoria, and that they have her best interests at heart. But the reality is it also gives him security for his family and position working with Lord Fitzgerald. He is also fighting off the thoughts of what a monster his beautiful daughter will be with for the rest of her life, however long that may last. For time with Lord Fitzgerald can be measured by how long he remains interested in you, not by longevity of life itself.

Deep down, Henry knows he is buying this lifestyle for his wife and his family by looking away from what goes on in the village. And he is sealing his status with Lord Fitzgerald at the cost of his beautiful daughter's happiness.

Shaking the thought from his head, he thinks of a way to change the subject. 'Well, children, as the conversation has started, what do you think of how the fairground looks so far?'

All the children start speaking at once – Oliver about the Punch and Judy stand, Edward about the prize ring, Rebecca about the jugglers and fire-eaters.

'Woah, woah, woah! One at a time!' Father says with a smile. 'Now, let's start with Rebecca. You were saying something about fire-eaters, my dear?'

* * *

Springer lives in one of the small cottages on the edge of the estate, a two-up two-down construction with an outhouse outside the back door. It has a small front garden for flowers and a fruit and vegetable area to the rear of the building. The freshly replaced thatched roof gives the house a golden glow, and the pink and white climbing roses on the front walls, along with a short white picket fence, give it the picture-postcard look. Inside, a small, middle-of-the-room brick fireplace keeps the house warm on all but the severest of cold days. Furniture inside this small cottage is limited, but what's there is functional and of sturdy construction.

Today has been a little different for Springer. He has been instructed to stay away from the estate and rest until nearer the time of his fight. However, his body clock still woke him at his usual time of around 6.30 a.m. He has been pacing around for almost an hour already, planning in his mind what he will be doing during and after the fight.

With time on his hands, he has cleaned out the fireplace and set the fire ready for the evening. It's a precaution as he may not be in too fine a shape to set one later, and the night ahead looks to be chilly.

He has also packed a large canvas bag with some personal belongings: food, two bottles of cider, several pieces of clothing and his spare pair of boots. The bag has been neatly placed by the side of the fireplace, with his jacket lying over the top. Sitting in the rocking chair, poking at the unlit fire with a long thin stick, Springer is thinking of all the ways the day could unfold. He may have to adapt to various options, depending on changing circumstances.

He thinks on the fight and how sore and painful he will be after it is over. The fight itself holds no fear for him as he has been in many a scrape in the past. In this case, it will actually be an easier proposition as he only has one opponent to worry about. However, today is different for other reasons. It is what happens after the fight that is a little daunting to him. For he has only one chance to get it right. The cost of getting it wrong will surely take away his freedom, if not his life.

There is a faint tap, tap at the door. He looks round, but it was so faint he thinks it's the wind and goes back to poking the fire. Tap, tap, again. This time it is a little louder and he gets up to investigate. Opening the door, he is surprised to see Victoria standing there in one of her favourite dark blue dresses. He stares at her for several seconds before he regains his manners. 'Please come in, me lady,' he says as he steps back.

'Thank you,' she quietly says as she steps through the doorway and into the main room.

'It be not much, but please sit thee down in that there best chair,' he says, closing the door onto the latch.

'Thank you, but no. I would sooner stand, and I do not have much time before I will be missed.'

There is a moment of silence that is not uncomfortable, just quiet. 'I tried to speak to you after the fight with those men some days back, but you left so quickly. I called and followed, but you went into the room with Father and *him* before I could get your attention. Since then, my life has been a bit of a blur and I have not seen you alone to speak to. Now, Mother is keeping me busy with her all the time to ensure that I am watched over continuously.'

He looks at her with deep regret in his eyes. For had he known she was following, he would have stopped just to see her again. 'I'm right sorry, lass. Had I—'

'Please, let me finish before I lose all courage. I wanted to thank you for protecting my brother from those ghastly men. It was very brave of you, and I am sorry to have put you in great danger.' She lets out a sigh of relief as if these words had been bottled up inside and needed to be forced out before she exploded.

'Danger? I be in no danger! Them there men were in danger, for they ort not to put a hand on young Oliver like that. Not while he be in my charge. Anyway, that's by the by now. He be safe and the matter be ended. Your father will see to that, I be sure.'

'That's not all, though. I know I should not have, but when I followed and you entered the room with Father, the door did not close fully and to my shame I listened to the conversation taking place inside the room.' Victoria pauses and looks around as if afraid somebody may be watching and listening to her. 'That horrid man – Lord Fitzgerald – he treats Father so poorly. I cannot understand why Father allows him to speak to him the way he does. And as for you!' She pauses to take breath. 'In Lord Fitzgerald's eyes, you are just an amusement to be used in any way he deems suitable. In this case, you are here to make him more money in bets and wagers from these guests he has arriving today. He does not care about you or worry who he hurts along the way. It's just so wrong, and I don't understand. He is just so evil.'

'Now, now, lass. Don't threat yourself. I'm sure your father knows what he be doing and can stand his own against the likes of Lord Fitzgerald and them that follow him around.'

'Well, if that is the case, why did he tell Father to control Oliver and Edward or he would deal with them himself?' Victoria's eyes start to well up. 'Oh Springer, I know there is something rotten with this place. I see it in every person's face wherever I go in the village. I hear it every time someone speaks to me. It's got to the stage that I despise every moment I am here in this godforsaken place.' Pulling a handkerchief from the cuff of her dress, she dabs her eyes as the tears start to flow.

Springer steps forward; he cannot bear to see Victoria upset. 'Cheer up, me lady,' he says. 'It be not as bad as all that. Time's just a testing, that's all. You will see, things will get better for thee, I am sure. You be a righteous person.'

Trembling, Victoria steps forward, holds Springer's shoulders and tucks into him. This takes him by surprise, and he tries to step back, but she latches on tighter, her head buried deeply into his chest. Slowly, he brings his arms up and cups hold of her tiny waist. He can feel her shaking and tightens his hold a little more.

Safe in his arms, Victoria composes herself. As she becomes more collected, she speaks to him softly. 'It gets worse. My mother has told me I am to be seen with Lord Fitzgerald today. It seems he has chosen me to be his, and I am to be his bride.'

Springer is rocked to the core. His eyes look to the heavens as he grits his teeth for a second, then shakes his head in disbelief. 'What? No, no, no, that surely cannot be.'

She turns her head slightly and stares into the unlit fireplace. 'Yes, it's true. It seems this is to be my lot, married to a monster so my mother and father can live in high society.'

Until now, Springer has been able to hold his feelings. But the thought of Victoria being given to Lord Fitzgerald is just too much. 'Surely this be a mistake – thy father is a righteous man. He would not see thee given to such a ruthless man.'

'My father has not spoken of it. But, as Mother has told me, it will be on behalf of my father, but planned and schemed by

Mother. You see, he is not a strong man. He is very skilled and clever at running factories, but in business, more ruthless and ambitious men have passed him over many times before. Coming here was his last big chance to become a pillar of society and show what he can do using his own abilities. Problem is, Mother is always wanting more, and she will push him for what she wants.' Victoria stops and takes a deep breath. 'And I fear now the price he must pay will be the loss of a daughter to that evil man. You see, Lord Fitzgerald knows how to prey on people like that. He takes advantage of their vulnerabilities to aid him in his success. To that extent, I am just a pawn in his game. And when he has used me for his purpose, I will be no more.'

Springer cannot believe what he is hearing. To be sure, he knows what Lord Fitzgerald is, as he has met many like him before.

But this time is different. This time it involves someone he cares about. This time it affects him personally.

He does not even realise he is speaking as the words come out before he has a chance to stop himself. 'Many a man would give their soul to the reaper willingly to have a lady like you in their life. You are a beauty to behold and a kindness beyond measure. There is only good in you, Victoria – I see it with my own eyes, and I feel it inside.'

She grips his shoulders tighter then slowly releases her clasp and pushes off. 'I should not have come here this morning. It is not for the likes of me to burden you with my misfortune. It is for me to bear and not to bother you with my problems. You have enough to think about, with the fight later today. I only wanted to thank you for defending my brothers. You see, they are all I really have now. They make life here manageable, and I love them dearly.'

Springer smiles. 'It was a pleasure to give out a thumpin', and them there youngerns will always be safe while I be here. As for the fight, well, I be no stranger to a bit of bother. It seems to find me wherever I be going these days.'

Victoria gives a raw smile. 'I have found someone true in you. I wish you well for the fight this afternoon, but forgive me as I cannot watch. It would break me up inside to see you hurt.' She steps forward and kisses him on the cheek, then steps back. Out of the corner of her eye, she notices the bag and coat on the floor. Not letting on that she has seen it, she turns to the door.

A thought crosses her mind as she reaches for the latch, beating Springer, who was trying to open the door for her first.

'I wish you well for the fight, Springer, I really do and thank you for your time.'

Springer smiles at her. 'Time spent with thee is time well spent. Fare thee well, lass,' he replies as she turns and walks away. He watches her as she moves off along the path with such elegance and grace. Her dress enhances her body movements, and he is just captivated by the moment, continuing to observe until she is clearly out of sight. Even when she is gone from view, he still stares blankly into the distance, thinking of what she said and how kindly she had spoken it.

Snapping out of his trance, he closes the door and returns to his chair by the fire with a lot to think on. He is not one for acting rashly or hastily but rolls all the information over in his head again and again, analysing every detail. Once he has it all clear in his mind and all avenues have been explored, he relaxes. He's come to a decision, and that is that.

His thoughts now switch to his own dreams and desires; his mind goes back to when he was younger, to an area on the border between Hampshire and Dorset where he was once sleeping rough in an old farmhouse on the edge of a small chestnut spinney. The roof had all but fallen in; however, the walls were all true and sturdy and the fireplace – although it had seen better days – was still complete enough to use.

But it is the view he remembers most. From the doorway of this old building, he could see all the way down the valley to the river. There was one big open meadow with woodland on the left and a stone layered wall on the right side acting as a barrier for grazing animals. To him it was a pocket of heaven. He always wondered what happened to the people who used to live there and why nobody had taken up residence. It must have been a fair sight in better times. The occupants must have lived like they were the only ones in the world, such was the remoteness and beauty of the location. It was the kind of place he wants to own for himself, forgetting his sins of the past and going forward under the sweat of his own brow. Making something for himself and, God willing, a family. Not for others to gain and profit from him fighting or some of the other things he had done just to have food on the table and a roof over his head.

Sitting in his comfortable chair, he dares to dream of the things he would like. For most, they are just normal things in life. But to a man with a past and a debt to pay to those gaining from his talents, he must endure and be patient. His eyelids slowly close as his body relaxes into the folds of cloth in the seat beneath him. Before long, he has drifted back into a quiet peaceful sleep.

* * *

Down at the fairground there is a hive of activity. Edith and the other children are walking around looking at everything as it is being assembled and put into place. They stop periodically to comment on various stalls and their contents and laugh at the Punch and Judy booth as they watch the puppeteers practise their routines. Edward can see Susan, Maddi and Megan in the distance standing by the tall, spiral slides and he runs over to greet them. Susan – the first of the group to see him – reacts to his presence with a smile and a wave.

'This is so exciting,' she shouts out as he approaches.

'I know! I've been watching it going up all morning from the window of my room!' he replies.

Oliver and Edith have also now reached the group of girls and they greet each other, all agreeing how wonderful the fair is going to be, when a man calls to them.

'Hey, you children! Do you want to be the first to try out the big slide?' They all look round to see a man on the top of one of the big slides, beckoning them over. The two boys look at him then back at Edith. 'Go on then,' she says with a smile, 'but be careful taking the steps.'

The group of five children go running over to the rides, with Edward, Susan and Maddi climbing the steps on one and Oliver and Megan climbing the steps on the other. 'Now, easy as you go!' the man calls with a wide grin. 'It's not a race to get to the top.'

One by one the children reach the top, take a mat from the pile and sit on it, then push off and slide down, hitting the three bumps that are built into each slide as it rotates round in a spiral before straightening out for the final third of the way. The bumps are designed to take out some of the speed but, as all children know, if they keep their balance and stay central all the way down, they can hold the speed at the bottom.

They all reach the bottom, but all have stopped before the ten-foot flat run-off has been fully used. 'That was so good!' says Oliver as they all run round for another go while Edith watches on.

'Well, you can have one more run before we add the decorations and boards to their sides,' the man replies.

This time, the children are more prepared and have a goal in mind: to reach the end of the flat run and finish by standing up.

Oliver and Edward let the girls go first and watch as they slide down exactly as before, stopping short of the full run-off at the bottom. The boys have a plan. At the top, they sit down together, one on each slide, and start to rock backwards and forwards using their hands to grip the edges of the chute. When their forward and backward motion is in sync, they both catapult themselves down the slide and lie flat on their backs. This time, they have more speed. And as they hit the bumps, there is a slight bit of light underneath them as they leave the surface of the slide and become airborne for a moment.

Oliver just about reaches the end of the slide and stands up, putting his arms out in triumph. 'Oh yes! That's how you do it!' he yells with delight.

Edward, however, with his extra weight and experience of these things, not only reaches the end of the slide, but is carrying so much speed that at the end he stands up and must keep running to stop himself from falling over. He runs for some ten or fifteen feet before turning round and punching the air in victory.

Oliver is in awe of his older brother. 'That was awesome,' he says as he runs back to the ladder for another go. But to his dismay, he is greeted by the man.

'That's enough for now, my young man. We need to finish off the sides. You can have another go when we've completed our work.'

Oliver's shoulders slump. He really wanted to try and beat his brother. 'Oh, that's not fair.'

Edward has set a standard that he needs to at least be the same as, if not beat for his own pride. He walks away from the slides with his hands in his pockets, kicking out at the floor in frustration. He re-joins the rest of the group as they wander around the many other attractions being tested out in readiness for the crowds to arrive in force.

As the group pass the second-largest marquee, they can see the jugglers throwing clubs to each other with a gap of around twenty feet between them. Maddi tries to count the number of clubs spinning in the air at the same time and thinks it is around nine, the others guess between eight and eleven. But with the speed and how fast they are thrown, it is difficult to be precise.

A man just outside the tent is launching flames into the air about ten foot high by spitting something in his mouth onto a burning stick. There is a short debate between the children as to whether he has a special gland in his mouth that allows him to do this, as they cannot work out how it is done.

The group pass many tempting food stalls and drinking tents on their way to the rifle and pistol ranges on the far side of the grounds. But with them all just being set up, and with the firepits only just lit, there is very little on offer to sample yet. The area has been roped off to stop people walking into the line of fire. Mounds of sand have been placed behind each target to stop the bullets travelling further than the desired distance. With a large lake behind the range, it has been well placed so that any stray shot will find its way into the water rather than the surrounding open fields.

There is a huge display of firearms and Oliver and Edward look at each and every one, commenting on everything they see.

Edith watches two men taking crates to a small wooden shed in the middle of the range. She observes them as they open rows of small cages and place pigeons, pheasants and partridges in each of the containers.

'Best we test one,' comments one of the men. He pulls back on a wooden lever. Moments later a pigeon bursts free into the air from one of the many pens and flies off, dropping a few feathers on the way. It is only then that Edith realises the birds are being positioned ready to be shot at, and her hand covers her open mouth as she takes stock.

'Come, children, it is time we all got changed and ready for the opening,' she says as she turns the heads of Oliver and Edward with her hands and pushes them on against their will, away from the guns. The other girls follow more compliantly for they have no interest in the weapons on display.

The group is soon lost in the crowds of people that have appeared, and that are wandering around like Edith's group, curious to know what will be on offer later that afternoon when the fair finally opens. The atmosphere is of pure excitement and as Edith and her brothers say goodbye to their friends before heading back to the house, they cannot wait for the event to begin.

CHAPTER 5

The Big Fight

It is just before 3.00 p.m. and at the main entrance to the fair, around five hundred people have gathered for Lord Fitzgerald's opening speech. It would seem that most present are employees of Lord Fitzgerald, including Henry and his wife and children. Beside them are Lord Fitzgerald's special guests and throughout the crowd his enforcers watch for any sign of danger or ill-feeling towards their employer.

Many more local people are hovering in the distance or hanging back in the village until he has finished his predictable lecture about himself and what he has done to put Pippinsford on the map. For they have no interest in him or what he stands for, just the fairground fun they can have with their families.

Sure enough, under a round of applause led by many of his own men and employees, Lord Fitzgerald takes to the stand. He is dressed in a rich burgundy outfit with flared layers at the wrists, frills on the front of his shirt and a triangular hat with huge feathers in the side. He carries a gold and silver tipped cane in one hand that he raises to the clapping audience.

'I would like to start by thanking all of you for turning up here today,' he begins. 'It gives me great pleasure to thank Henry for his assistance in helping me to prepare for the day's entertainment.' He points to Henry as the crowd applauds and Henry takes his hat off and dips his head in acknowledgement.

'I believe this to be the largest fair outside of the great city of London, and I intend for it to be as memorable – if not more so. But before I open the festivities, I would like to take a moment to talk about all the things I have achieved to help bring this fine village to the forefront of farming and industry. And why this is such a fine location to live, work and raise a family. It has always been a dream of mine to move to the country and improve on what it has to offer. With the right people and sound investment, the rewards are boundless…'

After twenty minutes of continuous talking, he finally cuts a red ribbon across a token entrance and opens the fair. The crowd claps and then begins to move into the fairground.

After his opening speech and a few minutes of handshaking with the people around him, Lord Fitzgerald also begins wandering around the stalls with Victoria by his side. She looks stunning in her new royal-blue full-length dress and matching bonnet and parasol. Only her smile is missing as she parades for all to see.

Lord Fitzgerald's guests follow close behind the two of them, matching the pace he sets to ensure they do not pass him. They stop periodically and observe all the stalls and view what they have to offer, participating in some of the entertainment as they go.

Lord Fitzgerald's final destination will be the prize fighting ring where, once he arrives, he can start to unleash his moneymaking scheme on his unsuspecting guests. Until then he will use the fair to entertain and impress his entourage and show what a model village Pippinsford has become with his guidance and expansion plans.

Such is the size of the fair that it takes ten minutes to finally arrive at the prize ring. Lord Fitzgerald leads them into the beverage marquee, which is right next to the main event. The long bar is packed with people – as are many of the thirty or so tables. Lord Fitzgerald makes directly for one particular table in the centre of the room and as he arrives, he begins his prepared speech to entice his guests.

'Ladies and gentlemen, I would like to introduce to you the undefeated prize fighting champion, Gripper "The Bear" Jones.' He extends his hand towards a man at the far side of the table, who stands up and acknowledges his introduction. Lord Fitzgerald begins to clap, and as soon as he starts, everyone else joins in.

Gripper is a mountain of a man – not a muscular shape or a defined physique, but a thickset man with hands twice the size of an average person. Standing a little over six feet tall, he is truly an intimidating size, and would put the fear of God into most who stand before him. His head is shaven, his nose is flat and bent from being broken so many times, his ears are squashed and look like old cauliflowers, and his face bears the scars of a person who has had many a conflict in the ring and probably a good few more on the back roads of England.

'Well, Gripper, would you like to tell these gentlemen your fighting record so they can appreciate your abilities and skills in the ring?'

'Since winning the title, I have had seventy-six fights without loss. Most don't last three rounds. And them that do wish they never had,' he growls with an air of confidence. 'I've broken more bones and skulls than most of you have had hot dinners, and I am yet to find a man who can match me inside or outside of the ring.' He boasts with the prowess of a man who is at the top of his game.

'Please be seated, Gripper. We will leave you for now and see you later when you demonstrate your skills,' Lord Fitzgerald says as he turns to leave.

Gripper answers swiftly as he sits back down. 'That will only be if the other man turns up.' He grunts. 'He would not be the first person to see me and run. It's happened on more than one occasion.' The group of men sitting round the table burst into laughter, while one man bangs the table with his fist and another toasts the health of Gripper before he downs his ale and slams the jug on the table.

'Well, has anyone seen the man I am supposed to fight yet? Cos I sure have not and it's getting close to the time when we need to start things off.'

Lord Fitzgerald takes full advantage in playing down his opposition. 'Well, I do hope he does turn up, or all this preparation would have been wasted and I will be out of pocket a substantial amount. And that would be something of an inconvenience to me and my esteemed guests.' After looking back at Victoria for a moment, he continues. 'I believe the man in question works for

Miss Victoria's father as a labourer on his estate just across the field from here, so he does not have far to come, or in fact far to be carried home should he lose.' The men around the table laugh loudly again. 'Still, we will know in less than half an hour, as the fight is due to start at five p.m.,' continues Lord Fitzgerald. 'In fact, gentlemen, I think it's time I take you to our platform to view the pending entertainment. We can order our refreshments there while we wait for the fight to begin.'

He escorts Victoria and the group of gentlemen out of the marquee and along the side of the prize ring. As they approach the raised viewing area, Victoria catches Lord Fitzgerald's attention. 'My lord, would you mind excusing me? The fight is something I would sooner not watch. I feel the time would be better spent with my mother, organising later events.'

Lord Fitzgerald thinks for a moment. 'Yes, yes, you run along to your mother. This barbarism is not for your delicate disposition, but I will expect you back at my side when the fight is over, my girl. We still have a lot of people to greet, and I wish to show you off to all who are around. After all, it's not every day I decide to get married!'

Victoria makes her apologies to the rest of the group and retires from the viewing area. Walking away from Lord Fitzgerald, she debates whether to find her siblings amongst the crowds, but in the end decides to head back to the house so she does not hear or see the impending fight. For the thought of seeing Springer hurt or even killed in the ring is too much for her to comprehend.

Lord Fitzgerald leads the group to the awaiting chairs and ensures all his guests are being supplied with the liquid refreshments and food they require before he starts to speak. 'Now, gentlemen. I think it is time we talk about a wager on this fight. I am prepared to offer three to one on Gripper to win, four to one for Gripper to win in the first five rounds, and seven to one for Gripper to win in the first three rounds. If anyone is prepared to bet on the farm boy to win, I will offer… let's say, for the sake of being generous… ten to one.'

'And how much are we allowed to bet?'

'My good man, you are my guests! I will cover any price you wish to offer. My benefactor here will write down all bets and you can sign them in acknowledgement. I will then countersign in agreement.'

'How does twenty-five pounds on Gripper to win in three rounds sound to you, Lord Fitzgerald?' The man laughs, thinking the bet will shock Lord Fitzgerald.

'My good man, I said I will cover all bets, however large or small they may be, even the tiny ones if it suits your purse strings.'

The man stops laughing. He does not want to look cheap in front of the others. 'Let's make it one hundred and fifty guineas then,' he says in a not-so-cocky voice.

'As you wish.' Lord Fitzgerald turns to a man who is standing beside the viewing platform, holding a small black book. 'Benefactor, mark it in the book and I will sign it.' This starts the ball rolling and before long all but one person has put a substantial bet down on Gripper to win.

'Do you not wish to wager, Pierre? For I know you are a sporting man,' asks Lord Fitzgerald.

'I think I will wait to see the opposition before I make my call,' says the Frenchman in a heavy accent. 'For your odds on the champion seem very generous. Perhaps just a little too generous for such a champion fighter.'

Lord Fitzgerald titters and lifts his nose in the air. 'My good man, I only want your stay to be a good one. If you wish to view the opposition first, I have no problem with that at all.'

Far away from the roar of the crowds, Springer is in his house, tapping out the old tobacco from a pipe he has just found sitting up high on the mantle. It is a weighty wooden construction with a lion's head carved on the front and the mane wrapping round to the back of the bowl. He fumbles in his pocket for his penknife, opens the smaller of the two blades and starts to scrape out the carbon residue inside the bowl. 'Now that there be a fine quality piece,' he says to himself as he puffs on the pipe to ensure it is now cleared through. 'And I know just the man to appreciate such finery.'

There is a sharp rap at the door. Springer looks up but does not respond. He knows what it is and takes a minute to place the penknife and pipe in his bag by the fire. There is another, louder knock and this time Springer walks over and opens the door. Standing before him is Henry. Behind him in the distance, Springer can see Lord Fitzgerald's man, Brannigan, watching intently.

'Are you ready?' asks Henry.

'Aye, me'lord, as ready as can be.' Springer steps out of the door and closes it behind him.

'I do wish you all the very best, you know,' says Henry in a solemn voice as they walk to the ring.

'Well, time be here now. Let's be seeing it through to end, shall we?'

Brannigan has not moved; he just watches Springer as he gets closer and closer. As Springer nears Brannigan, he looks at him and says, 'I hope thee be here watching when it be over, cos if I have anything left on my way back, I'll be sure to throw you another thumpin'.' Brannigan watches on. His instructions from his boss were to ensure that Springer arrived for the fight in one piece. He has no intention of tangling with Springer again in a fair fight, but he does intend to get even sometime soon.

For the rest of the journey, not a word is spoken, but as they get closer to the ring, the noise from the gathering crowd gets louder and louder.

At the one-hundred-yard mark, local people and others who know Springer are waiting for him – they wish him well and pat him on the back as he passes.

At the fifty-yard mark, he can see the ring in its entirety, surrounded by hundreds of people cheering and yelling.

Inside the ring the other fighter and his entourage are whipping the crowd into a frenzy.

'My God,' says Henry. 'The man is a monster. I'm glad it's not me getting in the ring with that.'

Springer looks at Henry and shakes his head. 'Thanks for that, me'lord. I feel much better, knowin' ye be right behind me, an all.'

They reach the rope around the ring and Henry turns to Springer. 'Well, good luck in there, my boy. Go get at him, and all that.' Henry pats him on the back and leaves to join Lord Fitzgerald's party in the raised stand.

A man wearing a white shirt opens the ropes wide, allowing Springer to bend over and step through into the enclosed arena. He stands up and is instantly met with the face of his opposition, staring at him, within inches of his nose, trying to get the upper hand by intimidating Springer with his sheer size and aggression. But it doesn't have the desired effect. Springer just steps round him and walks to his assigned corner, takes off his shirt and throws it behind the corner post. He then turns and faces Gripper, who is still in the centre of the ring shouting to the crowd about what he is going to do with his opponent.

By now there are around five hundred people crammed round the ring, watching the two pugilists with intense excitement, and all of them want to see a bloody and violent contest. The cheering, the booing, the shouting for their favourite is deafening. On the far side of the fairground, on the raised grassy slope, there must be another two hundred people. And any area with height that can hold a man's weight has a person attached to it or standing on it – all watching as the anticipation builds.

Small and large wagers are being taken from all areas of the ground – some between friends over a pint, others placing a week's wages or more. It would seem the champion is the heavy favourite to win the bout. However, there are a good few local people prepared to bet on Springer for the better return if he does just so happen to pull it off – although these in general are only small value wagers.

Springer stretches out his arms, twists his waist and rolls his neck, first one way and then the other. After a minute or so of this, he turns and faces the corner post, throwing a few shadow punches, dipping up and down between each volley, stretching out all his limbs before the conflict. Then finally he turns and faces his opponent again. Having heard of this man Gripper before, and knowing the brutal way he fights in the ring and finishes off his opponents in the fastest possible time, Springer now has to find a way to take down a man who has never been defeated.

Looking at his opponent properly for the first time, Springer watches for any signs of weakness. His neck is wider than his head, and his chin looks like a slab of granite. He is stocky, but there are no signs of a flabby waistline or any slowness in his movements. The only thing that stands out is his sheer size, with an ego to match, and to take advantage of this, Springer knows he has to draw the fight out over a period of time. Wearing the man down by using his own size against him may tire him out enough to make mistakes. But to do that, Springer will need to stand his ground and soak up a lot of punishment. He resigns himself to the fact that this may be a long and painful afternoon, and he will feel the effects for many days to come.

The man in the white shirt summons them both to the centre of the ring. The crowd – that has been deafening up until now – falls silent to hear what he has to say. 'Now, gentlemen, I want to see a good clean fight. No kicking, scratching, biting or gouging of eyes. Fists, elbows and head can all be used and all areas above the waist are fair target. No hitting the man when he is on the ground or in the gentleman regions. Each round will start with you both standing on the lines facing each other.' He points at two parallel lines on the floor about three feet apart. 'Each round will last five minutes and will be called by the timekeeper.' He points to a bearded man sitting at a table with a huge sandglass and a hand bell. 'Up to two minutes between each round can be taken to recover. Or, if you both choose to step forward to the line, this time can be waived, and I will start the round. In the event of a knock down, two minutes will be allowed to recover yourself and prepare to continue the fight. The winner will be declared when one man cannot get to the line within the two minutes allocated. Now step back to the corners and come to the line when you are ready.'

The crowd roars again as the two men turn back to their corners and prepare to step forward.

Lord Fitzgerald turns to Henry. 'I like these rules you have put in place. They make it clear and more gentlemanly.' Henry nods in agreement. 'As for you, Pierre, have you decided who to bet on?' asks Lord Fitzgerald.

'Yes. I think I will follow the crowd and place two hundred of your English guineas on the big man Gripper to win. Though I feel this other man may still yet have something to say, for I still think there is more to him than meets the eye. But I have made my decision and will stand by it.'

'Then it is done, by God. My benefactor is writing down the wager as we speak.' Lord Fitzgerald's net has finally been cast over all his guests. Now he just needs Springer to win to collect on his enterprise.

Back in the ring, the two fighters have both approached the line. The bearded man spins the sand timer over and the man in the white shirt shouts, 'Begin.'

Gripper springs forward and lets loose with a couple of swings to Springer's head. He ducks under one of them, blocks the other with his forearm and plants a body shot to Gripper's ribs. It has no effect, and Gripper turns and headbutts Springer on the side of his face, knocking him back and stunning him a little, but he's still able to trade punches with his opponent for the next five minutes. Neither one is prepared to give ground. Gripper has let loose far more punches, but Springer has had the more accuracy, and has produced the more damaging hits.

The bearded man hits the bell and calls out, 'Time, gentlemen, time.'

Both fighters stop and return to their corners, then turn and face each other and walk straight back to the lines. 'Begin,' is called and they start again instantly as the bearded man turns the sandglass, and the time starts again.

Gripper once again takes the lead, stepping forward and releasing a barrage of punches that has Springer back on the ropes. Although he is taking most of the punches on his arms and shoulders, enough get through in the next four minutes that they push his arms apart and allow Gripper to put a few to the body before he plants another headbutt on Springer's temple, sending him crashing to his knees.

'Time, gentlemen,' the bearded man calls, but Gripper does not stop. He continues punching Springer in the side of the body. The referee forces his way between the two men and helps Springer to his corner. The crowd is booing loudly, and Gripper is pleading his innocence as if he did not hear the man call time.

Behind the post in both corners is a bucket of water with a sponge in it, and a towel hanging from the back rope. Springer reaches for the sponge and splashes his face, then wipes it with the towel. He turns to look at Gripper and, to the amazement of the crowd, steps forward and walks straight back to the line.

Gripper has only just made it to his corner after all his showboating, but seeing Springer at the line, he also walks straight back, keen to get the fight over with quickly.

'Begin,' shouts the man. Gripper lunges forward with a barrage of lefts and rights to the sides of Springer's head. Again and again, he hits Springer's forearms and his shoulders, before moving back down to work on his body. Springer's arms start to waver. Seeing this, Gripper intensifies his assault, but this time as he positions himself to put in another headbutt, Springer has a surprise of his own.

He brings up a huge uppercut and hits Gripper in the stomach. The force lifts him up off the floor, and a second blow swiftly follows to the same place and has the same effect, taking the wind clean out of Gripper. A third delivery comes up and hits him square on the jaw. The impact throws him backwards through the air and he hits the canvas square on his back. The crowd screams with approval while Gripper is breathless on the floor. For a moment, he does not know what has happened, but as his head clears he rolls over onto his stomach and makes his way back to his feet. It is not often that Gripper is put to the floor. And never on his back. He yells and curses at Springer in a show of defiance, and to hide the fact that he was hurt by the attack and needs a few more seconds to get his wind back.

Springer knows it will take more than that to put Gripper down for good, but what it has done is make his opponent rethink. He now knows that Springer is better than he thought, and he will not be so foolish as to rush in again and try and finish him quickly.

Gripper is still clearing his head when the bearded man calls time, and both fighters return to their allotted corners. Springer wipes his face on the towel and returns to the line straight away. His plan is to keep Gripper moving and, if possible, give him no rest between the rounds, allowing the huge man no time to regain his strength. Looking back, Gripper sees Springer on the line and immediately returns to face him.

'Begin,' is the call and both men continue their brutal conflict.

The crowd are roaring with every punch thrown and the ebb and flow of this gladiatorial battle has everybody cheering and willing them on for more. On the grassy bank, Dan is waving a bottle of ale and cheering on Springer. Edward and Oliver have sneaked away from the girls and are watching the fight from behind a bush on the hill so Father does not see them. Oliver has put on his pirate bandana especially for the fight and is yelling with excitement as Springer puts in another couple of heavy punches to Gripper's body. Around the ring, Henry's gardeners and many of his other staff are willing Springer on, cheering every time he gets a good punch in. However, the majority of the crowd is pro-Gripper, for he is a well-known fighter with an impeccable record and fearless reputation. Some say he was born to fight, and all expect him to win out at the end of the day.

Lord Fitzgerald, for once, is not giving his opinion to everyone. Although he is watching the fight, he is actually working out how much money he is going to make if Springer wins or loses. He deduces that if Springer wins, he will have fleeced his party guests of nearly £1700. With all the other gambling on this fight that he is controlling, he may push £4000 by the end of the day. Not a bad return for doing very little.

Back in the ring, Gripper is getting the advantage over Springer again, and a combination of swift punches to the blocking arms followed by a few to the head put him down on his knees. Gripper again hits Springer's ribs over and over while he is down. The referee steps in to intervene and pushes Gripper back. This time, however, Gripper pushes the referee out of the way. He wants to end this now and lunges forward, sticking his knee into Springer's ribs with a nasty thud. Springer lets out a scream of pain and falls to the floor.

The crowd does not appreciate the move and starts to boo Gripper, but he does not care. He raises his hands, as he thinks he is the winner, and taunts the people watching. Springer is buckled over for a bit before he comes round, picks himself back up and steps towards the line again. He is still reeling from the pain to his almost certainly cracked ribs, but he must keep Gripper moving. He lowers his left arm to protect his side and beckons Gripper on.

Gripper, incensed that the man still stands, lunges forward, throwing punch after punch in an attempt to finish him off and end the fight. The barrage is relentless as he muscles his way onwards, leaning his weight on Springer as he goes. Springer bobs and weaves, nips and tucks, twisting his body to help take the sting out of the punches, but eventually the sheer volume of punches and the man's body weight pushes Springer onto the ropes. Gripper can sense victory and pushes on. The crowd are also screaming, willing the fighters on. Left and right the punches come raining in. Springer is still moving his body around, deflecting as many of the punches as possible.

Gripper throws a committed right-hand punch that misses and turns him round one hundred and eighty degrees. Continuing with the momentum of his movement, he extends his elbow and connects with Springer's eyebrow, instantly splitting the skin and opening a large wound that starts to bleed down the side of his face. The force knocks Springer into the ropes heavily, and he rebounds into the arms of the waiting Gripper. He tries to put his arms around him to hold on and recover for a few seconds. But Gripper has other plans, and with his head over Springer's shoulder, he bites into his left ear. Springer lets out a scream of agony as the teeth go through to the cartilage.

The referee pulls on Gripper, trying to detach the man's teeth from Springer's ear. Finally, he manages to separate them and pushes Gripper back into the corner. He has a mouth full of Springer's blood and spits it onto the floor, laughing as the referee checks out his opponent. The crowd is incensed by this act of foul play and boos Gripper continuously.

Springer staggers to his corner and grabs for the sponge from the bucket. He washes the blood from his eye, then feels his ear, and the part hanging down. To a large extent, he is numb to a lot of the pain, with so much adrenalin flowing, and rage at what this man has done. Gripper is taunting the crowd. But – more important to Springer – he is breathing really heavily. It's now or never.

He stands upright and walks to the line. The crowd cheers loudly as he approaches the start position. Gripper looks around, sees him at the line and rushes to take him on. As he reaches the line, they hear, 'Begin.'

Gripper lunges forward to take the advantage, swinging with his right hand towards Springer's head. This time, he blocks it early and delivers a straight right to Gripper's nose. The crack as contact is made confirms it is broken, and instantly the nose starts to bleed. Gripper is stopped in his tracks and steps back under the impact. Springer instantly switches the attack to the body with a barrage of right-hand uppercuts to the stomach, then one to the chin, then back down to the body and then again to the chin. Gripper falls back to the ropes.

Springer stays on him, toe-to-toe, another right to the head, a left to the head, an uppercut to the chin. Gripper is now bouncing around like a rag doll dancing to the impacts of Springer's punches. Left, right, left, the punches continue coming in from all angles. Gripper is slowing down to a standstill. A big right. Another big right. Springer steps back to reposition himself, bringing up another uppercut, but this time pulling from right to left as it makes contact with Gripper's chin. This twists his head up and to the right with the impact, and Springer snaps a left hook, twisting Gripper's head in the opposite direction. Springer steps back as Gripper drops to his knees before falling flat on his face.

Springer knows there will be no way up from this for his opponent. The crowd roar with approval as they watch for any signs of Gripper moving. The man in the white shirt bends down beside the stricken fighter and puts the back of his hand over his mouth.

'He is still breathing,' he comments to all who would listen and remains by his side, waiting for the timekeeper to call out the two-minute mark to end the fight. After what seems like an eternity to Springer, the bearded man calls out, 'Time's up.'

The mass of people clap and cheer as Springer's hand is raised in triumph by the man in the white shirt. It's not a minute too soon and moments after the man lets go of his wrist, Springer collapses to his knees. He is utterly exhausted. This fight has taken absolutely everything Springer had.

Henry tries to leave the stand to get to Springer's aid, but as he climbs over the fencing surrounding the box, he is summoned by Lord Fitzgerald to assist in another matter – discussions over more fights to be organised for Springer in the future, allowing Lord Fitzgerald's guests to be able to win their money back, gambling on another fight if they so choose to.

Henry knows Springer needs attention and is looking round the ring to see if there is anyone he recognises to help. In the front row, he spots two of his gardeners. 'Tom! Tom and James!' he shouts. The men look up and see Henry beckoning them over. 'You two, help Springer to my house. I will be along shortly to assist.'

'Yes, sir,' James replies, and the two men climb into the ring and help Springer back to his feet. Springer is exhausted, his vision is blurred, and he can barely stay conscious. Now the fight is over and the adrenalin has stopped flowing, the pain and discomfort is building. Blood drips from the open wound on his eyebrow, and his ear is bleeding profusely.

The men do their best to ease him through the ropes gently and without dropping him. Springer winces as the pain takes hold as they move him into various positions. Once through the ropes, they raise him upright and with one man under each shoulder, they drag him towards the main house.

In the distance, Dan is dancing a jig on the grass and cheering in Springer's direction, waving his cap in the air. He had put a tidy wager on Springer to win, along with the bet Springer had asked him to place for himself. And he'd got good odds for the both of them. Now he is looking forward to treating his wife to a gift and a night out somewhere away from the village.

Oliver and Edward spent most of the fight dumbstruck. The sheer brutality kept them totally engrossed in the action. Now it is all over, they clamber out of the bush and look at each other.

'He bit Springer's ear,' says Oliver.

'I know,' replies Edward. 'Springer smashed him for it though.'

Oliver is still staring at the prize ring. He can see men still inside the ring and wonders what they are doing. 'Let's go down and see what they are up to.'

Edward looks at Oliver and nods. 'Come on, then.'

They weave in and out of the people coming and going from various stalls that have restarted serving people now the fight has finished. As they reach the ring, they slow down to a walk. They can see the other fighter still on the floor with men around him, some kneeling, some standing and talking about the fight they have just seen. 'I never thought I would see the day Gripper would be out cold and flat on his back in a fight,' says one of the men.

'That man Springer certainly threw him a beating, that's for sure, even after taking such punishment,' another man comments.

'Aye, I don't think Gripper will ever be the same again. That kind of defeat takes a lot out of a man. Also knocks your confidence as well.'

A man carrying a wooden chair arrives at the ring. He puts it over the ropes and places it in the corner by the post. 'Give us a hand to lift him onto the chair, will you?' he calls out as he approaches Gripper. Several men oblige and they lift up the bloodstained, unconscious fighter and place him in the chair while another grabs the sponge from the bucket and wipes his face and chest, removing the blood and sweat, and cooling the fighter down.

Slowly, the cold water has its desired effect and Gripper starts to stir. First of all it's just a movement of his head and a twitch of his eyes and hands, then slowly his eyes open. A minute or so later, he starts to focus and look around at his surroundings. Quietly, he asks, 'Is it over?'

'Yes, my boy, it's over. You took a bit of a hard pounding at the end – now keep still while we look at you.'

Gripper's eyes slowly close back up. His body goes limp and slides off the chair and back onto the floor, banging the back of his head on the edge of the chair. He has taken one hell of a beating and his body needs time to recover.

'We need a doctor here,' yells one of the men. With no reply, he shouts out again, 'We need the doctor in here, now!'

Within seconds, a doctor is in the ring with his bag. He examines the fighter for several minutes, checking his swollen eyes, feeling round his broken nose and listening to his heartbeat and pulse before coming to his conclusion. 'We need to get this man to my surgery,' he says. 'He needs to be monitored until he wakes up. One of you get a carriage or wagon to take him to my house. The rest of you, help get him out of this ring.'

In minutes, Gripper is on a carriage with the doctor, heading towards the village. A few of the men watch as they disappear into the distance. A great champion has just fallen in a brutal fight, and a man who works in the local area has become a legend in less than an hour by his own hand.

Everybody will want to know Springer now. Some just to say they know the champion. Others will boast that he is their friend and show him off whenever they can to big themselves up in society. Then there are the worst ones: those who will look to make profit or gain at the pain and expense of Springer's abilities. They do not care who gets hurt or damaged, as long as they make money from the man before he is used up. These leeches of society exist in all walks of life and in all ages, past and present, manipulating and gaining from the abilities of others to climb their way up the social scale. In fact, they have no talent of their own. No skill, merit or ability worthy of note. Just the cold and selfish drive to use others to further themselves.

For Springer, only time will tell if what he has just put himself through was worth it. He has completed the first part of his plan, but will he be able to make the best of what he has just been through? Or will others gain from his great achievement while he becomes a victim of his own success? The next few days will surely answer that question.

CHAPTER 6

After the Fight

Springer is helped back to the estate house by two of the gardeners he knows well. He is barely able to walk, and his strength is sapped to the very core. The gardeners virtually carry him all the way back to the building.

He can still hear the baying and cheering from the crowd behind him as he goes, but it is more a blur and incoherent words to him. People passing by are cheering and patting him on the back, congratulating him on a fight well fought.

'What a fight!' one shouts.

Another yells out, 'The best fight I have ever seen!'

But to Springer, it's all just spinning around in his head, as he moves in and out of consciousness.

The cut below his left eyebrow has stopped bleeding but is showing a nasty open wound. His nose is still weeping a small blood trail and the bite on his ear is still dripping blood profusely.

All this blood mixed in with sweat and the heavy swelling around both eyes ensures that most who knew Springer before the fight would struggle to recognise him as the same man, such are his injuries.

As they near the front of the house, Cook sees them approaching. She has been waiting for Springer to arrive since the fight started. 'In here,' she calls to the men and opens the double doors to the kitchen side entrance. The two men turn sideways to fit through the doorway without dropping him and head to a large armchair which Cook has taken from the main hall and set up by the sink. She has planned this carefully, putting a large sheet over the chair to prevent staining, and an extra towel on each of the chair's arms to collect any blood.

Watching him closely as he passes her in the doorway, she can see the full extent of his injuries. 'Oh my godfathers!' she cries out. 'What have you done to yourself?' She holds back her emotions as best she can, but the state Springer is in is just terrible, and a complete shock to her.

She wonders how anyone could allow this to happen to a man, not least to a friend. 'Gently sit him down on the chair,' she comments while the men struggle to ease him around. Every time they try to turn and adjust his position, Springer lets out a small wince of pain.

'I said gently!' she yells.

They unwrap his arms from their shoulders and allow him to settle back into the covered seat, moving cushions around to hold him in the best pain-free position. The sink is full of warm water that Cook has just added to with more boiling water from the stove, as it has long since started to cool. She immerses a white cloth in its depths, part wrings it out and very gently begins to wipe the blood and dirt from Springer's face.

'How can anyone call this a sport? It's barbaric. Look at the state of this poor man,' she says to the two men standing by and watching everything she does.

Looking at his ear and the bits torn and hanging down, she can see it will need more skilled work than she can provide. Soaking a second cloth in the water, she wrings it out tighter and clasps it over the bleeding ear.

Turning back to view the two gardeners, she calls out to Tom. 'Hold this on his ear firmly and support the other side of his head with your hand to balance out the pressure.'

Tom does exactly as he has been asked, even though Springer is twitching with the pain as he applies pressure.

'As for you, young James, go and get the village doctor. This will need more attention than I can give him.'

James speaks up. 'I saw the village doctor in the crowd at the fight. I will see if he is still around the fairground.'

Cook raises her eyebrows. 'The doctor was in the audience watching these men fight? Words fail me! Well, go and get him, fast as you can. This man will need his help if he is going to get through this in one piece.'

'Yes, Cook,' James replies, 'I will go at once.'

As he slips out of the side entrance, the main door between the kitchen and the rest of the house opens and Cook looks up to see who would enter her domain at this time of night. To her surprise, it's Miss Victoria, who makes a beeline straight for Springer.

'I'm sorry, my dear, I cannot get anything for you to eat yet. I need to attend to this poor man first,' says Cook.

Victoria stops just short of reaching them and looks up and down at the state of Springer's battered, bruised and bloody body. Even though she had prepared herself for this moment, when you see it in real life, it always has more impact than you would expect.

'I'm not here for me,' she says, a slight crack in her voice. 'I'm here to help him.'

Cook, who is still wiping around Springer's face, does not look up this time. 'My dear, this is dirty work. Not for the likes of a young lady of society. Best you leave now and let me do what needs to be done.'

Victoria realises she needs to get stuck in or go. She walks right up to Springer, wipes her hand over his bloodstained neck, chest and shoulders and then rubs it on the front of her dress. 'There, now I'm dirty.' She picks up another cloth from beside the sink, soaks it in the water and starts work cleaning the blood and dirt from his shoulders and arms. Cook is shocked at Victoria's move but is proud that a woman of her status is not afraid to get her hands dirty and help a man in need.

With the two of them gently working away, they start to uncover the man below the sweat, blood and grime. Slowly they clean everything from the waist up exposing the true extent of his injuries from the conflict. As Victoria cleans his chest and moves down the sides of his ribs, Springer tenses up and lets out a grimacing moan. 'Careful,' Cook comments. 'I think some of his ribs are broken. You can see all that dark purple bruising already coming out.' Victoria nods while she continues to clean around the enflamed and damaged area.

During all this time, Springer has been in a semi-conscious state. With his eyes still closed, he tries to reposition himself in the chair to be more comfortable. It hurts him to move, but he needs to get in a better posture. Victoria supports his arm as he twists his damaged side more to the middle of the chair. His eyes slowly open, blink and focus on his environment. It is a slow process as his mind is trying to adjust to where he is and who is around him touching his body. The ladies continue to work on cleaning him up, regardless of all his fidgeting. Cook starts to work around the neck and ear, where Tom is still applying pressure.

'Thank you, Tom, I've got it from here,' she says as she replaces Tom's hand on the cloth being pressed on Springer's ear. Tom slowly backs off and stands at a distance, watching the women work.

'That will be all we need from you for now,' says Victoria as she looks him up and down and realises how dirty he is. 'You may as well go back and enjoy the fair for the rest of the evening. There is nothing more you can do for him here.'

Tom does not need much convincing. Coping with blood is not his strong point. And with his winnings still waiting for collection at the bet makers, he is only too ready to leave. Tilting his cap in the direction of Victoria and Cook, he heads off out the door to collect his prize and enjoy the rest of the evening.

After a while, there is only the area around his ear, eye, bruised ribs and his back to finish cleaning up. Gently they ease him forward and start to work on his back. He has been beaten black and blue, and the more they clean him up, the more the bruising shows through.

'My God, I cannot believe what I am seeing,' Victoria says with a sigh. 'To think this is inflicted by one man on another in the name of sport is beyond my comprehension.'

Cook looks at her. 'Er, you seem to forget, this is the man who won the fight. I expect the man who lost and never left the ring is in a far worse state.'

Victoria pauses for a second before replying. 'Yes, I'm sure you are right, but I do not know that man, nor do I want to. I know this man here and he protected my brothers and myself when we were in trouble. I could not in good conscience walk away from him now when he needs our help most urgently.'

Cook nods and smiles at her. 'It's the same for me. He had barely been here a week when he helped a man he hardly knew in a terrible situation. If it had not been for his kindness and quick thinking, my Dan would have been at the mercy of Lord Fitzgerald and would probably be dead, leaving me a widow.'

Victoria looks at her. She wants to ask her more on what happened that day, but before she gets the chance to ask, Cook continues. 'I will say no more on the matter, but to me this man is an angel and deserves better than what people give him here.'

Victoria is beginning to understand there is far more to this man than she first thought. He is not as slow-witted or stupid as many think, just old-fashioned and countrified in how he speaks. His ability to reassure and comfort people in need is admirable, and he has a sense of honour and decency that puts even her father to shame.

They finish cleaning Springer's back and gently lower him back into the chair as Cook looks round at the door and puffs out her cheeks. 'Still no sign of that bleeding physician. No doubt he is in a drunken stupor somewhere in the village.' She sighs heavily. 'We cannot wait any longer. Would you stay with him a minute while I get the things I need?' As Victoria looks up, Cook is already heading out of the kitchen.

Victoria reaches for the cloth on Springer's ear. She prises it back to see what it is covering and as the cloth moves the ear begins to bleed again. She can see the earlobe and back part of the ear are hanging by a thread. 'Oh my God, you poor man,' she mutters as she squeezes the cloth back onto the ear.

At this moment, Springer starts to come around to a more conscious state. As his eyes adjust, the first thing he sees is Victoria's blue eyes staring down at him. He looks at her as he speaks. 'Am

I dreaming?' he asks. 'I must be dreaming, for I be seeing an angel afore me.'

Victoria smiles. 'No, you're not dreaming. And I assure you, and I am no angel – as for that role I would need wings on my back. You are in Cook's kitchen, and I've been helping to clean up the wounds on your body.'

Springer tries to move. 'No, please don't move. You will start to bleed again,' she begs as she puts her hand on his shoulder and pushes him back into the chair.

'Your dress,' he says. 'It be all messed up.'

Victoria smiles again. 'The state of my dress is the least of my worries. Now sit back and lie still for you are in no fit state to be moving around. Cook should be back shortly.'

Springer's whole body must ache and hurt immensely, but while he is staring at Victoria, he can feel no pain. All he can sense is the warmth of a woman's hand on his shoulder, the compassion in her eyes, the smile on her face and the sweet smell of perfume.

Cook bursts through the door. In her hand are a needle, cotton thread and half a bottle of brandy. Both Victoria and Springer look round at the same time and watch as she heads straight for Springer, dragging a small side table behind her.

'Ah, you're awake then, Springer,' Cook says as she puts all the items she has collected down on the side table. She fetches a lit oil lamp from the far side of the room. Removing the glass top, she holds the needle over the flame to heat up the end, then she takes the needle and thread over to the sink and pours a generous dribble of brandy over the hot needle and roll of thread. There is a brief hiss as the heat is taken out of the needle before she threads it with around three feet of cotton thread broken off from the spool.

Cook pulls a large stockpot from the shelf, turns it upside down next to Springer's chair, covers the base with a cloth and sits down on it. 'You're going to wish you had stayed asleep a bit longer, my boy. For this is going to sting a bit,' she says as she takes the cloth away from the side of his head. 'I need to sew this ear back up while we still have a chance of it attaching.'

'It be bad then.'

'It's not a pretty sight, Springer. But I'm sure Cook can improve on it,' says Victoria.

'Well, get thee on with it, afore I have a change of mind.' Springer braces himself and Victoria moves round in front of him, kneels before him and clasps his hands.

'Now look at me, and keep your eyes on me,' she says. 'For I fear this will hurt some.'

Cook instantly starts to work on his ear, first splashing it with brandy, which must sting to high heaven. 'It burns now, but it will help numb the stitching,' she comments as her arm goes up and down like a fiddler's elbow, connecting the ear back together, stitch by stitch. In all the time it takes from the first stitch to the last, Springer makes not one sound, nor does he move. Just looks at Victoria in a constant trance.

'Now, that's as good a job as I have ever done,' Cook mutters as she bites off the thread and inspects the stitching on his ear. Moving straight on to the open wound above his eye, she speaks again. 'Now, young man, let's work on that cut by your eye as we cannot have that left open the way it is.'

She moves round behind him and closes the wound with her fingers, then begins to stitch the skin together, tying off each knot as she goes. This is a delicate area to stitch, and the pulling and jolting does make Springer grip Victoria's hands a little tighter. Victoria responds by leaning into him more and more, holding him a little tighter herself.

'Victoria! What are you doing?' comes a cry from the side entrance. She looks around as Father and Lord Fitzgerald enter the kitchen.

'We are attending to Springer's wounds, Father. They are quite severe,' she replies calmly.

'I have people to attend to that sort of thing, my dear. I do not expect my daughter to be on her knees before a common servant in this household.'

Victoria is about to reply but does not get the chance to comment as Lord Fitzgerald enters the conversation. 'My dear, look at the state of you. Not only are you kneeling down before a common dog, but your dress!' He points to the bloodstains on her front with his cane. 'It's all bloody! I could not possibly have you walking around with me looking like that. Please get changed into something more suitable. I cannot introduce you nor show you off to people in that attire as it is positively disgusting.'

Hearing this enrages Springer. If he was in a better condition, Lord Fitzgerald would now be on the floor picking up his teeth. But for now, Springer must be quiet and bite his tongue, for his time will come.

Victoria, on the other hand, does say something. She is angry and does not appreciate the way she is being spoken to. 'Father, I was helping Springer. Once I have finished tending his wounds, I will gladly get changed and Lord Fitzgerald can have his pet on a lead to walk round with as he sees fit.'

'Victoria! How dare you speak like that to Lord Fitzgerald!' Henry splutters. 'Apologise at once.'

Before Victoria has a chance to answer, Lord Fitzgerald speaks. 'Relax, Henry. The girl has spirit, and I like that. It gives me a challenge to overcome and break this wild streak once we are together.' He turns to Victoria. 'Now, my dear, when you have finished tending this brute, would you be so kind as to change and join me in the big marquee? It would be gratefully appreciated.'

Victoria is about to answer him back when Springer jerks her hands.

She will never know if it was a pain reaction to Cook stitching his wound or to prevent Victoria from saying the wrong thing, but it does give pause to the moment, and in that brief time she re-evaluates her words. 'Yes, I will, as soon as this poor man's situation has been addressed.'

Henry turns to leave the room, leading the way for Lord Fitzgerald, who is following close behind. Suddenly, Lord Fitzgerald stops and turns around. 'Oh, the brute! I almost forgot why we came here.' He walks back to Springer. 'Well done. That was a good display. For a moment there, I thought you were going to lose, but you managed to pull it off and beat a difficult opponent.

I don't think I will get as good odds on you the next time, but I'm sure plenty of coin can still be made.'

He fumbles in his pocket, pulls out several coins and throws them onto Springer's lap. 'Here, every dog should be fed, so here is your reward. Go spend it on booze, a woman or whatever takes your fancy.'

Springer is raging inside. He wants to ram the coins down Lord Fitzgerald's throat, but he needs all the money he can get for his plan. Also, he requires the situation diffused so that no one will be aware of his intentions later.

'Thank ye, me'lord,' he mutters in his finest yokel as Lord Fitzgerald leaves the kitchen muttering about the quality of Springer's language and how poorly the people around the village speak English.

'There, all finished. It might not be as good as the doctor could do, but I have sewn a stitch or two on Dan before and he's still kicking. Oh, and before I forget, Dan said he would be round tonight about eight to see how you are and deliver what you are owed.' Cook is careful not to say too much in front of Victoria as she does not want to expose any plans Springer might have for later.

Victoria, who has not let go of Springer's hands throughout, finally releases them and stands up. She picks up the coins from his lap, and the ones that have fallen to the floor. 'Eight, nine, ten, ten shillings and five gold sovereigns. All this pain and suffering for ten shillings and a few sovereigns?' she spits, absolutely disgusted with how Springer has been treated by her father and Lord Fitzgerald. She knows how much the others have made on the back of his efforts in the ring.

Springer slowly gets to his feet, helped by Cook. 'Easy, my dear,' she says quietly.

He almost manages to be fully upright before the pain of his ribs pulls him back down a little. He looks at Victoria. 'I owed your father a debt, for he helped me when I be in bother. That debt be now paid in full in my eyes, lass.' He takes a deep breath and coughs a little. 'Now I best be off and rest my bones and bother thee good ladies no more, for you have my gratitude for what thee have done for me. I know not how I be able to repay such kindness, but you have my thanks.'

As he steps away, he hears a quiet voice speak out behind him.

'No debt is worth this, Springer. Please, no more. I could not bear to see you hurt again,' Victoria begs him.

Springer looks back at Victoria and sees the sadness in her eyes. 'No, lass, this be the one and only time. I will fight no more for pay or line the pockets of them that do not deserve it. I give my word to thee on that.'

As he approaches the doorway, a figure appears in front of him. Looking up, he sees the doctor standing tall with his bag in his hand and beaming a huge smile. 'What a fight! What a fight indeed, my boy! You showed him a thing or two,' he says. 'You're also in a lot better shape than the other chap. He's only just left the ring a short time ago and is still unconscious. They have taken him away on a cart to the other village doctor as we speak. It would seem he is going to need watching over tonight, to ensure he does not fall foul of his injuries.'

The doctor instinctively starts to look Springer over. He touches the bruised rib area and Springer instantly buckles over with pain. 'Argh, old sawbones, you 'ave a touch like an 'ammer!' Springer yells out.

'I need to look at this in more detail, Springer. We must be sure the ribs remain in position and do not push in on your organs.'

'Well, help me home. Then thee can pull and prod as you see fit. We be done here, and I be needin' me to get some rest.'

The doctor tucks his head under Springer's arm and helps him to the door. Springer turns to the two ladies. 'Thank thee kindly for the help I be 'avin, but I will take my leave and no more time from those that be needed elsewhere.' He tilts his head at Victoria and Cook and disappears through the door.

As they shuffle along, the doctor says, 'I cannot wait to see you fight again, young man. It was an epic event this time, and yet I feel you have still better in you.'

Springer has a raw smile on his face as he replies. 'I hope you live that long, my friend. For it will be a while afore I step foot in that there ring again.' They are soon among the crowds of people still walking around enjoying the fair and the open grounds of the estate. Many of them cheer and congratulate Springer as they head towards his little cottage on the edge of Henry's land.

Back in the kitchen, Victoria turns to Cook. 'Thank you for all you have done for him.'

Cook smiles at her. 'You will not find many like that man. He is one worth keeping.' Victoria nods in agreement as Cook washes her hands. 'Yes, when you compare him to people like Lord Fitzgerald and Brannigan, you do see both sides of the coin.'

'Coin!' says Victoria. She looks down at her hand and the pile of coins nestled in its palm. 'I still have his prize money in my hand.' She turns to Cook and shows her the coins.

'Well, you will need to get them to him tonight if you want him to have th—' Cook stops mid-sentence and looks away from Victoria's gaze.

'What do you mean by that, Cook?' Victoria is quick to ask.

Cook thinks fast on her feet. 'Well, once the doctor's finished with him, I would think he will give him something to sleep and numb the pain. So if you wanted to return this money to him, I would do it sooner rather than later, or leave it a couple of days, as I think he will be resting for a while after what he has been through.'

Victoria thinks on Cook's words. She cannot help thinking there is more to this than what she is telling her. 'Well, I must go now and get changed. It is time for me to be dragged round the grounds like a prize pet.' Victoria heads off back into the house while Cook starts to clear up the mess they have made. She must do it fast as she has a limited time to meet up with Dan in the local tavern. Circumstances dictate that she can only see him when Lord Fitzgerald and his enforcers are elsewhere, like at the fairground today, for it is the only safe time to see her husband.

Victoria heads to her room and changes into another dress. She is dreading the idea of walking around with Lord Fitzgerald as his prize, but it must be done for now. While changing, she is thinking of Cook's words regarding Springer. For she is now scheming out a plan of her own.

It takes Victoria a good thirty minutes to get changed with the help of a maid she has called in to assist in tightening up the back of the dress. She finishes reshaping her hair and pins the matching hat in place correctly.

'Thank you, Alison. That will be all for now.' The maid curtsies and leaves the room. Now ready, Victoria begrudgingly makes her way down the stairs to find Lord Fitzgerald and be introduced to his guests.

She looks a picture as she glides down the large central marble staircase, walks along the main hallway, through the reception room to the main entrance. The doors are wide open, and she walks straight down the decorated steps onto the gravel driveway and forward about ten steps before stopping. She sighs heavily as she looks around to determine where to go next. There are many marquees and stalls in the distance, and she is not sure where her father and Lord Fitzgerald will be found.

Suddenly, a rasping voice calls out from behind her. 'I'm here to take you to Lord Fitzgerald.'

Brannigan is leaning up against the wall of the house with his arms folded and a clay pipe hanging from his mouth. He straightens himself up, taps out his pipe on the house wall, places it in his pocket, then walks towards her. Victoria looks him up and down. He is wearing a pair of black hobnail boots, a green and brown tweed suit and waistcoat, a kind of deformed cap that Victoria has never come across before, and in his hand he holds a wooden club-like cane which no doubt could be used to inflict severe damage if desired.

He walks straight past her with a smirk on his face. 'Come on, this way, my pretty. For it does not do well to keep the master waiting.'

He deliberately walks at a fast pace that would be difficult for any woman to keep up with, especially a woman wearing the kind of outfit and shoes that Victoria is dressed in.

Victoria is a smart and astute woman. Assessing the situation, and knowing what Brannigan is trying to do, she decides to walk at her own pace and quickly falls behind. It is several minutes before Brannigan looks back and realises Victoria is some distance behind him. He puts his hands on his hips and yells out, 'Hurry up! I've not got all day. He will be waiting for us, and I have other things to do rather than play guide to his bit of white meat.'

Victoria continues at her own pace and as she catches him up and passes him, she looks Brannigan square in the face with an expression of disgust. Brannigan is wearing a big grin as he chuckles to himself. He is enjoying intimidating Victoria.

Abruptly, she stops, thinks for a bit, then says, 'I see you still have the remnants of that black eye and bruises that Springer gave you some time ago. Perhaps Lord Fitzgerald should have better enforcers around him, for I am sure I feel safer with Springer watching over me rather than you.'

The grin on his face disappears instantly. 'The man was lucky. On another day I w—'

'You would what?' Victoria butts in. 'Two of you tried and lost. Seems to me, you are only good enough to bully young children and women. I have a feeling the only time you can take on a real man is when their back is turned or there are more of you to make up for your inabilities.'

Brannigan is incensed and scowls with anger as he responds. 'Why, you little whore. I'm gonna teach you a lesson you will never forget.' He steps towards Victoria, bringing his arm forward and raising his stick above his head. Victoria stands her ground. Inside, she is terrified. But she is determined not to show it to an animal like Brannigan.

'And what kind of lesson would that be, may I ask?' a man calls out in a heavy French accent.

Brannigan looks to his left and sees Henry, Lord Fitzgerald and the entire party of guests walking toward them. Out in front of them is the Frenchman, Pierre, who is pointing a small pistol directly at Brannigan. And he does not seem impressed by the way Brannigan is addressing Victoria.

'It would seem that the lady is right. Now, why don't you try your luck with a Frenchman and see what happens when a man fights back?' Pierre says, cocking his pistol.

'Now, now, gentlemen, it seems like there is a failure in communication here,' says Lord Fitzgerald. 'Brannigan, let me introduce you to Pierre. He is an acquaintance of mine representing the interests of Madam Kelly from 'La Fleur Blanche' in Paris. He is a kind of trouble-shooter like yourself, but just a little more sophisticated in his mannerisms.'

Pierre tilts his head in acknowledgement of his introduction, while Lord Fitzgerald continues to speak. 'You seem to be acting a bit above your station here. Return to my estate at once and I will have words with you on my return.'

Brannigan slowly backs away from the group, scowling and cursing, still staring at Pierre with a wild look in his eyes and gripping his club tightly. Pierre is following him with his pistol sights as he speaks. 'I would put this beast down now before he hurts someone. I myself do not wish to spend the rest of my time here in England looking over my shoulder, and Madam Kelly would be somewhat disappointed if I were not to return in good health.'

Brannigan takes offence to being called a beast and stops retreating. His arm slowly moves towards a bulge in his waistcoat pocket. Pierre reacts by raising the pistol slightly to be in line with Brannigan's head. 'Do it and I will finish you now, beast!'

'Please, gentlemen, there is no need for this to escalate. In fairness, it was my mistake. Brannigan has many uses to me, but his manners towards the finer things in life leave a lot to be desired. I should have sent someone with more understanding to escort Miss Victoria to us.'

A woman nearby sees the stand-off and a man with a pistol and screams loudly, attracting more people to take note of what is happening. Some start to run away from the scene, while others just stop and watch.

Lord Fitzgerald does not want this kind of public display. 'Brannigan, leave, damn your eyes. And Pierre, please lower that pistol. We are scaring the locals with our behaviour and that does not reflect well on me.' The tone in his voice has changed to a far more serious note and Brannigan knows his employer is not best pleased. He turns and walks away, swearing and cursing as he goes. Pierre slowly lowers his pistol and closes the hammer down on the pan. Eventually, after watching Brannigan move some distance away, he puts it away in his waist belt.

Henry rushes over to Victoria and comforts her. She is shaken but still manages to hold her composure. 'My dear Victoria, are you alright? I am so sorry you had to be witness to that,' Henry says softly as he holds his daughter in his arms.

'Come, everybody, I have so much to show you in this fine village. Let's not let this small debacle ruin a good evening.'

Lord Fitzgerald turns to Victoria. 'Take my arm and we shall escort these fine people to my tavern for some refreshments.' Victoria looks up from the comfort of her father's arms. 'My lord, I think I will retire back to my home. I think I have had enough entertainment for today.'

Lord Fitzgerald is not amused. 'My dear, I insist you join me now.'

She looks up at him and shakes her head. 'No, with the greatest respect, I think I will return to my home and safety.'

Lord Fitzgerald is fuming, but before he gets a word in, Henry speaks up. 'Quite right, my dear. Lord Fitzgerald, I will escort my daughter home and then re-join you at the tavern. She should never have been exposed to this kind of danger and I for one am most unhappy with the treatment my daughter received from your man Brannigan.'

Lord Fitzgerald sighs heavily and flicks his hand at Henry and his daughter. 'Fine, as you wish. I will speak with you when you return, Henry.' He stares at Victoria and speaks in a sterner voice. 'I will speak with you tomorrow and resolve this miscommunication, for I do not expect this sort of refusal from my betrothed in public.' Henry turns with his daughter on his arm and walks towards the family home, comforting and reassuring her as he goes.

'Well, gentlemen, please follow me to The Hare and Hound. I have laid on some fine food for you as well as some local ales for you to try, along with champagne and wine from Pierre's homeland of France. I will explain the rest of my plans for the expansion of this village and entertainment for the rest of the evening on our return to my estate. Tomorrow, we will continue the tours of the cotton mills and factory, the mining operation and fruit orchards that are the lifeblood of this community. I also wish to put forward my ideas of expanding into livestock breeding and horse racing.' The party moves off, following Lord Fitzgerald's lead towards the waiting carriages ready to take them to the village tavern.

* * *

On the far side of the fairground, heading for an ale tent, Brannigan is still swearing and cursing to himself. As he steps over the guide ropes holding down one of the marquees, he rounds the corner and bumps straight into a group of children, knocking several of them and himself to the floor. 'What the hell?' he yells as he gets to his feet and looks down at the children. As one of them turns to look up at him, he points at Brannigan.

'That's him from the other night!' says Oliver, who is still wearing his pirate's bandana. Brannigan instantly recognises him as the boy he fell over that night in the village. 'Aye, you recognise me, don't you, boy?' Brannigan reaches down and picks Oliver up by the scruff of his neck. 'I think me and you had better have a few words.'

Edward has also been knocked to the ground and as he rolls onto his back, he sees his little brother being held in the air by Brannigan.

Bracing his elbows against the floor, he kicks out and his heel connects with Brannigan's kneecap.

'Aah!' yells Brannigan as the impact buckles his leg and he drops to the ground again, taking Oliver down with him but letting go of the boy on impact.

'Run, Oliver, run!' shouts Edward as the brothers both get to their feet and flee the scene. As the boys run past the entrance to the ale tent, Sykes and Crossy reach out and grab them by the shoulders, holding them fast while Brannigan gets back up and hobbles towards them.

'You little bastards!' he yells at them. 'I will show you what we do with nosey children.' He whacks Edward round the back of the head, knocking him sideways.

'How dare you lay a hand on my brother!' shouts Rebecca, who is standing and watching the events unfold with Susan, Megan and Maddi. 'My father will hear of this,' she continues as she steps forward.

Brannigan was unaware of the others, such was his concentration on the brothers. He also realises that many other passing people have stopped and are now watching his actions. He thinks quickly and yells out for all to hear, 'I caught this one trying to pickpocket me while the other had me distracted. They will be detained and be going to the magistrate for punishment.'

The people in the crowd start to talk amongst themselves and Susan speaks up. 'That's a lie, and you know it. You just walked into us and knocked them over!'

Brannigan stares at her. 'Young lady, you better be careful what you say, or you might end up with them.' He turns his attention back to Rebecca. 'As enforcers, we represent the law here. And I say they were attempting to steal from me. Now we are taking these criminals to the magistrate's office, so I suggest you run along to your father and tell him these two thieves will be in a cell tonight and he can come down in the morning and see the chief magistrate.'

Brannigan gives Sykes and Crossy a nod and they start to drag the boys away. Brannigan turns to the growing crowd of disgruntled people. 'All of you now be on your way. There is nothing more to see here unless you wish to join them in the cells.'

The crowd shows its disdain by shaking their heads. 'You're the only crooks here,' a woman yells out while pointing at Brannigan. 'I know these children well. They are no thieves! Not like you and them murderers around you!'

More and more people advance towards Brannigan and the enforcers that have now joined him. He responds by taking out his pistol and raising his club-like cane. 'Anybody fancy their chances, then? Well, bring it on! For there will only be one winner here today,' he bellows with wild eyes and a growl in his voice.

Soon the crowd of people start to disperse, as they do not want any repercussions with the likes of Brannigan and Sykes. Rebecca, however, stands her ground and looks straight at Brannigan.

'My father is going to hear about this right now, for you are no more than a dishonest scoundrel.' Brannigan takes exception to the way she speaks to him, but as he moves forward to grab her, the people around have stopped moving off and are now watching him again. It is just enough to stop him advancing and as he pauses, Rebecca turns and swiftly heads back across the fairground, closely followed by Susan, Megan and Maddi.

It takes about ten minutes for the girls to reach the driveway to the house. As Rebecca runs up the steps and bursts through the door, she is calling out, 'Father, Father! They have taken Edward and Oliver!' She rushes around the house, followed by the others, until she finds Father in the lounge talking to Victoria.

'Father, that man Brannigan has taken Oliver and Edward!' she cries, tears running down her cheeks. 'He says they have stolen from him, and he has taken them away. But it is all a lie, I tell you. Just a terrible lie. I saw it all and so did many others.'

Father rushes to comfort her with the assistance of Victoria and it takes a few minutes to calm her down enough to explain what has happened. With the same story coming from her friends and the fact that he also observed Victoria having a confrontation with Brannigan less than an hour ago, Henry grabs his coat and walking cane from the chair beside him.

'Victoria, look after your sister. I am going to see about my boys and get them back. I will not be long.' Henry storms out of the room and they hear the front door slam as he departs in a hurry.

At the magistrate's office, Edward and Oliver have been escorted inside the building and are unceremoniously being marched into one of the cells used for prisoners. The idea is to put the fear of God into the children, to keep them quiet about what they saw that night. Oliver is terrified as Sykes pushes him against the wall inside while Edward is angry at being treated this way. He holds his trembling brother in his arms and stares at Sykes and Crossy. 'My father will come for us and then you will be sorry, you just wait and see.'

The two men simply laugh at him. 'Your father will do what he is told. I have no fear of him,' says Sykes.

'That may be so,' replies Edward. 'But when he tells Springer to get you, he will tear you apart for touching little Oliver, for I know how he feels about him.'

These words hit a nerve with both Sykes and Crossy as they look at each other and stop pushing the brothers about. They put on a brave face, but Edward knows he has put one over on them, as they have gone quiet. They leave the cell, locking the door behind them as they walk off into another room.

Edward can just about hear them speaking and makes out some of the words. They are indeed talking about Springer and their father. He hears the footsteps of one of the men leave the building before everything goes quiet. With nothing more to hear, he takes his brother over to the bed and sits him down. 'Don't worry, Oliver. Father will be here soon to get us out of here.' Edward sits down beside his brother and holds him in his arms.

Some time passes before Edward hears voices again. He can make out his father yelling at someone in a room nearby. 'Oliver, Father is here,' he says to his traumatised brother. He gives his brother a shake, but he just stares at the wall. 'Oliver?' he says again, but Oliver does not respond, just sits there motionless.

'Father,' he yells. 'There is something wrong with Oliver! He's just staring at the wall and won't move.' Within minutes, Henry is outside the cell with Sykes, demanding the door be opened. Just as Sykes is about to do as requested, more people arrive. Brannigan and Lord Fitzgerald enter the room, being led in by Crossy.

'Do not open that door,' says Lord Fitzgerald, before he turns to look at Henry. 'Could I have a word with you in the other room?' The two men walk through to another office and close the door.

Henry starts the conversation. 'Your men have arrested my boys on a charge of pickpocketing Brannigan. Why would—'

'No,' interrupts Lord Fitzgerald. 'Your sons were arrested because the young one recognised OUR men who silenced that local publisher and his wife that night in the village. I told you to control your children or I would do it. NOW I am doing it. You had your chance to sort this mess out some time ago and failed. I have total control of this enterprise and you can be part of it, or the rest of your daughters can join your sons in jail, and you and your wife can go to the factory. And believe me, when I use the word *wife*, I use it very lightly in her case.'

Henry clenches his fists. He cannot believe what he is hearing. 'I set this whole thing up with you! Don't think I have no cards to play, for I am not as stupid as the murderous henchmen you have next door. Nor am I as gullible as I once was. Yes, I know what my wife was before I married her. You and your corrupt father made her that way a long time ago, while you ensured she used her talents on me to keep me working for your father's company. I had no idea then, the depths to which you would stoop to control me. But somewhere along the way I grew to love her. She does not know I am aware of her past and that is the way I choose it to remain.'

For the first time, Henry presses home his opinion.

'Don't think I do not know what you have done to get where you are today. The fate of your family and siblings is no secret to me, nor the way you expand your workforce and land acquisitions. Because of that I have learned to cover in duplicate many things over the past few years and store them where they would do best should they be needed. I would not push me too much more for I also have everything invested in this and I will fight for the little – and I mean little, compared to you – piece of the pie I have.'

Lord Fitzgerald is taken aback by Henry's stance. 'You show more promise than I first thought, Henry. Perhaps you are the right man to support me and my ambitions. I tell you what, you leave the boys in my care for now. Then, providing I have no more issues tonight, I will square it up with my men and release them tomorrow morning. I feel the fright we have put in them today should do the job and keep them quiet.' He sighs heavily. 'You see,

I have to show authority over my men, or utter chaos will reign. So you give me this tonight with your boys, I will forget this has happened and we can continue to work together. I do not want this to sour what has been such a good relationship between us.'

Henry thinks for a moment. He was not expecting to confront Lord Fitzgerald in the magistrate's building, and he has pushed as hard as he dare against a man with absolute power in the area. If he agrees now, he has done all he can for his sons and will still leave on good terms with his employer. After a few minutes pondering on his options, he answers. 'Agreed.'

He walks out of the door and leaves the boys behind.

It is a terrible feeling, but for the good of his whole family, he must walk away and get his sons back tomorrow.

Back at the house, Henry's wife and daughters are all sitting around in the lounge waiting for Father to return. They have all been told by Rebecca what has happened and are hoping to see Oliver and Edward return with Father.

The bell on the front door rings, and everyone sits up in anticipation. Then the door to the lounge swings open and Henry steps through on his own, head hung low and his pride even lower.

Victoria runs out of the room with tears in her eyes before Henry even speaks. 'Edward and Oliver will be back with us tomorrow,' he says, his mouth turned down. 'I could not get them out tonight.'

He turns to catch up with Victoria, but his wife holds him back. 'Leave her, Henry. She has been through a lot today. We will talk with her in the morning. Now come and sit down with me and tell me what happened.'

CHAPTER 7

The Price of Honour

Springer and the doctor arrive at his cottage. The journey has taken its toll on the exhausted fighter and the physician leans Springer against the porch wall while he opens the door and enters the building. He looks for a suitable place to set Springer down before going back to collect him. With his bed being upstairs via a tiny stairway, his options are limited to the large chair by the unlit fire, or on the floor at the back of the main room. For now, his favoured position is in the chair. Returning outside, he once again lifts Springer onto his shoulder and side shuffles him through the doorway and into the room, slowly easing Springer into the seat.

Springer has been gritting his teeth, but as he sits down in the soft chair, the pain eases to a more tolerable level and he moves a little to one side to help reduce the pressure on his damaged ribs.

The doctor gently feels his side, adding slight pressure to the parts that need assessment. 'Yes, as I feared, I think you have one, possibly two cracked ribs. They flex a little, but they are still holding their shape, so they are not broken away. I will need to wrap a bandage around your waist to compress the area and keep the shape of the ribs as they heal.'

He fumbles around in his medical bag and pulls out a large, long cotton bandage. 'I put some items in here that I thought might be needed to repair you after the fight, and it seems like I was right to do so.'

'That thee be right, old sawbones, for it was a brutal affair for sure and I be feeling the pain now and no doubt the morrow will be worse.'

'Now you need to sit up for a minute while I wrap this around your ribs. I know it will hurt a little and be uncomfortable for a while, but if the ribs splinter or dig into other organs, the problem will be far worse.'

Springer does his best to sit up, and the doctor gets to work wrapping the bandage strips around his chest and shoulder to hold it in place. In total, the bandage goes around Springer's body four times before the doctor takes both the ends and ties them together to hold it all in place. It is a little uncomfortable, but nothing he cannot live with, especially if it helps to support his ribs and possibly aid him to repair sooner.

The physician then starts to look over the rest of the damage, first the wound over his eye, then the area of ear that was hanging off just a few minutes ago. 'Cook has done a good job, stitching these up,' he comments as he works his way around Springer's body. 'I would say to cut out the stitches around the eye in about a week to ten days, depending on how quickly the area heals up. The ear is a different matter. If it goes black, it has not taken due to lack of blood flow and will need to be removed. If it remains pink and you can feel it when you touch it, the repair has worked, and you can take the stitches out in about two to three weeks and not before. Whatever you do, don't leave any stitches in as they will go septic and if they get buried into the skin, you still may lose the ear.'

Springer nods his head.

'I will leave you with a bottle of laudanum – a mixture of opium and alcohol used to numb pain. It has a glass rod built into the lid; just swallow a few drops as required to ease the pain.' He unscrews the bottle and moves towards Springer. 'Now, open your mouth.'

Springer obliges and the doctor drips the dose to land on his tongue.

'Be careful with this, as it's powerful stuff and a small amount goes a long way.'

Springer smiles and nods at the doctor.

'I will come back and see you in a day or so, my boy. But for now, the best thing for you is rest, for your body has taken one hell of a beating.' With that the doctor picks up his bag and heads for the door.

Springer is still a bit disorientated, but as he collects his thoughts, he calls out after him. 'Thanks be to thee for all that you have done, and cheery bye.' But the physician is already out of the door and gone. Heavy on the doctor's mind is the fact he still has time to get down to the tavern and have a few drinks. After all, he also won a tidy sum, betting on Springer to win the fight. Never has the physician so swiftly walked across the meadows, through the park and along the path into the village. From the speed he is moving, you would think he was a man half his age.

Springer leans forward and faces the fire. He spits out the solution the doctor put in his mouth, but not because he could not do with the pain relief. He knows full well what laudanum can do. But he is expecting a visitor tonight and he cannot afford to miss them, so he will have to endure the pain for a while longer while he waits for his guest to arrive.

For now, he sets himself another task: to light the fire he built up and set ready for his homecoming, knowing he would be in a poor state upon his return. Picking up the matches he left on the mantle, he lights the paper and old clothing under the kindling in several places. He watches as the paper burns out fast, but it still holds a flame long enough to set the old clothing alight. This burns a little longer and in turn starts the kindling ablaze. Finally, the larger pieces of wood start to take on flames and the fire takes hold. He sits back in the best position he can find to reduce the pain and waits for the arrival of his friend.

As the room warms up and he starts to feel a little more comfortable, he relaxes back into the chair and recalls the fight in his mind. It hadn't gone on as long as he'd anticipated. He thinks of the noise from the excited crowd cheering the men on, and the sheer number of people who turned up to watch him fight in this historic battle. He reaches up and touches the area above his eye where the cut was stitched up by Cook. It's painful, but bearable. Then he touches the lower part of his ear. That really is painful and throbbing as if it has its own pulse.

He comes to the realisation he's lucky to have people like Cook ready to step up to the plate and help him in his time of need, and if Dan also manages to come through with his part of the plan, he can move on with his life and take back his freedom.

Then there is Victoria. What a prize she is. To come round from the fight and see her kneeling in front of him, holding his hand. That smile she shows when she is happy, and the sadness in her eyes when she sees him hurt. What a lady she is. What a prize. What a woman she would be for some lucky man, any man. Any man but that weasel, Lord Fitzgerald. The thought of HIM being with her knocks Springer's train of thought back into the present moment. He stretches out as best he can then settles back into his chair. The heat of the fire and the exhaustion from the fight along with the effects of the trace of laudanum have made him very tired, and it's not long before he cannot help but fall asleep where he sits.

He wakes suddenly, looks round but sees nothing. The fire is still burning away nicely, and nothing seems out of place. He wonders what woke him up so sharply, then he hears someone banging on the door. 'Come thee in,' he shouts. 'The door be open.'

The door opens and quick as a flash Dan steps through. 'I've been banging away for nearly five minutes, so I have!' He grabs Springer's hand and shakes it strongly. 'By 'eck, man, you made me feel proud, you did. That fight was something to behold!'

'Ease up then there, Dan, I be as sore as 'ell.'

'Oh, sorry, I did nar think.' Dan drops his hand and moves forward to take a closer look at Springer's wounds.

'Looks like you took a fair throw of a beating yourself to win that fight. But what a fight. I felt I was in there meself with you on that one.' Dan moves to the side of the chair to look at Springer's ear and pokes the stitched area.

'Ouch!' Springer yells.

Dan jumps back. 'Sorry about that. It looks nasty, but the stitches seem well sewn.'

'Slow down, Dan. Stop moving and speaking so fast. I'm too sore to keep up with thee. As for the stitches, it be your wife, Cook, who put them in, and I be right grateful she was there to 'elp when I be needin' it.'

Dan smiles. 'Well, she's had plenty of practice on me – stitching, setting a bone, even putting a joint or two back in when they have pulled out. She be a wondrous thing, my Cook.'

Springer nods in agreement. 'Now, how did ye fare with what I needed to be done?'

'Well, there is good news and bad news when it comes to that.' Dan burrows into one of his deep pockets and pulls out a black pouch. 'The watch and two rings did not have value and the offer on them was not worth accepting, so I kept hold of them. The jewels were a bit better– a poor-quality diamond, a reasonable ruby, and the multicoloured one was a black opal with all the colours in it. I got nine gold sovereigns. So, fourteen gold sovereigns in total at odds of six to one gave you eighty-four gold sovereigns.'

Springer nods again. 'Well, it be better than a poke in the eye with a stick.' He takes the bag and opens it. Taking out three gold coins, he passes them back to Dan. 'For the time and risk ye took for me.'

Dan reaches forward and closes Springer's hands back over the coins.

'No, my friend. I made good enough from my own poke on your pain. Me and Cook will have a grand time with the gains I made. You keep what you have earned the hard way.' He looks down at Springer's bag and coat by the fireplace. 'Besides, you will need it more than me, by the look of things. If you are to go, make it quick. While down the tavern I overheard Fitzgerald speaking to Henry. Between them, they made nearly £4500 on you and the share they got from the fair. Talking they were. Talking about you and the setting up for another fight in the very near future.'

'Hell will have froz over afore I fight again for them scallywags.'

'That it might be in your eyes, but they have other plans. For you have the potential to make them a lot more money and to ensure you're still around, they be sending a man to watch over you here tonight. Just in case you decide to do something they would not approve of.'

Springer gives a wry smile. 'I sort of expected as much from them. For that be how they see it with me – just a man to bleed for them.' There is bitterness in his voice. He leans down by the side of his chair and pulls out the pipe he had been working on earlier. 'I found this 'ere pipe on fireplace. Been working on it for a while now to clean it up. I thought with you being a pipe man an' all, that this be of use to thee.'

Dan's eyes light up as he sees it. 'It be a grand piece, Springer.' He takes it and cups the bowl in his hand. 'Like it I surely do. It even feels good to the hand.' He views the carving on the front before testing the draw through to the bowl. 'This be of fine work, Springer, and I thank thee greatly.'

Dan puts the pipe in his pocket and passes a piece of paper to Springer. It lists three names and addresses and a rough map to each location.

'If you are to leave here,' says Dan. 'You will need some safe places to hide up until you are healed and out of the area. They are three of my poaching contacts. Each of them for a small fee will hide you up for a day or so. I trust them true as I have used them many times in the past.'

'Many thanks, Dan. They may be of use if I be in need of a place to stay and rest up on my way from here.'

Dan shakes Springer's hand. 'Time I was gone. I wish thee well, my friend, and fair happiness wherever you go.' He heads to the door, opens it and looks around before stepping outside.

'Fair thee well, Dan. And many thanks for the kindness you done me.'

Dan nods at Springer then closes the door behind him as he disappears into the darkness.

Springer takes a deep breath, closes his eyes and breathes out slowly. He has a lot to think about. He picks up the pouch and places the three coins back inside. Taking out the watch, he unclips the clasp and allows it to spring open. 'One minute afore nine,' he comments to himself. Just as he has called it out, the park clock starts its build-up before striking the chimes.

'Still close to good time,' he mutters.

He has a big decision to make. When should he leave? Does he wait for his wounds to heal up for a day or so? Or should he leave and heal on the way? The question sits in his mind as he stands up to test how his body feels. His ribs hurt a bit, but getting to his feet is not too bad. He slowly moves over to the window and looks out into the darkness. The moon is but a tiny sliver in the sky, so there is very little light reflecting anywhere.

Just as he turns away, he sees an orange glow to the right, about thirty yards away. It grows brighter for a second before lowering and disappearing. He thinks for a second. Could that be someone smoking? If it was, then Dan was right. He is being watched already by one of Lord Fitzgerald's men.

Grabbing the iron poker by the fireplace, he decides to find out. He walks to the kitchen and quietly lifts the latch on the door leading to the outhouse, opening it just enough to get through. He quietly moves round to the corner of the cottage, allowing himself some time for his eyes to acclimatise to the light conditions. He waits for a while before peering round the side. To start with, he can hear and see nothing. Then in the distance there is a muffled cough followed by an orange glow. There is someone about, and being downwind, Springer can smell tobacco smoke.

Knowing the house and garden well, Springer can work out that this person is standing between the two holly bushes at the end of the garden path. He decides to approach this unwelcome guest by moving out in an arc and coming up behind whoever they are from the footpath side. Taking his time, he silently moves into position to ambush this night stalker. Against the skyline, he can make out the silhouette of a person with a hat. He moves closer, keeping as tight to bushes and small trees as he can without disturbing their branches. Being within ten feet, he prepares to strike out, but just as he is about to move, another sound travels through the air. Someone is walking down the path towards the house. Springer slowly lowers himself down, crouching low and holding his rib area to reduce the pressure and pain.

The footsteps get louder and louder, and Springer can see the outline of a person walking past just a few feet away.

'Come here,' a man shouts out as he grabs the person walking past. Springer instantly recognises the voice as Fletcher; his dulcet tones and gruff voice are unmistakeable.

The new arrival lets out a scream.

'So, who do we have here at this time of night?' Fletcher pulls down their hood. 'You!' he yells. 'You have cost us nothing but trouble, and a month's pay for Brannigan.'

'Let me go!' cries the woman. She twists and turns to get away, dropping a large case to try and break free with both arms, but Fletcher's grip is too strong.

'I'm gonna teach you a lesson, just like the one your little brothers are going to learn where they are going.'

'So, you were the one who took my baby brothers. I suppose it took a whole group of you to grab two little boys?' Victoria swings round and scratches down the side of Fletcher's face with her nails.

'Aah,' he cries out in pain. 'I will teach you to interfere, you little whore.' Gripping her tight around the throat with his left hand, he raises his club and goes to strike. As he swings down on Victoria, the stick stops mid-flight. Fletcher looks up to see what is going on and notices another hand holding the middle of the stick. He looks along the arm, to see whose hand it is, just in time to get the full force of Springer's fist – still holding the iron poker – impact him square in the face. *Crack.* The force of the blow is immense, splitting Fletcher's nose, cutting his eye and taking out some of his teeth all in one go. He falls through one of the holly bushes, taking part of a low-lying fence with him.

The impact also releases Victoria from his grip as he falls to the ground. Victoria herself was pulling so hard that upon release she has fallen in the opposite direction, over her own case and onto the floor as well. Fletcher rolls onto his hands and knees and from his waist pulls a large, wide-bladed knife. Getting to his feet, he pushes it out in front of him and waves it around in Springer's face. 'I'm gonna gut you like a fish!' he yells.

Springer has already moved forward, anticipating Fletcher's next move. The poker drives down out of the darkness and onto Fletcher's hand, shattering his fingers and releasing the knife from his grasp. The man yells with pain, cursing as he looks at his disjointed, broken fingers. With that hand out of action, he fumbles for his pepper pot pistol with his other hand. As he begins to raise it in Springer's direction, the next heavy blow from the poker finds its target, striking Fletcher round the side of the head with a chilling thud. This time, he hits the ground like a sack of potatoes. His body twitches a few times before going limp.

'There be no getting up from that, you turncoat,' Springer says as he can see blood already seeping from the side of his head. He throws the poker down beside Fletcher. 'You will never touch my Victoria again with that hand.' He turns and helps Victoria back to her feet, brushing her down to remove the dirt and pieces of grass and twigs that have attached themselves to her coat. She grabs him round the neck and holds on for dear life, tears flowing down her cheeks as she looks up to see Springer's face.

'Easy, lass. Let's get you inside. There be a warm fire to take off the chill of the night, and we can see if thee be injured.'

Victoria does not release her grip around his neck. 'Oh Springer, I hate them all,' she cries as he tries to turn her towards the cottage.

'You have to let go, me lady,' he asks quietly. 'For I cannot hold you, carry this here case and hold my ribs all at the same time.' She reluctantly lets go and turns to look at the man lying flat out in the flower bed.

She steps up and kicks him as hard as she can, just to make a point and to show that she is not afraid to stand her ground. 'That man is an animal,' she says before reaching down and picking up the poker.

As they enter the cottage, Springer drops her case on the floor and indicates that Victoria should sit. He turns and slowly lowers himself into his armchair beside her. There is a moment of silence before she reaches out and holds his hand in both hers and looks him in the eyes. The glow of the fire reflects in the tear tracks on her cheeks.

'Oh, Springer, I cannot stay here anymore! I have no love for this place or any of the people here. It's all just a front for that man, Lord Fitzgerald.'

Springer nods in agreement. 'I be seeing the same thing for a time now. They be a law unto themselves, and them that fight back pay a terrible price.'

Victoria is still trembling. 'They took Oliver and Edward away tonight on a charge of pickpocketing Brannigan. But it was a lie, a wicked lie. It was revenge for me getting Brannigan in trouble and walking out on Lord Fitzgerald at the fair. Father tried to get them back, but he could only get them to release the boys tomorrow, after a night spent in the magistrate's building. Just so he could appease his men and not lose face in front of them.'

Springer is raging inside. 'Them there youngerns would not be stealing, least not from him, I be sure of that. So they must be wanting to show control on your father and have a hold on thee.'

'Yes, I have seen it myself. Lord Fitzgerald keeps most people on edge to ensure their loyalty and compliance. He puts his will on others through fear, extortion and intimidation. Playing them off against each other while secretly making both sides think he is supporting them.' Still trembling, Victoria squeezes Springer's hand to ensure she has his attention. 'I have waited long enough for you to say it. But you're just too stubborn to tell me. The only person I have left here is you, Springer. So please tell me now…' She takes a deep breath. 'Do you feel the same way I do about you? Or would you sooner see me end my days at the hands of Lord Fitzgerald? For I need to know.'

Springer stares intently at Victoria. 'No woman has ever stirred my blood like you, Miss Victoria. But I could never give you such fineries that thee deserve. I am but a humble man, and my needs are simple. What could I possibly give to thee that could match what them there overs can gift you with money, status and position? All I have are these here hands to work with and my nature to stand for righteous and truth. Surely that is not enough for the likes of someone like you.'

She leans forward and kisses him gently on the lips, holding for a few seconds before moving back. 'You could tell me that you love me, and you would be by my side through good and bad. Promise to never hurt me and be there when I need you most, like you were tonight.'

Springer looks at her with reassuring eyes and an expression to match. 'There be not a day go by that I think not of you, Miss Victoria. And I will already love thee for the rest of my life, such is the impact you be havin' on me. But I must go from here tonight. More so now I've done what I've done to that there wrongun outside. For Lord Fitzgerald and your father, they have their plans for me and will be coming 'ard to find me now, you mark my words. Come the morrow, when they find Fletcher dead on the ground, I will be a hunted man with a price on my head.' He turns from her to look into the fire. 'I am not certain where I be going from here. I have a mind to head for a small farm holding in a valley I once used in a time of need. The views over the hillsides and river below damn near took my breath away. That is if it still exists, for it was many a year ago that I be there. But if it does, it be well out of the way and needin' a lot of work to put right again. Should I be able to get it with the small poke I now be in possession of, it would be a fine start for one such as me. But for you, what life is that for someone so fine as thee? You deserve much more than a simple homestead.'

Victoria just stares at him. 'That is all I needed to hear.' She leans forward and kisses him again. This time he responds with passion.

'As kind as you are to me, Springer, I am of a mind to leave this godforsaken place off my own back this very night. I have packed as little as I could – some clothes, money, jewellery to trade – and I will be departing with or without you once I leave this cottage. If you do not want me with you, I will find a way to reach my cousin in France and make a fresh start there. But I saw your bag packed when I was last here, and I felt you had feelings for me like I have for you. I hoped you would be of a mind that we could at least travel together away from here. I know there are risks, for I am not a child anymore. But a life as the woman of Lord Fitzgerald is a life not worth living to me. If I had a choice, I would far sooner try a life of challenges and hardship with a man I love than a life of luxury with nothing but misery and sadness for company.'

Springer thinks for a moment, then replies. 'Dear lass, as soon as they know I be gone, he will have people hunting high and low for me. He be a proud man and would not want to lose face. If you go with me, the risk I take will be a fatal one should them there men get their hands on me. And what he would put you through would make my fate a better choice. For thee, I would willingly give my life and more a hundred times over, but could you take what be coming your way if he finds you with me in the years that follow? For I be sure he would make you suffer each and every day that thee be living and I would no longer be around to protect thee.'

Victoria releases Springer's hand and fumbles around in her pocket. She pulls out of it a white handkerchief tied up at the top and places it in Springer's hand. 'This is the prize money chucked at you by HIM for a beating that knocked you senseless. You can take this and go find a place to hide on your own and hope he loses interest in finding you over time. Or you can use this money along with what Dan dropped off to you earlier and what I have with me, and we can find a place together and build a home of our own choosing, and a future that we both have a hand in making.' She glances at the window. 'You must decide as I need to leave soon, for I have only the night to walk as far away from here as possible before I am missed. And there will be precious little in the number of places a single woman can hold up while travelling without raising suspicion.'

Springer thinks on what Victoria has said. He wonders how she knows about Dan, then nods to himself as he realises it would have been Victoria working her charms on Cook in the kitchen earlier. He stands up and readjusts, feeling his ribs gently. Victoria stands too and looks into his eyes. He takes her gently in his arms and softly kisses her lips. She responds by clasping both his shoulders and holding him in a loving embrace.

'I would not have thee travelling alone, whether I love thee or not. But as I do, it looks like we best be going while there be time enough to go. For I have already arranged a place to stay two days' walk from here. Be it two people or one, it would not make a difference to them there folks. They are good people with a deep hatred for Lord Fitzgerald and all the wrong he stands for.' He thinks for a moment, takes a deep breath then speaks again. 'We must get the going now and be as far away from here as we be able afore light comes and Fletcher is found. With luck, we be long far gone enough by the morrow to be safe with friends before they catch up to us, as come they surely will.'

Springer picks up his bag and Victoria's case while Victoria takes his coat and opens the door. He grimaces a little with the pull on his ribs from the weight of her baggage. But he would never let Victoria know the extent of the injury; he is far too proud to have this beautiful woman making this journey with him, and no matter what the pain, it will be endured without complaint.

Outside, they can still see Fletcher's boots sprawled out on the side of the path. Springer drags him a little further from the track, throwing some branches over him from a nearby bush to cover the body a little more. Then, as a final check, he gives his boot a firm kick and watches to see if there is any response. With no movement, he collects their belongings and walks on, only turning once to look at the cottage he once lived in before it is out of sight.

They walk for the best part of the night, stopping only for short rest breaks or for Springer to adjust his grip on the bags and put his thick jacket around Victoria to stay off the night chill. They have only what little light the sliver of moon and stars are prepared to give up to guide their way forward. Through the woods and across the fields they travel. It is an eerie time, with only the odd hoot of an owl, call of a fox or the startled scurry of a bird or deer to break the silence of the still air.

For several hours they do not speak, both deep in thought over the events that led to them making this decision. Finally, Victoria turns to Springer. 'Do you have directions for where we are going?'

Springer stops and, putting the bags down on the ground, holds Victoria in his arms. 'Aye, lass. Up here in my head, safe that none can find the people who would help us. In an hour or so, we be at the village of Emmetsdale. There be a small farm on the left side of the village run by a friend I know well. Old Bob be his name, and he be a goodly man. On Mondays he hooks up a wagon and delivers cheese, butter, milk, eggs and meat from his farm to the local town of Earlchester. If luck be with us, he will have room to take us up yonder in his wagon and save a long step and a hop of walking. We can sleep right safe and quiet like in the wagon while he takes us on through the morning. Come midday, we will be near a place belonging to a friend of Dan's and for a small fee there be a place to eat, rest and for me to recover from my wounds.'

Victoria is trembling with the damp of the night, and he rubs her hands and shoulders to warm her up. 'I be glad thee is with such a man as me; it's been many a year since I have felt wanted or needed by anyone, and you be the first lady that I be feeling this way for in a long time.'

Victoria smiles at Springer then tucks her head into his shoulder. 'Why, Mr Springer,' she says in a posh accent, 'am I to presume I am the first woman to seek your affections?' She leans back so as to see his face as he responds.

Springer pauses for a moment, then looks deep into her eyes. 'You be the first and, God willing, the only and the last lady that I be allowing to seek my affections in many a year. You have set me on a road I cannot turn from. Now until my end it be thee and thee alone for me.'

She leans forward and kisses him gently on the lips. 'Well then, let's hope I don't disappoint! For I may not be the angel you think I am.'

Springer looks at her in awe. 'That, my dear, you could never do. For even now you're beyond what I be deserving for what I have done in my life, angel or not.'

He reaches down and picks up the bags. 'Come, lass, let's be finishing off this next bit of our journey. For come the morning a whole heap of people will be wearing themselves out trying to find where we be.'

Victoria tucks her hand under Springer's arm. 'I guess you could call this our first date together, though I don't much like the distance we have to walk on it.'

Springer chuckles. 'Many an age ago, when I were but a littlun, my ma said that when I be finding a woman of my own, my life would be one big journey. How right she be.'

The darkness slowly turns to the light of dawn as the rays of a fine sunrise slowly reach out and spread warmth and glow through the branches of the trees over what has been a chilly night. The mist is thinning and rolling away on the open fields, while in the thickly wooded areas and ditch lines, it has its final last valiant stand before its inevitable defeat as the bright warming sunlight cuts through its defences and vanquishes the mist for another day.

Springer and Victoria arrive at their destination and follow a farm track down from the main road. They see old Bob hitching up the wagon to a pair of horses. His boy is rolling out the last of the milk churns, rotating it round on its base to reach the loading point at the back of the wagon.

'Allow me to give thee a hand, young man,' says Springer as he arrives on the scene, putting down his bags and picking up the churn. Even with his injuries he lifts the container and places it in the back of the wagon with ease.

Old Bob comes round from the front of the wagon. 'That there was one mean fight you put up last night, Springer. Well worth the trip to see. My boy and I watched it all from the hillside a fair way back. Thought you were going to lose for a spell, but what a comeback! You were right on how the fight was going to go. I'm glad I listened to you, as I had a pound on you to win and walked away with six.' Bob laughs. 'Wife is in the house now writing out a list of clothing, pots and heaven knows what else she wants me to get when I head off into town shortly. Seems I will not be hanging on to my winnings for long in this household.'

'I be glad you got something from it. Good folk like you deserve a little extra when it be there for the taking. For me, it eases the pain to know you took from them that have a lot.'

Old Bob turns to Victoria and tilts his cap. 'I'm sorry, my dear, where are my manners?' He looks at her for a second then realises who she is. 'Why, Miss Victoria, what are you doing here at this time of the morning?'

Springer cuts in. 'Victoria and I have seen fit to leave this place on the quiet like, and I was hoping we could hitch a ride together to where you be going with your cart this morning.'

'That will be no problem; there be plenty of room inside the wagon. But you have been walking all night, looking at your shoes and the bottom of Miss Victoria's dress. Come inside first and have some bread and cheese and rest your feet. You be safe now you are here, and the wife would like to see you and we can talk about this great escape of yours.'

They head over to Bob's house for breakfast, and Springer lets out a stark warning. 'You know that by mid-morning they will have people looking for us high and low. No stone will be left unturned as they seek to take back them that they think they own.'

'Well, what do you say to that, young Robert?' Bob says to his son as he rubs his hand over his head.

Robert looks up, down, then all around. 'I see no people here, Pa. Must have been like one of them mirages the teacher was talking about in class last week.'

Springer smiles in acknowledgement of the lad's words. 'Thank thee I do, young Robert. You are as goodlier man as your father.'

Bob's wife Emily opens the door as they approach. She has been watching from the window that overlooks the yard and as Springer enters the room, she greets him with spread arms and gives him a hug. 'Hello, my dear,' she says before inspecting the wounds to his eye and ear. 'That looks nasty. I would say you poor thing, but I have a feeling the other man faired far worse than you.'

'That be true, Emily. But before we talk about that, I would like you to meet Victoria. She be dear to me and could do with some warmth from your fire. For it be a long walk and a cold night's travelling to get here.'

Emily approaches Victoria, again with her arms wide open in a warm hug. 'Welcome, my dear. A friend of Springer's is always welcome here.'

It's not the kind of welcome Victoria is used to from another woman, but it is comforting to her and makes her feel at ease. 'Thank you kindly. It is nice to meet you and your family.'

'Now sit yourself down by the fire and warm yourself, and I will fetch some bread and cheese.' She guides Victoria to a rocking chair. 'It's the best spot in the house for warmth in the morning, my dear.'

'I don't get a greeting like that from the wife when I come through the door anymore,' moans Bob as he takes a seat.

'That's because you always want more, and your hands have a mind of their own,' Emily yells as she comes back through carrying a tray with two loaves of bread, butter, cheese and preserves. She slides it all onto the table then turns to Victoria. 'Men only have one thing on their mind, and it is down to us women to nip that kind of thinking in the bud.' She smiles and winks at Victoria then turns and disappears into the next room, returning swiftly with a pitcher of milk, some cutlery and a handful of assorted-sized plates. 'Pour the milk, Robert, that's a good lad,' she says as she passes the plates around the table. 'I should be angry with you for fighting, young Springer, but I now get to have a lot of needed items in the house with the three pounds Bob won betting on you.'

'Three pounds? I thought it be s—' Springer stops in mid-sentence, but the damage is already done.

Bob's head sinks into his hands.

Emily swiftly turns to face him. With a dagger-like stare, she quietly and politely asks Bob, 'And how much did we win on the back of poor Springer's injuries, my dear?'

There is a total quietness to the room. Victoria and Springer smirk at each other across the table, before they both look down in an attempt not to give the situation away. Bob's head slowly rises, and he shifts uneasily in his seat.

He swallows. 'Well, my dear...' As he is speaking he cannot help but notice Emily slowly raising a large wooden spoon from the table and pointing it in his direction.

Emily's gaze turns to poor Robert. Still with cup and pitcher in hand, he tries to pour the liquid without raising his head towards his mum. 'Robert,' Emily utters in a tone that shakes Robert clean down to his boots. 'And how much did Father win, may I ask?'

He stops pouring and places the cup and pitcher down. 'I'm not sure, Ma. I did not see Father bet on the fight. Nor did I see him collect his winnings after it was over.'

The spoon in Emily's hand continues to slowly rise and move towards Bob. While still looking down, Springer is the first to break out with a smile as he tries with all his might not to laugh. Meanwhile, Victoria is looking at Springer and gripping the arms of the rocking chair tightly with both hands. She also is barely hanging on to just a smile.

'Now Emily, put that spoon down,' says Bob. But the spoon continues to move ever closer. 'Dear woman, I am the man of this house and I wear the trousers here. Now put down that spoon at once.' But the spoon continues on its way. 'I demand it!' he says in a higher-pitched voice, pointing his shaking finger back at Emily.

Both Springer and Victoria are now trembling as they desperately hold their laughter in as best they can. Robert is starting to break into laughter and sits down and holds his head in his hands to try and hide it from his mum.

Whack, the spoon has whipped round and smacked Bob on the back of his pointing hand. Bob yells out and jumps back, taking his chair with him. Springer, Victoria and Robert burst into heavy laughter, while Bob is left holding his wounded hand and rubbing it to ease the sting.

'Hand over the rest before I set the dogs on you,' Emily demands in a growl, still pointing the spoon at her husband in a menacing manner. She starts to rotate the spoon again. The three others are flat out laughing. Springer has tears in his eyes and is holding his ribs as they hurt so much. He watches Bob struggle to put his sore hand into his pocket and drop two more pound notes and a few coins onto the table.

They are willingly collected by Emily, who puts down the spoon, walks over to the sideboard and adds some more items to an existing list. Sitting back at the table, she smiles at her husband. 'It would seem we can afford those additional things after all, my dear. I have found some savings I did not know we had.' She leans forward, grabs Bob's cheeks and gives them both a jiggle. 'That's my man,' she says.

All at the table are now laughing, including Bob, who has resigned himself to the fact that no matter what he may think, Emily wears the trousers in the household.

As they eat the bread and cheese and drink the fresh milk, they talk about the farm and the fine produce they sell from such a modest smallholding. The conversation inevitably turns to Springer and Victoria and why they are heading away from their friends and family. The couple explain many of the things they have seen, and Lord Fitzgerald's intentions to make Victoria his wife, much to the disgust of Emily.

Emily says, 'Seems like you stepped up just in time to stop a tragedy, young Springer. For Victoria is a fine woman and you two make a good couple.'

'Here, here,' says Bob, tapping the table with his cup of milk.

Springer looks at Victoria with a smile. 'I think ye be as right as can be said, for I be happier now in this moment than at any time I can recall.'

'Well, if we are to keep you two ahead of the game, I think it is about time we be on our way,' Bob says before turning to his son. 'Robert, be a good lad and finish the horses ready to go.'

Robert instantly gets up. 'Yes, Father,' he replies before heading outside.

'Now the boy has gone, I will tell you something you do not know,' says Bob. 'Lord Fitzgerald's so-called dealings and climb up the status ladder are not all they are made up to be. The man's past is as dark as pitch and as cold as ice. For I knew him when he was a younger man. His father was big in the whale oil industry, at one stage owning two score of boats. These boats were only in port for as little as three months every couple of years. Just enough time to unload the oil, repair and restock and pressgang at least half the ship's crew from the surrounding towns and villages. It's no easy life being at sea and when the crew got paid their share of the oil price, some who lived on their own would be like kings for a few months, be penniless at time's end and be ready to go back to sea. Others with families in the port would have little choice than to go back to sea to keep their families fed. They were exploited by the shipping company on rent, supplies and necessaries needed to survive.'

'Oh my!' says Victoria, her eyebrows raised.

Bob looks at her shocked expression and continues. 'You see, all supplies in a whaling port can only be bought with whaling tokens. So if you live in the area, you had to buy the whaling tokens with your share of the purse, in order to purchase food, drink, clothes, supplies and pay rent. And whaling tokens were up to five times more expensive than buying the same items with cash away from the whaling ports. You could never bring goods back into port as the protection were always patrolling and would confiscate any goods brought into the area.' Bob pauses to drink some milk and looks at Emily. 'The smart ones took their money and that very first night would try to get as far away as they could from the port. With the protection not knowing who was who, many made it into the surrounding towns and away from those employed to keep them trapped in the ports.'

'The protection sounds very like Lord Fitzgerald's men,' says Victoria, her lips pressed tightly together.

'That's as maybe,' says Bob. 'These men are ruthless and vicious, and if they caught you trying to abscond, they were entitled to half what you were carrying. So many got away that the ships were delayed while looking for replacement crew. The old Lord Fitzgerald came up with a plan. Every time a ship came in, the oil was unloaded and graded, and the value of the cargo would be confirmed. They would set up table in the local whaling office, line the crew up and pay them in front of all who was there. The owners would have a large amount of protection present, explaining they were there to ensure safety due to so much money changing hands. But the real reason was to ensure their so-called protection could look at all the faces of the people being paid. Then for the next week or so these groups of protection would patrol just outside the port, and if any of the crew were caught making a run for it, they would apprehend them, take their money and leave them to borrow from the whaling industry to survive. That way, they would be forced to crew a ship for another couple of years to pay off a never-ending debt.'

'That there be mighty bad for them that be family men,' says Springer.

Bob takes a deep breath. 'You see, a man who had been at sea whaling for a year or so knows what to do, and mores to right he knows how to survive, so he is worth his salt. Whereas a man who has never known the harshness of whaling is more likely to lose the will to live and do something stupid. This leaves the ship one less – take that several times over and it is harder work for those left, and they be at sea longer to fill the barrels needed before they come home.'

Victoria shakes her head. 'That's terrible! How could they treat people and families so badly?'

'That is not the worst of it,' Bob continues. 'The old Lord Fitzgerald was a brute of a man. As his family grew, he would send his sons and daughters to the finest places for education all over the world – Vienna, Paris, Italy. The cost was not an issue as he had made an obscene amount of money from selling whale oil. Oil was in huge demand for lighting everything from streetlights to lanterns in houses and factories. By the age of fifty-five, he had seven sons and five daughters alive – having lost two at a young age to consumption – and was on his third wife.'

'Third wife?' says Victoria.

'Aye, the first wife died in childbirth. The second, failing to produce any more children after the first three, apparently had an accident and broke her neck falling down the stairs drunk in the family house. Two weeks later he remarried and five months after that she had their first child. So you can make of that what you will.'

'It's certainly an unhappy tale,' says Emily with a frown. Bob takes another drink from his cup before continuing with the story.

'But one day his world was to be turned upside down, and all his harsh ways would come back to haunt him. It started with his oldest son, Darius. He had just returned from another scrape in

Paris, pleasuring himself in the fun houses on the entertainment scene, if you know what I mean. Not for the first time, a woman had become pregnant, and another influential family was up in arms over the condition of their daughter, demanding satisfaction. This meant yet again a lump sum of money was required to pay them off, or another unfortunate accident for the woman involved. This time though, he decided to do something about it and confronted his son. To cool his blood, Lord Fitzgerald decided it was time to send his oldest son on a whaling trip for two years. As you can imagine, this did not go down well with Darius, who in his time away had become somewhat of a dandy. The thought of him doing anything outside of whatever he wanted was unacceptable in his eyes. Several furious rows erupted over the course of the next couple of days and when one of Lord Fitzgerald's ships returned to port, Darius hatched a plan of his own to resolve his problems.

'The ship was unloaded of all its barrels as usual, and the quality of the oil was inspected. A price for the cargo was decided in the assay's office and the following day the crew were paid, as was the custom. However, that night a terrible thing happened, and when morning came, Lord Fitzgerald and his wife – along with his two youngest daughters and youngest son – were found with their throats slit in bed. It was concluded they had been murdered while they slept, by four disgruntled crew members off the ship that had just docked. They had extracted their revenge for being pressganged into service on the whaling ship by killing him and some of his family.'

Bob looked at Victoria's shocked face. 'This just gets worse!' she says.

'By a strange coincidence, some of the protection men caught the four men escaping the port, still carrying the bloodstained knives. The trial lasted all of one hour and all four men were hung before noon that very day, still pleading their innocence right up until their last gasps.'

Victoria's mouth hangs open as she looks at Springer, then back at Bob.

'I know,' he says. 'It's not good. It didn't take long for Darius to take his father's title, and his rule over the people around became far worse. As for his siblings, the three daughters were allegedly sent to France to continue their education, some say they never survived the boat crossing. Others say they were sold to some of his associates in the Parisian prostitution racket. Whatever the truth, they were never seen again.

'His five younger brothers did not fare any better. Over a period of eight months, each one was sent on a whaling ship under the advisement of the new Lord Fitzgerald to oversee the collection of barrels of oil. For whatever reason, none were ever to return to the shores of England alive.

'Some say it was the curse of whaling that had killed off this family, but I tend to believe Darius was in fear that one of his brothers or sisters would end up doing to him what he had done to their father. Three years later, with the finding of black mineral oil on land and its cheaper process of extracting lamping oil, Lord Fitzgerald sold off the entire whaling fleet, port and all items connected to its running to the East India Trading Company for a princely sum of money. Then several years ago he ended up in the village of Pippinsford, where he now intends to take over the entire trade for the area and rebuild an empire in fruit, fabric and other commodities on the backs of others, just like before.'

Bob stares into his empty cup as Emily leans forward and rubs his shoulder gently.

'How do thee know that the Lord Fitzgerald in Pippinsford is the same man as the one who be the murderer of his own kin?' asks Springer.

Bob rolls up his sleeve and shows Springer and Victoria a tattoo of a whale and above it a ship with the words *Not Forgotten* inked over it.

'I was on the ship that returned, having been pressganged from a farm outside of the port two years and three months prior, at the age of fourteen. I was also with the four men when they were caught that night trying to leave the port. You see, I was a bit behind them four as I was carrying Emily, who had twisted her ankle in the dark. Emily's father, William – or Bullseye to them that knew him as the best harpooner on the ship – had taken me under his wing while at sea, and it was only thanks to him that I made it back alive. For life at sea on a whaling ship is harsh, to say the least.' He turns to look at Emily and gives her a grim smile.

'The six of us had planned to run on the first night. Emily was the only family any of us had left alive, so we collected her from the people she had been staying with while her father was at sea. We knew the protectors were watching everyone, as they always were when a fresh ship arrived. But like everyone else who tried, we took our chances and made it out into the surrounding woods.' Bob lowers his gaze, and stares at the table.

'They were out in force that night,' he says sadly. 'Being the youngest, I was to stay a bit behind with Emily, in case the others had to deal with any protectors we could not get round. Bullseye did not want his daughter to see anything that might go on. So, when she tripped over a root and twisted her ankle, we fell behind. We heard footsteps and people talking, so we took cover tight to some gorse bushes and hid in fear. That's when we heard them being attacked. They were only twenty or thirty yards ahead and they had been ambushed by around fifteen protectors. We watched as Bullseye dropped two or three people before they overwhelmed him and pinned him to the ground. All four of them were clamped in irons and the protectors pushed them towards us on their way back to the port.

'Two of the protectors were talking as they reached the path beside Emily and myself. I remember the words even now. They were not happy that Bullseye was amongst the four caught, as they knew their boss wanted him back on the ship harpooning whales when it next went to sea. But they needed some people to take the blame for what had gone on earlier, and these four would fit the requirement perfectly.

'Bullseye himself had seen us watching from the bushes, and as he passed he dropped a pouch from his pocket and flicked it with his foot in our direction. He whispered, "Take it and go. You can do no good for me now." We waited five or six minutes for it to go quiet before Emily reached out and grabbed the pouch. When we opened it, it was all the money he had been paid for the voyage. Being the number one harpooner on the ship and top whale killer, it was a princely sum.

'We knew if we went back to the port to find out about her father, we would be rounded up, so we continued with the plan and went on our way. With the protectors escorting Emily's father and the others in, we had a clear walk to a neighbouring village and from there we headed to another place inland and away from any port.

'Our thoughts were that he would be sent back to sea when the ship left, so we would not see him for a year or more. We made a decision to invest his money and mine in a farm. That way, when he next returned, he would have a place to call his own.'

Bob looks at Emily, who now has tears streaming from her eyes.

'By chance, we came across this farm when we were travelling. It was run down and needing a lot of work. The old woman who lived here, being too old to work the land anymore, wanted to move to the city with her daughter. We found it to be available to purchase, bought it on the spot and renamed it Bull's Farm in honour of Emily's father.' He cleared his throat. 'Thought he would be proud of it when he returned from whaling and would have a proper place to escape to. We only found out about his and our friends' fate three months after they had murdered them for a crime we knew they did not commit. Even now we cannot visit his grave as no one knows where they buried the four men. Some have even said they were put back on the ship and cast out to sea so they would never be found.' He stops to take a deep breath.

'Ever since then, we have lived here. Two years after our arrival, Emily and I married and now we have a wonderful boy. The farm has grown, but we never forget how it came to be and the price that was paid by Bullseye and the others to get us here. Out the back, past the trees, I have a small fenced-off plot with four headstones. It is the only place you can read their names. Although their bodies are not there, it is the least we can do to remember that night and honour our friends and my Emily's father's sacrifice.'

Emily speaks up for the first time. 'Imagine our shock a few years back when we saw that bastard Lord Fitzgerald in the village. Since then, we have watched him slowly destroy all that is around him for his own gain at the expense of others like before. Soon, though, he will slip up. And when he does, I will be there. I will wait my time until I get that evil man, for we will have our revenge.'

Victoria holds Emily's hand as she can see that the telling of the story has deeply affected her. 'How do you know this is the same man? The man who I was intended to marry?' she asks.

'The men who set up, framed, then murdered my father and our friends are the same ones that killed old man Fitzgerald and his family. They were some of the protection men and they still work for the man who masterminded the whole show, the new Lord Fitzgerald. You may know them: Brannigan, Sykes, Fletcher, Cribbs and that new one Crossy. Cold-blooded murderers the lot of them, and now they are here doing the same thing again. Enforcing Lord Fitzgerald's will on others, murdering, removing people from their homes. But this time it's not whale oil or just the pricing of goods. It's cotton mills, factories, fruit farming, mining tin and coal with cheap and free labour taken from the surrounding lands. Also, the buying and selling of all the new houses and shops in the village. How I hate him and all he stands for.'

Springer looks at Victoria and waits for a sign. She nods at him and so he begins to speak. 'Well, there, Emily, I might be having news that thee would be glad to hear. Last night, one of them there men – Fletcher be his name – put his hands on my Victoria in a way not to be done. I took offence and set to him with a vengeance.'

'Did you hurt him bad?' Emily asks.

'That I did. The last we be seeing of him he was down in a flower bed not moving and that be before the cold of the night came a knocking. By now he be as stiff as a board and not for this world.'

Emily does not hesitate. She just grabs Springer in a fierce hug and gives him a kiss on the cheek. 'Thank you. I can only hope he suffered badly.' She turns to Victoria. 'You have a good one there, my dear. Enjoy all life has to offer you both.'

Victoria smiles. It seems this is not the first time she has been told that. Inside, she feels leaving the village has been the right thing to do. Going forward with Springer will be much better than going back to HIM.

The front door opens, and Robert pokes his head inside. 'Pa, the horses are ready.'

The four of them get up and Springer and Victoria thank Emily for her hospitality. Emily gives Bob the list of items she wants him to purchase in town and the money to buy them with. She holds him tight and kisses him a fond goodbye. With a grin and a wink at Springer, Bob takes his chance and grabs a handful of Emily's bottom.

Springer bursts into laughter as Emily grabs the offending hand and brushes it away, clipping the back of Bob's head with her other hand. Emily points at Bob and shakes her head before she turns away with a small but cheeky smile that Bob cannot see.

By the time Bob arrives at the wagon, Springer and Victoria have climbed in the back and are tucked out of sight of any prying eyes. He climbs up on the front of the cart and takes the reins from his son. 'Thank you, boy. Now look after your mother while I be gone, and I will bring you something back from town.'

The rickety old cart heads off up the track from the farm to join the main road at the top of the lane.

CHAPTER 8

Victoria Gone

Back at the estate Victoria once called home, Henry awakes early. It's been a restless night with the worry of his sons being held in the magistrate's cells. And the decision to marry his beloved daughter to Lord Fitzgerald does not sit well with him. He slides out of the bed quietly to ensure he does not wake Mary, and dresses himself in the room adjacent. He still has a lot on his mind and once clothed he heads straight down the elegant stairs and into the dining room. As he walks in, Nancy is setting the table for breakfast. 'Morning, sir,' she says with a small curtsy.

'Yes, yes, good morning to you as well, Nancy.' Henry looks around the room, then peers into every doorway leading off the dining room. 'Have you seen Victoria this morning?' he asks. 'She is usually the first to be up.'

'No, sir, Miss Victoria has not come down yet.'

'When she does, please let her know I am looking for her and to find me at once.' Henry walks around the room as fast as he walked in. His mind is a blur and his words do not seem to make sense. He appears not to know what direction to go in, then decides to head through to the kitchen, leaving Nancy to ponder where to tell Victoria to find Henry as he did not say where he was going. She watches as he slaps the side of his leg before leaving the room, then continues to set the table ready for the family breakfast.

'Morning, Cook,' Henry says as he briskly walks through the kitchen. Cook looks up from kneading the bread, but before she has time to speak, he has opened the door to the garden and is calling his dogs. 'Zeus, Apollo, come,' he says to the two Great Danes. Instantly, they are up from their beds and heading for their master at the door. They run out into the open space, matching each other stride for stride as they bound down the gravel path.

Henry can see in the distance that people are deconstructing the tents and side stalls that were so heavily used the day before. Yesterday's entertainment went down well with the locals, and all the stalls and rides made a tidy profit on the side. It also had the added benefit of putting himself in a good light with the local community as well as his employer.

The fight had also paid off handsomely for Lord Fitzgerald and himself, while also putting him in a favourable position with him. But he must resolve his daughter Victoria's attitude towards his employer. She needs to understand that sometimes you have to sacrifice for the better good. In this case, she must comply with Lord Fitzgerald's needs and demands so Henry can look good and continue to have Fitzgerald's good graces for the benefit of the whole family.

As for his two sons, it is not for Victoria to question his decision to leave the boys in the hands of his employer to be disciplined. They were potentially out when they should not have been and due to that they saw something that was not to be seen. He sees no problem with putting the wind up his children to prevent something worse happening to them; after all, he is the man of the house, not Victoria.

Since finding out about Lord Fitzgerald's personal interest in Victoria, he has convinced himself the matching of his daughter with Lord Fitzgerald will not be all that bad for her. It will also secure his future and position within the Fitzgerald empire. She may not find true love with this man, but financially she will be secure, and in society she will be in a prominent position and that should be more than enough. Maybe love can come at a later date along with children. For that alone would keep her entertained and busy, or so he tries to convince himself.

Henry must also see how severe Springer's injuries are, for Lord Fitzgerald wants to put on another fight in a little under three weeks – this time in the garden of his own estate, with the aim to make more money from a selection of high-profile guests he will invite down from London for a private party and weekend of entertainment.

Although it has only been one night since the fight, Henry decides his first point of call should be Springer. He'd have a look at his injuries and assess how much time he needs to recover. In his mind, he has already decided that three days' rest should be enough before he will expect Springer back at work supervising his affairs on the estate. But if his ribs are cracked – or worse, broken – it may be three or four weeks before he is ready for another fight. Yes, Henry had better check out his prize fighter for himself.

Changing direction and making a beeline for Springer's little cottage, he walks across the meadow at pace. Zeus and Apollo notice his variation in course and tear through the undergrowth towards him. Both dogs are again matching each other stride for stride, each attempting to play-bite the other's leg. With the length of each bound being near to eight feet, it takes the dogs seconds to cover the open ground, overtake their master and blast into the distance. Each dog is not prepared to give way to the other; wherever one goes, the other is always close by as if attached by an invisible cord that binds them to within feet of each other.

By the time Henry reaches the house, the dogs have long since arrived and are busying themselves around the perimeter, sniffing and digging at anything of interest.

He knocks on the door, waits a short while, then raps on the door a little harder, calling out at the same time. With no reply, he opens the door and enters the cottage, calling Springer's name. The kitchen and fireplace area are empty, and the curtains are still drawn, making the room very dark. The fire has long since burned itself out, leaving the hearth cold to the touch and the room with a chill in it.

Before climbing the stairs to check out the bedroom, Henry calls out again in hope of a response. With nothing forthcoming he ascends the steps to the rooms above and looks around. The bed is made up and there is no sign of Springer in either room. Returning downstairs he wonders where on earth Springer could be. As he turns to leave, he clips something heavy on the floor.

Bending down to investigate, Henry picks up a fire poker. He thinks nothing more of it and goes to put it back in the slot by the fireplace. It's only then, as he reaches forward to place down the item, that he notices the red staining on the end. He moves to the kitchen to take a closer inspection in better light and realises that the red staining is dried blood.

'What on earth has gone on here?' he wonders to himself as he places the poker on the kitchen table. He's so intrigued by the poker he doesn't hear his dogs barking outside. But as his attention shifts, the barking of the dogs becomes more noticeable, and he turns and exits the house to investigate.

Both dogs are about twenty yards up the path, barking at what looks like a raised flower bed.

'Zeus and Apollo, come here, boys,' he calls. The dogs turn and approach their master, opening up the area for Henry to see the ground. On the path he notices nothing out of the ordinary, but looking further back into the garden itself, loosely covered in a few branches, he can see a pair of boots pointing skywards. As he gets closer, he sees Fletcher lying on his back, facing the sky with his eyes wide open.

'Oh my God,' he says, as he leans forward and touches the man's stone-cold cheek. There is no need to check for signs of life. Henry can see by the amount of blood on the floor and the condition of the body that this man has long since passed away.

Henry knows Lord Fitzgerald asked Fletcher to keep an eye on Springer's house until the morning in case their prize fighter decided to abscond. Now, putting his thoughts together, it is clear Lord Fitzgerald's fears were well-founded. Henry deduces that Springer must have bushwhacked Fletcher with the poker and absconded during the hours of darkness.

A feeling of dread comes over Henry as he realises Lord Fitzgerald will not be impressed at the loss of his new moneymaking fighter, nor the death of one of his valued henchmen. He turns and rushes back across the meadow, calling out as he goes. 'Help. Help! There has been murder here!' The dogs rush past him and bound towards the house, still challenging each other as they go.

As he reaches the grounds of his estate, the first to hear his calls for help are three of his gardeners. They rush over to assist, and Henry explains what he has just seen. He sends one to get the local magistrate, another to cover the body with a sheet and stay with it until the magistrate arrives. The third, he sends to Lord Fitzgerald to inform him what has happened.

He rushes back to the house and calls to his wife and family. Mary, Edith and Rebecca come to the top of the stairs, wondering what all the commotion is. He looks for his sons, then remembers the boys are in the care of Lord Fitzgerald at the magistrate's office. But where is Victoria?

He rushes up the stairs past his wife and Edith and bursts into Victoria's room, calling out her name. She is nowhere to be seen and the bed has not been slept in. Panic sets in and he looks around her room and the adjacent changing room. Mother and Edith arrive just as Henry notices a letter addressed to him leaning up against a perfume bottle on the dressing table. He stops in his tracks and stares at it. Countless thoughts go through his head as he slowly makes his way over to the small wooden table and reaches out a hand. Inside the envelope is a folded sheet of paper. He flips it open and starts to read its contents.

Dear Papa,

I cannot in good faith stay here anymore after being treated the way I have. It's terrible to see the amount of control Lord Fitzgerald has over you and Mother these days. For you to think that man would be an ideal suitor to be my husband does not fill me with encouragement. I do not want the rest of my life to be an endless time of misery and despair being owned by that hated man.

I can only imagine the fear on Oliver's and Edward's faces as they were being escorted away under that man's instructions, and the thought that you left them incarcerated for a crime you know they did not commit will stay with me forever. They idolised you, Papa, and you did nothing to protect or defend your own children from the actions of that evil man. To me and my way of thinking, this is unforgivable and beyond disappointing. They are your own flesh and blood and deserved better, being only children.

I love you all most dearly and do not wish to hurt you in any way, but I have decided to make my own way in life and be a woman of my own choosing before Lord Fitzgerald has a chance to take it away from me. Fear not for my safety for I am sure I will be in good hands wherever I go.

My love always,
Victoria.

He lowers the letter from view. There is great sadness in his face as he wonders how could it have come to this? That his own daughter would choose to run away rather than follow his wishes. How could she betray him this way, for he only wished her a secure and safe future.

'What is it?' asks Mary. 'What does it say?'

Henry passes the letter to his wife. As she takes it from his hand and starts to read, Edith and Rebecca are either side of her and read it at the same time.

Henry is motionless, as if frozen to the spot. He closes his eyes and shakes his head in disbelief, then looks back at his wife.

'We need to find our daughter,' she says. 'Before anything happens to her and we lose favour with him.'

Rebecca has also finished reading the letter and her eyes fill up as she starts to cry. 'Control yourself, my dear, and get a grip,' says Mother. 'That is not going to help the situation.'

'Edith, take your sister to her room and comfort her while I discuss this letter with your father. We will talk about this shortly.'

Edith wraps her arms around Rebecca and ushers her away from the top of the stairs and back to her bedroom. 'Come,' she says, 'let us leave Father and Mother to their own counsel. They will get our sister back to us.'

'But it's our sister Victoria! She has left us!' Rebecca says in disbelief.

'Yes, I know, my dear sister, but I am sure Father will be able to resolve this. Just let them worry about it and find a solution. They are older and much wiser than us.'

'I blame you for this,' Mary says. 'You gave that girl far too much freedom, and now look what she has done to us. All that planning and setting up for our future and now just look what has happened. How are you going to explain this to Lord Fitzgerald? He will not take kindly to us losing his bride-to-be.' She crosses her arms and lets out a big huff. 'If I was him, I would think you incompetent, and that doesn't sit well as you're the person he expects to run his affairs in his absence.'

Henry looks at his wife. He takes the note from her hand and crushes it into a ball, throwing it in the direction of a nearby empty vase. 'That's typical of you—'

Henry interrupts her. 'Why don't you shut up, woman, and let me think? I know what is at stake here, and I also know how much you have manipulated the situation to better yourself at the cost of our daughter.'

Mary opens her mouth to speak but realises this may not be the time to push her luck and answer him back.

Henry continues, 'Victoria cannot have gone far. I'm sure if we send out riders this morning, we can find her today before people even know she is missing. There are not that many roads out of here and she has nowhere to go! What I am more worried about is the fact that Springer has betrayed my trust and absconded as well, leaving the body of Fletcher dead on my land.'

'Springer gone? Fletcher dead?' she repeats back to Henry. 'Could this get any worse?'

Henry is deep in thought when he hears a noise coming from outside. As he listens, it gets louder. Soon he can make out the sound of cantering horses coming up the stone chip driveway. Without even looking up, he knows who it is and turns to his wife. 'He is here. Say nothing and let me do the talking.'

Mary reacts instantly. 'I will do nothing of the sort.'

'For God's sake, woman, for once in your life, do what I say before you disappear the same as all the other people in this village do. I am tired of your scheming and planning. At this moment, I am three of my children down, so do not test me, for I am not in the mood for it.'

It is one of the few times Henry has enforced his will on Mary and she knows when it happens that it is best to be seen and not heard.

The horses come to a stop and within a few seconds the front doors burst open. Lord Fitzgerald leads the way through, flanked by Brannigan and Sykes. Behind them is Crossy, Cribbs and a dozen or so other men. 'Where is the body of Fletcher?' bellows Lord Fitzgerald.

'In the flower bed by Springer's cottage,' Henry replies. 'I found him lying there this morning when I went to check on Springer's injuries.'

'That man has been with me nearly twenty years and saved my life on more than one occasion. Who would have the audacity to do something like that to one of my enforcers?' He cracks his riding crop on the side of his leg.

'I found a fire poker on the floor of Springer's house with what looks like blood on the end of it,' Henry replies.

'And pray, may I ask what the dog Springer says about its presence in his dwelling?'

Henry's gaze drops to the floor. 'I'm sorry to say he was nowhere to be seen. I believe he may have absconded in the night.'

'What? You mean to say you have lost me my prize fighting asset as well?'

Mary improvises and burst into tears. 'That's not all, sir. Our beloved Victoria is missing as well. We are beginning to think the worst and that he might have taken her with him as a hostage.' She looks at her husband, knowing she has set it up for Lord Fitzgerald to draw his own conclusions.

'By God, this is too much,' Lord Fitzgerald says, thrashing his crop through the air. 'Are you telling me he has abducted Victoria as well? I will have him fighting dogs in the pit with nothing but his bare skin for the rest of his short miserable life, so help me.' He turns to Cribbs. 'Take a couple of these fellows and check out Fletcher and the poker in the house. See if you deduce the same findings as Henry.' Cribbs tilts his cap at Lord Fitzgerald, turns and points at a couple of the men as he walks past them. They both follow close behind and all three depart the building.

'Brannigan, split the men up. Half to the north road out of town and half to the south. Follow and split up as the roads divide. I want this man's head on a pike by lunch time.' Brannigan leads the men out of the house and back to the waiting horses.

'Twenty guineas to the man who gets Springer,' Lord Fitzgerald shouts after them. 'Thirty if you get my Victoria back unharmed.'

There is the sound of horses whinnying and hooves stamping and crunching on the gravel as all the riders mount at the same time. They bump and jostle with each other as they turn and gallop off in all directions under the instructions of Lord Fitzgerald and the guidance of Brannigan and Sykes. All of them are thinking of the bounty Lord Fitzgerald has offered. For most, it is a princely sum that will change their lives forever. Every one of them will move heaven and earth to be the person to find them and claim such a reward.

'Now, now, my dear, worry yourself not. We will have Victoria back before you know it,' Lord Fitzgerald says to Mary. He then looks towards Henry. 'Get some of your men and horses ready. We will go cross country to the east and see if they went through the woods and back roads to the neighbouring villages.'

'Yes, I will see to it personally,' Henry says and leaves immediately for the yard to organise his people and arrange the mounts for the hunt ahead.

Lord Fitzgerald remains with Mary, awaiting the return of Henry and his people. He has time to think on the current situation and, after lining up all the facts in his mind, he speaks. 'My dear Mary, I cannot help but wonder why Victoria would have been taken by Springer. To him she would be nothing but a burden to slow down his travels. The risk for this man to take a lady with him would almost certainly see him caught. He would also know his fate would be a one-way trip to the gallows for such a crime. So I wonder what would make a common man do this and take such an unnecessary risk of dragging her along.'

Mary swiftly responds. 'Do you think Victoria went willingly with a common labourer? I would have you know that Victoria has been brought up to be a proper lady. The very idea she would abscond with such a man is insulting and preposterous.'

'My dear Mary, I do not for one minute think that an injured man would burden himself with a lady unfamiliar with common ways and the means to survive unless there was reason to do so. The only conclusions I can think of would be if he is being paid to take her, or they are…' He pauses for a minute to maximise the impact of his next comment. 'They are intimate with one and other, and if that be the case, she is of no use to me as I would not want a used whore of a commoner as a wife.'

Mary is about to explode in a fireball of rage, but before she gets the chance to vent her feelings, Lord Fitzgerald continues.

'Just remember, I know exactly who you were, what you were and where you came from before you married Henry. So do not think for one minute you can manipulate me.' Raising his voice louder to prevent Mary from speaking and ensuring she listens to every word, he continues. 'Now at present I am prepared to take it that Victoria has paid Springer to take her somewhere. And that – being the lady we hope she is – she will have kept her virtue pure. If I find out later this is not the case, then you are down to only one option if you want to enjoy the life you have here. As one daughter is due to be married and has unfortunately already been deflowered, according to my sources, that leaves you only the one option. Admittedly, she is a little young, but I'm sure she will be a fair second choice should the matter arise.'

Mary is speechless. All the wind has been knocked out of her sails as she stares blankly at the wall opposite. 'But Rebecca has barely sixteen years. She knows nothing of this world yet.' She turns to look at Lord Fitzgerald. 'She is but a babe! What kind of a monster are you? That little girl knows nothing of the evils of men. Your world would destroy her.'

'That is exactly the point – she is untouched. A blank canvas you might say, yet ready to be shaped and moulded into the ways of society. If I remember correctly, you were barely fifteen when my father broke you in, but you still made it to a reasonable level in society for one with such humble beginnings.'

Lord Fitzgerald sees Henry rushing back to the house. He looks back at Mary. 'I think it better we keep this conversation between us, don't you? Let's hope all will be well with Victoria, then all of this would just be talk, rather than reality.'

Mary is completely stunned. Still in a trance-like state, she nods towards Lord Fitzgerald, but inside she has been completely stripped bare to the bone.

Henry comes dashing through the doorway. 'My men and horses will be round the front shortly. I have eight good riders with me and four more of the magistrate's men that have just arrived.'

'Splendid, we will leave at once,' Lord Fitzgerald says as he heads towards his mount at the front of the house. Henry looks to his wife. He sees how sad and distant she looks and walks over to give comfort.

'Fear not, my dear, we will have Victoria back with us shortly, I promise you.' He holds both her hands in his and kisses them gently, then follows Lord Fitzgerald out the door to await his men and horse.

Mary watches on as her husband leaves. She thinks on Lord Fitzgerald's words and her mind goes back many years to the time of the docks and the fleets of whaling ships returning and disembarking.

In those days, she was from a noble family, a beautiful young lady of society. Her father was a successful businessman who for a while was doing very well with his dealing and trading ventures. That was until the day he went into partnership with the original Lord Fitzgerald. He loaned a ship of the fleet and crew to travel to the Middle East to collect spices, oils and other tradable goods, then continue on to India to collect as many boxes of tea as would fit in the hull of the ship. Its aim was to return to England within a year with all the goods it could hold. Sell them for a high profit, pay off the crew and the loan of the ship and send it back out on the same venture to repeat the process.

In the case of her father's invested trip, the ship arrived back to England in a little over a year and three months, fully loaded with all they'd set out for. But it was quarantined off the coast for a week for an alleged cholera outbreak on board. During this time, a fire broke out and the cargo and vessel along with most of the crew were lost to Davy Jones's locker. Her father could not prove it was deliberate, but during that week – and for months after – a huge amount of tea, oil and spices was available from Lord Fitzgerald's merchants throughout the area, making a fortune for those selling the products. With no ships arriving from the Middle East or India during this time period, how could these exotic items have arrived, if not from the burnt-out ship? They must have been smuggled off during the nights before the fire broke out, on smaller boats under the instructions of somebody with great influence.

With no income back from his huge investment, along with the cost of the lost ship and its crew to pay for, the family business was in ruins. To help pay off her father's debt, Mary was handed over to the first Lord Fitzgerald. She did whatever his lordship required and to whomever he required it done. Most of the time, it was to find out information or to entertain high-ranking officials to find out who they had allegiance to. Henry was one such target. He never knew it at the time, but he was being tapped for information on steam engines and his engineering knowledge for future projects.

When the new Lord Fitzgerald took over his father's empire and was going through his father's accounts and records on all the people he associated with, it included a special ledger on all the bribes, extortion and leverage information. He found Henry in one of these books, marked up as 'easy to manipulate and a potential candidate in a new enterprise away from whaling'. Lord Fitzgerald's father thought this man would be of use to his plans going forward. His methods and ideas in modernising factory working and using the power of mechanical, steam-driven machines to reduce labour and improve profit were a revelation. Fitzgerald had already realised he would need people like Henry around him to keep his lifestyle and enterprises afloat. Especially with whale oil beginning to be replaced with easier-to-access mineral oil from the land without the dangers, time and cost to obtain, he needed to diversify his operations to continue his empire. Taking over his father's empire, the new Lord Fitzgerald was no fool and also realised the potential of this man and his need to expand away from the fleets before they lost their value.

Mary, however, was written in the book as a tool to be used, not trusted, as well as being neither as young nor as attractive as she once was. By now, she was well-known for her abilities amongst his father's business associates, and this meant she was coming to the end of her usefulness. So the new Lord Fitzgerald hatched a final plan to use her to trap Henry, and when she fell pregnant, a marriage to Henry was swiftly organised and funded by Lord Fitzgerald as an ideal way to keep Henry under his control. Whether or not the child was indeed Henry's was never discussed – Henry thought it was and Mary was only too pleased to be married off to a prominent man, especially when pregnant and with her future looking bleak.

Mary's past would keep her under control by fear of the truth coming to light – hence controlling both Henry and Mary at the same time. His father once wrote, 'A man with a family would be more easily manipulated to play along with the ideas of others, by using children and wives as leverage against them, should the circumstances dictate the need.' In this case, how true it has been.

The new Lord Fitzgerald has no conscience about using family members to bend his will on others. He all but wiped out his own family without his heart skipping a beat. But he is not opposed to taking full advantage of others who held these moral standards and used it often it to his gain. Just like now, in the case of Mary. Putting her down and destroying her self-esteem is bread and butter to the likes of Lord Fitzgerald. She will not be as fast again to try it on with him and will always wonder how much he truly knows about her, and where the information came from.

* * *

Lord Fitzgerald is mounting his horse as Henry's men arrive on horseback leading his favourite mount, Millie. Though not the biggest horse in the yard, nor the prettiest bay in the group, there is something very special about this mare to Henry. She has a heart like a piston and a turn of speed to match any of her rivals, with the bravery to take on any fence or hedge Henry would have the bottle to face her at.

'Hello, my girl,' he says as he pats her neck. She stamps her rear foot, grinds her teeth and swings her head round to butt him in the back in defiance of his kind action. This pushes Henry forward and he clasps the saddle for stability as he turns and looks at his adversary. 'Really?' he says as they face each other in a stand-off. To most, she would seem to be a scary proposition to ride. But Henry knows it is all pomp and show; this horse has a character that needs to be understood, and once known she will ride the shoes off her feet to get you where you want to go. He grabs the reins and top of the saddle, puts one foot in the stirrup and bounces twice on his other leg before hopping up and preparing for the off.

Lord Fitzgerald is cantering off towards the woods and Henry gives Millie a gentle kick with his heels. It's all he needs to do as she is off like a rocket, ears forward with excitement as she moves off. In the distance, Millie can see another horse. To her, this is instantly the target to aim for and without any prompting she redirects her course to intercept and – like a scalded cat – she rips up the ground between them.

Whether Henry wants it or not, Millie tears past Lord Fitzgerald in a flash to take the lead. Lord Fitzgerald is not to be outdone and kicks his horse to catch up with Henry and away they both ride into the woods. The rest of the group has barely started moving and it takes them a full-on gallop just to catch up with the two leaders. By the time they do, they are half a mile into the woods following a narrow track to the next village.

It takes the riders over an hour of hard riding to get to the village of Emmetsdale. Upon arrival, the riders split up and question everyone they meet – some more than once as a different rider meets the same person at another location. After around twenty minutes, most of the riders are back in the centre of the village with nothing to report.

'Nothing, damnit. Not a single sighting of either of them,' Lord Fitzgerald yells at Henry.

'We need to split up and check the farms on the edge of Emmetsdale, as they may have avoided the village altogether,' Henry replies while trying to control Millie by turning her in a circle. Lord Fitzgerald nods and pairs the men up, sending them in different directions. He leaves the last direction to Henry and himself.

'We will go this way,' he says, pointing his crop towards a road heading off from the main street. They follow the road for about a mile before coming across a wooden sign for Bull Farm, with an arrow below pointing down a track lined on both sides by tall hedgerows. Lord Fitzgerald points it out to Henry. 'There,' he says. 'Let's go there.'

The pair of them trot down the winding track and before long it opens up, showing the farmhouse, several outbuildings and a large barn. The two men ride up and stop by the front door.

'You, in the house, come here,' bellows Lord Fitzgerald from the back of his horse, looking around at the other buildings for signs of life. From the side of one of these buildings, a young man appears, carrying a basket full of eggs.

'You boy,' Lord Fitzgerald calls out. 'Come here at once.' Robert stops in his tracks and looks up at both the men. 'Hurry, damn your eyes, I do not have all day to wait!'

Robert walks at his own pace towards the two strangers, taking care not to bump or roll the large basket of eggs. It takes him about thirty seconds to get to the two men.

'Took your time about it, didn't you, boy?' says Lord Fitzgerald.

'My mother would have the skin off my back if I was to drop these eggs, sir,' he replies, putting the wicker basket on the floor beside him.

'I am looking for a man and a woman who may have come this way early this morning. The woman may have been a captive of the man.'

Robert instantly knows who they are talking about but does not let on. Instead, he starts to put on a show of his own. 'Captive, sir? What be that mean?'

'Oh my God, it's another one of them who cannot speak the Queen's English!' Lord Fitzgerald rolls his head in frustration. 'A prisoner, boy. A prisoner of the man. The woman may be a p-r-i-s-o-n-e-r of the man, held against her will.'

Robert thinks on it, scratches his head and looks back up at Lord Fitzgerald. 'Seen some cows this morning. A few pigs. Some goats and a dog. But I not see no man or woman, unless thee be talking about Ma an' Pa. Would they be a man and a woman, sir?'

Henry tries not to laugh as Lord Fitzgerald starts to lose control. 'Where do these people come from?' he mutters. 'How do they manage to survive long enough to breed more of them? How do they even manage to procreate?' Lord Fitzgerald holds his head in his hands, then looks up and shouts, 'Is there anyone else here?'

'Yes, sir, I am here. Emily is my name. And what can I do for you gentlemen?' She is standing at the front door, holding a quart of milk with the farm's working collie dog sitting by her side.

Lord Fitzgerald takes his head out of his hands and looks towards her. 'I am looking for a man and a woman who may have passed this way this morning. The woman's name is Victoria, and she may be a captive of the man. His name is Springer, and he has killed one of my men and is now on the run, wanted for the brutal murder of Bill Fletcher.'

Emily must control her emotions, for standing in front of her is the man who had her father hung with their friends for the crimes he and his group of thugs committed. The hatred for this man runs deep and it is the closest she has been to him since running away from the port with Bob. The wanting for revenge wells up inside her. If only she had a gun. But then again, at least Springer disposed of that animal of a man Fletcher.

She calms her feelings and controls herself before answering. 'I'm afraid not, sir. I've seen no one around the farm all morning, and if they sneaked in, the dogs would have kicked off an almighty fuss.'

'Would there be anyone else who worked on the farm this morning that we may speak to?' asks Henry. 'For the missing woman is my daughter Victoria, and I am desperate for her safe return.'

'The only other person here this morning would have been my husband, but he is not here at present.'

Lord Fitzgerald looks at Emily. 'Oh? And where might he be, then?' he asks.

Emily realises she has made a mistake. But then thinks he must have reached town by now. 'He delivers milk, eggs, cheese and meat to the local villages, including Emmetsdale, on a Monday.'

'We have just come from there and we did not see anyone delivering produce,' says Lord Fitzgerald as he thinks on her words. 'He would have to deliver his goods by cart, wouldn't he?' he says. 'Would your husband be going to Earlchester, by any chance?'

Emily pauses for a moment. 'It could be possible. He does deliver to many areas and it's not like we have a set route. He goes to many places until he has sold all his stock, then he returns home.'

Lord Fitzgerald turns to Henry and quietly speaks. 'There is something about this woman, but for the life of me, I cannot put my finger on it.' He turns back to Emily. 'I'm sure you will not mind if I have a look round?' As he goes to dismount, Emily nudges the dog, Flash, with her leg.

'Foxes,' she says. The dog is straight up on his feet, hackles up, ears flat and teeth bare in a growl. With the lead dog up, two more come running from the house, barking and growling. As Flash steps forward, the other two dogs take positions either side of him, slowly moving as a unit toward the two riders.

The horses sense the change in atmosphere and become agitated, moving around and facing off with the three canines.

Lord Fitzgerald thinks twice about dismounting his horse now there are three dogs on full alert moving forward in a line. He repositions himself upright on his horse and takes stock of the situation.

Emily gives Lord Fitzgerald a stern look. 'What would my husband say if I allowed two strangers to walk around his place while he was at work? I think you had better go now, while there is light enough for you to continue looking for your missing people.'

Lord Fitzgerald is not impressed at being spoken down to by a common farm woman, but without his henchmen to do his dirty work, he will have to bite his pride until another opportunity arrives. He speaks to Henry, while watching Emily for a reaction to his words.

'We will take the road to Earlchester and see if we can find this man delivering milk and cheese and find out if he has seen anyone on his travels around the local villages.'

Emily has had years of hating this man. There is no change in her expression or mannerisms, and she just stares at him with a dagger-like gaze.

Lord Fitzgerald stares back at her, trying desperately to work out what it is about this woman that reminds him of something. He turns his horse and kicks off back up the track, while Henry is more polite. He tilts his head at Emily. 'Thank you for your time,' he says before following Lord Fitzgerald to the main road.

Emily watches them all the way up the path until they are out of sight and off their land, then turns to her son, who is now by her side. 'That man who spoke to you was the person I have told you about all your life. He was the one that had my father, your grandfather, murdered so he could wipe out his whole family and take control of his father's estate.'

'You did not have to tell me, Ma. I see it in your eyes.' He hugs his mum. 'One day, he will get what he deserves. And when he does, I hope it is slow and painful and I get to watch him suffer every bit of it.'

Emily looks at her son and smiles. 'That man changed the course of our lives. Perhaps if it was not for him, your father and I would have not been together, and you would not have been born. Just remember, he did not change or make the people we are. That is down to us. He just changed the circumstances we live in.' She gives a deep sigh. 'That man has made many enemies who want to see him suffer as much as me and your father, not least one of his own brothers, who he does not even know is still alive.'

'He still has a brother?' asks Robert.

'Oh yes, he has a brother alright. But many years at sea and living in faraway lands has left him very different from the child I once knew.'

Robert looks at his mother curiously. 'You have never mentioned that to me before.'

His mother smiles at him. 'Well, Robert, perhaps at the time I thought you too young to understand. And maybe now it is time I tell you the rest of what your father and I know.' She turns to walk back into the house. 'Well, come inside and I will tell you as I peel the vegetables.'

They walk into the kitchen, closely followed by Flash, who wastes no time weaving between the two of them and jumping back in his willow basket by the side of the stove. As top dog he has the best position, usually beside wherever Bob is. But when the master is away, he is always beside Emily while the other two dogs remain in the hallway sharing a folded-over thick red blanket.

Robert takes a seat at the table while Emily lifts a large bowl containing a mixture of carrots, onion and celery from the sink and carries it to the kitchen table. She spots a small piece of cheese on the table, possibly a piece broken off from this morning when they had guests for breakfast. Picking it up, she turns to Flash, who is always alert watching his master's every move. As Emily throws the cheese in his direction, it is snatched out of the air and swallowed whole. With a lick of his lips, he lowers his head back on his front paws and continues to watch Emily's every move.

Taking a carrot from the bowl, she scrapes the skin away then chops it up into bite-size chunks and drops them in the pot by her leg. She collects another carrot and repeats the procedure.

'Now, let me see… it was around seven or eight years after your father and I escaped the grip of the whaling port. We had been living on this farm for most of that time, and we had just finished fencing the large paddock. Your father had commissioned the town blacksmith to make four large hinges for the gates and a dozen brackets for shelving in the house and that day we had gone into town on the cart to collect them. When we arrived at the forge, I went to buy other goods from the general store, while your father went directly to the blacksmith to settle his account.

'To be fair, your father is not much of a haggler, so the buying of goods is best left to me. I collected all the items needed and waited in the cart for some time before I got bored and decided to join Bob inside the forge. On arrival I could see your father talking with the blacksmith and another man. As I got closer, they stopped talking and all turned to look at me. The stranger with them stood out, as half his face was covered in tribal markings which extended down his neck and around what was showing of his arms. I know what he was, as I had seen his kind many times, leaving the boats on the docks. He was one of the harpooners from a whaling ship. The tattoos represent his clan, fearlessness of his trade, and in some cases the marks can be read as a history of the person's deeds, whales taken, ships served on and place of origin.

'But in this case, the man was different. The closer I got, the more he changed. His appearance was not of a man from far away. For a start, he was white – well-tanned but white. Many of the words in the tattoos were English, like *Not Forgotten*, below a portrait of a lady wearing a bonnet. Now standing right beside him, I could make out the tattoo of the ship your father and grandfather served on – The Endeavour. It was something all sailors tended to do if they volunteered to the life at sea.' She looked at her son with misty eyes. 'The man smiled at me and spoke. "Hello, Emily," he said to my face. Well, you could have knocked me down with a feather.' She absent-mindedly selects another carrot from the bowl.

'Before another word could be spoken, your father shook the blacksmith's hand and ushered us back towards the cart, thanking the blacksmith for his parts while emphasising that we must be on our way. I remember being swiftly loaded in the back of the cart and the two men climbing up on the front bench. The stranger threw a heavy bag in the back of the wagon next to me and several harpoon tips poked out of the top of it. Your father quickly flicked the reins to get the horses moving, and it took about ten minutes to get back on the road towards our farm. It was only then that the stranger spoke again.

'He turned round to face me and asked, "Do you have any idea who I am yet?" I remember looking long and hard at the man's face. The tribal tattoos were such a dominating feature it was difficult to look past them to the man behind. I tried to imagine him without all the tattoos and his skin in a lighter colour, but I could still not picture who this man was. Then I saw it, a small scar on the right side of his chin. A boy I once played with got that same scar, catching his chin on a burr while jumping from a tree branch. It had bled profusely all over my clothes and we'd had a terrible time getting the blood out of my favourite dress.

'"James? James Fitzgerald? Is that really you?" I asked him. I cannot forget his face as he smiled at me. He seemed relieved I had remembered him. Or perhaps we were the first and only friends he had seen in a long time that recognised him. He rolled up his sleeve and high up on his shoulder was a tattoo of a rope knot – the friendship symbol. He'd put it there as a reminder of good times before his brother's betrayal.

'James explained what had happened to him – all about his adventures and how he ended up back here with us. As best I can remember, this is how he told it… It started with his brother, Lord Fitzgerald, ordering him to sail out on the ship that had returned my father and your dad on the previous voyage. He was to learn about the business and understand all about whaling and what it involved out at sea. After serving with the crew on the ship for over a year, harvesting whale oil, the hull was near to bursting and it was finally time to return home. Unknown to James, his brother had also given the captain another more personal instruction: to throw James overboard at the end of the hunt before returning home. If not, the captain needn't bother coming home at all.

'The captain and his crewmates had a problem with this and could not bring themselves to carry out the instructions. Partly because he had become a friend to all, but also out of respect for my father and Bob and the others. The crew felt ashamed for the way they were murdered for a crime they all knew they did not commit. However, they also knew they could not return home to their loved ones with James still around, as the punishment would probably have been death for them as well as their families. So they decided on the only option left to them – to set him adrift with enough supplies to last a couple of weeks. That way, they would have given him a chance to survive, and their consciences would be a little eased by the fact they had not directly killed him themselves.

'The captain himself passed a bag of gold coins to James. "This was the money your brother paid us to end your life. To us it is blood money and has no place amongst us. Please take it and I pray you have time to find a use for it."

'James explained how he understood what the crew had to do and bore them no malice for the decision they had come to. In the end he made it easier for them by getting into the boat himself and rowing away from the ship. That way, they parted as friends, and not as enemies or murderers.

'He was adrift for nearly three weeks before sighting land. It took a further two days to reach its shore as the tides and reefs combined with riptides and upsurges around the island made a near impregnable barrier. His boat took an enormous amount of damage getting through the reef, being dragged against hard corals and semi-submerged rocks and battered by the unrelenting waves. By the time he beached the half-sunken boat on the shoreline, the craft was beyond seaworthy. The planks were all cracked and the main beam running the length of the boat had been split in half.

'James went on to explain how he lived on this island for nearly two months, using up all his supplies and all the meagre resources the island had to offer. He lived the last two weeks on coconut flesh and milk. Fish were also on the menu, but the shoreline was constantly covered in small box jellyfish pulsating along in the warm shallows and it was difficult to get through them without being stung. And the sting from these little brutes was near fatal – as he had found out the hard way, being stung on his ankle and spending three days in absolute burning agony.

'Rescue came in the form of a group of tribal fishermen who arrived at the island on a very high tide to bury a village elder in the traditional way. They were shocked to find a white man on their island but took it as a good omen for the village as he must be carrying the souls of the dead within him and that was why his skin was so white. With nowhere to go, he spent the next five years living with these people, learning their beliefs and customs, marking himself with tattoos in the traditional way using charcoal instead of ink, even taking a girl from the village and starting a family.

'His life now was very different, but considering everything he had been through, he was content with his newfound position with these people. They had become his new family, and over the years he fought in several bloody battles against other tribes, slavers and pirates to ensure his and their safety.

'But when the tropical storms hit the village, he would always wake up sweating and screaming. Each nightmare was a little worse than the one before. Soon it came to the attention of the village elders, who worried for their white son – so much so, they called in a great witchdoctor from the next island to read the signs. After he spent a day in the village and several hours staring, poking and pulling James, the conclusion was that the lost souls of James's siblings were calling out to him to find them. At least one – if not more – was alive and they needed him to collect them and bring them back to him.

'To the village elders, this was his quest. All men in the village would have a quest in their lives, and this was his. James needed to leave the village, find his missing siblings and bring them back into his life. If he did not, it was believed the nightmares would be passed down to his family and children and they would suffer even worse.

'James did not want to leave his woman and child. Nor did he want to go back to his old life. But deep down he knew he needed to find out if any of his brothers or sisters were still alive. After agreeing to accept the quest, the village elders all wanted to help James back to England and waited for the opportunity. He was presented with many leaving gifts, including a final tattoo, but this time it was done by the witchdoctor himself to mark the occasion. As it was tradition for the whole tribe to help a man on a quest, all the villagers on all the local islands were looking at ways to help get him back home. After talking with various people from the surrounding area, it became known that a Dutch whaling ship had arrived at one of the islands, looking for hardwood for repairs after it had taken damage in the latest storm. The village nearby struck a bargain with the captain of the ship. They could have all the hardwood they needed if they took a person back to Holland on their vessel.

'The captain had no choice but to agree as he needed the wood. He also dared not upset the locals, as he would be unable to get enough supplies of food and water for his crew to survive the journey home. So a bargain was struck.

'With a heavy heart, James said goodbye to his new family and the rest of the village that turned up to see him off. He climbed aboard a dugout canoe for the two-day paddle to the waiting ship. The village chief, his wife's grandfather, accompanied him. James knew this man well as he had lived with him for six months when he first arrived at the village. The man spoke of his sadness that James, his adopted son, must leave on his quest, but understood it must be done even though he may never see him again.

'Two days later, the canoe approached the ship. As they pulled up beside the vessel, the village chief turned to James and said he had one more gift. He took out a small bag and poured a dozen large black pearls into his hand. James knew they were very special and extremely rare and thanked the chief. Then the chief pulled a cloth from his hip belt and unfolded it. Inside was a beautifully made mother-of-pearl-handled knife. On the top of the handle was a cylindrical shell. The chief pulled the shell off the top, exposing a thin, one-inch hooked blade coated in a clear resin.

'The chief explained it was made by the medicine man with one purpose in mind. The blade was made from the gill cover of a fish and had an edge sharper than any made of steel. The elder explained that the blade had been cursed by every person in the village, and if James chose to take revenge, he should cut the brother who caused him so much pain, and he would be cursed the rest of his life with ill health and bad luck. He explained the blade was coated in the secretions that cover the spines on a stingray and he must never touch it, just use it if he desired and then destroy it.

'James thanked the man for his wonderful gifts. He had learned to understand these people and their ways, including how they believed they were part of everybody in the village. Part of his spirit now resided in every member of the tribe, and all in the tribe will reside in his spirit forever. What happens to one happens to them all. Whether or not James chose to believe in their superstitions we'll never really know. But they believed in it, so out of courtesy he never questioned their heritage and ideals.

'The captain of the whaling ship got the surprise of his life when James climbed the rope ladder and stood on deck. He was expecting a local native looking to see the world and one day bring back tales of his journeys to his tribe – not a European man. And especially not one that dropped a bag full of harpoon tips on his deck.

'He looked at James and asked him if he knew how to use the harpoons, explaining he had lost all his experienced harpooners when a big bull whale dived deep then came up and leapt onto the two boats attached to it, killing all on board. The storm that followed had damaged the mast and rudder, so they had been in the lagoon repairing the ship for a month. With less than fifty barrels of oil in the hull, the trip was a disaster. But if James was prepared to work for the captain, he would offer him double pay and full passage home to England instead of Holland.

'James agreed to the deal and spent the following six months as the only harpooner on the last rowboat they had. But in that short time, he took down three dozen whales, enough to fill the hull and make the trip worthwhile to the crew and its captain.' Emily gives up pretending to peel the vegetables and places the knife down on the table.

'He explained how he had travelled from the Galapagos Islands all the way back to England, where the ship dropped him off before heading to Holland. In total, he'd been away for nearly eight years. Imagine his surprise to find the whaling ships had all but gone, the port had fewer than five hundred people left out of the tens of thousands that once worked and lived there. His brother had long since moved away, the family house had been stripped and the land and buildings sold off in pieces to the highest bidders. What was left of the old house had fallen into ruin, abandoned by all who used to live and work in the once great building. In the local tavern he ran into one of his old crew members from that first ship, now missing a leg and one eye after a whale crushed the boat he was rowing. Peg Leg Jones was now of no use to anyone and had nowhere to go, so he stayed in the port and scavenged a living as best he could.

'With the assistance of a few glasses of rum and knowing James could be trusted, he hinted that Bob and myself could be found around this area. And with no other people to ask about his family, he decided to try and find us. It was purely by chance that James bumped into the two of us at the blacksmiths. He was there to sell his harpoon blades for scrap as they were heavy and he had no use for them. The price offered was too low and he was about to leave when Bob walked into the forge.

'He stayed with us for two or three days, talking about his family, travels and of course his brother, the new Lord Fitzgerald, and his henchmen. His feelings on that man were no different from your father's and mine. I explained that none of his brothers ever returned from their whaling trips, but there was a possibility his sisters may have been sent to Paris and could still be alive. We told him of the rumours of where they had been sent and what they could have been forced into. This broke him down to tears, but we thought he needed to know all that we had been told.

'Then one day we found a note on this table from James. It thanked us for our time and wished us well for the future. He left us one pearl, that your father had fashioned into this ring.' She quickly thrust out her hand to show her son the ring. 'He asked us to use or dispose of his harpoon tips as we saw fit, for he only needed one and the rest were of no use to him anymore. He was going to Paris to find out if any of his family were still alive. James also said there were a few ships' captains he would visit on the way, and one day he would see us again before visiting his brother. All this was several years ago.

'They are his harpoons that are hanging above the fireplace in the next room. We could not convince ourselves to throw them away, as they represent where we all came from and are a part of what we once were. But a visit from an old friend two years back did fill in some missing pieces.

'It seems James must have tracked down the captains of the ships that had taken his brothers on their voyages, as one by one they all succumbed to the same fate. Each has had their right hand cut off and been marked with a branding iron, for now they have the word *murderer* burned onto their foreheads. It would be just like him to make them live with a reminder of what they did for a bag of gold. I would think the branding iron was made from the harpoon spear that he kept, as it would have served no other purpose.

'The only captain to not have been visited by James was the one from the ship he himself sailed on. I think he understood that letting him row away was the only option left to him and his crew if they wanted to go home.'

Robert has not said a word, such was his mother's story. He cannot believe how much this man James has gone through in his life.

Finally, the words come to him. 'Do you think he will ever come back and see you again?'

Emily thinks for a minute as it is a question she has often asked herself. 'That's a difficult one,' she says. 'If he has managed to find some family in France, he may have decided to head back to his own people and new home in the Caribbean. But he is also a man with honour, with truth and principles to satisfy. I personally think he will return, and we will see him one more time, for I do not believe his honour will allow him to leave without first seeing his brother and repaying him for the betrayal of his family.

'James was very close to his brothers and sisters and loved his mother dearly. I also think Lord Fitzgerald now knows one of his siblings is still alive, as the branded captains are sure to have made contact and told him of their fate. By a process of elimination, he may well know which one of his brothers is alive. It would just depend on how many captains made contact. One day, I'm sure he is expecting to get a visit from his brother to settle what has been long overdue. Perhaps that is why he has so many villainous men around him. Maybe he thinks by having them close, it will put his brother off making contact. Who knows? I just hope I am still around to see James when he does finally visit, as I am sure it will be a fitting end to a bad man.'

CHAPTER 9

Difficult Choices

Bob has been delivering his goods to various taverns and manors along the road to Earlchester. The cart has off-loaded a little under half its cargo of farm produce so far, but the main drop will be at the Blue Boar Hotel in the middle of the town. They usually take all he has left on board, as it is a very busy establishment. It's a well-known landmark in the area; in particular it has a reputation as a gentleman's club, allowing for a feast of entertainment ranging from gambling, drinking, cabaret shows and provocative ladies for all occasions and requirements.

It has over one hundred rooms available for rent and three restaurants to dine in – two of which are open to the public, and one strictly private for guests and their associates staying at the hotel.

It remains busy most of the year round, which is good news for Bob as they take most of the cheese, milk, eggs and butter that he and his family produce. When there is excess meat from culling the bulls and rams for the season, they will also buy all that he can spare.

Juddering along the well-worn track, Bob is about half a mile from the stone bridge that spans the river on the outskirts of the town. Springer is in the back of the cart looking at the small map given to him by Dan the poacher, with Victoria curled up fast asleep in his arms.

Springer frequently leans forward to look out of the cart, waiting for some special feature to come into view. As they round the next bend, he finally spots what he has been looking for: a huge yew tree surrounded by its own stone wall with two branches posing like a man showing off his biceps.

The tree itself is hundreds of years old and has a history all of its own. To the locals it is more commonly known as the Widow Maker, as it has a chequered past of being the place that criminals were once regularly hung from. It is just on the town border and in days of old was a good place to set an example that would offend the people travelling to and from the town.

The fact that both branches have a pronounced dip in them is testimony to the number of people that have hung from its branches – highwaymen and witches and poachers of the king's deer to list but a few. They would be left to swing for days as a deterrent to others. Before recent expansions, it was a mile mark from town and far enough away for the smell not to cause insult to the people living there, but close enough to be a visual deterrent to those who would break the law.

'Hold up them there horses, Bob. We be where we needs to be,' calls out Springer from inside the wagon.

'Woah.' Bob pulls back on the reins, the horses slow down to a stop, and the brake is applied via a wooden hand lever.

Springer shakes Victoria softly. 'Time we be on our way, afore them there others come looking, my dear.'

She looks at him for a second or two to collect her thoughts before straightening herself up and getting to her feet.

Even half-asleep and dishevelled as she is, he is captivated by her beauty and just stares at her in disbelief that she is in front of him. As Victoria looks back, he has a smile on his face and a pride that brings her a warmth she has never known before. 'Why, Mr Springer, I do believe you are making me blush,' she says with a smirk.

Springer does not stop looking at her. 'It be 'ard for me to put into words what I be feelin', for I know not how to say them. I stand here afore ye and it be 'ard to draw breath. All I know is that I be right proud thee be by my side.'

He snaps out of his trance and climbs out the back of the cart, then lifts down Victoria's large case and his bag. He turns his attention to Victoria, lifting her up by the waist, over the lip of the backboard and onto the ground. A sharp pain stabs at his side and ribs, making him twitch, but he makes no sound.

Victoria notices his grimace but says nothing, as she knows it would hurt him even more if he knew she had seen him in pain.

'Thank thee kindly, Bob. We shall take our leave of you now in hopes of finding this place afore nightfall.'

Bob turns around to look at them both. 'I hope the pair of you find what you are looking for, and may God keep you both safe and away from prying eyes.' He turns back to face his horses and raises an arm. 'Cheery bye, my friends,' he yells without even looking back.

Victoria and Springer watch as the cart that had taken them this far now moves on without them. It follows the track for about thirty yards before it turns a corner and disappears from sight behind hedges and dense foliage. Springer puts his arm around Victoria's shoulder. 'Well, my dear. We be now truly on our own. Everything we be doing from this point on will be at our own making.'

Victoria smiles at him. 'Shall we be off, then? From the look of the map you have been studying for so long, we have about three miles to go?'

'Aye, lass, that be about my reckoning too.' He picks up the case and his bag and looks at Victoria. 'Let's be getting afore the going gets 'arder. For I be getting as stiff as that there tree up yonder.' He sets off along a narrow path that starts by the misshapen yew tree.

Victoria stands for a minute, trying to decipher what Springer has just said, then smiles to herself, shakes her head and skips to catch him up.

They have barely made it thirty yards along the track before they hear the sound of horses cantering. At first it is very faint, but gradually the thundering of the hooves echoes louder and louder as they draw ever closer. Springer grabs Victoria by the hand and pulls her under the overhanging branches of a hawthorn bush. They both crouch down in silence, looking back at the road they just left as the horses come into view. Cantering hard, they swiftly pass, with white sweat and froth marks on their heads and necks

– caused by the oiled reins and tack rubbing on wet fur – showing the horses have been pushed hard and have travelled far in a short time. Leading the group are Lord Fitzgerald and Victoria's father Henry, with around half a dozen riders following in a staggered formation behind them. They disappear around the bend, in the same direction as the cart. The sound of hooves hitting the ground fades as quickly as it arrived as the speed of the horses takes their riders far from sight.

Springer and Victoria come out from under the branches. 'They be a mite faster than I was a reckoning,' says Springer.

'My father was with them, Springer. They chase after me as if I were made of gold, but in truth it's because I have a purpose for them by being a puppet wife to that horrid man.' She moves closer to Springer and puts her arms round him. 'And you, you're only needed because you make them lots of money. When you have taken all the beatings they can throw at you and are no longer able to win, they will have you working in one of their factories or mines, until you fade from existence.'

It saddens Victoria that people think of Springer in that way, but after a moment's pause, she continues. 'When it comes to my baby brothers being held by him on nothing but lies and my father doing nothing to protect them, it upsets me greatly. If only he would be so keen to protect his family, get Edward and Oliver back home and away from Fitzgerald's evil clutches. But all my father and mother are worried about is keeping in that man's good graces and keeping their positions in high society, regardless of cost.'

'Easy, lass, you be not with 'em now, and nor will you ever be, not while I live and take breath. We might not have much at our beginnings, but we be free and making our way while beholding to none.' He picks up the case and bag. 'Time we be making the best of the light we have left, for I know not these woods like the ones back yonder.'

They walk along a little-used path as it winds in and out of trees and bushes, moving ever upwards. Before long, they are on the edge of a hillside, looking out at all that lies before them.

Springer looks across the landscape. 'Look there, Victoria,' he says, pointing into the distance. 'That there be the river flowing down the side of the town of Earlchester.'

From where the two of them stand, they can see the huge stone bridge at the eastern entrance to the town, showing all twelve of its arches across the whole river. In the middle can be seen two walled turrets, one on either side of the bridge, hanging out over the river. In days gone by these were used by the guards who were stationed there to collect a small tariff from all using the bridge, to help pay for its upkeep and build costs. Between the turrets is a pair of iron grid gates that could be closed to protect the town in the case of an attack by hostile forces. Nowadays, the turrets are used by people as a viewing platform or meeting point. It shows great views overlooking the river in both directions and is the ideal place to take a break. The constant supply of goods and commodities by cart, horse and hand-drawn barrows coming in and out of town to supply its population means there is always traffic on the bridge. With both the old iron gates fully open, the bridge is so wide it has two lanes for access, allowing for travel in both directions at the same time by even the widest of wagons and carts.

'Look! There at the front of the bridge, Springer, it looks like Bob is just about to cross with his cart.'

'Aye, lass, it seems like Lord Fitzgerald and Henry will reach old Bob as he be about halfway across.' They watch as Henry and Lord Fitzgerald move along the bridge, stopping and speaking to all they come across. Soon they are beside Bob and his wagon. They cannot hear what is being spoken, but moments later two of the riders from the group dismount and start to search the back of his wagon. One man can be seen climbing into the back of the cart. He pokes around for a bit, then falls from view for a second before reappearing, brushing something off his arm. They watch as Bob gets up from his seat on the front of the cart and disappears inside the wagon.

Springer turns to Victoria. 'I think that there man must 'ave broken some of Bob's eggs or something.' He starts to chuckle. 'Someone's about to get a clobbering if that be the case.'

They can see Bob pointing at something in the cart, and then pointing at the man. It is clear to Springer that an altercation is now in full swing in the back of the cart. The man starts pointing at Bob then shakes his fist at him and pushes him back. Bob repositions himself before delivering an uppercut to the man's chin. He goes upwards and back at the same time and falls straight over the side of the cart. Springer laughs out loud and even Victoria has a smile on her face.

'Hell's teeth, that there old boy still has it, by 'eck! He be feeling that come the morrow.'

They watch on as the rest of the men with Henry and Lord Fitzgerald dismount their horses. Some of them help the fallen man to his feet, while others are pointing and waving their arms at Bob in the back of his wagon. As one tries to mount the cart, Bob swings something at him and knocks him back to the ground.

More men try to get aboard, while Bob is still swinging something around above his head. The unknown object has the desired effect and keeps the men on the ground. For a moment, Bob is heavily outnumbered. But this soon changes. Two carts coming from the direction of the town stop beside his wagon and four men – two from each vehicle – start pointing and waving their arms. The people travelling behind Bob drop their packs and join in and before long there are twenty to thirty people arguing in the middle of the bridge.

Springer and Victoria can only watch. They are too far away to give help. Even if they could, they would be seen and captured and all that they have done so far would be for nothing.

Lord Fitzgerald waves his riding crop at the men in his party. They all mount their horses, surrounded and heckled by an ever-growing crowd of people. Henry moves his horse forward through the angry group towards Bob, passes him something and waits for a response. Bob looks at it, then flicks his hand up at Henry, who in turn pulls his horse away and re-joins Lord Fitzgerald and his men.

The crowd of assembled people disengage and start to go their own ways. The men who stopped their wagons next to Bob remount and move on.

'I think your father just be paying Bob for that there damage rendered to his stock.'

'It would certainly look that way,' Victoria replies, still watching the bridge.

Lord Fitzgerald points towards the town of Earlchester and rides across the bridge with Henry by his side and the rest of his group close behind.

Bob returns to his seat and collects the reins. He is about to flick them on when he pauses for a minute then looks in the direction of Springer and Victoria. He watches for a while before taking off his cap, raising it and waving it in a circle as if to say goodbye.

Victoria looks at Springer. 'Do you think he can see us?'

Springer chuckles. 'No, my dear. The man sees not like a hawk, but he be knowing we were probably watching, just not where we be watching from. More I think it be a chance that we see him take the upper hand from them that stopped him.'

He picks up their bags. 'Let's be moving on. Time be a wasting and I would like to find this place afore dark sets in.'

As they walk along the winding track, Victoria clasps Springer's arm. The path takes them around the hillside and down into another small, wooded valley. When they reach a small brook, Springer takes out his map.

'We go down this 'ere stream for about half a mile to a cottage with a green door and a large wind chime hanging up above.'

They follow the brook and eventually come across the small homestead that fits the description on Springer's map.

'Stay thee here and I will see if somebody be home,' says Springer as he heads over to the cottage.

He raps on the green door and awaits a response. For a while, nothing happens. Then, just as he is about to knock again, he hears a shuffling from the inside. A minute or so later, the catch clicks, the door slowly opens, and Springer is confronted by an old man with a hunched shoulder. 'Can I help you?' he asks in a quiet voice.

'I be a friend of Dan, Dan the poacher. He said thee could help with a safe place to rest up for a day or so, or until I be fit to travel on.'

The old man looks him up and down. 'Um, he said that, did he?' He looks at Springer's battered face. It still carries all the bruising, black eye and stitches from the fight. 'You must be Springer then! And if that is the case, you will soon have many a man looking for you, if they are not already doing so.'

Springer is shocked the old man knows his name. 'That be me and them that thee be talking about be close to a hair's breadth from finding me not a short time back.'

The old man gives a small smile. 'Was a fine fight, my son. Best I've seen in many a year. Dan put me on to you, and what a time I had. I don't get out much these days, but on word of Dan I went with some of the old boys to watch you at work. And what a good day out we had! Even left with a little more coin in my pocket than I went with! I was told to expect you and here you be. Jack be my name. Was an old sea dog in my time, but age has caught me up and the sea is not a place for an aged man with my ailments.'

He peers past Springer and sees Victoria standing in the distance. 'But not alone I see!'

'It was not my intent, but it is what it is. The lass be with me now and I be glad for it.'

The old man looks back at Springer. 'Makes no odds to me. There be room enough for two. On occasions there's been room enough for four to hold up. It be a safe place for you and your friend to rest until fit to move on.'

He points down towards the brook, past his house. 'Lodge is just out of view. Use all the wood you need. I will replace what is used every day when I stock up my own pile. There are two loaves of bread inside for you and the lady. It's two shillings for the week in advance, three if you want me to supply some food each day. That should give you time to heal up and be ready to move on.'

Springer puts his hand in his pocket and takes out some coins. He passes Jack four shillings. 'A week be time enough to heal my wounds, but here's an extra shilling for any unseen needs I not be knowin' of yet, along with a thank ye.'

The old man picks up a stick that is resting by the side of the door and uses it to lift down the wind chimes, placing them in a wicker basket by the front door. He looks back at Springer. 'To them that need to know, the lodge is now taken until I put the chime back up. It saves others from approaching my home. Goodbye, my son. It is best we do not see each other again, as then I know nothing and can say nothing to those who may come asking. The food will be by the door each day around lunch. It may be game or fish, just depends on what gets dropped off by Dan or his fellow poachers.' Jack turns and coughs a sickly gurgling noise, before turning back to Springer. 'After the fight you've had, I'm sure you could do with the rest and time to heal up. For I have never seen such courage, bravery and sheer will to win a fight before and I doubt I will see it again in my lifetime. You put it all on the line when you go for it, that's for sure, lad.'

'Thank thee kindly, sir. We best be on our way now – old bones are weary, and I could do with a rest.'

Springer walks back to Victoria. 'Come, my Victoria. The place be but a quick step and a holler from here.' He reaches for the bag and case, but his strength starts to leave him. He is tired and weak, and the day has taken its toll on his abilities.

Victoria sees him struggle and grabs the bag from his grasp. 'It's time I carried my weight,' she says, holding Springer's side to aid him as they move along the edge of the brook. They follow it for two hundred yards and come across a narrow path that disappears into a tight thicket of scrub willow. As they pass through this narrow gap, they are confronted with four steps down to a round, thatched cabin. It is almost impossible to see on the approach due to its low level and the well-positioned bushes.

The building has been purposely thought out to ensure minimal exposure to the outside world. But the interior also hides a secret or two of its own. As they step down to the entrance and open the door, it becomes clear this is not just a shed in a forest, but a good-sized room with a large bed on one side and up and down bunk beds on the other. There is a large open stone fireplace – already set with kindling and small logs – with a black iron cooking pot hanging from a hook. Below one of the many windows is a sink and there are various chairs stacked around the room.

'Well I be damned,' says Springer. 'I thought them there poachers hid in small dark squalors living rough like. This be more like a home than a place of refuge.' He takes Victoria in his arms and kisses her passionately. 'That be for all thee have done, for I be right proud to have you with me.'

Victoria just smiles. She takes the matches from the lintel and lights the fire in several places. The flames dance left and right, growing in size and intensity as the fire takes its grip on the wood. As she watches the fire in a trance-like state, her mind is at work, thinking of the right words to say to Springer. For she is happy to be with a man who loves her as much as he does. Rich or poor makes no odds to her feelings. They may be from different tiers of society, but together they are whole and content.

Finally, she gets the words right in her head and turns to tell him how she feels, but her face changes from radiant excitement to disappointment. Springer is lying before her, sprawled out on the bed fast asleep, fully clothed and still wearing his boots.

She puts her hands on her hips and comments to herself, 'Typical, just typical. When I finally find the right words to say, he falls asleep.' She stands and watches him for a while before going over and undoing the laces on his boots, taking them off and placing them under the bed. She then takes her own boots off and places them next to his, massaging each aching foot. With a big sigh, she climbs onto the bed and, placing one arm on his chest, she curls up by his side and whispers something in his ear before giving it a small kiss. Tucking her head tight into his shoulder, it does not take her long to fall asleep – for they both have been up for the best part of two days now, and most of that has been walking.

* * *

Springer awakes to the smell of burning. Sniffing the air, he opens his eyes and sits up, looking around for the cause. It takes him a few seconds to come to terms with his new surroundings, but soon his senses become accustomed to the room and its layout. The source of the smell soon presents itself. Over by the fire, two pieces of bread have been hung to toast on a piece of improvised metal wire, but the hanging bread on one of the hooks has rotated, putting the corner too close to the fire – causing it to not only blacken, but to actually catch light.

Springer jumps to his feet and slowly unhooks the wire from its mount. He opens the door and swings the burning offering outside.

To his horror, Victoria is within feet of the doorway, heading towards him, looking down at some flowers in her hands. Before he even has time to warn her, the burning projectile bounces off her shoulder, narrowly missing her face.

She jumps back, shrieking loudly as the toast falls to the floor beside her, then looks up and sees Springer full in her face and jumps again. She lets out another squeak and drops the flowers. By now the adrenalin in her body has fully kicked in. Her heart is pounding, and she is trembling following two frights in as many seconds.

Springer rushes forward to comfort her. Holding her in his arms, he says, 'Easy, lass. I did not mean to give thee such a fright like that.' He rubs the top of her arms and shoulders. Victoria looks round and sees the burning bread smouldering on the floor.

'Oh damn! I cannot even toast a piece of bread without trying to burn the building down.'

He laughs. 'Is that what it be, lass?'

Victoria looks him in the eyes and starts to laugh. 'I dropped my flowers.' They are still chuckling as she bends down to pick up the small posy of wildflowers she has collected from beside the brook. 'I thought they would brighten up the place while we are here,' she says as they move back into the wooden lodge.

Springer eases himself down and sits on the corner of the bed. 'They be a grand thought, my dear.' His side is giving him discomfort and he needs to inspect the damage. He carefully takes off his shirt, then undoes the dirty, sweaty bandages that have been wrapped around his ribs and throws them into the fire.

It's two days since the fight and the full extent of the bruising can now be seen. His cracked and bruised ribs are swollen and sore, but not too hot to the touch – so there is no heavy infection or leaking bones to cause him concern. Which is a good thing, considering they are in the middle of nowhere. The skin surrounding the area ranges in colour from dark purple to yellow with patches of blue and red for good measure.

Victoria is watching from the sink, where she is placing the cut flowers in a glass jar she found in the cupboard. 'Oh my days,' she comments, staring at Springer's wounds. She stands the jar on the window ledge then pours water from a jug into the stoneware bowl in the sink.

'Lie back on the bed,' she says, placing the bowl on the floor beside her. Placing one hand on Springer's shoulder, she gently pushes him back and pulls forward a cushion to place under his head.

Slowly Springer lowers his head down. Victoria sits beside him and, leaning forward, she soaks her handkerchief in the water before wringing it out and laying it over his bruises. The coolness of the water helps to reduce the temperature of the wounded area and she wipes down the damaged side of his body, repeatedly re-soaking the cloth to keep it clean and cold. She moves on to the cut above his eye, and follows the same procedure, wiping the dried blood and dirt away from the wound. Finally, she moves on to the ear. This time, as she makes contact with the stitched lobe, Springer grimaces. 'Easy, lass. That bit still be a mite prickly to the touch.'

'Sorry,' she murmurs; however, it does not deter her as she cleans and inspects all the damaged areas on Springer's body. Speaking softly as she works, she says, 'It must have been a brutal conflict.'

'It needed to be done to free me from my owing to your father.'

'Promise me you will never fight in the ring again. I do not think I could bear to see you again in the state you were in after the fight ended. It near broke my heart.'

Springer smiles at Victoria. 'Have no fear, little'un, I have no intention of fighting again for the entertainment of them there others. Not now, not ever. My life be now yours and yours alone. Our fate be for us to decide, not for others to dictate. To that end I promise thee.'

Victoria wipes the last of the bloodstained skin around Springer's neck, then throws the dirty handkerchief into the red water. She places both her hands on his shoulders and kisses him on the lips, slowly moves to his neck and then back to his lips.

Springer responds by holding her waist with one large hand and moving the other up over her breast, cupping it and gently rubbing her nipple with his thumb. As she moves back down his neck, trailing feather-light kisses, Springer whispers, 'By hell, my dear, you bring the fire out of me, you do.'

His grasp becomes stronger and his hand slides down to caress her bottom. Victoria is more confident in her actions, brushing her fingers through the hair on his chest.

Kissing her neck, he unbuttons the fasteners on the back of her pale blue dress and slides it over her head. As her hair falls back into place, he looks down at her plump, firm breasts. Her nipples have become erect, and he leans forward and nibbles each breast in turn.

Victoria feels the heat rising as he tweaks one nipple between thumb and forefinger while gently sucking on the other.

Her body quivers as the more experienced Springer gently works his way around her entire body, gently touching every part of her intimately. This is further than she has ever gone before with any man, and she is as much nervous as she is excited. Springer's kisses move upwards, around her breasts, up her chest, around her neck and back onto her lips. All the time his fingers are sliding in and out of her, and she trembles as she starts to feel light-headed and very responsive to his touch.

She slides her hand between his legs and feels his large, swollen penis. She pretends not to be shocked, but in truth it is the first time she has touched one.

Instinctively, she begins rubbing her hand up and down over his full erection and Springer thrusts his fingers deeper into her.

'Ohhhh,' she lets out a moan as his fingers start to get her juices flowing and a hot flush comes over her body as he gently explores every part of her.

Is this good or is this bad? she wonders as her body quivers with enjoyment. *It feels so good, so it must be right.*

Springer slowly rolls her across him and onto the bed, until he is on top of her, resting on his elbows. He gently opens her legs, allowing him to lie between them. She is still passionately kissing his neck as she feels him fumbling below. He looks her in the eyes to judge her response as he prepares to penetrate her, then he thrusts something a lot bigger than his fingers into her and her eyes light up as she releases her emotions.

He is well equipped and thrusts again and again, pushing deeper and deeper each time. Victoria moans with every thrust, holding on to his shoulders with her fingers and nails gripping tight. Each stroke stimulates her more and her body pulsates with pleasure. Again and again he thrusts and again and again her body trembles with delight. Soon, there is a welling up in her body that grows bigger and bigger with every thrust, and she is becoming more light-headed with every stroke. Her moaning gets louder and louder as her body quivers, encouraging Springer to thrust faster and faster.

He starts to sweat with the effort, and she is perspiring with the physicality of the engagement. The pain from the damage to his side is also building, but his desire is winning that battle, hands down. He is now thrusting faster and faster and she is gripping tighter and tighter, shaking with every deep penetration while her body is building up to something she does not understand. Her body quivers. The intensity inside is coming to a head as he thrusts deeper and harder than at any point so far.

Then he moans as he ejaculates into her body. She can feel the warm liquid spurting into her in pulses with every thrust. At the same time her body bursts with her first orgasm. In her head, the room is spinning, and her heart pounds as if it will leap out of her chest at any moment. She grips him tighter and trembles with delight and fear.

His thrusts start to slow, slower and slower before he stops and holds his position above her. Both are panting heavily at the physical effort and emotion they have put into this moment. Springer raises his head from her shoulder to look into her eyes. Victoria is still trembling and shaking. Her emotions are at near bursting point, and she does not fully understand them. She has tears weeping from her eyes as every part of her body tingles, while the pain from Springer's ribs is growing with intensity the more he comes down from the high of his actions.

This is an event that has never happened to Victoria before, and it takes her a while to calm herself and her body down. Springer goes to slide off, for fear that he is hurting her, but she holds him tightly and quietly whispers, 'No, stay with me. I need you to stay with me.'

Her body slowly settles down over the next few minutes. The quivering has subsided, and she strokes Springer's hair. She kisses him gently on the lips, then speaks softly into his ear. 'That was my first time.'

Springer is surprised by the statement, for she started this and had turned him on more than any other woman he has ever known – not that he was all that experienced to start with either.

As Springer slowly slides down and off her, she notices blood on his shoulders. 'Wait,' she says as she wipes it away to see where it has come from. 'Oh,' she murmurs as she realises it was her own nails that caused all the scratches on both his shoulders and upper arms. 'Looks like you have been in a fight with a wildcat or something.' She gives him a cheeky grin to match her words.

Springer smiles back. 'Or something! By God, lass, you bring out the fire in me, you do.' He does not roll away from her, but turns gently onto his good side, taking Victoria with him. He holds her lovingly in his arms and they stare into each other's eyes, sharing small kisses and rubbing noses for many a minute.

'I could get right used to being here with thee,' Springer comments as he looks over the scratch marks on his shoulder and upper arm, then plays on something Victoria said earlier. 'Mind you, it looks like I've been in a fight with a wildcat, an' a vicious one at that.'

Victoria is still beaming. 'Meow,' she whispers, laughing and pawing at his chest.

Springer could not be prouder. He has the love of his life wrapped in his arms. He may not know what the future holds or where they will end up, but with Victoria at his side, he is prepared to face and – if need be – fight anything that is thrown his way. 'Thee be worth your weight in gold to me, my dear.' He gently rubs his hands over her naked body, stroking with just his fingertips.

To Victoria, this is soothing and relaxing. It helps her body and mind to calm while allowing her to think about what she has just done with her man.

Now she has regained her composure, she feels back in control of herself again. It may have been her first time and she was a little afraid to start with, but now she feels good and excited inside. A new, more confident woman has emerged. Above all, she knows beyond all doubt that Springer is the only man for her. Sitting up, she starts to put her clothes back on. She has a desperate urge to go to the outhouse but is the kind of woman who is not prepared to go outside naked. Although not fully done up, the dress is on, and she slides her feet into her boots.

Looking at Springer, she says, 'I will be back shortly, my dear.'

She heads to the door and slips outside, closing it behind her. Springer can hear her footsteps on the path, the outhouse door being opened and closed, and a brief silence before, 'Oh my God, that is disgusting! And the smell! It stinks!'

Springer chuckles as he hears the door open and then slam back closed, followed by Victoria's footsteps as she stomps off into the woods, kicking things as she goes. He is trying not to picture what she has seen, but knowing the setup and what kind of people would be using this cabin, it was inevitable that the outhouse would not be in a pristine, woman-friendly condition.

'There will be no living with her now,' he comments to himself as he sits up to check out his ribs, touching around the bruised area. It is still very tender and painful, but mobility is an improvement on yesterday – especially after what he has just been able to do – as long as he ignores the pain.

Looking around the cabin, he spots a fly-fishing rod, net and a small wicker basket. It's enough to give him an idea, and he puts on his trousers and boots. In the basket, he finds several folded leather pads filled with an assortment of flies and a crude type of centre pin reel. He knows Victoria is going to come back in a fiery mood after the outhouse incident, so he takes the rod, basket and net and leaves the cabin.

Victoria is still in the woods, and he shouts out, 'I be back shortly' and heads for the brook. As he looks downstream along the narrow waterway, he can see where it widens out and he heads off to investigate. Sure enough, the brook joins a small river with overhanging willows and elder bushes on the far side. He crouches down and approaches the bank. The water is near to gin-clear, and he can see brown trout and what look to be grayling darting in and out of the cabbages, snapping at insects and flies drifting by in the current.

The rod is out and assembled in the blink of an eye, the small wooden reel is attached, and the line is put through the ring. He attaches a short catgut leader and views the available flies. He goes for a gold-headed hare's ear – a classic for this kind of water. Within minutes of his arrival, he is shooting out a line just short of the far bank and running a fly through the water in front of the cabbages. The first few casts have the fish showing an interest, but they only follow the fly and do not strike at it. With pinpoint accuracy, Springer puts the fly in the same place time after time. Eventually, he gets a take, and he strikes into a fish. It darts in and out of the current, lifting its large dorsal fin to get more purchase on the line as it shakes its head violently to try and shed the hook. After a strong but brief fight, a grayling weighing about a pound graces the net.

Springer takes the priest from the wicker basket and dispatches the fish with two swift strikes to the head. It was not his main goal, but it is a good, edible fish often referred to as the 'lady of the stream' – and a fine start to the fishing stint. He takes no time in cleaning and recasting his fly to the same spot on the river. On his third cast, he strikes into another grayling and again the fight is fast and furious as it darts in and out of the current. This time, though, the fish catches the side of a reed bed and slips the hook, much to Springer's annoyance.

He checks the fly, cleaning some weed off the hook and re-fluffing the fur trimming, then watches the water. He can see no sign of any more fish and concludes that the disturbance caused by the fish he lost has spooked the other ones away. He moves downstream about twenty yards to a bend in the river, where the flow speeds up on the far side and there is a large, submerged boulder making a good ambush point for a predatory fish. He recasts the fly five or six times to the same area before he is happy with its positioning, then he lets the fly drift past the rock. Just as it reaches the darkness of its depths past the boulder, a shadow shoots out and hits the fly. There is no need to strike as the split cane rod doubles over with the impact of the take. The rod is raised just as the fish leaves the water with a jump of around three feet. The flex in the rod takes the pressure but only just. The fish dives down to the depths before coming up and leaping out of the water for a second time. Only Springer's skill and experience keeps this fish on the end of his hook – knowing when to give some line out and understanding when to keep pressure on the raging fish.

In and out of the depths, it tears line off the reel. Springer gains a few feet before he loses ten. Assessing his choices, he is left with no option but to follow his foe downstream while reeling in all the line he dares. He keeps enough tension on the line to prevent the hook from pulling out, but also enough play in the rod to absorb the constant barrage of runs.

While playing the fish, Springer looks for a suitable place on the bank to land his adversary. Just as he thinks he has the upper hand, the fish goes on another run, this time rubbing the line on some submerged willow roots as it tries to shed the hook. Springer applies as much sideward pressure to the fish as he dares, to get it away from the underwater obstruction. He knows the line will be frayed from the dragging along the roots, so he must end the fight quickly or risk losing his prize.

Slowly, with pressure applied, the fish is teased back into open water, where he allows it to swim around in circles to wear itself out. With the fish's energy all but spent, Springer moves to the edge of the river and, crouching down, lowers the net into the water. He gently coaxes the fish towards the net before scooping it up at the last minute. 'Oh yes!' he yells as he swings the fish back onto the land behind him. Unfolding the net reveals a plump, three- to four-pound spotted brown trout. 'What a prize,' he mutters as he grabs the priest and, with a crisp crack to the head, dispatches the fish instantly.

Not being greedy, he packs the fishing gear away. He has all he requires for a meal or two and will not need to catch any more for a while. He grabs a length of willow from a nearby tree and peels off the bark and leaves, then threads the pliable branch through the gills of each fish and uses it to carry them back to the lodge.

There is a large grin on his face as he enters, wipes his feet on the mat and places the fish in the sink. Victoria, now fully clothed and presentable, is standing by the fire, brushing her hair. Coughing loudly and raising his eyebrows, he points to his hard-won prize in the sink.

'Is there something wrong with your finger?' she asks.

'No, my love. Over there in the sink,' he replies.

She gracefully walks over and peers into the sink and nods her head in approval.

Springer puffs out his chest. 'Man will provide, me lady. Be not afraid I cannot supply what is needed for the table when you are with me.'

Victoria smiles and points delicately at the sideboard. He cannot believe his eyes, for sitting on the side are two fully plucked pheasants – heads attached – a large bowl of assorted wild mushrooms, a bowl full of blueberries and blackberries and a dozen or so eggs.

'What...? When...? How...?' Springer's words do not come out well, for he is totally lost for what to say. He walks over to inspect the goods on offer, checking the mushrooms and berries to ensure they all are safe to eat. The pheasants are still slightly warm to the touch. Beside them is a bowl full of freshly plucked feathers which Victoria has used to sit the eggs on.

'Where be they come from, then?'

Victoria puts her hands on her hips and thrusts out her ample chest. 'Man may provide food, but a woman provides a feast.' He looks at her, looks back at the bounty she has provided, and looks back at her again.

'Well I be blowed. There be more to thee than I be thinking,' he utters with a shake of his head.

Victoria raises her eyebrows and lets out a cheeky smile. 'Ask and I will never tell, but you are not the only one with abilities, my dear.'

Swinging her hips, she walks over to the fireplace and takes off her boots, leaning them up against the fire guard to dry out, then stands by the bed. 'Now, come over here and finish what you started, before I begin the dinner.'

Springer is, again, lost for words – for this woman is full of surprises.

He holds her in his arms and kisses her passionately. Leaning back, he looks into her eyes. 'I fear I created a monster in thee. This man be needing his rest and recovery.'

She puts her arms round his neck and slowly leans back onto the bed, gently pulling Springer down on top of her. 'A woman needs to know that her man can satisfy her needs. Now let me think… How many rounds did you fight in that ring the other day?'

Springer's eyes widen. 'By 'eck, lass, I'm just a man, not an army.'

Victoria slides her leg around him. Her hands work on taking off his shirt, pulling it over his head and flinging it onto the floor. 'Let's see how many rounds you have left in you, shall we?' she says with a grin.

CHAPTER 10

A Place to Call Home

It's a damp, cold and misty morning on the border between Hampshire and Dorset. A large, heavy cart travels slowly along a disused pathway, cutting a new route through the overgrown, dew-soaked undergrowth. On the front of this wagon sits the lonely figure of a woman wrapped tightly in a thick, red-and-black blanket to help keep out the early chill. She shakes the reins, encouraging the two horses to pull on, knowing they cannot stop for fear the heavily loaded cart will sink into the soft ground.

It is evident she has given her all and is tired from the effort she has put in for a long time. She is near exhaustion, but her will is strong and she is determined to stay the course – as her great journey is near to completion and she is about to see the land she has come so far to make her own.

In the back of the cart there are many lengths of timber, working tools, a large metal fire grate and – on top of the wood – one large cage containing a dozen chickens of varying colours and a smaller cage housing three Gloucester Old Spot piglets.

Tied to the back of the wagon on a length of rope is a young tan-and-white bull and beside him a red-and-tan cow. They are followed by a ram and four ewes which have been kept in close order by a man and his large crook, who ushers them on with various clicks and noises. Perched in this man's arms is a small black-and-white Border Collie puppy. Its legs dangle over his forearm and rock with the motion of his walking and it is constantly looking around at anything that moves, happily chewing on the man's sleeve as it enjoys the free ride.

The cart continues for about another one hundred yards before it reaches the entrance to a small spinney of sweet chestnut trees. 'You can stop here, my love,' the man calls out. He walks up to the front of the cart, places the puppy on the floor and lifts the woman to the ground.

Pushing open the old, well-worn gate just wide enough to walk through, he takes the lady by the hand and leads her through the entrance and under the canopy of trees.

On the right, there are the remains of a farmhouse in need of a new roof and various other repairs. The windows have seen better days and the front door is broken and hangs to one side. In front of them is a huge, open meadow of long grass and wildflowers that dance and shimmer as they sway left and right in the morning breeze.

A river snakes its way along the valley floor, turning this way and that as it finds its way through the fields, only to fade and finally disappear into the last of the morning mist.

On the left, in the distance, a mature wood of mixed trees stands firm and tall, sheltering two rustic barns and the wooden frames of holding pens. The sun is attempting to break through in patches, but this early in the morning, it is still a struggle to shrug off the veil of morning fog.

The trees show off their thick canopy of greens and browns, while within the uppermost branches a parliament of crows is hopping from limb to limb, announcing their presence to the world and each other in the noisiest of fashions.

Finally, beyond the farm building a thick drystone wall sparkles like a million diamonds as the emerging sun reflects off the dew drops resting on the moss-covered rocks. Although some areas have collapsed and are in need of levelling and rebuilding, it is an impressive sight with most of the remaining wall still standing at around five feet. It runs from the top of the hill all the way down to the mist at the river's edge, enclosing the meadow.

It's been over six months since the fight, when Springer and Victoria left the village to seek their safety and happiness away from the evil hands of Lord Fitzgerald and his kind. Many obstacles have been overcome and challenges faced and defeated on this journey, just to make it this far. With so little in the way of help and support to start with, and so many people looking for them, it has been no small undertaking to finally get here. But now, going back to the place Springer once used as a refuge and had often dreamed of owning, they have a chance. Here they have an opportunity to start their new lives together in the quiet of the English countryside.

'I know it be not much at the moment, but it be ours now and in time enough it will be a sight to behold, of that I am sure,' Springer says while holding on to his beloved.

Victoria stands in awe as she looks over the valley and takes in all the view has to offer. Taking a long, deep breath, she turns to him. 'It's as beautiful as you said it was. I am sure it will do us just fine.'

He gently squeezes her and cups her swelling stomach. 'I won't have long to fix this there house now, will I?' he says with a beaming smile. 'That there youngern will be here right quick like to this world, I'm sure.'

He releases his hold on Victoria and walks over to the ailing house. Stepping through the open doorway, he pushes some of the rubble away and pulls an old wooden stool from the debris.

'Now sit thee down there while I unload what we need first.' He lowers Victoria gently onto the stool, picks up the fallen blanket and wraps it back around her shoulders. 'There thee be, my love. We needed to start on rebuilding our home at some point, for it be our land now and I be wanting this dream for so long.'

Victoria smiles at him. 'I know, but at nights we still have George's place for now, and he is a good man.' Springer returns to the wagon and unhooks the cattle, leading them to the huge meadow and releasing the head collar on the cow and the rope on the bull's nose ring. The animals run into the field and instantly start to graze. The sheep are soon to follow as Springer guides them through the gate and watches as they tear down the hill not knowing where to go first. Before long, they too start to graze on the knee-high meadow of grass. He turns to Victoria and smiles. 'We be farmers now, with livestock on our own lands.'

Victoria watches him as he dismantles the contents of the cart. First the cages are placed on the ground beside the wagon, then the metal grate is upended and rolled off the back onto the grass.

Suddenly, she feels something cold and wet touching her leg and she twitches. The little puppy is prodding her with his nose. Desperate to get her attention, he paws at her leg, his tail wagging so frantically that his whole body wiggles. He lets out a small yap, as if to ensure he has been seen.

'Hello, little man,' she says as she reaches down and picks him up, folding him into the blanket. She strokes his ears and massages the top of his head, as they watch Springer.

Victoria's mind starts to wander, back to the time a few months earlier when the place they now own was just an idea in Springer's head. They did not know who owned the land, nor whether they would be prepared to sell it to them for a price they could afford. But Springer was determined to find out, either way. They had eventually arrived at the village of Stockton. Hungry, cold and tired, they'd headed for the local tavern – ironically called The Travellers Rest.

Being in the situation they were, they had the routine down to a fine art – coats on, hood up on Victoria, cap down on Springer. She would find the quietest area of the tavern, preferably near the open fire if there was one, and sit quietly, not looking at anyone. Springer would collect some drinks from the landlord and enquire after some food. They would avoid drawing any attention and would not speak to any of the locals if it could be avoided.

But in this case, it was different. They needed to know who the main landowners were to the south of the village. This meant they needed to strike up a conversation with someone and make some enquiries. They thought the best person to talk to would be the landlord, as he would have good knowledge of the area and know all the local people – as the village tavern in all places is usually the focal point of village life.

As the landlord arrived with their food, Springer brought up that he was looking for work as a farmhand and was wondering who best to ask in the area. It soon became clear that the same person owned most of the land around that side of the village. A man by the name of George Todd. They also found out that he rented various plots to farmer tenants and lived on an estate about three miles away. They decided to board a room at the inn for the night, have a good rest and seek out the landowner in the morning.

With all that Springer and Victoria had been through, they were mentally and physically exhausted. All that was left of their belongings now fitted into one medium case. Just to get this far and still be hiding out from Lord Fitzgerald was a small miracle. Their journey had taken a huge toll on the pair of them, especially Victoria in the condition she was now in. Perhaps now they were finally close to the end of the road, as they could be just days away from starting afresh with a safe place to rebuild their lives.

The following day, they got up, packed what little they had, paid the innkeeper their board and made their way to the farm where the landowner lived. This final leg of the journey was making the pair of them very nervous, and they didn't talk much as they both thought about all the possible outcomes. Victoria in particular had given up everything and now didn't just have herself to think about. She had never seen this bit of land that Springer talked about so much, but she had been willing to go on the faith of the man she loved so dearly.

With the pace that Victoria could move at, it took them nearly two hours to reach the entrance to the farm. Part way down the track, they stopped and took stock of what they saw. It was not a huge mansion by any standards that Victoria was used to, but a large, two-storey country farmhouse – no doubt with several rooms on each level. However, there were many buildings, barns, stables and sheds of all sizes surrounding it. Clearly this was a busy working farm with a great deal going on. It just looked a little scrappy and run down to the eye.

They knocked on the front door and waited for several minutes with no response. Springer knocked again and – with still no response – they started to look around. It was then they saw an older man walking towards them, flanked by two Border Collies which – although they walked in step with him – both had their eyes firmly fixed on Springer and Victoria.

'Yes, can I help you?' he asked.

'I be here to see a man by the name of George. George Todd,' Springer replied.

The man was stocky, pushing his sixties and about five foot eight. He bore a white moustache and wore a tweed jacket, waistcoat and cap.

'I see,' he replied. 'And what would you want to talk to this man about, then?'

'I be here to see if he owns a piece of land up yonder with a house in need of repair and a meadow with an old stone wall down its side. I be askin' to see if it be available for us to purchase an' claim as our own.'

The man looked them up and down. 'Well, that would be me then. My name is George and I know well the land you are talking about.' He walked past them to the entrance of the house, opened the door and turned to his two visitors. 'Well, you had better come in then.' He clicked at his two dogs, who sprinted at the sound, running through the door and down the corridor and diving into a large wicker basket with a chequered blanket. They turned and dropped instantly while facing George intently. 'You can hang your coats on the hooks in front,' George said. 'And leave your case on the floor below. It will be safe enough with Harley and Meg watching it.' He pointed at the two dogs in the basket. 'You will both find chairs at the end of the hall, and I will be with you shortly,' he said and walked into another adjacent room.

Springer and Victoria walked down to the room at the end. It opened up with a large oak table and eight chairs in the middle of the room. A fireplace smouldered at the back and the wooden beams were covered with dusty ornaments and brasses of various shapes and sizes. It was a well-used room but had clearly missed the attentions of a woman cleaning for a long time.

George returned after cleaning himself up. He joined them at the table, still drying his hands on a towel. Now that Victoria was without her hood and Springer had removed his cap, George took another good look at the both of them before speaking.

'Seems to me I have seen your faces before somewhere.'

They both looked at George nervously – especially Victoria, who was coming to the end of what she could take from this ordeal. George thought for a moment. 'It would be when I go to the bigger town at Newark, some twenty-five miles away, to deliver stock. I have seen your pictures posted at various places all over the town in the past few months.'

Victoria started to tremble, and Springer went to stand up.

'Now, now, lad. Sit yourself back down. There is only me in the house and I'm not here to judge.' Springer paused, then sat back down again. 'I am only saying that in more populated places, you are still being looked for to a more intense level.'

'Oh God,' Victoria let out. 'I don't think I can take much more of this.' She was starting to panic, and Springer took her hand in his.

'Easy, lass, there be none alive I would let harm thee while I draw breath. Now calm theeself down. It will do you no good to be upset.'

'Please, please do not upset yourself. There is nothing to fear here. I am not going to endanger you – I just needed to be sure, you see.'

From the moment George saw them, he'd known there was something about them that was different from all the others who had asked after the land. During the conversation, it did not take long for him to put two and two together. With all the searching, posters and attention created by Lord Fitzgerald's men, it would be impossible not to know who Springer and Victoria were, where they came from and why they were looking for a quiet smallholding in the middle of nowhere.

'So if I be not mistaken, you, young man, are the infamous Springer – murderer and wanted criminal with an offence list as long as your arm. Making you Victoria, an abducted and helpless woman, dragged away by this man against her will when he made his escape.' He chuckled and smiled at the pair of them. 'That is if I were to believe all I heard of late. Now tell me, how have you been able to stay hidden for so long, with so many looking for you?'

'I can't say it be easy, but we have met a few kindly people who have been good enough to help. But now my Victoria is soon to be with child, I need to find a place for her to be safe. And many a year back, when times were 'ard, I slept in that there shell of a house on the land I ask thee about now and it served me well enough on a cold night more than once. But more so, the view and location – it be grand on the eye and away from them that seek to find us and claim the reward.'

'Yes, that it be. I could put no better word on its beauty or position myself. And the well… it may need to be cleaned out and the stones reset around the top, but it is spring-fed and is as sweet as it comes.' George went on to explain that he started out in that very cottage with his wife nearly forty years ago. Every stone, brick, tile and piece of wood had been through his hands. He had built the house from scratch, and carried every stone used in the retaining wall on the edge of the field from the rock edge on the hills above and the riverbed below.

'We lived there for twenty years before I had enough to buy all the land around the area, and with the additional land and several good years, I could afford to have this larger house built and purchase more land. Now with my wife long since gone and not being blessed with any children to inherit these lands, I am left with just squabbling distant relations who are waiting for me to die so they can claim my farm and all my hard work for themselves.'

George paused for a while as he thought on his words. 'There is more to me knowing about you two – or should I say where you both came from – than you are aware. For I know Pippinsford very well. I spent a lot of my youth there working for my older brother, Steven Todd. He was one of the original farmers who had a large estate there and had cleared much of the land for the growing of fruit. He was one of the old group of farmers that used to own land in Pippinsford before Lord Fitzgerald and his associates moved in and slowly started to take over the whole village.'

He talked about how Steven and his family were one of the last groups of original landowners to have allegedly sold up and left the area, never to be seen again. Try as he might, he could never get to the bottom of his disappearance. He still looked to this day as he knew his brother, like him, loved the land he lived on and would never have given it up – not with two sons to continue working the farm after he would pass away.

They continued talking and George set the fire with Springer and made tea for the three of them. Springer and Victoria gave George all the information they had about Lord Fitzgerald and his operation and the people involved. It did not give hope to his brother being alive but did give him valuable information on Lord Fitzgerald and the key players involved.

'I have some good friends who will help me have words with one or two of these men, in particular this Brannigan and Sykes,' George said as he poured Victoria another cup of tea with a smile. 'I afford me these luxuries like tea now I have the wealth to do so. It is one of my only vices, and having people to enjoy it with is a real treat.'

Springer looked at George and reached out to hold Victoria's hand.

'If thee intend to pay them there two a visit, that you be speaking about, I would like to come along If I may. A debt needs paying for what was done to Victoria's young kin. And though I not be there when they needed, I will end their wrongdoing permanently.'

Victoria looked at Springer, but she did not oppose his call. For she had as much hate for these men as he did.

'Well, that being said, I can only allow you to come along if I know where to find you when we go, which brings us to the reason you are here.' George paused. 'The land you want is dear to me, as it was where I started with my wife. I have fond memories of that place, and the sweat and the graft it took to build it and clear the meadow and build the wall. So, with that in mind, how much are you prepared to give for this piece of land?'

Springer reached into his pocket and pulled out a pouch containing sixty-eight gold sovereigns. He spread them on the table along with a handful of silver shillings. Victoria placed a bag containing all the jewellery she possessed.

George viewed all what was on the table. 'Is that all you have?'

Victoria took off her locket containing the pictures of her two brothers and added it to the pile. 'It is of solid gold, with a few precious stones in it.'

Springer spoke up. 'I will add more when I am up and running as I know this be not near half what the land be worth to you. But to survive these last few months and keep to moving from so many that be out to have at us has cost us dear.'

'Indeed,' said George as he stood up. 'You travel here in great peril with a woman who is with child and near to exhaustion. What you offer is not enough, but it is everything you own. And you are willing to help a man you have never met avenge the loss of his brother! No, no, no,' he says slowly, sliding the jewellery and locket back to Victoria. He takes fifty-five gold sovereigns off the top of the pile and pushes all the other coins back to Springer. 'How many people take the risks you have? Who else offers everything they own, and more to come as they earn it, in this day and age?' He stacked the pile of coins in front of him. 'This is all I want for the land. And I have a request. If your first be a girl, consider calling her Molly after my good wife. For hearing her name being called out would make me feel like she is still around. You see, if you love the land half as much as I do, it will be worth it to see a family take it on and make it live again. For it's been too barren and dry here for too long. Laughter and the sound of children playing in the fields has been gone for many a year, since my labour force no longer be families.'

They could not believe what George was offering. 'Thank you,' came out from Victoria, for she was fit to burst with relief and excitement. 'If it is not a girl at first, we will try until we have a Molly.'

Springer could not speak; he was lost for words at such generosity and kindness, something he had not come across often in his life. So, he just shook George's hand.

'You will find out the back a large, heavy cart. Use it and the money I gave you back to get all the supplies from the village to rebuild the house. There is a good sawmill just outside the other end of the village. He will have some stock you can have, and within a few days of asking, he will have made the rest of what you require to finish the job. You just mention my name and he will see you well. When the time is right, I will have a few spare livestock cut out to help you get going. You can pick them up when the walls are better repaired and replace them when you have bred your own,' he said with a smile. 'Be mindful though; I will ask for help on my farm when needed as I am not as strong as I used to be and for some things, I could use the help of a stronger man.'

'That be not a problem. I will help thee when an' where you need it, so help me. I swear it,' replied Springer with great excitement in his voice.

George had not told Springer or Victoria yet – and he may never do so – but six months ago he was at the fair, watching Springer fight. At the time he was visiting a friend who lived in the village, as he was still hoping to find out more about his missing brother and where he might have gone. He had seen Lord Fitzgerald sitting up high and mighty in the viewing box, saw how he treated the people, heard how he spoke to those around him. Now sitting with Springer and Victoria, he could see how he pursued people who tried to get away from him, or who would not bend to his will. His friend had highlighted that if any wrongdoing was going on, then that man would be at the centre of it. And after hearing about him and his goings-on from Springer and Victoria, he was sure he would not need to look any further than that man for answers.

'Now there is a small problem to be overcome,' he said. 'I need to register the land to the new owner, or it will not be yours. But it would not be safe for me to put your names down with so many people looking for you. So for the moment, should you wish, I will put down Mr and Mrs S. Todd on the deed and bill of sale. No one knows my brother's sons in these parts, so you could go about your daily business without interference. And who would question me over having my brother's son on his own family's land? It would help me out as well, as Molly escaped from an orphanage and has no family. So, my land would be protected from those distant relations who would rob me when I'm weak of mind and near the end. Not saying I am there yet – I have many a summer left in these old bones, and I intend to be here for as many as I can.'

'You offer so much for so little in return,' said Victoria. 'Pray tell me why you would do such a thing for us?'

'There comes a time in life when money and wealth are not all it's made up to be. I want to see new blood on these lands again, and the sound of laughter in the air. I want to see the land being used and people making a living from their own efforts like I have. You, my dear, have given up a life of luxury to be with this man Springer… Wait!' He turned to Springer. 'What is your first name?'

'It be Springer, sir. That be all.'

'No. First of all, I'm not "sir" and second of all, if I am to have a close neighbour disguised as a nephew, surely knowing your first name is not too much to ask?'

Victoria raised her eyebrows. 'Yes, until now I have never thought of it. But I would also like to know as well.'

Springer paused, and quietly uttered, 'Bartholomew.'

Victoria choked back her laughter, but George took it a bit further. 'I'm sorry? What was that?'

Springer looked at them both and shook his head. 'I believe it be Bartholomew Benedict Springer, though I be not sure for certain. My ma was a right one for church and the words that be spoken by them that were righteous.'

Victoria burst into laughter and George by now was also holding on to his emotions for dear life. 'Well, that is a bit of a mouthful,' he said, then also started to chuckle.

'I think I will stick to Springer,' Springer said politely. 'Yes, well, now that be known and over with, I think I would prefer it to be between us so not to give them there others any ideas of laughing.'

'I think I like Bartholomew better,' Victoria said with a grin. 'Perhaps I should call you that always.'

'Eh, I be not having that from the woman I love. There's pride at stake here and I cannot be seen as a bible thumper.'

George's expression turned serious. 'Victoria, I think it best if you and your man stay in my house for now. It's cold at night and you are in no fit state to spend nights outside or be too long working in these damp conditions. That cottage will take some time to be near to habitable again for a woman with child. Anyway, this house could do with opening up a few more rooms, and I would enjoy the company.' Springer and Victoria looked at each other as George continued. 'You can work on your house and the land during the day, but it makes sense not to push yourself too much in your condition.'

Springer spoke to Victoria. 'It be a fair and wise move, my dear. There be a lot for me to do and fix. You being safe and warm would ease my mind while I get the doing done.' He turned to George. 'I cannot thank thee enough for your kindness, George. Victoria is my life and the child to come is precious and more than I deserve, I'm sure. I have not had faith or reason to trust in people in many a year, and now I have two – Victoria and you. We do not want to be a burden to you and if you say go, we will get the go. But I would like kindly to take you up on this offer. I will do all that you see fit to repay for such goodness shown by thee.'

Before George got to answer, Victoria added, 'I must ask you, George, why would you offer so much when before today you had never seen or known of us at all? We bring you the risk of trouble and strife and yet you offer us your home to stay at. We cannot fully afford the land we ask for and yet you give it to us for less than it is worth. We do not have much to offer you in kind except for our friendship and gratitude and the promise to always be here to help in any way we can. But is this enough for you?'

George paused and thought his answer through carefully. 'Over the past few years, since Molly passed away, I get up in the morning, feed the animals, organise the labour and start in the fields and orchards. I finish after dark and return to the house. Every day is the same repeat performance. Don't get me wrong; I'm not complaining. I love my life and all my animals and what I do, but it can be a little bit lonely, and I do miss good neighbours, social contact, seeing the land being used for the better and people who are prepared to work to better themselves. I enjoy the company of friends and the laughter of children, and I want to see this place go forward with deserving people for many years to come, even after I have gone.' He took a deep breath. 'You see, I do receive many people asking for that plot of land. I must have had a dozen or so people ask to farm on that patch of dirt in the last year alone – some of whom I know, in other cases they have offered me a great deal of money for the land you now own. But they did not have that something that I feel the land needs – that sparkle in their eyes, that passion and desire to make a go of it. You two have that by the spade load. And most of all, I want to see you succeed and achieve all the things that you desire from it.'

He smiled at Victoria. 'Who knows, you two might inspire me to go and find someone to share these latter years with.' He laughed and sipped his tea. 'But for now, a lot of my time is spent working out constant issues on the farm. I need to work on where all my game goes in winter. Why the salmon catches in the river seem less and less each year, though I see a lot migrating during the season. I see a lot of everything throughout the year, but when it comes to harvesting, I seem to get less than what I expect from the fields.'

Springer raised an eyebrow. 'What be the problem? Land seems good to hold game, and the fields look sizeable enough.'

'Well, I hatch and rear additional pheasant and partridge to add to the wild stock, leave some of the maze and root crops in the fields unharvested to let them feed on when released. This also helps to keep them in the area of my land, as they tend to stick to a food source if you provide them. But come the days of the shoot, the game is sparse to say the least. The same with the salmon and trout. The river is full of fish all year, as you will find out with it on the land you now have. I have five miles of that river, near to one hundred and fifty glides, holes, pools, eddies and bends to fish. Three ghillies on the books running the beat, but my return is poor, and I do not have as many people want to fish it as I used to. Stockbreeding herds show less calves making it to maturity and the deer and wild boar don't show as they used to. My grain and other crops are also lighter than the samples I take to predict for the fields' take.'

Springer looked at Victoria then back at George. 'Seems to me that you must have poachers or employees who be looking to themselves before thee. What you be needin' is a master poacher and scrounger. A man who knows the workings of the trade. One not known to them that do the taking around here. One who has seen and used all the tricks and where the gains be sold, but having him work for thee, not against.'

'Yes, but where would you find someone like that who you can also trust to run the operation without stealing from you?' asked George.

'Aye, that be true. I know only one. Canny as a fox, slippery as an eel. I bear witness to his work – he be a master poacher alright. In the trade, I would say there be none better.'

Victoria chuckled. 'You're talking about Dan, aren't you? I always thought he was a poacher, by the way Cook always had the best of all meat and fish and lots of it. That would be why Lord Fitzgerald hated him so much and was always wanting to know where he was.' She laughed and shook her head. 'What a rogue that man be and shame on Cook for being married to him.'

'Springer, you know this man Dan – could he be able to help? I mean would he take gainful employment, and could he be trusted?'

'Know him, yes. But only one person has the reins on that there rascal, for even he dares not mess with that one. She would have the skin off his back and the flesh from his bones. Though me thinks it's more that he be married to her and loves her beyond all things.'

'Who is this woman you speak of?' George asked.

'She be the cook from Victoria's old home. Her name is Mira Beth, but we all just know her as Cook. If yee be needin' Dan, then it be Cook you need. For he would follow her like a moth to a flame.'

'A cook, you say?' George paused for a minute. 'I have not had a cook here in this house since Molly died.' In his head, he was working out an idea. He got up from the table and walked over to the fireplace. Grabbing the poker, he moved the red embers around and made a gap in the middle then placed two more split logs in the gap and pushed the embers up against the new wood.

Springer and Victoria just watched as he prodded the fire. They could see he was rolling things around in his mind. After a minute or so, he placed the poker back in the stand and returned to the table.

'In the last few years, I may not have made the best of what I have here. What with the loss of Molly and the disappearing of my brother, I seem to have allowed time to stand still while all around things have been deteriorating and going sour. But now, talking to you two, I realise I cannot dwell and just sit back anymore. I need to get stuck back in. It's me letting down myself to a degree. I need to start fighting back and take back control of my estate from those who may be taking advantage.' He took a deep breath. 'I do have an idea, but I would ask you first as there is a risk of your location being found out if you cannot trust the people you know, so it would be your call if I was to do this.'

Victoria started to feel a little uncomfortable. For the first time, she felt uneasy with what was about to be said.

'Now, hear all I have to say before you comment as it will make more sense as I go on. I have sixteen people working on this farm with the livestock, fruit trees and crops. Three ghillies, three woodsmen and many seasonal people during the five months of picking and sorting crops, fish and animals. It's a bit much for me to monitor all of them, run the farm and deal with the selling and buying of produce and feed.' He looked at Springer. 'Springer, you have knowledge of how things on a farm should run and how to organise people and get the best out of them. If you were to work for me four days in the week, I would have you as a foreman on this farm. I know it would slow the build on your house and land by a few months, but I would pay you fair and you and Victoria could stay here however long it takes until you are ready to move in.'

He turned to Victoria. 'My dear, I know you are well-educated, and I would presume you are good with accounting. In your spare time, could you view my books and help me to make sense of what I don't understand and assist me to become more organised? It may help me to understand where my weaknesses in the farm are. Give me guidance on where to improve what I am doing to better these areas.

'To all these farmhands, you would be introduced as my nephew and his wife from down south. None of them will know of you, so it would be good for you being here in this house for a while as it would be what an uncle does while building up your own place.

'Here comes the part that would expose you. I would like to seek this Mira Beth – or Cook, as you call her – and offer the lady the position of cook here in my house. I would offer her board here in this house to start with and a wage to fit the position. That way I could cater for fishing and shooting parties as well as leave her to do our food, allowing us to get more done on the farm.

'I would also like this husband Dan to arrive here and work as my gamekeeper and take charge of the ghillies and woodsmen and all gaming duties. But not before he has arrived on the quiet, spent some time in the area and found out the people who are doing me harm and offence. If he does this for me, they can have the old mill cottage on the river as part of their employment to make their own for as long as they choose to be here. It's a nice place with a small garden and a wooden jetty for a small boat launch.'

Victoria was rubbing her hands together, and Springer could see she had tensed up and was a little nervous about this suggestion. 'What be your thoughts on the offer, my dear?' Springer asked her softly.

'I'm not sure. We have come a long way, spent months looking over our shoulders. To finally be so close to a place of our own and risk so much scares me.' She turned to George. 'I do not just think of me but for Springer and what they would do to him if they found him. For I know with me in this condition he would not see out the night in their hands if he was caught. As for me, I am carrying Springer's child. I could not bear to think what Lord Fitzgerald would do to my baby and me. He is a monster with no thought for others. Even his own brothers and sisters were wiped out by his greed and evil ways.'

'It was only a suggestion,' George replied. 'I would not want to put you in fear. This idea only came to mind as you two have inspired me to wake up and look at what I have and see if I can better use what is around me. I will not bring it up again and am sorry to have distressed you.'

'No, please do not apologise. The idea is sound and of good logic and merit. I know when we left that Cook was in fear for Dan's life. Without Springer there to watch over him, the risk of them finding him are greatly increased. You see, they have never had a place to call their own. Dan sees Cook when he can, but he was always hiding out in the woods and various shelters. For them to have a chance like us would be something they truly deserve.'

Springer nodded. 'When I be thinking to leave, the risk they both took to help was more than I have words for… as well as Cook tending to my wounds and helping this here lass to find me when I knew not myself that she was for me. I owe her alright, more than words can say.'

Victoria faced George. 'You do know if you ask Cook to work here, she will expect to run the kitchen and have improvements made?' George dipped his head in acknowledgement. 'She runs a tight, timely ship and would not think twice to putting broom to arse and head if you interfere with her work or the kitchen.'

George laughed. 'She sounds like what I need round here alright.'

'Then I guess that I must say yes. The idea is a good one and I know we can trust Cook whether she comes here or not. If she chooses for her and Dan to come and work here, it will certainly have an impact on your life as well as theirs.' Victoria sighed heavily. 'The problem at hand would be how to approach Cook in the right way, that would not raise suspicion with my father. Or risk exposing us to our past and giving up the location of where we will be living. If she does decide that she would like to work for George and have this change in her life, how could she leave without raising any suspicion as to why?'

Springer spoke up. 'I be thinkin' we be needing to have words with Cook. To my mind, the best place by a long throw would be when she goes to The Hare and Hound tavern. She be seen a lot there, so none would be the wiser to her comings. An' that there landlord be a right friend to the both of them – switching messages from she to thee in exchange for free game and fish from Dan's activities.'

'Yes, I see where you're going with this, Springer. If we had someone there staying at the tavern as a guest, they would be in the bar when Cook arrives. Then we could arrange a place to meet and talk by giving her a message in a letter,' suggested George. 'But would she trust a stranger giving her a letter, given that the only reason she is there is to find out about her husband on the quiet? She will no doubt be very cautious and careful about giving him away, so she would need convincing that the message was from someone she trusts.'

'I do have one thing that she will trust and will know is from me,' said Victoria, placing her locket in front of them both. 'If that is in the letter, she will believe it is genuine, for she is one of the few that know I have this.'

George picked up the locket and opened it. Inside he saw a small picture of two boys, Edward and Oliver, and on the other side a picture of a young woman. Rebecca.

'These are, or should I say were, my brothers. And that is my younger sister. For I know not their fates at this time,' she said in a quiet voice. Thinking about them again really hit home. She stared at the locket in George's hand and even though she made no sound, tears started to roll down her cheeks.

Springer noticed the tears and got up to comfort her. 'Easy, lass.'

George looked up and realised her distress. He closed the locket. 'I'm sorry,' he said. 'I did not mean to upset you. Here,' He passed back the locket. 'I'm sure we can find a way without using this.'

Victoria looked at him with her watery eyes. 'No. This is the best way. It will have the same effect on Cook as it has me. It is not the locket that upsets me. I am just full of hate for HIM. If I were a man, I would ki—'

Springer butts in. 'Easy, my dear. Thee ort not be upsetting yourself while in this condition. George and I be dealing with HIM and them there others soon enough, believe me. Now let's best be working on a message to Cook and Dan and see if we can get them here and find any wrongdoing that be going on. Once we know, George and I can sort what be needing to be done.'

'As I have stayed at the tavern before, I think it best that I go and stay there again. What day does Cook usually visit?' asked George.

'By my thinking, it be Friday. Around three, after lunch. That's when she takes herself away from the kitchen for an hour or so without much fuss and bother,' replied Springer.

'I will write the letter and seal it with my locket inside. Shall we say to meet by the river crossing at four in the afternoon? That way she can be spoken to on her way back to Father's house.'

They continued to plan out the meeting for the next half hour before Springer changed the subject.

'George, I know this be important and I will do all that be needed to get the doing done, but is there any room that my lass Victoria can be resting in while we plan the day?' He pointed at Victoria, who was falling asleep at the table.

'But of course! Come with me and I will show you the best room in the house. It has its own fireplace, and it would be good to see it used again.' He led the way as Springer carried Victoria in his arms close behind.

George entered a room down the corridor and held the door open. As Springer placed Victoria on the bed and started to unroll a blanket to cover her, George was already at the fireplace, lighting the prebuilt fire. 'I have always kept this room ready for friends and guests, just like my Molly used to. But it is the first time I have had the chance to use it in a long time.' He turned to Springer. 'I would just like to say that no matter what happens, I am grateful you and Victoria have turned up on my doorstep today. I can see it will make great changes to me, my farm and the smallholding you have just purchased. All of a sudden, I feel excited at what could happen in the future. It makes me want to give it one more round and breathe life back into this farm of mine.' He stood up and placed a metal guard at the front of the fire to protect the room from spitting embers.

'I be a bit the same with them there thoughts in my mind,' says Springer. 'Seven months ago, I be alone in this world, wondering why I was here and with no real will to face the oncoming day. Now I have the love of a fine woman I thought was beyond approach, a youngern of ours near born and the place of my dreams to build and make our own. I've met a man willing to show compassion and help me at a time I be needin' it most, at no small risk to his own self should them that be looking find out where we be living and hiding. Words do not come easy to folk like me, but I be ever indebted to you for the kindness thee has done for Victoria, me and my soon-to-be youngern.'

George patted Springer on the shoulder. 'Perhaps there is a long way to go for the both of us, my boy. Now get some rest with your good lady and we will talk more tomorrow. I will show you around the farm and introduce you to the people I have working here. We will have more time later to talk about your friends and see if we can convince them to come and work for me. For now, though, I think you both be needing some rest.'

'You be right about spending time with my Victoria. She has given up her kin and all the fineries she did have to be with me. I have never seen her like before.' He looked at her asleep on the bed. 'How many women would do that for a common man of my indifference and disposition, for I know not of any.'

George nodded. 'It were the same for me and my Molly. When nobody else saw much in me, she did. Supported me and my dreams of this farm. Where would we be without a woman to support and believe in us, eh?'

Springer smiled. 'Be that the truth, right enough. But we still have that small agenda of Lord Fitzgerald and his group of lackeys to address and right a few wrongs they have put both our ways.'

'That can wait until later, for now I will leave you. It's been a good, if not different day and we can talk more in the morning.' George looked round the room and then back to Victoria sleeping on the bed. 'Makes me feel good to have guests in the house again.'

Springer was left staring at the fire. 'Cheery bye,' he called out after George as he went. Then he looked back at Victoria. In the background, the fire spat and hissed as the larger logs released their moisture to the intense heat of the flames. He watched as it gave off warmth and a light that filled the room with a yellowy orange glow. Moving over to the window, he unhooked the sash cords and closed the drapes.

Not wanting to disturb Victoria, he quietly took off his boots and placed them beside the fire to dry out. Satisfied that all was done, he sat in a chair and rearranged the cushions for more comfort before settling back. A lot had gone on today, and his mind went over everything.

He now owned his first home, but Victoria had never seen it. Would she even like the location? Within a few months, he would be a father. Again, a first for Springer. He contemplated whether he would be up to the task of looking after a baby, as well as providing for them all.

There were so many things for him to think about as his eyes started to close. He resisted for a while as he looked on Victoria sleeping in the bed beside him. He watched as the open flames danced and flickered across the logs. But as the room got warmer, Springer became more comfortable.

His body relaxed into the chair and his resistance to sleep weakened. Before long, the issues of the day had become just a memory and he joined Victoria in a quiet, peaceful slumber.

CHAPTER 11

Arrival of Friends

During the past six months, Lord Fitzgerald has had his men scouring the country far and wide, searching for any signs of Victoria and Springer. When they could not find them through searching alone, they changed their approach by circulating posters to find 'Missing' Victoria, and 'Wanted' signs for Springer – a thief, murderer of men and abductor of women. They had these notices pinned up in every village and town in the area and placed sections in all the newspapers across the country, moving in a wider and wider circle from the village of Pippinsford as time went by. With still no success, they added a reward for information leading to the apprehension of Springer and the location of Miss Victoria, but still no leads came to light. It was like they had disappeared without any trace.

People were paid to travel around villages and towns asking about any recent strangers in the area, and yet still nothing has been heard, seen or reported of them for six months. Whatever Lord Fitzgerald has tried to do so far has not ended in a good lead or positive identification. Every day that goes by, the chances of finding them reduce as people lose interest in old news and take no notice of old posters as they continue with daily life.

Being the kind of man he is, Lord Fitzgerald will never give up on his quest to find them as he has his reputation to think of. He has invested heavily – money, people and time – to continue the search and keep reminding everyone constantly to be alert for the only two people to have ever escaped his grasp and desires.

In all this time, with every resource he has put into finding the pair of them, he has never got close to the area where they are hiding. Even though Springer and Victoria are only in the next county, barely eighty miles away as the crow flies. It has also helped that George has proclaimed his nephew and wife to all on his estate, for all knew about his brother and that he had two sons around Springer's age.

It just goes to show that the low profile and caution they have maintained over the months has served them well, with little risk of exposure.

That is until now. For events are unfolding that could jeopardise all that Springer and Victoria have worked for – and all for the sake of helping others who have helped them to have a better life. For at this very moment, a carriage is heading at pace towards the village of Pippinsford, and inside is a man on a mission.

With four horses pulling hard at the front, the express carriage has made short work of the journey so far. With just the last couple of miles to go until it reaches its next destination, Pippinsford and The Hare and Hound tavern, the driver slows his team to a steady walk. It has been raining heavily for the past few hours and they will soon be on the cobblestones that surface the entire village road as it leads into the market square where the tavern is situated.

Horses can find it difficult to make the transition from ground they can grip well with each step to the cobbled streets of a town or village. This is even worse in the wet, as their iron shoes slip and slide, and the carriage's metal-rimmed wheels can skid on the slippery surface. Horses do not like this movement, nor do they like the sliding of their hooves on such surfaces. Less seasoned horses panic and become unpredictable without a good driver to steady them and a fine pair of experienced horses in the lead to keep the carriage straight and true. The younger, less experienced horses behind could slip, fall or injure themselves, but following others at a slow steady pace, these issues can be avoided as the younger horses learn how to handle the changing conditions better.

It takes a few minutes for the team to adjust their way of walking to ensure they do not fall foul as they negotiate the twisting roads. The high kerbstones and various obstructions – like shop signs that are put out to attract customers – are a risk not only to the horses, but to the coach's wheels. Clipping them can flick a wheel off the carriage in the blink of an eye, or twist and snap the leg of the horse as it buckles under its own weight, bringing down the others with it.

As the coach and team of horses move along the last few hundred yards of cobbles, the iron horseshoes flick off small sparks as they chip the flint stones used to make up the road surface.

'Woah,' the driver calls out, pulling back on the reins and stopping just outside the tavern. He swiftly pushes on the brake stick and locks it in position, then turns to the man beside him. 'That be it then, Ernie. Go let them out and we can go on to the livery around the corner for a team change and a welcome break and some food.'

The driver's mate dismounts the coach, opens the carriage door and rolls down the footsteps, then helps the travellers down. Two elderly ladies take the lead and Ernie steadies each one as they slowly and carefully step down to the safety of the ground. They are followed by two well-dressed men, then a woman with her small child in tow and finally the last man out of the door is George. As he takes the bottom step, he stops and takes in his surroundings then steps off and takes a deep breath of air. After hours being stuck in the confines of the stuffy carriage, it feels good to be able to stretch out his arms and straighten up his back.

He wriggles his shoulders and twists his waist to shake out the temporary stiffness, then a sweet smell catches his senses. It is a far nicer aroma than the smell of stale old mothballs (possibly from the two elderly ladies) he has been suffering within the carriage for the past several hours.

He sniffs the air again, wondering where the fine, sweet smell is coming from. Looking around while hoping to get some clue, he is distracted for a moment by the young mother and child as they walk off across the cobbled road hand in hand, their shoes clicking on the tips of the cobblestones as they head off into the distance. They are followed by the two elderly ladies, all be it at a far slower pace as they move on, locked arm in arm for stability purposes.

His eyes then turn to the two well-dressed gentlemen. They have also crossed the road and are entering a bakery. *So that is what it is*, he thinks as he views all the loaves and savoury pies displayed in the open shop window. He is debating whether to follow them into the bakery when he gets a tap on the shoulder. Turning around, he is greeted by the ever-smiling face of Ernie the baggage handler and 'general do everything' person from the stagecoach.

'Your case, sir,' he says as he passes it to George. 'Before you think of getting something from that bakery, I would advise you to get something to eat from the tavern, or the bakery round the corner. This one does not have the best reputation for what is in the bread and the pies. The ones in the window have been there for the last three or four days.'

George takes the case and passes him a coin in appreciation of his time during the trip. 'For your service, and thank you again for your counsel, Ernie.'

Ernie looks at the coin in his hand. 'Thank you, sir,' he says and tilts his cap towards George before unloading the rest of the baggage and parcels that are piled up on the top of the coach.

George enters the tavern and walks up to the reception kiosk. He raps the bell twice and a startled young woman pops up her head from below the counter. 'You gave me a fright!' she says as she stands up to address him, brushing herself down and placing a pile of books on the counter. 'What can I do for you today, sir?' she asks politely with a large smile.

'A room, my dear. A room for the night and some hot food in the bar by the fire would be fine.'

She thinks for a bit before answering. 'We have the first room at the top of the stairs still available, and that would be a shilling for the night. But the only hot food at the moment would be stewed meat and bread. We do not start to roast the meats for another hour or so, ready for tonight.'

'That would be fine, my dear.' George removes a pouch from his pocket and passes the girl two shillings. 'That's for the room and the food. The rest is for yourself.'

The girl is shocked. 'You do not need to pay now, sir. You can pay when you leave in the morning.'

'Tomorrow I may be gone early, so I feel better to pay my way now and be done with it,' he replies.

'Allow me to show you to your room,' she says as she reaches for his case, but George ushers her on.

'I will be fine to carry my own bag, my dear. Please lead the way.'

He follows her up the stairs and into the room. There is a washbowl, water in a jug and curtains at the window. By the bed is a side table with a bible on it and on the far side two regency chairs are back against the wall. He presses down on the bed and gives a nod of approval.

'I will see about the food next, sir. Shall we say half an hour? I will have it ready at a table near the fire.' George smiles as the girl bustles out of the room.

He sits down on the bed and pulls an envelope from his case. He is excited at the prospect of having people around him and – if these two are as good for him as Springer and Victoria have been – this will change his life forever and he will start to get his farm and businesses back in order. Not only that, but thanks to some new names and leads from Springer and Victoria, he is also starting to make headway into the disappearance of his brother.

Putting his fingers in his waistcoat pocket, he takes out his half hunter pocket watch, checks the time, then props the watch up against the oil lamp. He has had a lot to think about on his way up here. In the short time he has known Springer and Victoria, they have become like family to him. They have shown nothing but true friendship and compassion and worked hard to help with his estate and affairs – making him feel he has purpose and drive in his life again, something that gives him a new look on his own future. They have been totally honest and have trusted him with their lives – from when they first met and explained who they were, to now with a young one near to being born. He is conscious of the risk they are taking to help him acquire good staff. For he knows that should Lord Fitzgerald find out Springer and Victoria are nearby, they would not be long for this world, and he could not bear anything to happen to them. He thinks about how he will recognise Cook and what her responses will be to his approach. Can he really trust her? He leans back and rests for a while, thinking on the matter in great depth.

He hears a noise outside and looks at his watch for the third time. Nearly thirty minutes have passed. 'That's good enough,' he mutters. It is now quarter to three and the timing is perfect.

He closes the watch and places it back in his waistcoat pocket, picks up the white envelope and walks down the stairs. He looks at all the paintings and ornaments that have been placed in various areas of the tavern, but none of them holds his attention for long and he is soon walking into the bar area.

'Over here, sir.' The young girl beckons him over to a table by the large open fireplace. As he arrives at the table, she says, 'I've just put another log on the fire and your food is on the table.'

George looks at what has been provided: a large bowl of stew with a metal spoon resting on its edge, two chunks of bread and a jug of ale with a brass mug beside it.

'Just holler if you need anything from me, or if you require more ale just call to the barkeeper and he will assist you.'

George nods in approval. 'Thank you. You are most kind.'

As the girl walks off, George stirs his stew and views the bar area. The barkeeper is stacking washed tankards on the shelves behind the counter. He raises a tankard at George and nods his head in acknowledgement then continues with his work.

George takes his first mouthful of the stew. Chewing it, he instantly concludes it is hot and edible but nothing like what Victoria has been cooking for him back at home for the past couple of weeks.

He does not think about what meat is actually in the bowl, just that it will fill a gap in his belly and kill time while he is waiting for Cook to arrive.

For such a large place and just after lunch, the tavern is quite empty. Three men sit at the bar, a group of farm labourers are seated around a table on the far side, and five gentlemen stand at the end of the counter. Two separate couples are at tables in the middle of the room, and on the far side by the window, a group of three women watch all the men in the room intently. He knows exactly what they are and what they are after, and ensures not to make full eye contact with them, as it will be interpreted as a signal for them to come and join him at his table.

While chewing on his food, he observes the five young gentlemen as they laugh and joke with each other. They smile at the ladies, and one raises a tankard in their direction and, just like he'd thought, one of the ladies is soon on her feet and walking over. Within a minute, she is calling over her friends to join the group. One of the men calls to the barkeeper for more drinks and the group starts to get louder.

George chuckles as he wonders how much these girls are going to fleece the men for, and who is going to come away with more than just a good time. *Working girls, a trade that must be nearly as old as time itself*, he thinks as he wonders how long it will take for the group to split up and get rooms at the tavern.

With the food being so bland, George is slow with his eating. Breaking off pieces of bread and dropping them in the stew as he goes, he is beginning to think this is a waste of time and that Cook will not show today when out of the blue a woman quietly passes and sits at the table on the other side of the fireplace. She places a bag down on the floor and rubs the back of her calf.

Within a minute, the barkeeper is placing a small jug of ale and a small tankard on her table. 'How is he?' she asks.

'I've not seen him today, but he left two legs and a haunch of venison in the usual place when I got up this morning, so I'm sure I will be seeing him some time soon.'

She smiles and holds the man's hand. 'Thank you, Arthur. I miss him, so I do. And I worry about what they will do to him, should they ever find him.'

Arthur chuckles. 'It will be a cold day in hell before your man is found by them. As cunning as a fox he be and more lives than a dozen cats is what he has.'

She breaks out into a smile. 'Thank you so,' she says and discreetly places a small note into Arthur's hand.

'I will see he gets it. Now warm yourself up by the fire for a while for none of them have been around today.'

Cook turns to look into the flames, while Arthur returns to serve the people at the bar. She reaches for the jug to fill the tankard but then changes her mind. There is sadness in her face and the life seems to have drained out of her.

'Allow me,' George comments as he pours the ale for her. She is startled and as she looks back at him, he can see that she is afraid.

'Who are you? What do you want?' she asks, her hand pressing against her lips. 'I don't know where he is, so please leave me alone.'

George places the jug back on the table. He can see she is working herself up and fear is starting to take control of her. 'Please calm yourself. I am not here to look for your husband; I am here to give you a message from a friend of ours.' As he reaches into his pocket, the fear grows in Cook's eyes, and she leans back harder into her chair. George takes out the envelope and places it on the table in front of her.

'I am going to return to my table and wait for you to look at its contents. Be assured it is something that will not harm you.'

Cook's fingers tremble as she slowly reaches for the envelope.

In the background, Arthur has seen the man approach Cook and can see the fear in her as well. He reaches for a large wooden club he keeps under the counter and slowly moves towards her table.

Cook tentatively opens the envelope and the locket falls out onto the table. She recognises it immediately and picks it up. As she opens it and sees the boys on one side and Rebecca on the other, a huge smile comes over her face and a tear runs down her cheek. She clasps it in both hands and looks at George, then out of the corner of her eye, she sees Arthur making his way over with a club in his hand.

George has also noticed him coming his way and is now a bit on edge himself. Cook looks at Arthur. 'It's fine, I'm all good Arthur, just a little jittery, that's all.'

Arthur takes the hint and, looking at George, speaks quietly. 'She is worth her weight in gold is that one. I'm sorry if I gave you a fright, but I thought you were threatening her, and I could not have that.'

'No, no, my good man, that I would never do. I was just pouring her a drink, that's all.'

Arthur returns to his bar to tend to the other patrons while Cook takes the letter out and reads its contents.

The footbridge by the brook where you lost your shoe at 5 o'clock tonight,
V & S

She looks over to George, the fear in her face gone completely. 'Is it really from her? Is she OK? Do you know them?'

George smiles at her and nods. From all he has seen so far, he can tell this is a good woman, even though he has never met her before today. He leans forward and speaks quietly to her. 'My dear, I was asked to give you that letter. I can say no more at this time, but you are to keep the locket on you at all times as it is precious beyond its worth to a friend of ours. Now I must go back to my room and get ready to be on my way. I do not think we should be seen talking to each other again as I think we have caused quite enough commotion as it is. For I do not want to endanger the lives of our mutual friends who are risking a great deal at this moment. However, I do hope to see you again in the very near future and then you can explain yourself and why our mutual friends think you are so special and worth them risking so much.'

Cook is smiling for the first time in months. Her mind is so full of questions she knows she cannot ask. Is the letter really from Springer and Victoria? It must be, she convinces herself, for Victoria would never part with this locket for anything other than to prove it was from her. She places the locket around her neck and tucks it inside the frill of her blouse so it cannot be seen by anyone, then tears up the letter and throws it in the fire to burn. For she is a very careful woman these days.

Turning back to George, she is about to ask him one more question when who should walk in through the door but Brannigan and one of his lackeys, a weasel-like man with a face like a dead fish. Her smile fades as fast as it had arrived as they make a beeline straight to where she is sitting.

George looks up to see the two men crowding over Cook. 'Well? Have you seen that worthless husband of yours?'

Cook looks up at them, then turns to look into the flames of the fire as the last of the paper disappears into ash.

'I'm speaking to you, woman,' says Brannigan, poking her shoulder.

She turns and looks him in the eye. 'I've not seen my husband in weeks – you and your band of animals have seen to that. Now be on your way and leave me be. I have nothing more to say to you.' Cook turns back to the fire with tears running down her cheeks. She is absolutely terrified of these men, but somehow, as always, she holds her nerve. Her hatred of these bullies of men is intense, but for her own safety she must resist losing her temper – for these men know no limits when it comes to violence against men, women and children alike.

The weasel is next to speak. 'When we get him, he's gonna hang and I will make sure I am the one to pull the lever, as I likes a good hanging, I do.' He leans forward, pushing his face into hers, and pulls two fingers across his neck. 'Sometimes, the neck doesn't break cos the knot is too loose or there's not enough slack in the rope to allow for the neck to snap. It takes a lot longer for them to die that way, choking to death while twitching and wriggling, gasping for what little breath they can get in. I've even seen it the other way too, when the rope is too long and the drop has pulled the man's head clean off his body. I've seen it all, and believe me, I'm really bad at making knots, especially for them that deserve to suffer.'

Cook is shaking down to her very boots. Her arms are trembling, and she is holding onto her nerves by a thread as she grips the arms of the chair tightly and closes her eyes in the hope they will go away.

George can take no more of what he is witnessing. He has seen these men on his previous visits, and now after speaking to Springer, he knows who they work for now and that therefore they probably had something to do with the disappearance of his brother. Oh, how badly he would like to have words with them and extract the truth from their evil, twisted minds. But he knows it's not the time, for now he needs to defuse the situation and not cause too much attention while doing so.

'Gentlemen, gentlemen, enough is enough. Leave this poor woman alone. You've scared her half to death as it is. If she knew the whereabouts of this man you seek, I am sure she would have told you by now.'

Brannigan turns to George. He reaches into his pocket for the small, weighted club he carries for such occasions just to suppress a victim without leaving too much of a mark. But here, as he faces down George, he does not see fear in his eyes like most of the men he comes across. He sees a man prepared to stand by his words.

Arthur's hands are tied. He cannot get involved – as he would like to – as he works for the same man they do. Fortunately, the same cannot be said for the other people in the bar and they are not impressed. The five men at the bar have stopped talking to the women and are now walking towards Brannigan and his accomplice.

The group of farm labourers have also got up from their table and are facing towards them. The oldest in the group points directly at Brannigan and calls out, 'Best you be leavin' young Cook alone afore you start something you be regrettin' later.'

Brannigan looks at the number of men heading his way. 'I got the law on my side,' he growls in a grumbling voice. 'Her old man be Dan the poacher and he be needed for questioning. Poaching on Lord Fitzgerald's land is a crime, and we know he be doing it.' He looks round wild-eyed at both groups of men and slowly steps backwards towards the door.

One of the gentlemen continues the conversation. 'You may have the law on your side when it comes to catching poachers. But here, in our local tavern, when you start on a woman in this manner, in our presence, you are far from being within the law. Now get thee gone afore I forget my manners and something bad happens.'

Weasel-man is panicking and tugs on Brannigan's arm. 'Let's be going. We can continue this another time,' he says as he turns to leave the building.

Brannigan, still with his hand in his pocket holding his club, is slowly walking backwards, still facing the approaching men. He was not prepared for this and being forced to leave the building grates on his pride deeply. 'I'll be remembering this, Cook, you see if I don't,' he growls.

The two groups of men speed up their approach towards Brannigan, who turns and runs out the door at the last minute under a hail of laughter from the men.

'That be showing 'em who be in charge here,' says the older man in the group of labourers. He turns to Cook and holds her shoulders. 'Now worry thee not, Cook. Dan's a fine man and they will never find him. As for you, there be not a man, woman or child in this village that would not be by your side, should thee need it.'

Cook looks up at him. 'Thank you, Jethrow. That swine, he just caught me off guard, that's all. I was not prepared for them as I had other things on my mind.'

Jethrow speaks again. 'Now finish your drink and we will walk with thee back to the manor, right safe like.'

She wipes the tears from her face with a handkerchief passed to her by George, then looks round at all the men who came to her aid. 'Thank you all. I am grateful beyond words. I do not know what I would have done if I was on my own. It seems that my life and my husband Dan's is plagued by these animals. Every day someone in this village has them or others like them to deal with. I have seen with my own eyes, families, men, even the children beaten or taken or just gone missing.' Looking down at the floor, she starts to cry again and dabs her eyes with the handkerchief. 'Oh God, poor Oliver and Edward,' she says, putting her hand on her chest over the hidden locket. 'What has become of them fine boys, I wonder.'

All the men around her nod in agreement, angry at what they have just witnessed. They are all fed up with how Lord Fitzgerald's men throw themselves around, intimidating all they see fit, with no repercussions. Even the three working ladies are now talking about how unsafe the area has become. They all feel the same way about Lord Fitzgerald's men and want to comfort Cook in her time of need. She and Dan are such characters in the community, different from each other in so many ways but loved by all they meet – just due to their good natures and the way they are with people.

With one last dab of the eyes, Cook stands up. She holds her head up high and looks around at everyone then speaks proudly. 'One man stood up to them, and that man Fletcher is in a better place for it.' All the men cheer at once, for they know who she is talking about. 'God forgive me for feeling this way, but I hope one day he comes back and gets the rest of them.'

The men give a louder cheer. 'Now it is time for me to go. I have taken up much of your valuable time. Appreciated as it is, you must now get on with your drinking and—' She looks at the gentlemen with the ladies now standing behind them and gives them a wink. 'And you others, the entertainment that may or may not be on the cards.'

The whole group roar with laughter as Cook makes her way to the doorway. She turns to one of the farmhands, who has followed her to the door. 'I will be fine, Jethrow, they will not bother me again today as I have nothing to tell them. And besides, you have the rest of the men to be drinking with.'

'Are you sure you be safe to go alone?'

'I will be fine. I have some things to pick up for the housekeeper and food to prepare for the master's dinner party tonight, so go before you make me late and thank you for being there when I needed you.'

'Well, if you say you are good, then I still have a jug or two with my name on. But only if you are sure you're safe. You know Dan would never forgive me if something happened to you!'

'Jethrow, I am fine,' she says firmly. 'Now let me go and get on with my duties while you get back to your jugs.' They both pause for a second, then burst into laughter as they realise what she has just said.

'My word, Cook, it would seem you have gone a bit red in the face.'

'Off with you,' she says with a laugh. 'Or there will be no more pies for you and the boys when working near the house.'

She nods in the direction of George as she leaves, then checks the time on the carriage clock that is placed by the reception desk as she passes. She is working out how long she has to complete all her tasks before getting to the bridge by five o'clock.

George is still talking to the group of labourers. It is only when he asks about Dan and what he looks like that Jethrow goes quiet and realises he is talking to a stranger about his friend who just so happens to be a wanted poacher.

'And why would ye be asking to know what he looks like, may I enquire?'

'Could it be you're one of them there turncoats working for Fitzgerald to earn a piece of coin on the side?' another one of them comments as Jethrow starts to look George up and down.

'Good Lord no, I only ask because it struck such a nerve with the lady you call Cook when the two thugs asked her about her husband Dan.'

'And what is that to do with thee, may I ask?'

George understands why Jethrow is suspicious, but he cannot tell him why he is really here through fear of exposing Springer and Victoria, so he is as honest as he can be without risk to others. 'Absolutely nothing. I be a farmer with a smallholding nearby, and I came here looking for good corn and maize seed from the store. I always ask around on my visits to see if my brother has been seen since he left the area some time ago, as I have not heard from him since he left.'

Jethrow takes hold of George's wrists and turns them over. The thick calluses and hard skin along with split fingertips are all he needs to see. 'You be a farmer alright and, by the state of them there hands, an 'ard working one at that.' He lets go of George's wrists. 'Who is your brother? Perhaps between us all here we be knowing of him as a lot of us have been here all our lives and know many of the people who have been and gone.'

George ponders for a bit before speaking. 'My brother's name is Steven. Steven Todd. He was one of the original farmers in the area before all these changes and new people arrived.'

Jethrow takes a seat at the table where George had been eating, sighing heavily as he does so.

George is a good judge of people, and he can see by his mannerisms that this man knew his brother. He sits down beside him while calling to the barman. 'A round if you do not mind, for all these gentlemen. On me.' Arthur nods from behind the counter and the men around George cheer in appreciation and head towards the bar to claim their drinks.

It takes a while for Jethrow to speak. 'If you are the brother of Steven, then thee must be his older brother, Herbert.'

George looks at him strangely. 'He did not have a brother called Herbert, only me. I'm his younger brother, George.'

Jethrow taps his fingers on the table as he nods in acceptance of his name. 'I be sorry for the deception, but I had to be sure thee are who thee say thee be. You see, I worked for your brother, as did Albert and old Jack there.' He points to two of the men in the group of labourers now standing at the bar.

'We three worked for him from the first day he bought the fruit farm. There was another man called Jack, but we just called him Stumpy on account of his limp and we already had a Jack in the group. All our families lived on the land, in the beehive cottages that were around the farm. You can't have orchards and fruit crops without bees to do their thing and make for better fruit yields and each cottage had its own beehives nearby, hence the name.

'For years we served your brother. We pruned, weeded, planted and organised the harvesting of the crops when they be ready. All of us ran a quarter section of your brother's farm, with temporary folk from the village earning extra coin picking crops at harvest time. You could say he bought us with the farm as we were already here when he arrived. We learned and helped as your brother grew the place bigger and bigger each year. Watched him guide others to improve their farms and get better deals for their produce with the buyers by selling as a community. A good man he was to us, always being there in our times of need.'

'Helped put my children through schooling, he did,' comments a man from the group who has just returned from the bar.

'Hell, he paid to have the school rebuilt and enlarged in the first place to give our children a place of learning,' bellows out one of the others.

Jethrow continues. 'Your brother's farm was a great place to call home and work on. In fact, the whole village and surrounding farms owed a lot to him and his methods of production to make a good living. For it be him who started shipping our fruit and honey along with other produce to the towns and ports for a better price. I guess that's why it attracted the attention of Lord Fitzgerald and his so-called investors. For it was not long after we started shipping out to the ports and making better profits that THEY started to arrive, looking at houses, shops, farms, who owned what and for how long. Sometime after that, shops that had been in people's families for generations were bought for way more than they were worth and the people and their families were moved on. In fact, this 'ere tavern was one of the first buildings Lord Fitzgerald purchased. All my life this was the centre and heart of the village. Every night full of people laughing and joking. Almost all the farming business in the community was done across these tables, be it livestock, grain, dairy produce – you name it, it was bartered for here where we sit.

'Now you see precious few old village people here. It's more a playhouse for the rich and affluent. There's only a few of us who once in a while come here to remember what it was like. For over the past few years, it's been like the life and soul has been sucked out of Pippinsford.'

'Here, here,' comments one of the old farmhands returning from the bar with his ale. 'Bring back the good old days, for they be better times than what lays here before thee now.'

George is listening intently; this is the most he has heard about this place and what has happened over the past few years. He has so many questions to ask, but for now he is happy to listen to what they have to say.

Jethrow picks up the tankard that one of his friends has placed in front of him. 'Here's to you, George. And Steven, your brother.' He takes a long, slow drink from the jug, lets out a gasp of approval and places the tankard back on the table. 'By 'eck that tastes good. At least the ale comes from the same place still. Guess even Lord Fitzgerald knows a good thing when he tastes it.' He takes another gulp of ale. 'Now, where was I? Oh yes, after buying out most of the shops in the village, they went after purchasing all the farms in the area. First the ones where that damned factory now stands, then it seems the whole of the valley. Mind you, by this time – from what I understand from the people who were not afraid to talk about it – these buyers were becoming more forceful in their methods of acquisition, using men to enforce the purchase by any means needed. Your brother was one of the last large farms to hold out. He resisted them all, no matter what they offered. He even tried to stop them there others from selling up, but it was no good. One by one they got each of the farms around him, but it was always Steven's farm they wanted most. It was the biggest, the best and most profitable fruit farm in the area. That and the two deep spring-fed lakes on his land that never dried up in summer made it a prime location.'

He takes another drink from his tankard then speaks again. 'Steven allowed all the farms in the area to use the water from his lakes for their crops and livestock – whenever a drought was on or if the summer was long and very dry – free of any charge to the local farmers. But when Lord Fitzgerald forcibly acquired all the farms around him and demanded access to his lakes, that was another matter. Initially, your brother allowed any of the farms owned by Lord Fitzgerald to access his lakes, as before, in times of need. But when one day he was approached by a group of builders with equipment in hand looking for his lakes, he was shocked as he had not authorised any work on his lakes. He struck up a conversation with them and they showed him the plans for building a pump by the larger of the two lakes. It was to send water direct to Lord Fitzgerald's new factory on the other side of the village. His curiosity turned to anger, and he politely escorted the men off his land and, with immediate effect, banned any of Lord Fitzgerald's tenant farmers from using his lakes.

'That year was a very dry one and the crops on the surrounding farms suffered badly for it, whereas we had another bumper year. The farms around us had yields down by over half their expected amounts and the quality was on the poor side. Smaller fruit and not as juicy, so the sale price was far less, along with the added issue of a more reduced shelf life. Not so in the case of your brother though. With the extra money he made from the sale of his produce, he could start the building of a better school in the village. This had always been one of his aims, and with so many labourers out of work, he was not short of willing workers to get the project moving. If I remember right, it took from the autumn to the end of spring to be fully complete, and by summer the children were in the three new classrooms.

'From there on in, times became more difficult for your brother. It seemed like he had a mountain to climb every day, such was the pressure Lord Fitzgerald kept putting on him. Water access was difficult from the other side of the village and attempts to build other lakes near the factory failed as the ground be like chalk, and not spring-fed, so the lake continued to dry out and crack. Pumping from the river helped some, but it was too far away to be all that effective and uphill for long stretches. Such was the need for a large amount of water for the factory, Lord Fitzgerald tried to go through the courts and force access to Steven's water. Needless to say, the courts filed in favour of your brother, as he rightfully owned the resource, and he could choose who could and could not use it. This enraged Lord Fitzgerald even more. Over the following months, many of the people at the courthouse retired, left or just disappeared, never to be seen again. Within six months, he had managed to replace all the senior people in the magistrate court with ones of his own choosing.

'For a while, Lord Fitzgerald focused his attention on buying up all the houses in and around the village and knocked them down, replacing them with grander, larger houses. He sold them to wealthier people from the cities, attracted to the area with employment in his factories and shares in his ideas. He offered better amenities and a healthier standard of life to their families. It would seem the man has many fingers in even more pies. And he is a very, very greedy man.

'With all what he had going on in and around the village, the need for good water was growing more urgent and it was not long before Steven's farm was back on the agenda. It was becoming more and more difficult to keep the factory pool topped up with enough clean water to run all its needs. So, Lord Fitzgerald constantly had people visiting Steven at the farm, making offers and threats. I remember one time he got so fed up with people hounding him that he stuck an old blunderbuss in the ribs of one of Lord Fitzgerald's representatives – in fact, it was Brannigan, the man you confronted earlier who was leaning on Cook.

'Steven showed him who was boss alright – pushing him all the way up the lane with a piece of iron pointing at his belly to get him off his farm. Now that was a sight and a half. He was slipping and sliding in the mud, falling to his hands and knees as he tried to scramble away. Steven was not a man to be pushed, and his passion for the land he owned showed in everything he did.

'I still to this day don't know why he changed his mind and sold up. His family loved it here and his sons were coming of age and taking a larger role in running the land. We could not have had a better employer and if he were still here, we would be working with him right now.'

He downs the last of his ale, draining every drop. 'What none of us ever understood is why a man so adamant that he would draw his last breath on his farm would just leave it all behind.'

George shakes his head. 'He may well have taken his last breath here, for no one has seen him since he supposedly sold up. The last letter I had from him was years back. And even then, he was planning another orchard of damsons.'

Jethrow chuckles. 'I remember that letter,' he says. 'I was there when he wrote it, asking you about the best type of damson tree to grow in this chalky soil.'

'That be the one,' replies George. 'When he left, what did he say were his reasons for going?'

Jethrow looks at George. 'We never saw Steven before he left. All we got was a knock on our cottage doors from people from Lord Fitzgerald's estate, giving us the option of working for half the pay we were on the day before or we had one day to leave our homes.'

George looks surprised. 'I cannot imagine Steven would leave without speaking to his labourers first and ensuring you and your families were secure working for the next owner. That is just not Steven's way.'

Jethrow rubs the stubble on his chin. 'When I said no to the man's offer – and we all said no – we were pushed off the land within hours by Brannigan and a group of his men supported by the magistrate's office. We were left homeless with nothing but what we could take with us that morning. Some of us even now live in a disused barn in the woods with our belongings still in the cart we walked out with. Others have found low-paid work in the factory or as gardeners to the new people in the village. We only get by with all of us pooling together. If it were not for the talents of Cook's husband, Dan, and the food and clothes Cook drops off for the children, we would have been starved out a long time ago, and that is fact.'

George cannot believe what he is hearing. 'How can so much have gone on without the law getting involved and resolving the problem?'

'Lord Fitzgerald is the law round here. He owns everything and everyone – his men are everywhere. That's why we were all suspicious of you when you asked questions about Dan.'

Arthur delivers another two ales for Jethrow and George, and they both respond with a nod before Jethrow takes a long, slow drink. 'The last we saw of your brother was him going to bed after a few ciders by the lake with us. The next day we had visitors, and we were told he had sold up and gone to visit his brother, then would be moving on to live with his sister in Ireland.'

'Ireland? We have no sister in Ireland, nor any family in Ireland that I am aware of, and I am his only brother.'

'We watched as two carts of his belongings were taken from the house and headed off up the lane into the distance. They told us Steven had already left and his belongings were to catch him up. Come to think of it, the man driving the first wagon was the man with Brannigan today. Carlton, Dick Carlton, that's his name. Horrible little ferret of a creature, I'm sure of it. That is a face you cannot forget in a hurry.'

'Are you sure?'

'Sure as I be in front of you now.'

George leans back in his chair. For the first time he has a real lead and a chance to find the whereabouts of his brother and what happened to him. He puts his hand in his pocket and places several coins on the table. 'This will cover the cost of the round I ordered and another besides, gentlemen. I also thank you for your time.'

As he stands up, he asks Jethrow, 'Where will I find you if I need to speak to you again?'

Jethrow looks at him. 'There's thunder in them there eyes of yours, and I'm still not sure you are who you say you are. So, if you need to see me again, leave a message with Arthur and I will find thee.'

'That's fair to me,' says George as he tilts his cap to all present and makes his way outside.

Only one thing is now on George's mind. Even though he is supposed to keep a low profile, he must find that man who was driving the wagon with his brother's belongings. He looks up and down the main high street, sees a few people browsing the shops, but not the person he is looking for. With this Carlton not in view, he decides to turn left and see where it takes him, checking every road leading off the main street and in every shop window.

All he sees is Cook buying fabric in the general store and he cannot afford to approach her for risk of exposing himself. He returns to outside the tavern after about half an hour and this time he turns right. Again, he views every shop window and looks down all the side lanes off the main road, but still to no avail.

Hearing the village clock chiming quarter past four, George heads off in the direction of the clocktower he can see poking up above the stone and slate rooftops. Walking towards the tower leads him through the grounds of the larger houses being rebuilt at the end of the village, where it opens up to view the landscaped park. The clocktower is an imposing sight high up in the air, and the ornate designs on and around the clock face are way above what you would expect in a small village. He has seen it being built on previous trips, but now complete it is worth another look before he continues his search. To his amazement, there are more people walking around the park than there were in the village. Most are well-dressed and not your typical village folk, but as George is learning, Pippinsford is far from a typical village and the people here are far from the average yokel.

In the distance, above the trees that represent the border of the park, George can see two big houses towering above the trees. He counts the roofs of all the large state houses surrounding the open area. There are eight – two more than there were last time he was here.

He walks around the park, hoping to see the man he is looking for, but to no avail. Another half an hour passes before he decides he is not here. By now George is over the far side of the park, past the lake in the wooded area along the brook, walking along the hedgerow. He has just started on his way back to the tavern when he spots Cook walking along the river's edge with a large wicker basket on her arm. He decides to take a detour and moves past some flowering gorse bushes so she does not see him.

He stands well back behind a large ash tree and waits for her to pass by. There is a good thirty to forty feet between them when he suddenly notices someone poke their head out of the bushes behind her. They are back some way off in the distance, but the clothes seem familiar. George watches as the person weaves in and out of various undergrowth, crouching low to the ground where possible to keep from being seen.

Cook passes George without noticing him tucked neatly in his hiding spot. While George stays focused on the man following her, as he gets closer, he realises it's the man he's been looking for, Carlton. But what the hell is he doing, following Cook? he wonders as his brain ponders for a bit then realises if this man follows Cook for much longer, he may well see who she is going to meet with and that would put his friends at risk.

Needing to take preventative action quickly, George repositions himself to intercept Carlton as he passes, assessing all the possible routes this man could take and then deciding on the best ambush position. Sure enough, George's guess is right. Carlton continues to follow Cook at some distance behind, using the ground cover to his advantage. But as Cook rounds a corner out of sight, he speeds up to ensure he does not lose sight of her. George steps out from his thicket and bumps into him, knocking him off his feet and into a gorse bush.

'What the—? Mind where you be going!'

Carlton picks himself up, brushes down his clothes and looks at George, then arcs his neck round him to see where Cook is. With her out of sight and none the wiser to being followed, he turns his attentions back to George.

'Ye be lucky I've got things that need doing,' he says before pushing his way past. George grabs his coat at the back of his neck and throws him backwards to the ground.

'What be the rush then, boy?' he asks, standing over him.

Carlton looks up at him from the floor and pulls a large knife from his waistband. 'I'll cut thee for that, you mark my words,' he yells, jumping to his feet.

Slashing this way and that, lunging forward with every swing of the blade.

After several failed attempts to cut George, he pauses, pointing the knife right in front of George's face.

'You're going to need to get a lot closer than that to stick me, boy,' says George as he bobs and weaves in front of the frustrated man.

Carlton lashes out wildly with the knife and George clasps his wrist with his left hand and punches him square in the face with his right – once, twice, three times – before releasing his wrist and watching him drop to the floor, blood leaking from both his nose and mouth. As Carlton rolls to one side to get up, George steps on the hand that is still holding the knife, applying pressure until Carlton's hand opens, finally releasing the weapon from his grasp. Flicking the knife away with a sweep of his foot and stooping down, George grabs the blubbering man by the throat and drags him deeper into the undergrowth.

'Time me and you had a little chat,' George says while rough handling him through some brambles that catch and tug on his clothing. 'Now I'm going to ask you a series of questions and you are going to answer them. If I think you are less than honest in your answers, I am going to beat you—'

Carlton interrupts. 'Do you know who I work for, you idiot? I could have you imprisoned for this.'

George responds instantly, punching him hard in the stomach. The man leans forward and throws up instantly, dribbling liquid down the side of his face as George stands him back up and pushes him back against a tree.

'No, no, no, this is not the way. You see, I am the one who will ask the questions and it's your job to answer them.' George undoes Carlton's belt and uses it to tie his hands to a branch. 'Now, where was I? Oh yes… think back to a farmer called Steven Todd. You know, the one who had the lakes that now pump water to the big factory. He was a good man, an honourable man, a man who did good in the community. Until one day he suddenly sells up and disappears, never to be seen again! Now I want to know what happened to that man and the only lead I have is you. You were one of the men driving his belongings away from his farmhouse that day. Now as you must have been taking his belongings somewhere, I would like to know where. You see, in my mind the belongings must be heading towards their owner – in this case Steven – and I want to know where Steven is!'

Carlton looks at George and laughs. 'I don't know who you are talking about. I know nothing of this man Steven and even if I did, I would tell you nothing.'

George's knee swiftly rises and makes contact with Carlton's groin, and he screams in agony. After a minute or so, he looks at George and beckons him closer, then closer still. As George approaches, Carlton spits in his face and chuckles to himself.

Calmly taking a handkerchief from his waistcoat pocket, George wipes away the bloodstained saliva from his face then stuffs the cloth into Carlton's mouth. 'Now that was not nice, but then again, you're not a nice person, are you?' George paces around in front of Carlton. Anger is welling up inside him and – for a man usually so calm and collected – this is a side of him that rarely sees the light of day.

'Now let me tell you a little bit about me,' he says. 'I am not usually a vicious or nasty man, just a hard-working farmer who lives for the land he owns. But today, especially after seeing you bully that woman in the tavern, I can feel that bad side of me wanting to get out. And to be fair, that scares me a little, as I do not yet know what that side is capable of doing, or how far it will go.' George angles himself to the side of his victim and punches him in the ribs. Apart from a small moan, there is no other response. A second time, George punches him on the same side of his ribs, and again no worded response comes from his victim. George grabs the man's chin and turns his face towards him. He is now so full of rage that there is no turning back. This man will tell him what he needs to know, or it will go badly for him.

'I'm through fucking around with you, boy. Either you tell me where you were taking Steven's belongings, or where he is, or I'm going to push your ribs into your lungs, and I will watch you choke to death in your own blood!'

Carlton just smiles at him and shakes his head.

George pushes his head away, takes a step back, retracts his arm and punches him on the side, this time with much more venom. The crack from the impact and Carlton's muffled scream of pain leaves George in no doubt that he broke at least one rib, if not two. Carlton hangs limply from his hands tied to the tree. George removes his handkerchief from the man's mouth. 'Something you want to tell me?'

Carlton is struggling for breath. He now knows this man is not all talk, and that he is prepared to go the extra mile, possibly all the way. To hold out any more may well cost him his life.

'Alright, alright, no more.' Carlton struggles to speak between breaths. 'That farmer would not give Fitzgerald what he wanted, so as usual Fitzgerald just took it. I was told to clear out the farmhouse and take all the belongings to the factory.'

George is confused. 'Why the factory?'

Carlton does not answer.

'Why the factory?' he asks again.

Still there is no answer.

George pushes on Carlton's damaged ribs with his thumb, bending the broken ribs into his side.

Carlton screams in agony, and yells out, 'So they could be burned in the furnaces! Same as all of them, same as they always do. They all go the same way once he wants what they will not give him.' He sobs at the thought of all the belongings he has delivered over the years, all the people he knows will never be seen again, including some that were not unknown to him.

'He always offers more than the farms are worth, knowing they will never get to spend the money he pays them even if they accept it. And if they don't, everyone around thinks they took the money and left quietly through guilt or shame of leaving others behind.'

George is confused. Why would they burn all his brother's belongings? If his brother sold his farm, why not sell off the furniture if he did not want it? And what did he mean by 'same as all of them'? He thinks for a minute, looking down at the floor, then places his hands on his hips and looks skywards, as if for inspiration. He turns back to the gibbering Carlton. 'Where is Steven? Where was he taken?' He grabs Carlton by the hair and pulls his head back. 'Where did my brother and his family go?' Carlton screams again as George presses on his ribs once more.

'He's gone, man, he's gone! They took him and his family to the mines, like everyone else. There, they work them – man, woman and child – until they die.'

George's mind is going ten to the dozen. He shakes his head in disbelief.

'What mine? Where is this mine? How many people are—' The sound of a pistol being fired cracks through the air and Carlton's body judders with the impact of a bullet in his chest. As the bullet passes through the man, his blood splatters on George's face and body. Looking past Carlton's lifeless body, George sees Brannigan pointing a pistol in his direction with a plume of black powder smoke surrounding the barrel drifting off with the wind. He is not alone. Along with him are several other men, all brandishing weapons of some kind.

'Been looking for you, we have. Now get him!' calls out Brannigan.

George is off like a jackrabbit, ploughing through the undergrowth, down a gravel embankment and across the brook towards the woods on the other side. *Bang, bang, bang.* The pistols are being fired from behind him and he hears the fizz of the bullets as they whiz past his head and body. The third one nicks his arm below the shoulder, knocking him off his stride slightly, but the bullet has only grazed him, and he maintains his advantage over the pursuers into the woods and beyond.

While George is flat out, weaving in and out of trees as he runs, the men behind are reloading their pistols while trying to pick up his trail through the woods. 'Find him!' bellows Brannigan to his men. 'Sykes, go and get some horses and more men from Henry's house. We need to get this man fast, and Henry's house is the nearest option.' Sykes nods and scurries off.

Not far away, Cook is walking along a path on the edge of the brook with a meadow full of long grass and wildflowers on her right. She is heading towards a small bridge on the far side of the field. Although she's heard the gunshots echoing far off in the distance, she has no idea of the commotion unfolding. Living in the country, gunshots are a common sound as many people shoot game, cull pigeons to protect crops or remove vermin around the farm's grain stores. Her husband, renowned in the area as one of the finest poachers known, sometimes uses guns to fell larger game like red deer and wild boar out in the woods. So the noise of guns firing has been part of her life since she was young.

Cook continues on her way, now following the river's edge until the outline of the bridge becomes visible in the distance. Slowing down periodically to look around and ensure no one is following, she draws closer and closer to the bridge.

Just past the structure, sheltered by a small spinney of hawthorn bushes, she can see a wagon with two horses tethered beside it. Heads down, eating grass, their tails are swishing to remove flies hovering around their legs and rump. As she gets closer, she can see a person wrapped in a blanket with a hood over their head sitting on a small wooden stump, watching over the embers of a small campfire.

Cook slowly makes her way towards the person, who is presumably waiting for her. As she reaches the small encampment, she treads on a dry old branch that cracks under the weight of her foot. Both horses throw up their heads and look in her direction intently while still chewing mouthfuls of grass. The person sitting by the fire does not move or look up, just continues to poke at the fire with a stick.

'You would never make a good burglar would you, Cook?' they say.

'Who are you?' Cook replies, drawing closer. 'Are you the person I am supposed to meet?'

The stranger stands up and turns towards Cook. 'Why, don't you recognise me?'

Cook looks at the cloaked person from top to toe, trying to put a person to the shape in front of her. 'Looking as you do, all covered up, I would be lying if I said yes.'

'How about if I do this?' The stranger slides the blanket off their shoulders and flicks back their hood. Cook drops her basket and presses her hand to her mouth. She stares for a full minute. 'Is it really you?' she asks, staggering forward.

'Of course it's me,' replies Victoria with a huge smile, throwing her arms open wide.

Cook shuffles forward into her embrace and hugs her for all she's worth then leans back to look at her face. She realises something is pushing into her belly and says, 'I don't think much to the disguise.

It's pushing me away.' She lowers her hands to feel the obstruction. Her hands freeze and she looks straight back at Victoria. 'You're… you're… you're…' Cook cannot get the words out.

'Yes, I'm with child and all the better for it. We are both so very happy.'

'Both? You mean Springer is here?'

'Yes, he is here. I would never go anywhere without him, and he will never leave my side, more so now I am so big.'

Cook lets out a squeal of excitement. 'Where is the big oaf?'

'He went to check out some gunfire and will be back soon, then we must be on our way.' Victoria sits back down on her stump and Cook sits on the log opposite.

'Why have you come back? It would seem half the world is looking for you here, yet you have come back to a much worse place than before.'

Victoria holds Cook's hand. 'We came back to speak to you, Cook, and I knew the only way we could get to see you was to send you my locket in the hope you would remember us.'

'Remember you? Oh God, I think about you and Springer all the time along with Edward and Oliver. I cannot tell you how much you are all missed.' Cook undoes the locket from around her neck and passes it to Victoria. 'I'm sure you'll be wanting this back.'

Victoria takes the precious necklace and places it back around her neck, taking a quick look at the pictures inside before tucking it inside her clothes.

'Cook, I do not have much time to talk as we must leave here at nightfall and with a young one on the way, we will not be back, so hear me out. We have a lovely smallholding some distance from here, with a great friend and neighbour who you must have met, or you would not have had my locket.'

'You mean the man at the tavern, George? I think that was his name. He came to my aid when Brannigan and his weaselly friend set on me.'

'That's him. He is a very, very good man with a large farmhouse and estate. He is in need of good people to help run it better.

Springer and I thought that you might like to be the cook at a better place away from all the evils around here. The job comes with its own cottage by the river that is yours for as long as you want to stay.'

Cook thinks for a moment. 'I've never had a place of my own.'

'You would need to sort the finer details with George, but it is a chance to have a better, stress-free life, with a good employer and good neighbours in me and Springer and a third when he or she arrives.'

'Oh, Victoria, I would love to take you up on this more than fine offer, but alas, I cannot just go. Dan may not be much to many, but I love him. Rascal that he be, I could not move away from him, for I see little enough of him now and if I was to move, I would see less of him, and it would break his and my heart.'

'Leave Dan? My dear Cook, Springer has intentions to make an honest man out of that husband of yours. He would be part of the package! The cottage I spoke of is not just for you, silly – it is for you and Dan. Springer and George intend to put Dan to work doing what he does best for the good of the estate and employ him to run the gaming and fishery side of the farm.'

Cook is taken aback. 'But you know he is a rascal and poacher, wanted by the law around here as well as by Lord Fitzgerald's enforcers. There be a price on his head that has grown since I last saw you, even though he gives most of the meat and fish he gets to those that would starve without his help.'

Victoria smiles at Cook. 'What better way is there to prevent poachers than to use a better, wilier poacher to protect against them?' Victoria chuckles. 'I think the boys intend to make Dan earn a proper and respectable living while doing what he does best. The reward for you being that you have your husband at home most nights with you in your own cottage. Not having to worry about a knock at the door or where he is and if he is safe. The downside of this offer is that you would be starting again and not able to visit old friends or let them know where you are.'

Cook is left speechless. The opportunity to have a normal life with Dan, free from fear and dread, has never been on the table before. She has never thought of what life could be like with Dan by her side in public and in a home together. 'If I was to accept, how would we do it? I cannot put you and your family at risk. How would I even find you? Where would I be going?' The enormity of the change starts to sink in.

'It's difficult, I know. But the way I see it, you have two options – we leave in a couple of hours, and you join us now, leaving anything you have behind. Or you go back and give notice that you are leaving to return home to family, and we would then see you in a few months.'

Cook sighs deeply. 'Truth is, I have no family, own nothing and live in a room that is not my own. All my possessions add up to some clothes and a few trinkets. All my equipment in the kitchen is your father's and part of the house. For me, I could just leave with what I have, but I would need to let Dan know what is happening and where I was going.'

'Well, that bit is also not as straightforward as you would think, Cook. Dan would need to arrive separately and work in the shadows for a week or two. I'm not saying he cannot sneak to your house when it is dark, but his work would have him pretending to be a buyer of poached items for a while to root out the weasels on the estate.'

Cook laughs. 'My Dan doing poaching work for the good? Playing a thief-taker? Well I never. We would need to get a message to him before we go and a map of where he will need to find us.'

'Cook, if there is one thing Springer and myself know, it is that Dan will find you wherever you are, for he loves you and would not let you out of his sight for very long.' The pair of them laugh and talk on while they wait for the return of Springer.

CHAPTER 12

Being Hunted

A mile away from the campsite, George is tucked up in the hollow of an old oak tree, his heart pounding as if to burst through his chest. He can hear men shouting in the distance and the crashing of people running through the bracken and branches making up the undergrowth of the wood. He reflects on what has just happened and wonders if the bullet was meant for him or to keep Carlton quiet. The conclusion he comes to is that only the shooter, Brannigan, knows the answer, but he is still alive and one step closer to knowing what happened to his brother.

However, staying alive is going to be tricky as it's been many a year since George has had to move so fast, and now being much older, the stamina is not what it was twenty years ago. He must use more cunning and stealth than speed. While he catches his breath and listens for footsteps, George's mind goes over what he did to that man Carlton. Even now it is a bit of a blur, and he has to concentrate to pull it all back, for he is not usually a violent man. To tie a man to a tree and beat him like a piece of meat is more than just a reaction; it is the result of a build-up of anger and immense frustration.

He reflects on what he witnessed in the tavern and the state it left Cook in, how they treated the people who worked for his brother, and most of all the look in Brannigan's eyes when confronted by people standing up to him.

No, he was not in the wrong to throw a beating on one of the men who took his brother and his family to their deaths. He was put in this situation because this place has no proper law to protect the good people of the village. His heart has been slowing down as he thinks on these issues and his mind returns to the present moment. George looks around, working on how to get out of this wood and find his way to Victoria and Springer, who by now should be waiting for him with the wagon.

Pulling out a piece of paper from his pocket, he unfolds it to expose a rough hand-drawn map of the village. It shows a few landmark buildings like the tavern and school, the main roads and tracks in and out of the area, the park, Victoria's father's house and there is a small river running through the whole map, including the direction to the bridge where Springer and Victoria should be waiting for him.

George steps out from the safety of the tree and looks up at the sky for any sign of the sun to get his bearings. Alas, there is no sign of the yellow light filtering through the trees as it has already set too low and it is a cloudy evening. He tries to work out the direction he has run in a bid to see where he is roughly on the map, but as he has weaved this way and that through the trees for so long, it would still be a guess.

He thinks to climb a tree, but from what he can see around him, there are few trees with low-down branches to get him going, and those that do are not thick enough to hold his weight. Also, he would be an easy target for someone – if they saw him up a tree, they would shoot him down like a trapped bear.

Just as all hope seems lost, he faintly hears the quarterly chimes of the clock. He turns his head at different angles to confirm their direction and stands facing towards the sound. Then, rotating the map to show the clock in front of him and using his outstretched arm as a direction indicator, he deduces that if he turns ninety degrees to the right and keeps moving in that direction, he will eventually reach the river.

However, not knowing how far away from the clocktower he is, he could be upstream or downstream of the bridge when he reaches the riverbank. His next deduction is that if he is below the bridge, there should be a well-worn path leading from the village to the bridge. As he knows from Victoria that Cook and the farmhands use it all the time as a shortcut to reach the village from Victoria's father's manor. If he meets the river above the bridge, the path would be far less obvious as it heads into an unpopulated area.

With a plan set in his mind, George cautiously heads off in the direction of the river, fully aware that the people looking for him are armed and will probably kill him on sight. They will need someone to take the blame for the shooting of Carlton. So he takes his time and assesses every situation before moving across any open ground or tight spaces.

It might have been a time-consuming journey, but eventually George makes it to the river safely, having only a couple of sightings of people walking through the wood to contend with on his way. It is not much of a river – barely ten foot wide in some places – but the clear water looks quite deep. George surveys the banks and decides he must be above the footbridge. He follows the river downstream in the hope that he meets up with Springer and Victoria before darkness sets in.

He is mindful of walking along the path for fear of being spotted, so he uses the tree line away from the water's edge to ensure some kind of cover should he see anyone.

A noise breaks the silence of the wood. George hears what sounds like the cracking of a branch ahead. He crouches down behind a large tree, and soon he can hear hooves thumping on the ground. Keeping down and motionless, he quietly listens and watches to see what or who it is.

It does not take long for Brannigan and two of his henchmen on horseback to come trotting into view along the edge of the river. All have their pistols drawn and ready for action. 'I need him found, you hear me? I cannot have this man walking around here, not with what he might know. So find him and finish it,' Brannigan bellows out.

George spots another man running along the bank, calling for Brannigan to slow down. It takes him two or three attempts to get their attention, and a minute or so more before they pull up their horses and wait for him to catch up.

By the time the man reaches the riders, they are within twenty yards of George, who is still tightly tucked up tightly behind the tree. The man tries to catch his breath, but Brannigan speaks up. 'Well? What is it then? Speak up, damn yer.'

The man continues to puff and pant for a few seconds more before speaking. 'That man you're looking for, he came in on the stagecoach just after lunch. Booked into the tavern under the name John Smith and paid upfront for a room and food for the night.' He takes a few more deep breaths before continuing. 'We checked out his case in the room and it was full of rags and old clothes, nothing that could be worn or used.'

'I knew it,' growls Brannigan. 'I've seen him here before. I just cannot remember where or when, but I knows a face when I've seen it.'

'I've left a man in his room just in case he returns.'

Brannigan scowls and snaps at him. 'He won't be back. He was here to do something or see someone, then be gone from here.' He thinks for a moment. 'The only person I see him with was that bitch of a whore, Cook! Time we paid her a visit and got some long overdue answers, for I feel her luck has finally run out.' Brannigan kicks the sides of his horse and turns to head back towards Henry's house.

George remains rooted to the spot, waiting for all to disappear from sight and sound, then he waits a good five minutes more to ensure no one is around. After hearing Brannigan speak, he is now worried for Cook's safety if they find her. He is sure they will hurt her to get information but has no way of getting a warning to her as he does not even know exactly where she lives, just that it is at Victoria's old home. But even if he found the house, he could not approach without someone spotting him, and what could he say or to whom could he say it, apart from Cook?

He takes his chance and moves on as fast as he can without making too much noise or being too far away from any cover. Over the next twenty minutes, George scrambles along the tree line, following the course of the river. The light is fading fast and the shadows between the trees darken.

To George, this is a nightmare as anyone could be hiding behind any tree and he would not see them until it was too late. Moving on through the darkening light, he finally comes across what he is looking for: a footbridge over the river. As he quietly approaches the bridge, he looks around for tracks on the floor. There are many hoof marks in the soft soil, some no doubt belonging to the horses Brannigan and his men were riding, but he can see no wagon wheel marks.

He begins to wonder if he has the right place, when from behind he hears the click of a pistol being cocked. His heart sinks as he turns around and sees the runner who was with Brannigan pointing a pistol in his direction.

'He said you would be around here, and lookie, lookie, here you are, right where he said you would be.'

The fear on George's face slowly turns into a grin. To the amusement of the armed man standing in front of him, George starts to chuckle.

'For a minute there, you had me worried. I really thought I was in deep trouble,' George says, wiping the sweat from his face with his sleeve.

'You *are* in trouble! I'm standing here with a pistol aiming straight at your head and instructions to kill you.'

'Yes, I can see that. The unfortunate thing is that you will never get the chance to use said pistol before you succumb to the powers of my friend.'

'Pull the other one! You think I'm stupid enough to fall for that old trick?' says the armed man while readying his aim on George.

Swiftly, a hand comes over the top of the gun and holds down the hammer, rendering it unable to fire. The gun is then lifted up, so it points away from George. As the man looks to see who has grabbed his gun, a huge fist impacts with his face with a *crack*. This all happens in a matter of seconds, and the end result is a man unconscious on the floor in a heap.

'I have never been so glad to see you, Springer my boy.'

'Nor I you, George. We be a threatening and a worrying a whole bunch wondering where ye be. Victoria sent me a looking with instructions not to return unless thee be with me.'

'We can talk about it all later, Springer, but for now we need to find Cook. Brannigan has gone to the house she works at to find her, and he is not going to just talk this time. He intends to get answers, no matter what the cost. That man, he is an animal. I have just watched him kill one of his own men to stop him talking to me.'

'Calm thee down, George. Cook is right safe with Victoria in the wagon. We be more worried as to where thee be and how we be a finding you in this darkness.'

Springer heads towards a thicket of brambles some distance from the footbridge, closely followed by George. He grabs a stick on the side of the thicket and opens it up to reveal the two horses wearing food nose bags hitched to a wagon. As Springer leads the horse out onto the track, Victoria and Cook poke their heads out from inside the wagon.

'Looking for me, were you?' Cook asks with a smile.

'Thank God you are safe. I was worried we would not get to you in time,' George replies.

'For a person you never met until today, you seem a bit over friendly in your thoughts towards me. You do know I am a married lady with a reputation to think of?'

George responds swiftly. 'My good lady, I was worried for your safety, that's all. I have just been witness to what cruelty that man Brannigan inflicts on his own people, so when I heard him say he was looking for you, yes, I was concerned.'

Cook nudges Victoria in the ribs. 'Victoria, you were so right – George is such a gentleman. I was only teasing with you, George. With all that has now gone on, I could not go back to the house even if I wanted to. So I am afraid the circumstances have forced the issue and I must go. Whether it be to work for you or find other employment, I cannot stay here. Nor can I risk anyone following me if I gave notice and left as they may find where Victoria and Springer live.

'So, I go now, with no one knowing where I am and leaving all behind. The people in the village will think I have gone like so many others, and Lord Fitzgerald will wonder if his men have accidentally killed me and have hidden the evidence to avoid repercussions.'

George is taken aback by how practical Cook is. 'Springer and Victoria were right, my dear. If your cooking is half as good as you are wise and cunning, I would have made an excellent choice. And yes, of course the offer of employment stands. I would be a fool not to have you and your husband's services on my estate. In just a day I have seen how much the people of this village respect you and Dan. Not to mention how much you put yourselves out to help those in need. They are qualities I have sorely missed around me in the last few years.'

Cook gives him a stern look. 'I run a tight kitchen. Nobody enters without my say so or takes food without permission. I do all the cooking no matter how many people you need feeding and nobody else helps or interferes without my say so.'

George puts his hands up in the air. 'All yours. I will not touch a thing,' he says with a wink at Victoria.

Victoria chuckles while Cook tilts her head and stares directly at George.

'Don't think that I did not see that, cos I did,' she says with an even sterner voice.

Springer grabs the downed man under his shoulders, drags him to the side of the track and rolls him into the undergrowth, then goes back for the pistol and throws it into the river.

George is still looking at the floor. 'Where have the wagon tracks gone?' he asks. 'I was looking for them when I arrived but saw none.'

'Once I heard that there sound of gunfire, I wiped the whole area. It be safer with no tracks to see for them that come looking than to have them suddenly stop, so they be wiped from here to the road in yonder woods.'

Springer and George mount the front of the wagon and with a flick of the reins, the horses move off. 'We be needin' to be long far gone by morning to avoid what we stirred up today,' says Springer as they head off along the track into the woods.

After about half a mile, they join the first of several narrow roads that will take them back home, all of which have been carefully chosen to ensure they would not be seen by any who would wish them harm.

'How will Cook's Dan find us once we have gone from here?' asks George.

Victoria pokes her head out of the covered area of the wagon and hands the men two blankets to wrap themselves up in on this chilly night.

'That's easy,' she says. 'Cook has written a letter with directions to the neighbouring village of Tamworth. That letter will be dropped off by Cook to Jethrow at the barn on our way out while we will be parked up some distance away. I do not want anyone to see us or even know we were here. A week from today, you men can meet Dan on the village green at noon and plan his introduction to the farm and hopefully start to resolve the problems with poaching and thievery.'

Springer turns to look at Victoria. 'I be right lucky to have a lass like thee by my side, my dear.' As he smiles at her, he somehow manages to pass on an expression of pride and respect for Victoria in just a look. For she has managed to overcome so much with so little and given up everything in the pursuit of her love for him and now the safety of their friends.

Even being so close to bringing new life into this world, she risks herself and the unborn child to help others in danger and bring a better life to those that are prepared to take a chance.

Victoria has travelled for days in this wagon without complaint, and now must endure a few more days to get back home. All this she does without a thought for herself.

To Springer, Victoria is life itself and the fact she is his woman means everything to him. There is nothing he would not do for her.

'Cook, best thee be looking around and tell us where to pull over so thee can deliver that there letter as we be getting close by,' he says.

Cook's head pops out from inside the wagon. 'You have about half a mile to go. There will be a fork in the road with a small barn on the left with a scarecrow pinned to it. If you pull up there, it is a short skip and a jump through the woods for me to get to the other side where Jethrow and the others are residing. It should take me about ten minutes to deliver and return, providing I do not come across any of Brannigan's men like the one in the tavern earlier, for he made my skin crawl.'

George pipes up. 'I would not worry about that man anymore, Cook. His name was Carlton and Brannigan shot him while I think he was aiming at me, though I cannot be sure.' All of them look to George. 'Jethrow explained at the tavern that this man Carlton had driven my brother's furniture and belongings from his house the day after he disappeared.'

George breathes in and lets out a deep sigh, for now he must explain what he had been doing and why he deviated from the plan.

'Once I heard this, I was a bit hot-blooded. I left the tavern looking for Carlton and Brannigan. I searched everywhere from the shops along the high street to the lanes off the main village road. With no luck in the village, I moved on to the clocktower and around the lake in the park, where, by chance, I came across you, Cook! And caught sight of Carlton following you in the woods.'

Cook gasps. 'Following me?' she asks, her eyebrows raised.

George nods. 'I knew if I let him follow you, he would see Springer and Victoria – something I could not allow. As I needed to ask him a few questions about my brother's whereabouts, I took my chance and intercepted him quietly, so you did not hear me. After a small physical exchange and a right good thumping, I overpowered him and tied him to a tree. I had just started to get information out of him about my brother when Brannigan showed up and shot him. Or shot at me and hit him – I just don't know which.' George shakes his head. 'That man is worse than any I have known before, utterly ruthless and a dangerous one at that.'

'That he be,' says Springer.

Victoria leans forward and puts her arms on George's shoulders to comfort him. Instantly he flinches as she touches the area where he had been clipped by his pursuers. She swiftly retracts her hand and notices the smear of blood on her wrist. 'George, there is blood on my sleeve. Have you been hurt?'

'It is nothing. A bullet clipped me as I was running, but it can be seen to later once we are away from here.'

'Let me help you off with your jacket so I can take a better look at it,' she insists while giving Springer a stern stare. 'I thought you were looking out for our George; this does not look like you did a very good job.'

Springer shrugs and looks at George. 'I knew not that thee be hit, my friend.'

'It is naught but a scratch, young Springer. Worry yourself not. I have done worse coppicing a hedge back home.'

'I will be the judge of that, George,' Victoria says as she wipes away the blood to check out the wound. 'As for you, Springer, I will deal with you later.'

George begins to chuckle as Springer sighs and shrugs his shoulders while shaking his head, resigned to the fact that he will receive an earbashing later from Victoria. Her simple and caring actions help to reassure George as he continues with his recollection.

'Seems that his job that day was to take all my brother's belongings to the factory to make it look like they were being sent on to him, but the truth was different. They burned all his clothes, belongings and furniture in the factory furnaces. That way, no one would ever know where they went, and they could make up any story as to where my brother had gone.'

'Did you find out anything about where Steven could be?' Victoria asks in a quiet voice.

George puts his hand up across his chest and taps Victoria's hand where it works on his shoulder. 'Some information, my dear. You see, by now Carlton was getting upset and emotional about what he had done and to how many people – friends and strangers alike. He was talking about a mine or a pit where people were worked to death in poor conditions. I was just getting into that when Brannigan showed up and shot his pistol. He hit Carlton in the chest and at that point I just ran.'

Springer speaks. 'I be hearing some talk when I be present with Lord Fitzgerald and your father, Victoria. They be arguing with some engineers about safety of strip-mining ore they discovered while building drainage underground. I be not knowin' the words they used, but a geologist, I thinks that be him, he be sayin' it was a fault line, with high grade deposits and additional mineral veins. Somewhere below the factory I think, but I knows not where.'

Victoria lowers her head in shame and stares at the bed of the wagon. 'I have also heard them speaking about this. Lord Fitzgerald used to brazenly enhance his ego in front of me, talking about the prisoners from the courts, vagrants, drifters and homeless people from the local ports and towns being sent to work in his mine as free labour. He would bribe officials to look the other way or to send their prisoners in his direction. They would talk about getting six good weeks before they were spent and needed replacing. He was always looking for ways to find unwanted people. If they went into that place, they were never seen or heard from again. Oh George, if your brother and his family ended up there, they would have been there years by now.'

George wipes the tears from his eyes. 'It is not your fault, Victoria. And perhaps my brother is not there − he is a very adaptable man, you know. But if they were sent to this place, they would have long since been lost to me, so me charging in would be a fool's error.' He turns to look at Springer. 'It is a lot to ask of you, Springer, when you have done and risked so much already. But in time from now, when we have my farm running well and Victoria has her young one in the world, would you come back with me to this place and see if we could trace what happened to my brother?'

Springer reaches over and places his hand on top of George's. 'When the time be right, I will come back here, and I will tear this place apart with thee. I owe it not just to you, but as a debt to Victoria, whose younger brothers also have been missing for some time too. There be men here undeserving of being amongst us and I intend to give full retribution to them that be doing the hurting to the people around here.'

They continue for a short while, always wary of meeting anyone along the road. Fortunately, so far there has only been a couple of deer, a badger and a fox. With darkness in near full effect, the way forward is only lit by the moon's glow.

'Pull over here and I will be on my way,' says Cook as she makes her way to the back of the wagon.

Springer has barely pulled up the reins on the horses when Cook leaps out and hits the ground. She takes a minute to check all is quiet and clear around her, then heads towards a slight orange glow permeating through the wood.

Just seconds after she disappears from view, Cook comes running back to the rear of the wagon. Victoria is waiting for her with an outstretched arm, holding the letter in her hand. As she reaches Victoria, Cook looks at her with an embarrassed expression and Victoria starts to chuckle.

'Not a word,' says Cook as she whips the letter out of her hand, turns and heads back to the woods for a second time.

'I hope she cooks better than she remembers,' comments George with a chuckle.

To the surprise of all of them, a voice echoes back from the empty darkness. 'I heard that.'

George looks at Springer. 'My God, that woman must have the ears of a bat.'

Springer laughs. 'You have no idea of the abilities of that there woman. After that fight I had, it was Cook who stitched up my ear and eye, not a sawbones, and a right proper job she did do as well.'

George calls to Victoria to join him and Springer at the front of the cart. 'While we are alone, I have something to tell you before we return home. I hope you do not mind this old man interfering, but with you helping so much on the estate, Springer, and you working in my house cooking for us and cleaning, Victoria, it has not gone unnoticed by me that you are not as far done on your own cottage as you would have liked. Springer, the roof you have repaired looks very good, almost as good as when I first built it.' He chuckles with Springer for he knows Springer hated working on it, as he has a fear of heights, and every corner was not quite as square as it should have been.

'So, while you have been on this adventure with me, I arranged for a friend of mine to come over and fit the last three windows and finish the back stable double doors to the kitchen. His stonemason brother with his two boys have been reseating the stone steps and path leading to the front door. They are also going to reline the well and repoint the top stones if time permits.'

Springer is speechless. 'Words fail me. I've not known a more kindly, decent man than thee in my lifetime.'

Victoria gives George a big hug. 'God bless you, George.'

'Before you say anything more, understand you two are important to me. From the day you arrived on my doorstep looking to purchase that plot of land, my life has got going with new vigour and purpose. You have helped me without any thought to yourselves and I feel like I have family around me again. Not to mention the adventures I now seem to be getting into. My heart has not stopped pounding for hours and this trip is still far from over.'

The sound of snapping branches breaks in the air and all three of them turn to face the woods. A faint shadow can be seen weaving this way and that between the trees, but it takes a minute to make out the figure coming out of the woods is Cook. She runs straight for the back of the wagon and jumps in.

'Go,' she whispers. 'Go now. Brannigan and some of his men were arriving as I was leaving. They have been here three times so far tonight, looking for George and myself.'

Springer flicks the reins to get the horses moving, and they are soon back onto the road. He shakes the reins again and the horses start to trot. 'I'll keep this pace up until we be away from this here.'

George moves to the back of the wagon to look and listen for anyone following. In the direction of the barn, he can make out the sound of muffled yelling. It is faint, but he can just about hear it.

Suddenly, a white flash illuminates the sky, quickly followed by another. It is a second or so before they hear two pistol shots, then more shouting and screaming.

Nobody speaks for a while as the horses trot on and the sound of yelling fades to nothing. All is silent except for the muffled thud of the hooves on the soft dirt road as Springer follows the path as best he can under the faint veil of moonlight.

'I hope they are all OK,' Cook says.

'I'm sure that be all puff and wind by Brannigan trying to put the frighteners on Jethrow and his group of families,' says George. 'I saw in the tavern, he does not like it when the numbers stack on the other side and he will be well outnumbered there, that's for sure.'

Soon Springer is at a fork in the road. He takes the left turn and within minutes he is out of the woods and on a larger, more solid road heading home. He slows the horses down to a walk as they have been trotting for nearly half an hour and are sweating up with the effort of pulling the wagon over the soft ground they have just left.

Victoria turns to face Cook. 'Well, Cook, two days from today you will be at George's estate with Springer and myself. Perhaps it might be a good idea for you two to discuss employment duties and for you, George, to talk about the cottage for her and Dan. I am sure I know of a couple of neighbours who are more than happy to have Cook as a nanny, should the offer not be goo—'

George butts in. 'My good lady, I have been to the end of another county to rescue a damsel in distress from an ugly ogre and his weasel-like friend. I've got into a fight, been shot at, been hunted through a forest like some kind of wild beast, and now, at this present time, I'm stuck in a wagon on the run with two of the most wanted villains in the land. All that, just to find this lady and her unique husband, who I may also remind you is a wanted poacher by many a landowner.'

Springer and Cook chuckle as Victoria holds a straight face and a stiff back. She is trying so hard not to laugh as George continues. 'With all this old man has been through, you want to steal her away from me before I have yet to make her an honest offer of employment!' He pauses for a second. 'No, I don't think so, thank you very much.'

'Honest employment?' says Cook. 'You don't know my husband! He would be terrified at words like that!'

George tries not to laugh, but it's no good; he cannot hold his serious expression anymore.

Even Victoria is laughing now as she says, 'I was only saying that Cook has options should she not find your offer good enough.'

It's now George's turn to take the advantage. 'All I have to do is scream and call for help and pretend I have been abducted against my will by two villainous criminals.'

Victoria gives a shocked expression. 'But I am an innocent, heavily pregnant lady. Surely you would not do such a thing to a defenceless woman?'

Springer speaks up. 'By God, my dear, he be right, knowin' who be the villain here.' He turns to George. 'Sir, you be right. That there woman took advantage of me when I be tired, weak and wounded from battle. She had her wicked way with this naive innocent man when my guard was down and I were unable to defend myself.' He points to Victoria's stomach. 'Took what she be a wanting and cast me to the wolves.'

George nods deeply. 'Yes, I understand fully now. I can see how you have been taken advantage of, my friend. For I fear this woman be a wolf in sheep's clothing, and you were caught off guard by her wily ways.'

All of them are now laughing heavily. Cook has tears rolling down her cheeks. 'Enough,' she says. 'Please, I cannot laugh much more. It hurts my sides.'

Victoria turns to Springer with her eyes and mouth wide open. 'Weak and wounded? Unable to defend yourself? Taken advantage of?' A wicked smirk appears on her face. 'Perhaps that is why I do not remember any of it, as the events were so unsatisfying and unworthy of recalling.'

Springer shakes his head and looks down. 'I'm only a mere man, my dear, not one of them there new-fangled steam thrashing machines.' As he raises his head back up, he continues. 'So weak and wounded be I, still I tried. For king and country, I tried… pushed through the pain barrier, fought off the exhaustion of the demands made upon this broken man by this strong-minded woman.'

Cook controls her laughing to speak. 'I must be fair, Victoria. I tended Springer's wounds and he had taken a fair bit of punishment at the time. In fact, I would say he was barely conscious when I was stitching him up.'

Springer shakes his head and lowers it again. 'If only you knew, Cook. Trapped there was I, in one of your old man's poaching huts, defenceless and weak.' He shakes his head again. 'That fight, that be the easy part. The forced-on demands set by this here rampant rabbit masking as a woman made that there fight just a warm-up to what be to come. I be nearly a stone lighter now and leaner than a polecat with all the effort. I can't say I am not glad for my love's condition now as it gives me time to rest and recover.'

Victoria clips Springer across the top of his head. 'That will be enough of that! You are lucky to have my attentions at all, considering you have made me a wanted woman,' she says.

George breaks in on the conversation. 'I still remember the day these two strays arrived at my doorstep. I knew who they both were, as I was at the fight watching Springer duel with the other man. And I had seen Victoria walking round before the fight with that man I will not even mention. I would never have taken them for a couple, but now after knowing them for a while, I could not imagine one without the other. However, in this case, Victoria, I must side with *Bartholomew*. Victoria, you are a magnet for danger and risk for the same men are now hunting Cook and myself as they are you. Well, minus the one that was picking on Cook. It just goes to show they will turn on each other just as easily as they will on the innocent.'

'And good riddance to that horrible man,' Cook says. 'But who is this Bartholomew?'

'Oh God,' Springer mutters. 'There be no living this down now.'

Cook looks at Springer, who turns his back and looks away. Her curious look changes to a huge smile. 'Nooooo…' Victoria is nodding her head behind him as he looks forward over the backs of the horses and flicks on the reins. 'Well I'll be. Springer, was your father a preacher by any chance?'

Springer turns to give George a solemn stare and grits his teeth.

George smiles back. 'Well, my son, the good book shows itself in many ways, and he who helpeth others in need will surely be rewarded in this life or the next.'

Springer clenches his fist and shakes it at George, muttering under his breath. 'I'll be givin' thee a helping soon.'

Victoria moves to the front of the wagon and hugs Springer. As he turns to look at her, she kisses him gently on the lips. 'Don't worry, dear, I will protect this weak and wounded battle-worn man from the evils of Cook and that nasty man George.'

Springer takes in a deep breath and lets out a huge sigh. He knows when he has been outgunned and outmanoeuvred. He holds up his hands and just concedes to the loss of pride. Cook laughs again, with Victoria and George soon joining in. Even Springer starts to chuckle. The roar of laughter and banter from the wagon continues as it trundles down the road into the distance.

For the next two days, they travel night and day at a near-constant pace, Springer and George taking turns to lead the wagon and its team back to George's estate. They stop only to rest and feed the two horses and to cook hot food over an open fire for the party of four.

It is late afternoon when the wagon turns down the track leading to George's farm estate. His three dogs are sitting in the porch and, as soon as they see their master in the distance, they are up on their feet and awaiting his instructions. George lets out a short, sharp whistle and the three of them sprint towards the wagon. They don't bark, as they are trained not to, but jump up and down by the side of the wagon to get a look at George and who else is inside.

As he steps down off the side of the cart, the dogs go wild with excitement, tails thrashing and teeth showing. They are so happy to see him after several days of being away.

Fern, the young bitch in the pack, takes her chance and jumps clean up in the air at George's chest and he catches her as he has done many times before. 'Hello, my pretty,' he says as he hugs her before putting her back down with the others.

The girls disembark and enter the house while Springer surveys the farm buildings and land from his position at the front of the wagon. He can tell something is not right, but he cannot put his finger on it. All just seems too quiet and – for this time of year –

there is far too little activity. He turns the horses and heads to the large storage barn adjacent to the house. George follows him with his pack of three collies walking along beside. He opens the barn doors and swings them out so that Springer can drive the horse and cart into the waiting space.

There is an unpleasant odour in the air, and both George and Springer notice it immediately. The dogs run over to some loose hay on the floor. At this time of year, there is very little hay stored as it is early summer, and most has been used throughout the winter on feeding the livestock.

George walks over and kicks the hay away from the floor. Underneath is a pile of human vomit. As he looks around, he can see some of the ties of hay are broken while others are stained with more vomit.

Springer by now has jumped down from the wagon and is looking around as well. 'Seems the mice be a playing while the cat has been away,' he says as he moves a bale to one side to reveal empty bottles and tankards on the floor in a pile.

'I would not mind, but they have not even cleared out the rubbish. And this vomit-stained hay needs to be disposed of before it contaminates the last of the other ties.'

There is a groaning sound from the back of the barn and George goes to investigate. As he approaches, he sees items of clothing strewn everywhere. He hears another groan and turns to look into the bay at the end of the barn. To his amazement, he finds three of his farmhands butt naked on a blanket, asleep. Between them is a woman – again with no clothes on.

Springer arrives and stands by George.

'I know that there woman,' says George. 'That be Rosie. She works in the village tavern. For a few extra coins, she also performs a more personal service. If the hay does not make 'em itch, what she will have just given them sure will for a while.'

George takes a closer look at the blanket they are on. It is quite distinctive, with different types of seashells embroidered into the pale fabric.

'That blanket be from my house. It was my wife's favourite bed cover.' He walks away and returns with two buckets of water. Passing one of them to Springer, he says, 'Shall we?'

There is a big smile on Springer's face. 'Oh yes, this will be a pleasure.' They swing in tandem for a second or so before George counts down. 'Three, two, one.'

The content of both buckets is released at the same time, drenching all four of them. The woman screams and jumps to her feet, looking for something to cover herself up with. Spotting her dress hanging over a saddle hook, she grabs it and covers her modesty, while the men yell in disapproval while trying to get off each other.

'What did you do that for?' one of them shouts, wiping the water from his face.

'I did that because I do not approve of my employees lying around naked in the afternoon on my wife's blanket, let alone the mess and vomit that has been left to contaminate the last of the hay. Now get dressed and get this cleaned up, and as for you, young lady, get yourself out of here before I forget my manners.'

The woman grabs her shoes from beside the door and turns to the three men. 'I will collect what you owe when you are next down the tavern,' she says, then runs off through the building. As she reaches the doorway, she stops to put her shoes on and slides her dress over her head. With a wriggle of her hips, she positions the dress in place, turns to look at the group of men, blows them a kiss, giggles, then runs off up the track towards the village.

The three men, on the other hand, take a different approach. They are angry about being disturbed, and most of all about being humiliated by having the girl sent away. They stagger around, looking for their clothes and shoes amongst the hay and farm items spread around.

'You can start by clearing out the barn, putting all the contaminated hay on the manure heap and the glass bottles with the rest of the rubbish by the side of the barn,' yells an angry George as he walks over to the blanket and starts to brush it down, as seeing it reminds him of his late wife and better times.

His memory goes back to when they were in the shop purchasing it all those years ago. He recollects her smiling face and her pointing at the blanket for George to pick it up and display for her. He thinks of how much it cost and most of all how she fell in love with it, for it was on their bed for the last year they were together.

His mind returns to the present and he carefully starts to fold this precious item up. As he does so, he notices all the stains. It angers him that these people have treated it so badly and he turns to face up to the three labourers.

Springer sees the look in George's eye and knows he is about to do something stupid. Quickly, he steps in and pushes the men towards the piles of human vomit and contaminated hay. 'Now, be fast with it, lads. Clear that there mess up and don't be a sparing the horses.' As one of the men nears the area, he gets a nose full of the smell rising from the pile. Instantly it triggers a response and he projectile vomits a new heap on top of the old one.

'I bet that be a wakeup call to thee,' says Springer as he steps back to let the men get on with tidying up.

'Come, Uncle, let's be getting you to the house and I will deal with this on my return.' He puts his arm over George's shoulder and walks him and the blanket he is still carrying towards the house.

'This was my wife's, you know, one of the things she loved most.'

Springer opens the door to the house, and they see Victoria rushing around, trying to tidy up with Cook.

'I do not remember leaving it in this state,' says Victoria with a frown as she passes George and Springer to throw some dirty boots outside the front door. As she turns back inside, she notices George is quiet and stroking the blanket. Her demeanour changes as she realises something is not right and looks at Springer.

'It be his wife's and it has been messed up a bit by some drunken oafs,' says Springer while giving Victoria a nod. She does not need any more prompting and she takes George by the arm and leads him to his favourite chair.

'Come, George, sit down here. Cook's getting a fire going and then we will make you a nice cup of tea.' She reaches out for the blanket. 'Now pass me the blanket, my dear, and I will see to getting it cleaned up for you.'

George slowly passes the blanket to her then sits down. 'I'm sorry to get a bit silly,' he says. 'I do not know what came over me. I have kept that blanket safely stored away in my footlocker and the shock of seeing it messed up just got to me. I will be alright in a minute.'

Springer looks at Victoria. 'See to George, that be a goodly lass. I be needed to right some wrongdoing and I will be back shortly.' There is anger in Springer's eyes and Victoria can see it. She also knows this has been a long time coming and her man needs to start getting this sorted.

As Springer opens the front door, Fern slips in between his feet and runs straight up to George, jumping on his lap. The dog's distraction is just what is needed as it snaps George out of his state of mind as he interacts with the young collie. Springer, on the other hand, is fully focused. He storms back to the barn at a fast walk and as he enters through the open barn door, he can see the three men have been joined by a couple more labourers. They are standing in a circle talking and as Springer approaches, they stop and turn to face him.

John, or Big John as he is known to his friends, steps forward with a pitchfork in his hand. He lowers it so it is pointing at Springer. 'This was a right sweet setup before you arrived. George's nephew or not, we control the show here, not you. This farm be run by us now, not the likes of you and that old man George.'

Springer eyes the man up from top to bottom. He has seen many like this in his time, but this time it is personal. George has become a great friend and bad behaviour from these disrespectful farmhands will not be tolerated.

'My Uncle George be a goodly man who has given thee all homes on the estate and coin in your pocket. He has treated all of thee with more respect and decency than what thee be showing in return. Now as it be his estate and him that employs you, not thee controlling him, you be wise to be more respectful of them that be your employer.'

'I think not,' says John, taking another step forward. Springer is in no mood for messing around. He grabs the pitchfork below the prongs and pushes it up out of the way, then steps inside and delivers a right hook to the jaw.

Big John hits the ground like a sack of spuds, but Springer does not stop. This is real life, and he must ensure that all are aware it is changing around here. He steps forward and plants his boot heavily into John's balls. The man lets out a yell and curls up into the foetal position. Springer steps back then lunges forward and kicks John again, this time on the chin. The impact knocks him unconscious.

As Big John lies there motionless, Springer hears the rustling of hay behind him. On the floor beside the motionless John is a dark shadow cast by a man approaching him from behind. 'You bastard, I'll get you,' yells the man as he is almost on top of Springer.

Without turning around, Springer pulls his elbow back, impacting the man on the bridge of the nose. With a *crack* it splits wide open from the force and as the man falls to his knees, blood pours down his chest and onto his trousers. Numb with pain, he tries to hold his nose gently in his hand, cupping the blood as it flows. 'Aaaaahhhhhhh,' he cries out in shock.

'Any other bugger feel the need to try his luck? For I be in the mood to educate some more learning today if it be needed,' yells Springer as he looks around at the rest of the men with hate-filled eyes and his fists clenched tight. The rest of the men around him are rooted to the floor, fear making them shake to their very boots. Never before have any of them seen such brutality and swift discipline dished out so fast.

This has been the moment Springer has patiently been waiting for. He has wanted to straighten out this group of people but needed to set the foundations and understand who the ring leaders were before he got the ball rolling. It might have been a little sooner than they were planning, but as George was so let down by his farmhands, the time felt right. This will be a good shock start to them all. With luck, from this event Springer and George may well see who is worth his salt and who is needed to be cut loose from the farm to better its working ability.

Springer sets out his demands. 'Well, as thee all seem to be done with me, finish off that there clearing up of this barn. You with the bloody nose, Tibbins, unhitch and rub down them there horses then start a feeding and watering the rest of that there livestock. For I can see from here that the water butts be near empty. Young Ivan, throw a bucket of water on that there waste of space on the floor, then feed the chickens and bring the eggs you find in the hen house to the girls indoors. For once don't stash the half thee been hiding up each time, for I be tired of the game thee be playing at George's expense. The inn in the village will have to buy the eggs they be needing from now on, not trade for ale and cider.'

At first no one dare move, all still in shock at the events that have just unfolded. 'Move afore I takes to thee as a duck does to water,' yells Springer.

The men fly into action, all of them moving faster than they have ever moved before, as Springer walks over to Big John, who is just getting to his feet while still holding his balls in his hands. 'You've had your last laugh at my uncle's expense,' he says as he throws a few coins on the floor in front of him. 'That there be severance pay, now pack what belongings thee be owning and be gone by dark afore I be needin' to end what thee started.'

As Springer turns to walk off, Big John pulls a knife from his belt. 'Nobody tells me what to do,' he says, lashing out at Springer.

Springer was half-ready for a response and leans over to one side to slip the sweeping blade, but slicing back the knife cuts through the edge of his shirt, putting a small cut into the top of his arm. The response is instant: a left and right punch to the head, two uppercuts to his stomach, which buckles him over, then he's finished with a knee to the face that catapults him up into the air and onto his back, leaving him out cold to the world.

Springer turns to the others. 'Before thee unhitch them there horses, throw him in the back and be taking him from this land. Don't be forgettin' to put the coins in his pocket, for he be needin' a sawbones for sure.'

For the first time that Springer can remember, the labourers work as a team. Two of them place John in the back of the wagon, one collecting up the coins and another mounting the front to drive the wagon up the road.

He leaves the labourers at work and walks back towards the house. To his surprise, George and Victoria are standing in the doorway watching as events unfolded. As he approaches them, George speaks. 'Fine display, young Springer. I'm just sorry I was not there with you, but I was caught off guard by the blanket and my mind was at another place for a moment.'

'My friend, this be my job to handle now, not thees. You have been good to Victoria and me and I be a man of my word. I will not see your life's work ruined by them that be of no honour. We will put to right the wrongs that them there be putting afore thee soon enough and you will have your farm back how thee remembers it.' Springer walks in through the front door. 'Now where be Cook when she be needed, for I feel a few stitches may need sewing and we also have eggs coming our way. George, you need to see what fineries Cook can put together with a few eggs and what's in your pantry.'

As Springer closes the door behind them, he knows the scene has been set. It is now down to the farmhands to prove their worth. On top of that, it will be only a week before Dan is expected to arrive.

CHAPTER 13

A Stranger Arrives

It's mid-afternoon on a hot, sticky Friday near the end of July. There is a heat haze across the fields, and it is another still, dry, energy-sapping muggy day. The ground has not seen rain for two weeks and the grass has started to dry out in the scorching conditions. Laughter in the local tavern – The Thatcher's Arms – can be heard outside by the people sitting on the extra benches put out on the edge of the village green for the fine summer weather. Four children have set up a target board and are shooting what looks to be a selection of small bows and assorted-length arrows. They take it in turns to shoot off five of the projectiles each before running over to the target to count up the total value and see who has the best score in the round.

A group of labourers, fresh from the land, have just arrived. Laughing and joking, they head inside to take a drink in their local watering hole. Over the next hour or so, several more groups of people arrive to begin what is the start of another social weekend. For some it is just a pitstop before they return to their families or to the fields to continue their work, while for others there seems to be a lot more cash to spend than the average labourer for the area.

The innkeeper does not mind as long as everyone is drinking, as he is making money on every tankard and pitcher filled. At this time of year, he employs additional staff who are always pretty girls with some cleavage showing to keep the men coming back from the fields and spending their wages in his tavern. He encourages the girls to flirt with the men and any additional money they make outside of the tavern's hours entertaining them with a more personal service he does not care about, for he only has three or four months to make the most of his income for the year. After that, the girls and seasonal farmhands are gone until the following harvest time. It is the time of year when there are a lot of fresh faces in the village as pickers and planters arrive in numbers to work the land and harvest crops for the nearby farmers. Even the local shops have a large increase in the sale of goods in this bounty of times.

George's farm is no different from all the others. Despite having several farmhands working full time, more are always needed when the harvest arrives, and he employs around thirty more people at this time of year – with most of them being the same people that work for him year on year. George is wise enough to have different crops ranging from fruit, root vegetables and some salad produce as well as bean and grain crops. Not to mention the dairy, poultry and livestock that require harvesting and slaughtering over the coming four months.

This extra-long seasonal work makes it an attractive offer for good casual workers, as it is a constant time of employment for those who work hard for him on the estate. It also makes for having a good supply of regulars that know what will be required when they arrive.

George is out walking the fields with Springer. They are checking on each crop for its readiness to harvest and trying to work out the best time to put the workforce on the crops being inspected. They also estimate the volume each field should produce, how long it will take to harvest and a rough price that can be expected when the crop goes to market.

'You know, I do this every year and yet in the past few years, I have got it so badly wrong. It's like the middle of the fields are hollow and the crops have been just too thinly planted. Even though the edges look fairly thick and uniform,' says George as they walk along.

Springer chuckles. 'The edges should be the thinnest as the rabbits and deer take their sneaky share during the night – but they pay the price come autumn, as good meat be on hand for the table and excess can be sold or traded. But you be knowin' this already, George. Your loss of product I think is down to them that be sly of hand and stealing, a problem that will be right resolved in due course. Anyway, I think we move them there men on to the strawberries and raspberries come Monday. With three or four days picking, we split half the men to cut and turn the hay fields while the other half start the re-pick of fruit again as it will ripen in this heat faster. Now don't forget, George, be using the same people to deliver the produce to market as you usually do, so none be the wiser to us looking for the loss.'

George looks at Springer. 'I only use my own farmhands for the deliveries. I never use seasonal people to take the goods to the market and most of them have been here years.' George and Springer continue to walk around the estate, viewing all the produce and animals while planning the next few weeks' workload before heading back to the storage barns to check on current stock.

* * *

Back at The Thatcher's Arms, the afternoon is well on its way for some. The ales have been flowing for a few hours and the patrons are enjoying the attentions of the barmaids as they work round the men, assessing who has money to burn. Once they work out who has been paid or who is being flash with the coin, they focus their attention on them – knowing there is money to be made later after the tavern closes, providing they hook their men correctly.

By far the best of the girls is Rosie, a buxom lass with fine assets who does well enough to live in the village all year round. Showing more than her fair share of cleavage, she has a seductive personality and can tempt many a coin out of the farmhands during the summer period. Being a seasonal veteran and a lot smarter than she acts, the fair-haired girl plays the foolish, cute, girly type very well. And with her way of teasing the men until they are so very aroused, she can work through two or three men after a shift as they are easy to tempt and quick to be satisfied. Unfortunately for many, they will collect an additional dose of something that will need attention later from the village doctor as the burning and itching grows into a more severe rash and painful swelling with time.

For Rosie, she shows and feels no ill effects visually or otherwise to what she carries. All she has on her mind is to earn as much money as she can, as fast as possible, and get out of the village for a better life. Her dream is to set herself up with a place of her own before her looks fade and she is unable to find the kind of man she wants to settle down with and have a family. A fresh start where nobody knows her name or how she has earned her living in the past. By her own reckoning, at this moment she has just this season to go before she has enough squirrelled away to make the transition to a better way of life and will no longer need to be pawed and groped by dirty, sweaty, drunken men.

Like so many others who are trapped in this way of life to survive, the consequences of what she does to follow her dreams cost a high price, and it is already too late. For what she carries has already robbed her of the ability to bear children. She will eventually find her man and purchase a house, but within the coming years he will have died from the pox, and she will rot from the inside out, leaving her to suffer a lonely, unpleasant and painful existence right up to the bitter end.

Inside the tavern, leaning his chair up against one of the wooden beams covered in leather strips of brass souvenirs, a man puffs on a lion's head pipe full of tobacco. He is a tall, thin man with long black straggly hair. His clothes and mannerisms allow him to blend into the crowd without collecting any attention from those around him. He rocks backwards and forwards on the hind legs of his seat, quietly biding his time.

Like the barmaids moving round the room, he has been watching all those in the tavern who have been drinking and bragging for the last couple of hours. It does not take him long to form a picture of the people who may be able to supply him with what he requires. He just observes the barmaids and those with whom they hang around the most – for some of the patrons are flashing more money than a farmhand would earn, and this attracts the girls like moths to a flame.

A group of seven labourers who are getting louder and louder with each round of drinks fits the bill perfectly. He waits for the right moment to present himself and start his act. As the loudest one of the lot walks up to the bar to order the next round of drinks, he knocks back the last of his drink and makes his move. Stepping up to the bar, he slams the tankard down on the counter to get the innkeeper's attention. 'Another of your finest ales before I leave to return to my employer, my good man,' he says in a disappointed manner.

The labourer looks round at the man who has butted in. Dan slaps a large pouch on the table and rummages round inside for a coin to pay the server. Little does anyone know the pouch is full of bits of metal, nails and small stones. For all who do not know, it sounds like a large pouch of coins.

It has the desired effect as the man next to him is drawn to the chinking of metal. 'Aren't you worried about having all that coin with you?' he asks.

Dan looks at him, still rummaging around. 'No, not really. I have two armed men watching my back at this very moment.'

The man looks at all the people in the tavern to see who is looking in their direction. With a bar full of people and lots of new faces, many people catch his eye as potential candidates, some even look back at him.

'And who might they be?' he asks.

Dan shrugs his shoulders. 'I have no idea.'

'What? You have no idea who be watching for you?'

Dan places a coin on the counter. 'Thank you,' he says to the innkeeper before turning back to the man beside him. 'I have no idea who is watching me because my master, Lord Fitzgerald, does not tell me. He sends me to find produce and gives me money to pay for them. I make the deal, arrange a collection point and supply wagons and drovers to receive the goods. When I have checked out the quality of the merchandise and it is to the standard required, I pay the supplier the price that we have agreed.' He sighs heavily before continuing. 'Only in this case, the contact man has not shown up and I cannot wait any longer. So, I now need to go elsewhere before my master loses patience in me.' He raises his tankard to the man. 'Well, good day to you, for I must drink this and be on my way.'

Dan goes to turn away, back to his chair with his new tankard of ale, but the man pulls him back round. 'What kind of goods would you be looking for?' he asks.

Dan places his drink back on the counter and fumbles in his pocket before pulling out a sheet of paper and stepping back from the man so he cannot read the sheet himself.

'Now let me see… On the livestock side of things, two dozen highland cows, a stud bull, twenty Gloucester Old Spot pigs and four dozen sheep. Other requirements are thirty sacks of grain, five barrels of salted salmon and trout, five dozen hens. Then on the butchered meat side, six sides of pork, three sides of beef and, if possible, six sides of venison.'

The man scratches his chin. 'Now that be an order. Supposing that list can be made, how much is it worth?'

Dan does a bit of thinking. 'Well, if the produce was good, and the livestock young and of good breeding stock, around three hundred and fifty guineas.'

The labourer's eyebrows raise at the price, and he nods slightly. 'When would you be needing all this stock by?'

Dan shrugs. 'If it were to happen, I would need to leave on the Friday next week as I have commitments to supply produce to the large estate. But it is now not happening, and I need to stop the arrival of my drovers, so I will bid thee well and get back to my drink before I leave.'

As Dan turns to leave, the man pulls him back again. 'Now wait just a minute. I may be able to fulfil that order myself, as I happen to have a fair size freeholding that I work with a group of likewise-minded people. If you were to give me but a moment of your time, I would have a word with my fellow farmers and see if we could supply such an order.'

Dan sighs. 'Well, if you want to talk to your friends, you can do. For I am here for another half hour before I must leave. I have another meeting on the supply of winter root crops to feed the cattle – and that is for thirty wagons for December.'

The man's jaw drops. 'Thirty wagonloads?' he says. 'Please take your ale and wait a while, for I need to speak to my associates.'

As Dan heads back to his chair by the wooden beam, the man moves back into his group of friends. With a few words, they file out of the building and walk over onto a part of the village green away from the crowds of people.

Dan watches through the window as they debate the tempting offer he has placed before them.

'This be the chance of a lifetime! No more odd sacks here and one or two animals there. We do the whole lot in one go, take the money and spit it between us. Almost all the requirements we can take from that old fool George and his tenant farmers around the village. The meat I can get from my new employer's estate,' says Big John. 'What do you say? This man is a big player, and he represents a lord – Lord Fitzgerald. He also wants thirty wagons of animal feed in December. Let's take what we can and make a better life for us. Having George under our control for years since the loss of his wife has done us all well, but not to the scale this could take us.' The other men nod in approval.

'Think about it, since the arrival of his nephew, it has been a little different and pickings have been a little thinner for us all. But with the money we could make, we could deal with that inconvenience of a nephew and George would be back under our control. Then we could work on getting his land for ourselves just as we had always planned. That old fool's not getting any younger and we nearly had him broken once. With a little help, the end could be sooner rather than later. He has had his life – time for us to have ours. Let's just take this opportunity to line our pockets with some real spending money, while the loss of stock will maybe even finish him for good.'

Young Ivan has been standing on the fringes of the group listening to all John has said. Finally, he speaks up. 'My mother told me about what happened with George's wife. Never sat well with her, what happened that day. Even spoke of it on her death bed, telling me the way it really was that night.'

'We did what was needed to have a better life,' Big John says. 'If she had told George of all the missing stock, we would not be here now. We'd be strung from a rope – or worse, sent to a penal colony in some country on the far side of the world.' He looks at Ivan. 'Anyway, you should count yourself lucky you're still with us at all, considering you have no family left, my boy. And while we are on that point, you should know you will only be getting a half share, as you are not yet a full man and have not put enough time in yet to earn a full stake in the game.'

Ivan stares John down. 'No,' he says, shaking his head. 'My mother would turn in her grave if I was to do this, for George paid all to have her properly buried in the church and have the priest say the words over her body. For that reason, I want nothing to do with what you are planning. All I want is to be paid a fair wage for a fair day's work, that's all. I will say nothing of what I have heard, but I will not take a hand in your plans to steal from that man. Collecting eggs and moving stock for you was bad enough for me.'

With his point made, Ivan turns and walks away, leaving the others to bicker amongst themselves as to the best way to collect all that is required to fulfil the order.

The fact that the lad has walked away from the others has not gone unnoticed by Dan. As he watches the young man walk back across the field, he does not know for certain, but his guess is that the young man wants nothing to do with the bargain he has just struck. He also notices the men looking at the lad in a way Dan has seen before in the likes of Brannigan and Sykes.

Dan has nearly finished his drink by the time the man returns to him and stands up as he approaches, takes another sip and places the tankard on the table.

'I've had a word with the others, and I believe we can have all that order ready for Friday next week for three hundred and fifty guineas. But you must supply the drovers for the livestock and bring wagons to transport the other goods away.'

Dan thinks for a minute. 'I set the price when I see the goods and not before. But if the stock is good, I see no problem in three hundred and fifty guineas, maybe even a little more if the quality of the animals stands up to my inspection.' Dan knows he has hooked the right people. 'Now where do we meet? For we cannot drive the livestock to and from the tavern as they will be hard to control and what they leave on the ground will not be appreciated by the villagers.'

Big John scratches his head. Dan knows this man will need a place where nobody will see them do the trade or him and his group will be known to all as being thieves.

'Come outside with me and I will show you on the village map,' John says.

Dan picks up his tankard and knocks the rest of the liquid back before slamming the mug down on the table. Several people look round and he nods in their direction. It's an old trick, but it never fails Dan, as John looks to see who he was nodding to. It is always better to keep the people you are dealing with on edge, something that has kept Dan alive in some of his darkest times.

With so many people noticing them together, Dan feels safer and more confident – it should deter this man and his friends from mugging him for his pouch later if they had a mind to do so. He follows him outside and across to the village green noticeboard.

'This is the village, and that is the road beside us along this green. Follow it down for about two miles and you can see this small track leading off to a meadow behind a small wood. There is a large black barn on the corner of the lane, so you cannot miss it and I will have someone waiting for you on the road. The grass will keep the cattle feeding for a while and there be space enough for several wagons to transfer the rest of the stock.'

Dan looks closely at the map, then the road beside them to get his bearings. He nods, as he has it right in his head. 'What time of day shall we do the trade?' he asks.

'Early,' John replies swiftly. 'Early so the cattle can be moved in the cooler part of the day. You don't want to be moving big cattle during the worst of the heat as they can get a bit moody, so shall we say six in the morning?'

Dan deduces they will rustle the animals and supplies overnight and will want them gone from the area before people notice them missing. 'Six is good with me,' he says. 'Now with whom am I making the trade on the day, should the produce be of the correcting standard?'

John stands a little more upright and puffs out his chest. 'Why that would be with me, sir. I will be there on the day to go through with the trade. My name is John, or Big John to them that knows me best.'

Dan takes his hand and shakes it. 'My name be Dan, and on behalf of Lord Fitzgerald, I will take you up on this offer, providing you can supply the goods requested on time.' He pulls out his list of requirements and passes it to John. 'This be the list, and this be a down payment of intent.' Dan passes him five gold coins. 'We have been seen together, so it is only fitting that I should deposit something to show my good faith to the deal, so until next Friday, I bid you farewell.' Dan turns and leaves. He heads back towards the village and once out of sight of prying eyes and disappears down a side road. For now, he has far more important things on his mind and his pace quickens.

Big John is still standing on the edge of the green, beaming as he stares at the five gold sovereigns in his hand, moving them around in his palm with his finger. He is soon joined by the rest of his group. 'Well, lads,' he says. 'It looks like we are going up in the world. He has even given me a deposit.' The men look at the gold sovereigns as John moves them around in his hand. For most, this is the first time they have seen gold coins and they pass them around to look at.

'You should have seen the bag of coin he was carrying. He even had guards watching him in the tavern!' says John.

'No, surely not!' says Laurence.

'I swear down, I sees them with my own eyes. He works for a man called Lord Fitzgerald, and we have all heard stories of how rich he is,' says John.

The other men nod, some because they have heard of him, others as they do not want to seem ignorant of knowing who he is.

'Are you sure we can pull this off, John?' one of them asks.

John turns to him and opens the list. 'We have been doing this for near six years now, Derek. This is just on a grander scale, that's all. Just think what you can do with all the money we are going to make! It should keep us all going for a blooming year if not longer.' John studies the piece of paper. 'What we need to do is find out where each item can be found and decide how best to take it on the Thursday night. Then a way to get it down to Pigeon Wood meadow for Friday morning, where we will hand it all over to his drovers and wagons.'

John thinks for a bit. 'We can deliver and stack the grain and other goods in the black barn, as long as one of us keeps an eye on it constant like. Once they take control of the stock, it will be on the lands owned by Lord Fitzgerald within three or four days. Nobody will question where he got his produce from, and we will be in the clear. Just think! If we get this right, we can maybe get the feed order for the winter as well, then we would be really living like kings.'

The men go through the list, breaking it down as to where the produce can be obtained and assigning people to the task of getting each item for the Friday deadline. It soon becomes clear that some of it will need to come from other farms in the area, as George's estate and his tenant farmers do not have it all as John had first thought. They hatch a plan and work out they can even afford to pay an additional couple of people to assist in the thievery, and still make a whole summer's worth of money in one night for all present.

With the initial plan marked out, the men go back to the tavern for more drinks. 'It would seem to me that the best thing George and his nephew ever did for me was to kick me off his land,' says John. 'For soon we will have taken enough of his produce to have a yearlong celebration.' He opens the door so the other men can file in. They laugh as they make their way to the bar for some more drinks and see the night away using Dan's deposit to keep them fully supplied with alcohol and the attentions of the pretty barmaids.

* * *

On the outskirts of the village, Dan is looking for the farm his beloved Cook is residing on, as he was delayed in leaving Pippinsford due to other priorities. He is two days late and is in the village by George's farm, not the neighbouring village in the letter. He knows the name of the owner and the name of his farm and saw the area on the map where the farm should roughly be located.

He is heading in that general direction but is still a little lost, but as usual with Dan, he has a touch of luck as he spots the young man who left the group at the tavern. He is slowly making his way in the direction Dan is travelling, so on a hunch, Dan decides to follow him discreetly at a distance. His thinking is that he must be a labourer on the estate he is looking for as there cannot be that many large farms in the same small area.

Sure enough, within the space of fifteen minutes, Dan can see a large farmhouse in the distance and many assorted outbuildings surrounding it. Breaking away from following the young lad, he makes a beeline for the farmhouse, stealthily making his way closer and closer to the building using the cover of the trees and bushes.

He already knows some of the men doing all the thieving in the area and has set them up before his first day is over. Now he must find his beloved and see how she is – only then he will make contact with the others.

The only thing that ever draws this man out into the open is his wife. For she is everything to him, and now he is searching to see if his lady is in this farmhouse. He moves round the building from bush to bush, looking through all the windows from some distance away – as all farms have working dogs and he does not want to be spotted or smelled by them before he has checked out the lie of the land.

He also cannot afford to be seen by any of the farmhands, as it might cause a problem with the deal he has been setting up in the village. So for now he keeps his distance, choosing to settle down under one of the bushes and watch the windows. After nearly an hour, he is finally rewarded as he sees his beloved Cook walking past the window with Victoria. Even from a distance he can see Victoria has a bump on her front.

'Well I be blowed,' he mutters while raising an eyebrow and smiling to himself. He maintains his position until late in the afternoon, watching as the many seasonal workers leave the fields and return to their lodgings in one of the large community barns. In the distance, he can see four of the group of men from the pub sneaking down the lane, trying to not be noticed by anyone. They stagger off towards the far side of the meadow, separating as they go. Dan can see several buildings in the direction the men are travelling in and deduces they must be farm cottages for the permanent labourers.

He can smell the roasting of chicken in the air and instantly knows Cook is the one responsible as it carries the scent of the herbs tarragon and thyme she likes to use. Within minutes, the unmistakeable figure of Springer arrives, walking across the yard towards the farmhouse with another older man at his side. Springer opens the door for him to enter first and as he is about to follow him in, he stops. Just freezes on the spot. He does not look around, just stays completely still for a moment or two before entering the house and closing the door behind him.

Inside, George and Springer pull off their boots and hang up their jackets. They both head off to wash up before dinner. As Springer passes the table, he gives Victoria a hug and a kiss and feels her belly, where their child be growing. She is setting the places at the table for the four of them. He whispers in her ear, 'You had better be setting another place at the table tonight, for I be thinking we have a guest arrive soon.' Victoria looks at him curiously as he walks away to get cleaned up before they eat.

George is the first to sit at the table with Fern as always pinned to his leg. She is not so much interested in the food but wants to be by her master, who she cannot do enough for. That being said, she is a smart breed of dog and knows a few discreet scraps will come her way if she is lucky. Springer is next to arrive, adjusting the fire with another log and a prod with the iron horse-head poker before taking his place at the table. As he sits down, Victoria arrives with the plates while Cook follows with the first bowls of food.

Soon the table is full of fine items – roast chicken, various vegetables and potato dishes, bread and butter and a pitcher of ale. Cook and Victoria join the men at the table, and it is only now George notices the extra place setting. 'Do we have a guest today that I am unaware of?' he asks the girls.

Victoria shrugs and Springer chuckles to himself.

Suddenly, Fern stands up and walks to the middle of the room. She is alerted to something but does not know what it is yet. Her ears are pricked forward as she tilts her head left and right in an attempt to get a better understanding of what she is sensing.

Springer turns to Cook. 'He's been out there watchin' for near three hours now, given the time I be aware he be at the top of the lane following young Ivan, so are thee going to fetch him in?'

Cook smiles. 'I know. I saw him through the window a while back. Let's just see what he does when we sit down to dinner.'

George and Victoria are none the wiser, but within a minute Fern is facing the door. Her hackles are up, and she is in silent growl mode, with her teeth showing but no sound being made.

Cook yells out. 'If you think I'm coming outside to find you, you're going to be waiting a long time, my dear. Now get your arse in here while the food is hot and introduce yourself to your new employer.'

Barely a moment passes before the door clicks on its catch and opens, and Dan slips inside, closing it behind him after a quick look back.

Springer stands up and speaks. 'George, I would like thee to meet your new gamekeeper and ex-poacher, Dan. Dan, this be George, the man I feel a mite bit sorry for as he has the challenging task of keeping you to hand.'

George stands up and Dan steps around Fern. 'It is a pleasure and an honour to meet you, sir,' he says as he wipes his fingers on his chest and shakes George's hand.

'I have heard so much about you, my boy, that it is hard to think there is anything I do not know. But it is nice to finally put a face to the legend that is Dan the poacher.'

Cook laughs. 'Try being married to him. You would be surprised at what this man has been up to in the years I have known him.'

'All what I do is always for you, my dear, for I can only work with the talents that God gave me, and the ones he chose for me are just a little different than most.'

'Oh, is that so? Well, the talents he gave you must have been all the leftovers from everyone else, because they at least see their husbands every now and then. Whereas mine is usually found sleeping in a barn or under a hedge.'

The group laugh at Cook and Dan bickering, before Victoria speaks up. 'Well, to be fair, when Springer and myself fled the village, he was heavily bruised from the fight, and we ended up two weeks in one of the poaching lodges that Dan recommended. It was not half bad. A large room with water, a sink, fireplace, bed. Outside toilet was not pleasant, but it was a liveable place.'

Cook is taken aback. 'Is that so?' She turns back to Dan. 'I never hear about these kinds of places, just how you have been living in the hollow of a tree or a disused chicken coop.'

'Er, well, um, some places are a little better, but I very rarely see those nicer places, my dear,' he says as Cook stands up to give her husband a kiss.

Behind her back, Dan is shaking his fist and gritting his teeth at Victoria and Springer as they continue to smile at Dan's misfortune. As Cook releases him, she takes his coat and cap and places them on a hook in the hallway. Fern has finished sniffing Dan's legs and has returned to her master's side, sitting by him and awaiting instructions.

'That there be a fine animal,' says Dan.

George smiles. 'All the better now she's had a whiff of you – for I reckon she will be able to find you anywhere on this farm should your good lady chose to know where you're hiding.'

'Anyway, that's all about to change,' says Cook, 'as my husband is going to have an honest position, a home to look after with me and I will be seeing a lot more of him going forward. Otherwise, I may well borrow Fern if that is alright with you, George?'

'As you wish, Cook.' George nods. 'As you wish.'

The group sits back down at the table and starts to eat. There is a lot of laughter as they go through some of Dan's antics, and a few more that he is now only prepared to divulge with the others around the table. They explain to Dan the setup of the farm and the place where he and Cook can live down by the river. Cook lays down her own rule that she does not want to move there until her husband has joined her, so for now she will remain in the farmhouse with George, Victoria and Springer.

There is great camaraderie at the table, and as they finish their meal, George sits back in his chair with a satisfied smirk on his face. As Cook gets up to clear the table, he reaches for her arm and beckons her to sit down again before he speaks.

'I know I have said similar things before, but I would just like to say it again while it is fresh in my mind. Two months or so ago, I was sitting here probably eating leftovers and seeing out my time.' He looks at Dan. 'A cold, empty existence with little to look forward to since my wife passed away in a tragic accident a few years before, or so my charge hand explained.' Several of them try to comment, but he waves them all back down. 'Now hear me out, because from the day Victoria and Springer walked onto this farm, my life has changed. In fact, I would say it is a new life for me. Far different from the one before – for I have been on a non-stop ride of adventure, thrills and events that I would never have expected at my time of life. You see, I have been shot at, hunted, run with villains, gained a nephew, loved a girl like a daughter, stolen a fabulous cook, watched a great fight and seen a man stand up for me when none before ever had.

'I've seen my estate take on new purpose while I am still alive, and this farmhouse regain a warm, living, breathing soul again. I cannot begin to say how much I appreciate all of you around this table, for it is more than words can express.

'Dan, I've not known many poachers, and them that I have I would sooner have put a shot in rather than employ them. But Springer has convinced me that, if I were to put my trust in you, we could both benefit from a better life, and this could be a far greater place.

'Who knows, in the future – if this place can get back to the potential it should be able to achieve – I may well be able to invest in improving the village and build a school like my brother did in Pippinsford, that he loved so much. The way Cook talks about you, Dan… I have watched her with my own eyes stand by you when men have threatened her to tears to find your whereabouts. I think you owe this lady the opportunity to have a stress-free life with you by her side.

'Now you could help me and be part of something great here, as we work to build a better future for us all. For that, I am willing to give you employment and fair payment as head gamekeeper, along with the cottage down by the river for as long as you want it as a home for Cook and yourself. No more hiding in the woods or being on the run, a clean slate from this very moment. A complete start from fresh with no baggage to carry with you, now what do you think of my offer?'

Dan looks at George, then turns to the anxious Cook beside him. He lowers his head to think on it a moment. 'You seem to have left out the bit about finding who be doing all the stealing around here before I can take the position on, so there is no way I can take your offer.'

Tears start to flow down Cook's face as she holds her man's hand. 'But these are good people, Dan. We would have a home of our own and I am to be a godparent in the weeks ahead. Why—'

'Let me finish, my dear,' he says. 'There is no way I can accept the position until Friday next week.'

The group of friends look at each other, mystified by Dan's answer. Finally, Victoria asks the question on everybody's mind. 'Why Friday next week, Dan?'

Dan looks back up at them all. 'Well, it may come as a surprise, but I have already been here for a day or so. I've walked the two rivers, seen where they be netting the fish in the pools. Found the pens in the woods for keeping deer and rustled stock and been in the local village, more so the local tavern where all the farmhands drink. But it was not until a couple of hours ago I found the farm where my dear Cook be working, and I could not approach until all your seasonal farmhands had retired from the fields.

'For at this present moment, I am a buyer for Lord Fitzgerald, and I have just placed an order with a man called Big John for this merchandise to be delivered to me next Friday at six in the morning.'

Dan places a copy of the list on the table for them all to look at. 'Now from the seven or so people with this man John, only the lad I followed here would not be involved in the theft. For that I fear he may well be marked for what he has done, as I also saw four of the others from the tavern sneak back to your far side cottages the same time your seasonal labourers called it a day. No doubt to mask their arrival back here.'

Springer takes a deep breath. 'That lad be Ivan. I be watching him arrive when I saw you ferreting around in them there bushes behind him.'

George looks at Springer. 'That lad lost his mother some time back,' he says. 'I helped pay for her funeral as they never had a lot, but she was a good woman and a close friend of my late wife. Her lad is also a fine boy just like his father was. Springer, I would appreciate you watching over him for a while as he is dear to me, though he has been distant from me since his mother passed away.'

Springer nods. 'It be as good as done.'

Dan continues, 'As for the rest of your residing labourers, I fear most of them are involved in what is going on here. Also, the woodsman as the holding pens are well-used, the ghillies as there are several areas of the river regularly netted, and your farmhands have a routine of thinning out your crops and livestock at harvest time – spending most of what they get down in The Thatcher's Arms on women and drink.'

George thinks for a bit. 'Young Ivan and his mother were the last family left on the estate – all the others are single men with no ties to anybody. Drinking and womanising down the tavern is all they do outside of the work they do on the farm – and from the sound of it, that is not always good for me. But what do we do? I am part way through the harvest and can ill afford to have no farmhands on the land at this time of the season and it's far too late to find replacements.'

Dan leans forward and taps George on the shoulder. 'Do not worry – that is mine and Springer's job now, and I have already taken care of it. It might be a bit of a scramble, but it will all get done in time, of that you can be sure.' Dan goes through the rest of the plan with Springer and George while Cook and Victoria clear the table.

After another hour of debating and organising, Dan says to them all, 'I need to go, for we cannot afford for me to be seen here by anyone until Friday morning.'

Cook looks up, saddened – a sight not missed by George. 'Well, at least spend a few hours with Cook in her room,' he says. 'She has been looking forward to seeing you for a while now. Besides, we can do no more for now and it is getting late, so shall we all call it a day?'

With pleasant goodbyes, the group disperses. George takes his usual seat by the window with Fern by his side, not yet ready to retire to his room.

Victoria returns and pours him a glass of brandy, smiles at him but says nothing before leaving the room. He has a sense of newfound pride as he strokes his dog and thinks on his growing community of friends. The thought that his farm is starting to come back to life fills him with joy as he takes a sip from his glass then settles back in his seat.

CHAPTER 14

The Deal Is Done

Morning arrives and the first into the kitchen is Victoria. For the first time since her arrival, Cook is nowhere to be seen. The cooking range is cold and the fire in the hearth has not been set alight. Both were prepared the night before as it is the last thing done to make the morning an easier start and Victoria wastes no time in striking a match and getting both fires lit to warm the room and stove.

Minutes later, Springer arrives in the kitchen. He looks round the room, then at the fire that has only just started to take and finally at Victoria, who just shrugs at him and smiles.

Five minutes pass and George arrives with Fern as always beside him, her nose level at the side of his leg. He is rubbing his hands together as he walks into the kitchen, then suddenly stops and looks around.

Springer opens the door to the yard and George sends off Fern to do her business away in the bushes behind the house. As the door is closed, George looks at Springer then Victoria and gets the same shrug from both of them. Springer moves to the hallway and points out Dan's jacket and cap and the three of them chuckle quietly as it seems Cook and Dan have overslept.

Suddenly, there is a shriek from the far side of the building and seconds later Cook comes thundering down the hall and steams into the kitchen to the waiting smiles of the other three. She is red in the face and flies round putting pans of water on the stove and checking out the condition of the fires. Realising there is nothing she can do without heat, she stops and holds up her hands. 'OK, I overslept. I'm sorry.'

Springer tuts and shakes his head, then starts to speak. 'If this be what we are to expect in the morn—'

'Don't say another word, my boy, not another word. It's bad enough I overslept for the first time ever – I do not need you to add more misery to the moment as well.' She turns and looks remorsefully at George. 'I am sorry. It will not happen again.'

There is a rustle from the hallway and Springer and George look through the doorway to investigate. Some of the coats are still rocking, but Dan's jacket, boots and cap are missing. They move over to the window in time to see Dan running away from the house and scurrying between the bushes with his coat, cap and boots in his hands. Fern is snapping at his ankles as he runs, tripping him up as he makes his escape. He tries to push the dog away, but to no avail as the dog is far too quick and agile for Dan to handle.

Fern gets her teeth into one of Dan's boots and is tugging hard to remove it from his grasp. As Dan fights back, the dog switches her grip to his cap and manages to pull it from his fingers, running ten feet towards the house before turning to face her adversary. Dan lets out a muffled curse and shakes his fist at the dog as he tries to approach her. Fern just drops to the ground and waits, then as Dan approaches, she jumps backwards several feet before dropping to the ground again and waiting.

This is repeated three more times before Dan realises he will never get near her. He abandons all hope of getting his cap back and makes off again. He turns and only makes two or three paces before he steps into something warm and soft and looks down at his bare foot. His shoulders drop as he shakes his head. 'You have got to be fucking kidding me,' he yells out as he starts to drag his foot through the grass.

The people at the window are in stitches, laughing uncontrollably. Cook has tears running down her cheeks as she watches her man dragging his foot along the ground in an attempt to remove the unwanted substance from between his toes.

Finally, after several yards of foot scraping and dragging, he disappears from view over the ridge at the top of the driveway. The group in the kitchen is still laughing as they hear scratching at the door. Springer opens it and Fern trots up to George. She sits down in front of him with Dan's cap still in her mouth. Still smiling, George takes the cap and passes it to Cook. 'You might want to give this back to him when he next pays you a visit, Cook. But I would suggest he takes a bath or at least washes his feet first.'

The four of them are still chuckling as they all pitch in to catch up with breakfast and set out the day's requirements. With the new information Dan has provided, there is additional work to do between now and Friday, as well as still keeping all the labourers harvesting the crops for market. Half an hour later than planned, Springer finally leaves the house. He is carrying a mug of hot tea in one hand and his cap in the other as he heads to the large barn. He opens up the kennel to release the two elderly collies as he passes by. 'Off thee go and find them there rabbits,' he says.

As he arrives at the barn, he spots Ivan picking up a long hoe ready to head out to the fields. 'Morning, young Ivan,' he says.

Ivan looks up. 'Morning, sir.'

'Lad, I be not of that yolk. Springer be my name, so just be calling me that. Now put back the hoe for I be tasking you with several other jobs this morning.'

The young lad's brow wrinkles. 'I be a good worker. I will work faster today, I promise!'

'There be nowt wrong with thy work,' Springer replies. 'I just have other things for you to do, that's all. First of them being to tack up George's horse, for he will be needing it shortly.'

Ivan puts back the hoe and leads out George's horse. Tethering him to a post, he picks out his hooves, checks the fit of the shoes, linseed oils the front of the hooves and gives a quick brush over the horse's body before tacking him up ready to ride.

He has just finished when George arrives with crop in hand. As always, he checks over his horse and tightens up the girth strap one more notch before mounting up while Ivan holds on to the reins and steadies the animal. 'Thank you, me boy,' George says before turning the horse and kicking off up the lane.

As Ivan watches George head off, Springer calls to him. 'Help me finish setting up the light wagon, for Cook and my Victoria will be going to town this morning to pick up some supplies.'

The ladies emerge from the house and Cook climbs straight up on the buckboard, taking the reins from young Ivan while Victoria gives Springer a kiss before struggling up onto the front of the wagon. Being heavily pregnant is making it difficult to climb around like she used to. Springer knows not to comment or ask her to take it easy, as it will hurt Victoria's pride and the tongue-lashing he will receive is best avoided.

'Now, young Ivan,' Springer says as they watch the ladies leave. 'Hitch up that there heavy horse to the big wagon, for I be needing thee to collect three full loads of seasoned logs from the woodsman. Unload them by the cottages in that there far meadow. Then a wagonload each for the three cottages in the low valley and the disused one by the river. When done, return the wagon and bed the horse down. By my way of thinking, that will be your day as good as done. Then, from tomorrow until it be all but complete, take an axe and stone and chop the logs to fill all the woodsheds for all the dwellings. Be sure to chip up plenty of kindling as well, for it be needed to start the fires.'

Ivan's heart sinks at the enormity of the physical task ahead. What's more, the thought of filling the woodsheds for the horrible men who are going to steal from George and Springer really does not do the world justice. But it has been asked of him, so it will be done as requested. 'That will take me the best part of a week,' he says.

Springer nods. 'That be true, lad, but it be well worth the effort for times ahead be a changing and we have a lot to prepare afore the reckoning to come. So, stay the course, lad, and all will be fine, you will see.'

It takes the lad a few minutes to translate what Springer has just said and get it right in his head before he speaks. 'So are there changes coming for this place then?' he asks.

Springer stops what he is doing and walks towards the young man. 'You stood up for George against John yesterday, did you not?'

The lad's mouth falls open. 'Well, yes, but how do you know? I did not see you there.'

'No, but it be not the point. I be knowin' all that be needed to be known and in your case my friend thinks you put yourself in harm's way with them that be plotting bad things. So he be asking me to watch over you like, until the doing gets done.'

Ivan sighs deeply and lowers his head. He sees a saddle rack nearby and sits down on it. 'George is a good man. Looked after my mother when she was sick. Paid to bury her in the church grounds next to my father and had the man talk the right words over her body. There was just me and George there at the church that day – all the other families had long since left the farm. He even put a stone on her grave sometime later with her name and a small poem she liked.' He takes a deep breath. 'You see, since my father died none of the others would bother with us anymore – we were outcasts as my mother was the last woman left on the estate and I was but a child. The other labourers were all men; they just drink and spend time with the girls at the tavern.' Ivan's mouth turns down at the corners. 'Ma loved George's wife Molly. They were the closest of friends and when they did that terrible thing, she turned from them all. Hated every one of them from that moment until she died. On her death bed, she told me what they had done. She was so ashamed that she could not stop them. But they had too much to lose and if she was to tell George what had happened, they said they would get me next. My mother died in torment of a terrible act and the fear of losing me if she said anything.'

The lad starts to break down and Springer is quick to sit down beside him and put his huge arm over his shoulders. 'There be no man on this estate who I would let touch thee, lad, and thee know I am a man of my word. But I will ask for the sake of asking what happened to George's wife, if thee have a mind to get it off your chest.'

Ivan rubs his hands together as he debates with himself. He finally decides that if anything should befall him, the truth should be known.

'Molly had confided in my mother that she was making some mistakes with the stock she was recording and asked her to recheck the figures again with her. Ma also found the stock numbers were reading light to what was held in the stores. They decided as it was dark by then that they would recheck the stock in the morning to see if the count was correct.

'Ma thought it must have been playing on Molly's mind like it was on hers, because later that night she went to the barn to check out some of the stock for herself. As she approached, she saw Molly with a lantern going through the barn herself. Passing one of the wagons, they heard a pig snorting and went to investigate. Inside the wagon, they found several young piglets, sacks of grain, baskets of eggs along with several other items I do not remember hidden under a large canvas sheet.

'The two of them managed to put all the stock back as it should be and decided to follow it up in the morning. But I was not well later that night and my mother, having been up all night with me, overslept and was late to the barn. By the time she arrived, Molly and John were in a heated debate, with Laurence and Derek watching them argue. She had confronted them head-on about the theft of stock and John was getting angry and frustrated with her getting on his case. When she said she was going to get her husband, John lashed out and struck her in the face with whatever he had to hand. In this case, it was the workings of a corn stripper, and it ripped her apart.

'My mother rushed to her aid, but the wounds were very deep, and the blood kept flowing so fast she could not stop the bleeding. Mother held Molly in her arms as she passed away on the very spot where we now sit. The three men started to panic. They hatched a plan about a fall of timbers and bails from the hayloft, but that would only work if my mother went along with it, and she refused bluntly.

'It was then that Big John suggested using me as leverage and threatened to dispose of me in another accident if she did not go along with their plan. What could she do? On her own with nowhere to go, the thought of losing me after her husband was too much for her to risk. So, she walked away while they rigged up a small area of the hayloft to collapse. They placed Molly's body under the impact area and set it off, then ran to get George and tell him of the terrible accident.

'They have played on his grief for years, thieving a bit here and a bit there, removing any people who were friends of his, wearing him down and taking more and more control of his estate. That is until you arrived. It seemed to bring him back from despair and breathe new life into him. It has been so good to see the old George back again for he is a good man.

'But for John and the others, it did not go down well as they've started to lose their grip on George and the farm. That beating you gave John before throwing him off the land really put the wind up them all. For nobody had ever done that to him before and I know he wants to get back at you, for he talks about it all the time.

'To her dying day, my mother despised those men and regretted not being strong enough to take the consequences and come clean with what had happened. I now feel it is time I told George what really happened that day and clear my mother's name, for she was a good woman.'

As Ivan goes to stand up, Springer pulls him back down. 'Listen to me, boy. Ye may yet have your justice the same as George be deserving of hearing what thee has to say, but for the now, do what I be askin' with the wood this week. For we be knowin' about Friday and a plan be in place to right many wrongs, so wait and see what happens to them that think they are above good judgement.' Springer stands up and young Ivan gets up with him. 'Whatever them there men ask thee to do, just do it and do not let on we know. I will task you with work and talk to thee as and when it be needed. Just trust to fate as come the time, it will be one day thee be remembering for an age to come.'

Springer rubs the top of Ivan's head and smiles. 'Now be on your way with the heavy wagon and tend to the wood, for many a good person will be relying on you a week from now.'

Ivan wipes the tears from his eyes and rigs up the big wagon. He tacks up Titan, one of the two huge Suffolk Punch horses they have on hand for heavy pulling and to plough the fields in winter. He mounts the wagon and heads off to the woods to get the first load from the woodsman.

Springer leaves the barn and organises the casual labourers who are starting to arrive in the yard. Once he has distributed the workers, he will check on the crops being harvested to ensure they are being picked at the right standard of ripeness to allow time for travelling to market and the big towns.

* * *

It's late afternoon when Cook and Victoria arrive back. The wagon is full to bursting with all they have purchased. Slowly, Cook manoeuvres the heavy load into the corner of the large barn.

George has also not long returned from his trip and is just brushing down his horse as it feeds on a hay net in its stable. He swiftly moves to the cart to help Victoria down from the wagon as he can see she is starting to struggle. 'I say this only as a good friend, my dear, but I think it is about time you stepped back a little. For you are getting close to having a child and you still have not eased up yet.'

She smiles at George. 'Yes, you are right, but with so much to do and so little time, I need to help while I still can.' George puts his arm round her and guides her back to the house, leaving Cook to finish closing the gate behind the wagon and collect a few items from inside the cart.

'You must understand that for all of us here, Victoria, you are the one who – by some kind of way we cannot explain – holds us all together and inspires us to go forward and be better people. Although it is you having a baby and Springer being the father, Cook and myself are just as excited. And whatever you say, we will worry and be protective of you because you mean so much to us. So please help us a little and take it a bit easy as it will help us to stop fussing over you.'

Victoria stops and kisses him on the cheek. 'You are always such a gentleman, George, from the first day I met you until this very moment, and no doubt going forward as well. I will take it easy from now on, I promise.'

'Don't let Springer catch you kissing another man, Victoria,' calls Cook as she passes the pair of them. 'For he might get jealous!' The three of them smile as they move towards the house.

'Oh, but I do see me lady kissing another man and if it be not for the condition she be in, words might not be all that's needed,' says Springer as he appears from around the corner of the barn.

The three of them roar with laughter as Springer gives his Victoria a kiss before he turns to shake George's hand. 'If I were a younger man,' George replies, 'I would indeed give you a run for Victoria's attention and believe me, my friend, in those days I was quite dashing and debonair.'

Cook looks George in the eye. 'Don't kid yourself; you're still as dashing now, George. I've seen you turn on the charm with that lady in the fields – what's her name? Er, Bernadette! That's it, Bernadette.'

George smiles. 'Oh, you mean Bebe. Yes, well, she is a very pleasant lady and I have known her a couple of seasons now.'

Cook immediately places the box of provisions on the ground and takes George by his left arm while Victoria grabs his right arm, and they walk towards the house. 'Please bring that box to the kitchen, Mr Springer,' Cook calls back over her shoulder. 'For we have things to talk about here.'

'Now, George, who is this Bebe?' asks Victoria.

'Is she married?' asks Cook.

'Does she have children?' asks Victoria.

Springer is laughing as he picks up the box and follows, while George is helplessly looking back at him for assistance as the women continue their cross-examination.

'Ye be on your own with them there, my friend, for I do not want the tongue-lashing they be abouts to bestow on thee.'

The group move into the kitchen and close the doors behind them. Suddenly, there is a shriek, the door opens, and Fern runs out with her head down low and her tail lower.

'It's your bloody dog, and you're the one who left it indoors all day – you clean it up!' yells Cook as a boot goes hurtling through the air towards the fleeing animal. The door slams shut again for about a minute before reopening and George and Springer step out, swiftly walking across the yard.

'Blow me, I forgot to check them there horses in the barn,' says Springer.

'Yes, yes, my boy, we had better check them right away.' The men hurry away while Cook stands in the doorway with a frying pan in her hand, staring at them with dagger-like eyes.

'I did but warn ye she be a bit feisty.'

'Aye, that you did, my boy. But running away from my own home is a bit extreme, even a bit scary, Bartholomew.'

Springer stops in his tracks. 'There be no need for that. Things be not that bad yet that you have to use that name with me.'

'I'm sorry, but I think that it is, my friend, and where the hell did that big pan come from? I have never seen it before.'

'I know not, but I think an hour or so away will calm the blood that runs through them there veins. If blood be what pulses in Cook.' The men chuckle as they disappear into the barn, closely followed by the evicted Fern.

For nearly a week, the routine is the same: up at dawn, organise the workforce and send stock to market or store what is for farm use in the outbuildings. They make a conscious effort not to check the items on Dan's list against stock on the farm.

Young Ivan has been splitting logs and chopping kindling for days, and each cottage has stock for at least a month, if not more. The men living in the cottages have been laughing about how they are putting one over on George and now he even has one of them cutting up the firewood for them to keep warm at night.

Ivan does not take kindly to all that is going on, but he does trust Springer. Gritting his teeth to all the comments, he finishes the wood cutting as requested. As he picks up the axe and stone to head back to the barn, Derek approaches him.

'Boy, we need you tonight to watch over the barn while we deal with the livestock. John has told me to let you know you will get a three-quarter share if you do this and if you don't… well, you do not want to hear the alternative.' Ivan thinks for a minute. He knows what he really wants to do with his axe, and where to plant it, but he is smarter than that.

'Tell your master I will watch over the barn for a full share or not at all.'

Derek's smirk turns to a frown, and he steps forward. 'Why you little upstart, nobody is my master.'

The young man swings the axe up onto his shoulder and stares back at Derek. 'Near six days I've been swinging this axe. Step one pace closer and you will see what all these blisters and calluses have produced in me as I see how good my aim has become.'

The man stops in his tracks. He can see the look in Ivan's eye is not of a child anymore but a young man prepared to go through with his threat and backs off a little.

'Now, now, let's not get all bothered here. If it is a full share you want, then a full share you will get. Just be at the barn at seven.'

Ivan watches as Derek walks away before picking up the sharpening stone and continuing his walk back to the estate yard. It takes him near twenty minutes to travel across the meadows, and as he enters the barn, he sees George struggling to lift a large wagon boom onto the side of the barn wall. He runs over and helps lift it the final foot onto its holding spot on the pegs.

'Well, thank you, young Ivan,' George says as he mops his brow with a handkerchief. 'It's too bad we have to get old, eh?' he says as he sits down on a barrel while Ivan puts his axe and stone away. 'Your mother would be so proud of what a fine young man you have turned into. Not that she was ever less than proud of you. I recall how you used to sit on my shoulders when you and your mother visited Molly and me all those years ago.'

Ivan lowers his head. 'You were always good to my mother and me, even more so when she passed away.'

'That's because she was a good woman like my Molly and good people deserve to be helped when they are in need.'

Ivan sits down next to George, his head hung low as he begins to speak. 'I have to tell you something that has been long overdue since Ma died.'

George puts his hand on Ivan's shoulder. 'Your mother told me several times what happened when I visited her on her death bed, my boy. Each time, I told her the same thing – she had nothing to be sorry for and neither do you. When you spoke to Springer, you just filled in a few of the blanks, but I already knew what these people had done and who was involved. I just have no way of proving it in the eyes of the law.

'On my own, it was never possible for me to take them all on without losing my own life. That was the reason I left the estate straight after her funeral, as I went looking for my brother and his sons for help. They would support me along with people they knew from their own farms. But they had gone missing, and I could not find them, so I was still alone, knowing of but not able to avenge my wife's murder. Now with the help of some new friends, I can put right many years of wrongdoing and still keep this estate running well. You see, lad, this farm was Molly's life, the people and animals on it, her reason for being. Somehow, and I know not why it happened, we got detached from our land and did not see the families disappearing from the cottages and these men taking over.'

Ivan takes some long, slow deep breaths before he gets the courage to speak up. 'They have asked me, or should I say told me, to look after the stock being stored in the black barn by Pigeon Wood meadow, from tonight until the trade in the morning.'

George thinks for a while. 'Then that is what you will do, for tomorrow morning when we close in on them, you will be in a safe area.'

Suddenly, at the back of the barn, some of the farm tools fall to the ground. The two of them look up and see the shadow of a person running to the barn door.

'Oh damn,' yells George. 'After him, Ivan. We cannot let him get away.'

Ivan is up like a shot and runs after the man with George following close behind. The sneak runs through an open storage barn and heads for the spinney of scrub willows around the duck pond. He turns the corner of the barn and runs straight into the arms of Springer, who clasps him around the shoulder and pulls him backwards onto his chest. The man pulls a knife from his waistband and raises it to strike down. Springer is prepared for this and catches the man's wrist as he attempts to plunge down with the blade.

'I think not,' says Springer as he squeezes his assailant's wrist so hard the knife eventually falls from his grasp, then he pushes him back up against the barn wall.

'Going somewhere be thee?' says Springer as George and Ivan arrive at the scene. With three of them now surrounding the assailant, Springer releases him from his vice-like grip.

The man straightens himself up, looks at Ivan and says, 'You're marked, boy. John will have your head when he hears of this, you turncoat.'

'It's Gatsby,' Ivan says to Springer. 'Or Long-eared Gatsby as he is known for always being around watching and listening for Big John. You would not have seen much of him as he is one of the ghillies and rarely seen around the farm.'

'We should have thrown you off this land when your whore of a mother died all of them years ago!' Gatsby replies.

Ivan's reaction is like lightning. He steps forward and punches the man in the stomach. As Gatsby hunches over, Ivan grabs the back of his head with both hands and brings his knee up, connecting with his nose. There is an almighty *crack*, and the impact throws the man back against the barn before he collapses onto the floor, out to the world.

'Well, I did not see that coming from you, Ivan,' says George.

'That man made my mother's last days a nightmare, hounding her for rent money on the room we lived in, demanding all the back pay from what my father owed before he died.'

George thinks for a moment. 'What are you talking about, Ivan? I charge no rent on the cottages, and nobody owes back rent – they are all free when working in this farm.'

Ivan looks at George in a strange way. 'No,' he says slowly, 'you took nearly three quarters of what we earned to pay for the room we rented after Father died.'

George shakes his head. 'I charge no rent on my cottages and you and your mother had a cottage of your own, not a room in a cottage – you had the whole cottage!' George's face flushes with anger. 'Who was collecting rent from you and your mother?' he asks.

Ivan looks down at the man on the floor. 'Him, Laurence or Derek. One of them would collect the rent the night we got paid from you. In the end, we could not afford the cottage, so they said we could have one of the rooms for a bit less money and with nowhere to go we had to take it.' George is near to tears as Ivan continues. 'That's why so many of our friends left; they could not afford to live here anymore. My mother and I were the last ones and when Mother died John moved me to the small room on the end of his cottage.'

'Oh my God,' says George as he falls to his knees. The final missing piece to the puzzle has now dropped into place with devastating effect. He had been so utterly betrayed by Big John and the other farmhands but had been so full of grief he had not seen it. He can hear Gatsby on the floor moaning as he comes round and tries to get up. George spots the knife on the floor and reaches for it.

'No, George,' says Springer quietly as he kicks the knife away and helps his friend to his feet. 'Not like that, my friend. Ye be a far greater man than that there villainous scoundrel.'

Gatsby is now up on his hands and knees, but not for long as Ivan takes two steps and kicks him in the head, knocking him back to the ground again. A line of blood detaches from his nose and sprays along the side of the barn.

'Nice kick, young Ivan,' says Springer. 'George, best thee get to the house and ready thyself for tonight, for there be a whole heap of things to do and barely time enough to do it in. Young Ivan and I will deal with that there wrongun and I be along shortly.'

George starts to stagger away. 'How could I have got it so wrong?' he mutters to himself as he walks a lonely path towards the farmhouse. Both Springer and Ivan watch their friend until he is out of sight, before Springer gathers some strips of leather and a length of cloth. He binds the man's hands, knees and feet with the leather and places a piece of the rag in his mouth before tying the rest of the cloth around his mouth and head. He then picks Gatsby up and slings him over his shoulder.

'We will stick him in the barn thee be watchin' over tonight, for it be easier to have him within eyesight than away from view.' The two of them walk off in the direction of the black barn at a good pace.

Nearly an hour later, Springer returns from depositing Gatsby in the barn. As he enters the kitchen, the table is already set up with bread, cider and a selection of vegetables. Cook serves him up a bowl of hot, thick stew with some corn cakes wedged in the side. 'Get that inside you, my dear,' she says, filling up his glass with a little more cider.

The meal is a little spicy but tastes superb and he nods in approval towards Cook.

While Springer eats, George has been explaining to Victoria and Cook what John and the other labourers had been doing to the families on the estate. 'I still find it hard to believe they could be so cruel, especially to young Ivan and his mother,' Victoria says.

George shakes his head. 'Made a terrible fool of me they have,' he says. 'I just had no idea they were profiteering from my farmhands that way.'

'You were not to know, George. At the time you were struck with grief from the loss of your wife. Those people played on your vulnerability, something I have had done to me by my family. In my case, they tried to make me an offering so they could live in a privileged position.'

Springer makes short work of the meal provided, but when Cook offers more, to her surprise he places his hand over the bowl. 'Not tonight, Cookie, my dear, for I do not want to feel bloated when the morrow comes.' He takes several gulps of the cider before he finally speaks on tomorrow's events. 'None here can change the past, but going forward we can right some of the many wrongs and make good from the here and now. Them there men that have taken from George and this here land be about to get retribution for past and present deeds.'

Springer turns to look at Cook. 'I be seeing your man near the woods just now, Cook. He's been back near a day watching and checking on that there man John, where the stock be coming from that they be hiding in yonder wood down by Applesford Bridge just past the lower meadow. John and his like have been lifting from your tenants and neighbours for many a past few years, more so in the last few days, George. Come the reckoning tomorrow, many of your friends will be better off for what is about to befall them there people. Now Dan, he be a right thinker. He has it all planned out and I for one be glad him be on our side – for a more cannier, devious man I know not in this world. I do declare when his time comes, God himself will need an army of angels just to watch that one man alone, or many will find their wings missing come the following day.'

He chuckles and takes another drink of cider. 'George and I are to meet with him on the morrow about a mile from the wood at near five in the morning. I be fearing this might not be for the fainthearted, so you lasses best stay here and do what be needed for our return. It will be a final reckoning for all but Ivan when this debacle starts.'

There is not much more for the group to talk about and after a few more words, they depart to get a few hours' sleep before the morning's events begin. As Springer and Victoria leave the room, Cook remains behind to speak to George.

'I know it is not my place to ask such things, but watch over my Dan would you, George? Clever and resourceful he might be, but he is more vulnerable than you all think. I've repaired that man of mine many times. I just do not want him hurt when I am so close to having a home with him.'

George stands up and gives her a hug. 'I fear for us all, but if we want a new start, we need to clear the stench that is affecting this land. I will do all I can to ensure his safety. Now go, my dear, for I wish to be alone with my dog in front of the glowing fire for a while and reflect on the things to come.'

As Cook leaves the room, George settles in his armchair with Fern tightly wedged up against his leg. He stares into the amber coals and lets his mind go back to times gone by. He pulls down a picture of his wife from the table beside him and stares at her image as he recalls some of their finest moments together. Slowly his eyes start to close and the picture leans ever forward before resting on his chest as he succumbs to a few hours of sleep.

* * *

On the far side of the estate in one of the labourer's cottages, John has a dozen men with him. He is going through the final preparations that will have all the required stock together for the trade in the morning. As he speaks, he is coughing and sneezing with a heavy summer cold and feeling under the weather.

The group of men has been bolstered by two farmhands from another farm and three from the estate John now works on. All of them are there for themselves and the quick money they can make at the expense of their employers.

'So, you three now go in the wagon and collect the sides of meat from the slaughterhouse and get it to young Ivan at the barn. If you go now, you can collect, deliver and get the wagon back before they notice it's been missing. Do not forget to ensure the meat is wrapped in muslin before taking it! Then help with the drive of cattle and sheep from the woods.' The three men nod and leave the house to start their part in the plan.

'Derek and Laurence, take a couple of the others and start moving the two wagons full of pigs we took from the Underwoods' farm down to the meadow and unload the crates. Our contact, Dan, will be supplying his own wagons and people to transport them away from the pickup point.' Derek nods as he leaves with the men to start the move.

'As for you two,' he says, looking at the two new recruits, 'collect the chickens you have been putting away for the last week and deliver them to the barn. Young Ivan can also watch over them until they are ready to be collected. I will see you right in the tavern tomorrow night and pay you for your assistance in this matter.'

The two men giggle as they leave the cottage, for Charlie and Ben are not the sharpest two people to have walked the earth – more like the village idiots. Their role in the theft is minor, so they will only receive a small payment from John for their services, not a share like the others.

CHAPTER 15

Sting in the Tail

It's a little after five in the morning. Springer is standing in the middle of the track while George is sitting on a log by the side of the road, holding the reins to his horse that is feeding on the grass round its feet. Softly to start with, but growing all the time, Springer can hear something in the still air. Over the next few minutes, the noise gets slowly louder and soon it becomes a rumble. 'Looks like Dan has made it with the folk he was talking about.'

George stands up. 'Folk he was talking about? What do you mean by that, my boy?'

'Calm yourself, George. All is about to be put to light, for this catching of all them that be sticky-handed and taking what not be theirs from you and many others round here. Once caught we be needin' good honest workers to replace them that be not trusting of your time and good nature. With the land still half heavy with this year's crops, we need them there workers in your fields within days for the crops to stay good for harvest.'

George is a little anxious about what he has let himself in for, but he trusts Springer like no other. Looking down the road, he can see several carts trundling towards him. There are people on the front of the wagons as well as some walking by the sides. As they draw closer, George can see women and children amongst the group.

The convoy pulls up to a stop in front of them. Sitting beside the driver on the lead cart is Dan, who stands up and stretches out before dismounting and walking up to George. 'Good to see you, guvna,' he says as he shakes George's hand.

'Who are all these people and where did they come from?' George asks.

'Well, funny you should ask that, for it took me a while to convince them to come here as they were all about to scatter to different areas of the country. I explained there may well be an opportunity opening up on your estate for hard-working people and their families if they were prepared to take a chance and see you today.' Several men have moved up to stand next to Dan. 'Seven families are here, and you may recognise some of them from times past.'

With that, one of the men steps up to George, pulls his hood back and beams a smile at him. 'Jethrow!' says George as he shakes his hand. 'You left a lasting impression on me the last time we met.'

'Dan said there may be a chance to start again on your farm and as it be only two days out of our way, we thought we would chance it and see if it was true. If not, we will move on as we could not stomach staying any longer where we were.'

George has a huge smile on his face as he looks at the other men. 'I recognise some of you,' he says. 'Yes, you worked for my brother! Albert is your name if I remember correctly.'

The man in question tips his cap at George. 'That be right, sir, for many a good year I did fine service for that brother of yours.'

'Three of these men worked for your brother, two more for Victoria's father and one for Lord Fitzgerald – or should I say for Dan on Lord Fitzgerald's land.' Jethrow introduces all the men to him in turn. 'All these men and their families are known to Springer, Victoria and Cook. We are all aware that Springer is known as your nephew around these parts, for Dan has explained the situation and you can be assured they would never let on or put them, Cook and Dan in harm's way.'

George thinks on it. 'Those two are like family to me and the risks they have taken to set all this up is beyond measure. But I am also aware and seen with my own eyes that you have been through troubled times, so please honour their trust.'

'There is not a person amongst us that would let you down, George. I promise you that. Also, we fear the wrath of Cook more than anyone else we know,' says Jethrow as all around him burst out laughing.

The conversation soon changes to the trade that is about to happen, the plan and route they are to follow as well as the probable conflict that may occur.

'We need to unload what little we have in the wagons quickly and leave the women and children behind, so we look like we are here to pick up the merchandise,' says Jethrow as everyone rushes to carry out the task at hand. With so few personal items left, it takes but minutes to unload the people's boxes of clothing and personal belongings from the wagons.

Dan turns to George. 'Time for you to ride to the Underwood farm. There you will find the Underwoods, the local magistrate and the owners of a few nearby estates waiting for you to bring them to the trading place. Be sure to come in via the woods at a walking pace where the spongy ground masks the noise of the horse's hooves. When you hear a hunting horn, come in as fast as you can. With luck, and so many people here, there may not be much of a debacle.'

Springer helps George up onto his horse. 'Be safe, George, and travel with care, for I be needing my friend back in one piece.' George turns his horse and heads off.

Springer unfolds a well-drawn map. 'Ladies and you youngerns, I have here a map. It be your choice to be waiting for our return or follow it up yonder and find my good lady and Cook waiting. For they have what thee be needin' for you to get settled in. Or, if you have a mind to stay or just be rested afore your travelling to come, wait here and we will collect thee once we be finished.'

Jethrow's wife, Abigail – Abby to her friends – takes the map and looks at it. 'It looks like three miles, girls. Let's pick up our things and get moving.' She turns to Springer and kisses him on the cheek. 'We know the risks you and Victoria have taken to give us this opportunity. God bless you, my lad. We will walk and let you menfolk get on with what needs to be done. Just all stay safe, you hear.'

With quick goodbyes between the men and their families, the women load up what few belongings they have and start the walk to

George's farm while the men mount and set off in the five wagons.

Jethrow and Dan are on the first wagon, while Springer sits as a passenger on the second wagon with a hooded cloak over his head to hide his identity from them that be delivering the stolen goods.

* * *

A few miles away, John has joined Derek and Laurence to drive the cattle to the meeting place. But cattle being what they are, and with two big bulls up front along with a few younger ones in the herd, they are more than a handful to move in the right direction. Nobody likes to move through woodland in near darkness and it is the same for cattle. They hate it even more when forced to go on a journey they have never been on before. They are hesitant and constantly spooked by any sound or breaking of a branch below their feet, making moving the herd a nightmare.

With a lot of pushing and prodding, the men finally get the animals through the wood and onto a footpath where it is much easier to move them along a straight track.

The toll on Big John to get them through the wood has been hard. He is coughing, spluttering and wheezing heavily as he tries to catch his breath. Eventually, it gets too much for him and he sits down on a stump to rest. Derek walks over to him in a bid to find out how he is. 'Take them on, Derek. Don't let them stop until you get to the meadow, or we will never get them going again. I will catch up in a while when I have my breath back, just get them there for the trade.'

He coughs again and holds his head in his hands. Derek nods and waves the cattle on, tapping them on the sides and their backs with a stick to keep them moving forward.

With the black barn visible in the distance, Derek turns to Laurence and speaks. 'That was hard work. I pity these drovers coming to take these beasts and push them on near a hundred miles.'

'Ha! I pity them just to move them a mile. They may be better beef, but by God they are stubborn and bad tempered. Just look at that lead bull with the big horns. He's been turning to look at me at least a dozen times on this trip. If he were a man, I would swear he be wanting a piece of me.'

'It's just a stupid cow,' Derek replies. 'In an hour we will be paid and think no more of this. In two we can be down the tavern for breakfast before going back to the estate and laughing at that old fool George and his nephew. How stupid they are to not know what we have been doing to them.'

Ivan is standing at the entrance to the barn to ensure the cattle do not push their way inside and damage the crates of pigs and chickens that are stacked just inside the near-to-full building. At the back, behind the crates of animals, the sacks of grain are layered four high and on top of them, wrapped in muslin, are the half sides of beef and venison. Behind that are several bushels of straw that hide Gatsby, who is still wriggling and shuffling, trying to break free now that Ivan has moved to the front of the barn.

Derek and Laurence do not even acknowledge Ivan as they pass. They just stare at him a while as more men are hollering and yelling from behind the cattle to keep them moving. Finally, they reach the open meadow where the men stop driving the animals, leaving them to put their heads down and graze along with the flock of mixed sheep that are already present.

There is nervous tension in the air – something that has not gone unnoticed by the ringleaders. 'Now calm yourselves, men. All we have to do is wait here a little while longer for all that lovely money to roll into our hands, lads. Then we will have a fine year,' says Derek in a vain attempt to calm their restless spirits.

A muffled cheer comes up from some of the other men as they rally a somewhat nervous enthusiasm while watching over the livestock in the meadow.

Twenty minutes pass before Laurence and Derek both check their pocket watches then look at each other. 'Well, it is nearly time,' Derek says as the two of them make their way back up the lane to wait at the intersection with the road.

They do not have to wait long before they see the convoy of

wagons turn a corner in the distance and come trundling up the long straight road towards them.

'Where the hell is John?' mutters Laurence. 'He should have been here by now. What are we going to do if he does not turn up in time for the trade?'

'Easy, Laurence. We will just have to go through with the deal ourselves. All the goods are here. Let's just get on with it and make the trade without him present.'

About five hundred yards in the other direction, John is staggering towards his men. He has just reached the footpath and is determined to get there in time to seal the deal when he has another coughing fit and pauses for one more rest on a large boulder before he pushes on. As he gets up, a sound catches his ears, and he stops to listen. The sound gets louder and soon he makes out the footsteps of horses coming up through the woods behind him.

Stepping back into a thick pocket of undergrowth, he crouches down and watches as twenty or so riders move past him, being led by George along with John's new employer, Sir Peter Jackson. As they move by, he can see there are magistrates mixed in with the group of riders armed with rifles.

'Oh my God,' he mutters in utter panic, while trying to hold down a coughing fit. The riders stop with the last couple in the group pulling up just opposite him, no more than ten feet away from where he is crouched.

If John yells to warn the others, he will be run down and caught. If he sneaks away and yells, he will be shot at or worse, captured and – having tried to help the others evade capture – the consequences will be severe, maybe even death. So he makes the only decision left to him under the circumstances and keeps quiet as a mouse and watches the events unfold.

Back at the meeting point, the wagons have reached Laurence and Derek. The first wagon pulls up beside them, while the other wagons pull up left and right, deliberately blocking the full width of the road.

Dan and Jethrow dismount and approach the men while the others also climb down from the wagons but stay a little further back. Dan looks round for John but does not spot him. 'Where be the big man John? I cannot see him amongst you.'

'Well, unfortunately he is a bit under the weather. He was hoping to make it here for the trade, but it looks like he won't get here on time. So you will be dealing with me now. Do you have the guineas with you?' asks Derek, putting out his hand for payment.

Dan steps into his act as if he was putting on a glove. 'My good man, before I surrender any of the money, I need to inspect the goods and ascertain the quality of the product. Only then can I give a fair price. Now lead on and show me what I am here to purchase for Lord Fitzgerald.'

Derek and Laurence lead Dan down to the meadow, where they first show him a mixed herd of twelve Cheviot, twelve Romney and sixteen Cotswold sheep. 'There be a few more than asked, total count being forty if you want them. If not, I will take them to market tomorrow,' Derek says while Dan inspects the sheep's teeth and coats.

'Cotswolds have a good shine to the coat, most have good structure and teeth, couple are a little on the old side, but they will do.'

He then focuses his attention on the highland cattle, moving through them all, inspecting each one as he goes, leaving the big bull to last. He has a ring through his nose and a man holding a rope attached to him.

Wide-horned and angry at being pulled around, George's prize bull, Winston, stands over six foot to the shoulder and is rippling with muscle and presence. He would give anything to butt the people poking him, but he is a wise one and bides his time, waiting for an opportunity.

'There be a younger bull that sticks with this one, so he comes as part of the trade,' Laurence says as Dan finishes his inspection.

'Nice, very nice. The bull is one fine specimen and should sire many a good calf. We will have them all, including the extra sheep.' He looks towards Jethrow and signals him forward with a hand gesture. Jethrow and the other men collect large walking poles from the front wagons and walk down to the meadow, taking charge of the herd animals now they have been approved by Dan.

Dan, Derek and Laurence move back up the road towards the black barn to view the supplies inside. They are followed by the rest of John's men, who have been released from tending the animals by the new drovers.

Jethrow looks around at where everybody is before instructing his men to move the herd of cattle halfway up the path and slow down, leaving the sheep to graze in the field behind them.

Arriving at the barn where Ivan has been standing watch, Dan inspects the caged pigs first, ensuring they are all healthy and well bred. Then he moves on to the chickens – a mixture of browns, Dorkings (for eggs and meat) and a few feisty bantams. Dan moves swiftly on to the sacks of grain, where he selects one at random and opens it to check how clean and plump the grains are. Finally, he inspects the sides of butchered meat. He unwraps several of the carcasses to view the quality of the meat, then nods with approval and wraps them back up to protect them from flies.

With all the inspections done, he walks out of the barn to the more open area and Jethrow comes over to join him. They enter into a small conversation for a moment before they turn back and walk over to Derek. 'Fine display of animals and stock,' says Dan. 'Well worth the three hundred and fifty guineas I said I would pay if they met my lord's demanding standards.' Derek and Laurence look at each other, for John had told them the deal would net three hundred guineas. They do not let on, just smile a little wider at the new price.

Dan flicks his fingers to the hooded man back by the wagon, who reaches into the side of the wagon and passes Dan a large leather pouch. He bounces the bulging bag in his hands a few times as Derek and Laurence, along with the rest of their men, crowd round. As the bag is passed over to Derek, he raises it up and shakes it for all to see. 'See this, boys? We will be celebrating tonight, that's for sure!'

So intent are they on looking at the bag of money that none of them sees Dan's men move up in front of the cattle and form a line at the intersection with the road, raising their poles into quarterstaff positions. Derek reaches inside the bag and pulls out a handful of its contents. 'Is this some kind of joke?' he demands, looking at the old nails and bits of metal in his hand.

'No,' says Springer as he pulls down his hood. 'It be what thee get when thee be stealing from the likes of me, you scallywags.'

Dan signals to Ivan, who blows on a small hunting horn several times, while Springer punches Derek in the face, dropping him to the floor like a stone, before delivering blows to some of the others. Panic sets in as they try to make a run for it. The ones who run towards the meadow find a barrage of blows from heavy polls hitting them and they turn to swiftly run back. The men running for the woods are stopped in their tracks by a line of horses charging towards them. They turn to flee towards the offset wagons that block their escape down the road.

Several of the riders dismount and get stuck into the thieves, with George leading the way as he knocks seven bells out of Laurence. 'I've waited a long time for this, my boy, and you're going to have every bit of it.' He lets fly with several blows that leave the man unconscious on the floor with blood dripping from his nose.

One of the men chances it and tries to climb over the blocking wagons. As he reaches the top, there is a loud bang, and the man is hit in the centre of his back by one of the magistrates with a large ball rifle. The bullet goes straight through him, bursting out of his chest with a splatter of blood. He is killed instantly and falls on the top of the wagon before rolling down the side and finally ending in a heap on the floor.

That single piece of lethal work knocks the fight out of all but one of the others. Resigned to their fate, the rest of them raise their hands and surrender to the magistrates. Ivan appears from the barn, dragging Gatsby by his arms and dropping him near the others.

Only Derek has made a part getaway, crawling past Dan's men and standing up between them and the herd of cattle. Springer goes to give chase, but as he passes his men, he hears George shout to him. 'Stop where you are, Springer. He's going nowhere.' Springer stops and looks at Derek, who is staggering about senseless from the punches he's received. He has slipped out of his jacket in the hope it would help evade attention as he crawled quietly away. As he looks back at Springer, he is now wearing a red-checked shirt.

A huge bellow from the direction of the cattle echoes through the air and Derek stops moving and turns. Winston is at the front of his herd, facing sideways on. Beside him is the young bull, watching intently as his leader stamps at the ground.

Winston has been pushed around one too many times by these people and now has no rope through his nose to hold him in check. This huge bull is about to dish out some payback of his own. 'I would not get any closer to that bull if I were you, for he can be hot-blooded if he does not like you,' yells George.

Derek waves George away. 'It's only a bull,' he shouts back as he stamps his feet and points back at the bull in defiance. All men from both sides of the law are now watching in silence as Derek steps forward and again stamps the ground in front of the bull. The challenge is met with an instant and reactional response, as Winston charges directly at him with the speed of a racehorse.

Derek turns to run, absolute terror written across his face as the bull bears down on him. At the last moment, Winston lowers his huge horns and impales Derek through his side and out through his stomach with his right horn. The bull lifts him off the ground with his massive neck muscles and thrusts his head to the left, flinging the stricken, screaming man near twenty feet through the air before he hits the ground. The side of his body has been ripped apart as it was torn away from the animal's horn. The massive bull bellows again in defiance and snorts at the man bleeding profusely on the ground with his intestines hanging out, before turning around and trotting back to the herd with the young bull companion back by his side.

'I hope that man has not damaged his horn,' says George. 'For that bull has a show next week and I am expecting good things from him.' Some of the men chuckle, while others are still in shock at the sight of a man dying at the side of the road.

'If that man dies, that bull will have to be destroyed,' says the younger of the magistrate's men. George looks up, disappointed, but before he can speak Springer comments in an angry tone from the far side of the group of men.

'That there animal protected his herd and stood to a challenge put on it. You shot a man in the back for running away. If you shoot that bull, I will hang you myself right beside it, so best thee make your choice now.'

The man is shocked by Springer's response and looks to his superior for answers. After a short pause, that man gives his judgement. 'We have caught or killed all the thieves in the area in one swift operation, except for the ringleader John Branson. Unless the others confess to his involvement, we cannot prove he stole anything and for now he is a free man. But his time will come, mark my words. As for the bull, it was an unfortunate event caused by provocation from a man who will not live long enough to put in a complaint. I think for now we will leave it be. It has been a good day's work.' He looks around at the remaining men, not noticing that Springer has put up his hood and moved behind one of the wagons, shielded by Jethrow and one other. 'Now I would like, with your permission, to borrow one wagon to take these men to town, along with the two bodies, for trial and disposal.'

Jethrow gives a nod, and the rest of the thieves are shackled in irons as they are assembled behind the nearest cart. With a few encouraging shoves from the magistrates, the prisoners collect the bodies and mount them and then themselves onto the back of the wagon.

'I will leave you farmers and landowners to sort out the livestock between you, for you all know who owns what far better than I do. As for these prisoners, I doubt you will be seeing these men again, for the courts do not take kindly to thieves. Especially in the case of this lot, who have stolen from so many places in one go. I would expect the punishment will be severe. I will have the wagon returned to you by tomorrow and again, thank you for your assistance, gentlemen. Who knows, there may even be a reward for you for what has gone down today. But for now, I bid you all farewell and I hope the rest of the summer goes well for you and your estates.' The senior magistrate mounts his horse, flicks his reins and leads his mounted men ahead of the wagon down the road towards town.

Springer and the others watch as they move down the lane and out of sight before they give up a great cheer and shake each other's hands. 'What a story I will have to tell the wife,' shouts Sir Arthur Jackson as he shares a drink with George from his hip flask.

It does not take the group long to sort out who owns what when it comes to the produce. The cattle and grain are George's, along with a dozen sheep. Another type of sheep, the meat and some of the pigs are from the estate run by Sir Peter Jackson. The remaining pigs, most of the chickens and the last few sheep belong to George's tenant farmers, the Underwoods. And finally, two cows, two pigs and the bantams were from the smallholder, Joe Harbour, who is still laughing with the others over the great fight he has just had. He finishes the conversation by commenting how he would like George's prize bull to sire him some calves, in the hope they would turn out just like Winston the Super Bull.

George laughs. 'Visit me in the spring and we will see what can be done, Joe,' he says with a smile.

Many of them have made new friends under these strangest of circumstances and they spend the next hour organising the people and wagons to return all the stock back to the farms.

It is nearly four hours later when George, Springer and the others arrive back at the farm. The cattle lead the way, then the sheep and finally the wagon of grain. All the other vehicles have been borrowed to deliver back the stolen stock and will be returned later. The cattle know exactly where they are and head straight for the field and feed rack, led as always by the bloodstained horn of 'Winston the Super Bull' as everyone now knows him, along with his young bull companion 'Champion'.

The sheep are driven back to join the rest of the herd with the assistance of George's two working collies that have just nipped in behind them from the hay barn.

With all the animals, wagons, horses and grain taken care of, George leads the men down towards the cottages to show them the dwellings available to his potential new labourers. To their surprise, they find all seven chimneys puffing smoke and a wagon by the group of four cottages that is now near empty of its contents. As they approach, they can see the women and children busying themselves with removing all the old rubbish from the houses and throwing it into one large pile ready for burning, while almost every window in every house is wide open.

George is confronted by Victoria, Cook and Abby. He is shocked by how fast everything is going and how organised the ladies are. Abby is first to talk. 'George, we love the area, and the cottages are beautiful. With a little bit of work, they will be fit for families to live in again in a few hours, thanks to the supplies provided.'

Victoria is next to speak. 'Now, by the smiles on all your faces and the fact you are all here in one piece, it must mean all went well with the capture of the thieves.' George nods with a smile.

'That's good, because while we have been waiting, we have sorted out the accommodation and you will be glad to hear that all the cottages have now been chosen by their respective families.'

It's hard to determine who is more shocked – the men who have not even had a say in staying, or George, who has not even needed to sell the idea of this group of people working on his estate.

Cook adds to the conversation. 'So, George, Springer and my husband, should you not be going through the duties of them men if they are to start work for you from tomorrow morning?'

Jethrow approaches Abby for affection and is rebuffed instantly. 'Us women have a lot to do here, and the day is only half done, so get on with what needs doing and come back at dusk. You have a lot of work to do, for I can see the crops needing harvesting from here. That casual labour has been put to task by Victoria this morning but will need overseeing.'

The men walk away chuckling to themselves. 'It looks like if you want us here, you have got us, George,' says Jethrow as he puts out his hand.

'Only too pleased to, Jethrow,' replies George as he grasps his hand and shakes it firmly. 'Only too pleased to.'

Only Ivan is looking dejected. He had been living in one of the rooms in John's old cottage before today. Now he has nowhere to live, as a family has taken over the cottage. He turns from the group with his shoulders slumped and begins to walk away.

Springer instantly notices. 'I be thinking, George,' he says with a nod in Ivan's direction, 'as your foreman, myself and Dan will organise the men with Jethrow while you deal with that there other issue.'

George nods. 'Yes, my boy. This is a debt long overdue and, to my shame, something that should have been done some time ago.'

Springer leads the men away with Dan as Victoria walks up and attaches herself to George's arm and the pair of them walk swiftly after Ivan. They catch up with the slowly moving young man and George begins to speak. 'Ivan, would you come with us, please?'

Victoria hooks her other arm around Ivan's elbow as they pass by and walks him towards the large farmhouse.

They move round to the side of the house and on to the next building – the guest lodge that the hunters and fishermen stay in during the season. It backs onto a woodland area and has a small patio looking over the fields to the right. As they arrive, the door opens and two of the new women pass them by, smiling at George and Victoria as they leave. 'I will bid farewell to you now and finish my duties in the house,' says Victoria as she releases her grasp.

George offers the way for Ivan to enter the building first and follows him into the main room. Ivan has never been in here before, and the first thing he notices is that it is very nicely furnished, with a stone-built fireplace in the middle of the room, a kitchen leading off to the left and two bedrooms on the far side. 'My boy, let me first tell you I had no idea how you and your mother were being treated these past few years, or that John was charging people rent for my cottages. If I had known, it would have been dealt with immediately.' George shakes his head as he thinks about it. 'Did you know your father was my best friend? He helped build the beginnings of this farm many years ago.'

Ivan shakes his head, surprised at Georges words. 'No, sir.'

'Oh yes, it's true. When Molly and I expanded from what is now Springer's farm – Valley View – and moved here to this land all that time ago, your father was the first man to work for me and this was the first building he and I worked on together.' Ivan's eyes grow wide. This is all news to him. 'It's true! Come here and look.' George takes him over to the fireplace and points to a spot at the foot of the hearth. Ivan sees his father's and George's names cut into the hearthstone and kneels down to touch it.

'I was never told this by my mother,' he says.

'That was because your mother wanted you to make your own way in life and leave your own mark on the world, not to live under the shadow of what your father did. Whether I agreed with her decision or not, I had to respect her wishes as it was what she wanted. What I will say, though, is over the last week you have made your own mark in life and stood up to be counted just like your father did all those years ago.

'I cannot make up for what John has done to you and your mother and I will never really understand what happened to your father that day as I was away with Molly. But I do know you are important to me, and I would like you to continue working on the estate but in a more deserving role, now you are older.' He pauses for a minute. 'I would like you to work with Dan the poacher and learn how to be a great gamekeeper, for I will need you in the years to come to help grow this place long after I have gone.' He gives Ivan a small smile. 'I also need someone I trust to keep an eye on him as he does have a reputation for being a rascal and a rogue!' He gives a light chuckle. 'In return, I am giving you this place to live in for as long as you want to work for us all here, and a wage per week reflecting that of an honest gamekeeper.'

Ivan stands up. 'This place! For me? All of it? But I could fit all I own in one draw in the bedroom,' he says.

'Well, I cannot say it was not noticed by Victoria and Cook when they were moving your belongings, but if you would follow me into the bedroom…' George leads Ivan into the main bedroom and opens one of the wardrobe doors to reveal an abundance of clothing, and on the floor are two pairs of boots and one pair of shoes.

'Those ladies decided to refit you out with a selection of clothing for work and leisure.' George grins. 'Those girls are something else, aren't they? And this is from me to you.' He reaches down by the side of the cabinet and picks up a gun bag.

Ivan opens the end and slides out a brand-new shotgun. 'It was made by Henry Nock of London, and she is a real beauty.' Ivan looks at the workmanship as he turns it in his hand, looking at it from all sides. He breeches the barrel and looks down the bores.

'It surely is a beautiful piece of work, but why would you give it to me?'

'My boy, I cannot have a gamekeeper without a shotgun, can I? And, well, I feel it is time you had the opportunity to make your own stamp on life. This is just a helping hand. You will find powder and shot of various size in the bottom of the wardrobe.' George looks at his watch. 'Well, I must be getting on. I will leave you to check out your new home for yourself.'

George walks away, then turns back. 'Oh, I almost forgot, breakfast and dinner will be in my house for you, boy, with the rest of us – should you like to join us. For I consider you part of our family group now and that includes sitting at the table with myself, Springer, Victoria, Dan and a few others. But don't dare be late, for that Cook has a furious temper and a vicious tongue.'

As George turns and leaves the lodge, he has a huge smile on his face. He has achieved so much in the past couple of months, after years of everything spiralling out of control and being so alone. He now is surrounded by real friends, removing unwanted problems, getting revenge on some of the men who have wronged him and his late wife in days gone by. His estate is slowly beginning to breathe with new life and real families have moved back into the cottages again. Children can be heard laughing in the distance and, most important to George, he has people wanting to make life better for themselves and the land on his property.

Where will this adventure take him going forward? God only knows. But what an exciting time for a man who was thinking his life was nearly over just a short time ago. He opens the door to his house and Fern charges down the corridor to greet him, near tripping Cook over as she is now back in the house preparing for dinner. 'That bloody dog will be the death of me!' she yells out.

George smiles to himself and shakes his head as he pats Fern. He walks through to his favourite armchair by the fire and takes a seat. With a bit of a shuffle, he settles back and thinks back on what a day it has been.

What is more ironic about the men who were apprehended today is that the fate to befall them for all the thieving and suffering they have put on others is about to return on them in a catastrophic manner. For what George and the others will never know is that within a week they will have been purchased and delivered to Lord Fitzgerald and will live what is left of their miserable lives suffering down in his mines digging up ore. For probably the only time in George's life, his biggest foe will be doing him the greatest favour of all: disposing of the people who had made his life a misery for the last few years.

* * *

Around the same time as George is settling back in his chair, content with how his life has now changed, some two hundred miles away in the English Channel, a man is returning after a journey that has taken near seven years to get this far.

Caught in a terrible storm, he stands on the rain-soaked deck of a stricken ship staring out at the coast of France. There is an unstoppable drive in this man to find out the truth, as well as a burning hatred and deep desire for revenge. To many who set eyes on him, he looks truly terrifying – more beast than man these days. To those who cross his path, pray stay out of his way, for you will find more pity in a pride of starving lions than you will in this man.